Draw Me In

ASH HOSKING

Table of Contents

Chapter 1

AELA

THERE'S A LOUD thud of a box hitting the floor behind me, and I turn to see my best friend and new flatmate impatiently shoving back her short blonde hair that has fallen into her grey eyes.

"Thank Jebus that's the last one. I don't know how you fit all that into your tiny car," Kara exclaims breathlessly. She tugs her black singlet into place over her faded denim shorts and then gratefully accepts the glass of cold water I offer.

"Determination and awesome packing skills," I state as I follow her gaze across the piles of boxes containing everything I need from my old room at my parents' home, which are now taking up space in our living room.

"It's not even noon yet, and I'm exhausted just looking at all the unpacking we have to do." Kara glances around the rest of the open-plan area of our new apartment in central Southport. She looks overwhelmed by all the bags and boxes piled chaotically on any available surface—most of which is her stuff mixed with the essential things we purchased together during the week.

1

"Why don't you test out the new lounge while I try out our espresso maker, and we'll have a coffee break?" I cheerfully suggest. Before I can even finish the sentence, Kara has flung herself over the length of the mocha suede three-seater lounge, bare feet dangling over the arm as she stretches gratefully with a moan of agreement while I make my way to the kitchen.

It's a well-deserved break for Kara because she's never done so much physical labour in her life as we just did, hauling stuff from the basement parking lot to the lift then down the corridor to our apartment.

I know this because I've known Kara since before we could walk. We grew up on opposite sides of a cul-de-sac that housed seven families, the only two girls of fifteen kids that resided in the dead-end street. We quickly learned it was easier to stick together and have each other's backs when it came to defending our Barbies from evil boys or having an alibi or a helping hand in mischief.

Kara is the three-day-older sister I never had, and we hardly ever fought.

So, of course, when we were getting ready for our second year of Uni and Kara mentioned she was thinking about leaving home and finding an apartment closer to campus, I jumped at the idea to be flatmates. Not just to get out from under my parents' overprotective and overbearing roof, either.

I love them dearly, so don't get me wrong. I had a great, loving upbringing and never wanted for anything, but I think being over twenty is too old to still have a ten-thirty curfew and check-in calls after sunset. I couldn't imagine living there without Kara being within walking distance. She was the one who helped me breathe when I felt like I was being suffocated in that house. So while Kara was lagging in energy to get the apartment set up, I was so excited to have our own place and a little slice of freedom that I felt like I could run rings around her.

2

"I knew there was a reason I wanted you as a flatmate. You're not just a pretty face," Kara jokes, sitting up to grin at me over the back of the lounge. I smile as I remove the plastic covering from the sleek black and stainless steel machine that matches the kitchen.

"We both know you would be rocking back and forth in the corner, lost without me. You wouldn't survive a day," I mock then duck laughing when a throw pillow flies over my head as she lets out a hard, sardonic laugh.

"I'm sure I could find a strong, capable guy willing to do all this moving business and fetch Zarraffas for me. That's all I'd need," Kara assures, and I shake my head as I insert the freshly ground coffee.

"You just love me for my mad coffee skills," I jokingly complain over the noise of the machine while I wipe out two new mugs. The 'Bitches Brew' cup for Kara, while I stick with my favourite, 'Never trust an atom. They make everything up.'

"You know it, babe. That and your gorgeous face and body I get to use anytime I want." Kara winks, making it sound like an innuendo. Of course, she's referring to the times she talks me into posing for her camera when the mood strikes her. It doesn't take much convincing, actually. What she creates with her photos is truly amazing. Looking at myself through her art makes me feel beautiful, which is always a nice boost.

"To our first apartment—freedom and happiness, bitch," Kara exclaims as she holds her steaming mug out to toast with mine after I pass it to her, so I grin and follow her lead.

"To all the joys of adulthood. Doing our own cooking, cleaning, paying bills and having to take out bugs on our own," I joke, making Kara choke on the mouthful she had sipped after the first half of my toast.

"Just so you know, I shotgun not dealing with roaches. They're all yours if we find any. And spiders," Kara warns after clearing her throat.

I grin in amusement before replying, "We'll see about that. Enjoy your break. I'm going to get started on my room. Hopefully, I'll still have enough time and energy when we're settled in to hit the gym downstairs." I start down the hallway with my coffee.

"Better you than me. But then again, we both know it's not the workout you're going down there for but the view, and I'm not talking about from a window," Kara teases knowingly as I'm pushing open my bedroom door.

"Well, it is a great view," I grant jokingly, smiling in amusement as I hear her laugh.

"You creepy perve. It's okay, though. I still love you!" I shut the door on Kara's loud chuckling about my admittedly (at least to myself) verging-on-creepy fascination with the guy Kara dubbed my 'Gym Candy.'

I've seen this guy enough since joining the gym two months ago to know his workout schedule—not because I camped out to see him. That would definitely be creepy. I just noticed the repetition in the times I'd see him there.

He is kind of hard to miss, covered in tattoos from halfway up his forearms to over his shoulders and an owl piece on the back of his right calf. Tall and lean, muscled, unlike the majority of bulked-up-apes who go to the gym to pose and flex in front of the mirror. He always wears a baseball cap shading his eyes, a hint of blond hair peeking out from the back and has a piercing on the left side of his bottom lip.

My fascination with him is absurd. I don't even know his name nor have I had the guts to approach him. I've smiled politely as we passed in the hallway to the change rooms but never even managed a friendly 'hi' to him.

That didn't stop me from watching him lifting weights through the reflective windows while I ran on the treadmill, though. I don't know a single thing about him except he mostly keeps to himself, preferring to work out solo with his headphones on while doing sets, unlike the apes who usually inhabit the weight room in packs, socializing more than anything.

A bang on my door distracts me from my daydreaming as Kara yells, "I don't hear any unpacking in there. Stop fantasising about Man Candy and get your arse moving before I set up the kitchen totally wrong just to mess with you."

I huff out a laugh then get to work.

Chapter 2

DECLAN

"THAT'S IT, WE'RE done," I announce, setting down my machine. I gratefully straighten my back to stretch the kinks out of my spine from being bent for the last several hours over my last client for the day. I examine the butterfly and floral piece that now crawls up her left leg, double checking I haven't missed anything while she sits up.

"Oh, my God. Dec, you are freaking amazing. I love it!" Laney exclaims as she eagerly attempts to bend awkwardly to view the latest addition to the work she has been regularly coming in for.

Her eyes lift to mine with an interested gleam I know all too well, and then she flutters her overly fake lashes.

"Let me buy you a drink to thank you." It's more of a demand than a question as she curves her back so her double-Ds are within inches of my face. I stand to reach for the salve and try not to watch the lone button struggling to contain her breasts in the two-sizes-too-small top. I smile politely before gently smearing the ointment over the raw skin around her fresh piece.

"Sorry. I already have plans," I refuse and try to ignore her shiver and sigh as I apply the ointment up the outside of her thigh. *Damn, she's eager.*

"Well, you have my number. Call me, and I'll show you

what I'm amazing at." Lainey shoves the money she owes me deep into my pocket, but I pull back before she reaches my junk she's clearly aiming to find.

I have to give Laney props for being so ballsy. If it were a few weeks earlier, I would have taken her up on the blunt offer. But lately, I've found myself not even slightly interested in these girls—the ones with barely any clothing or inhibitions, who don't want to see past my 'bad boy' tattoos and piercings, and who are usually forgotten when the sun comes up.

I can't pinpoint what changed. I used to love these girls and swore it was the only type I'd ever want or need, but now they just make me feel... tired, empty, and much older than my twenty-five years.

Alex, my best friend and also self-appointed wingman, doesn't understand it. I've copped a lot of flak, but he's more than happy to pick up my slack, which is why I give her my smile that's been dubbed 'the panty-flooder' by the guys, as I wrap her leg in cling wrap.

"We'll see," I reply non-committedly as I hear the front doorbell ring, followed by heavy footfalls headed this way.

"Yo, Dec. You still down he—oh. Hell-lo."

Speak of the devil. I look over to see Alex leaning against the doorframe, ink-covered arms crossed over a black singlet that states he loves all pussy with pictures of different kinds of cats in the background.

Alex tilts his head so his messy mop of dark hair falls into his jade green eyes while blatantly looking Laney up and down with his devil-may-care grin.

"What's up, bro?" I snap off my gloves, throw them in the trash, and begin to clean up. I'm already being ignored by the other two as they introduce themselves, making eyes at each other.

"Uh... I was going to see if you were busy, but I may have

plans. You free, Laney?" Alex replies. He doesn't take his eyes off her as she slides off the table without hesitation to link her arm around his.

"All yours, baby," Laney purrs, trying to sound sexy—which makes me cringe.

"I'll spare you the care instructions since you know it by now, but just remember no friction to the tat while you guys… do whatever you do." My warning falls on deaf ears as they are off down the hall with a wink from Alex as he leads the way.

I chuckle to myself as I clear everything up then check the clock and groan before moving to jog up the stairs to my apartment above the shop. If I don't get my workout in before the gym closes, I'll be in for a restless night's sleep. Exhausting every muscle in my body seems to be the only thing that works lately to stop my mind from running once my head hits the pillow.

I dump the leftover chicken pasta Mum made me bring home last night into the microwave. Then I stumble with getting my shoes off, dodging Tom, who comes over to rub against my legs, begging for food.

No, I don't have a creepy housemate. Well, I do. But he's an overweight, smoky-coloured tabby cat, so his behaviour isn't so unusual. I nudge him out of the way with my foot while I retrieve his meat from the fridge, and he attacks my socked foot with his claws, eliciting a very unmanly yelp from me. I jump out of his reach and hold his food out for him to see.

"Cut it out, or I'll leave you with only dry food until morning, you fat jackarse," I threaten, watching cautiously as he slowly sits back on his haunches to glare with his tail twitching threateningly. Yes, I said he glared at me and was threatening. If you don't believe me, then you clearly never owned a cat and had to deal with it being pissy at you for leaving it cooped up inside all day alone with just biscuits and water to eat. You would think he'd be happy to see me, but no, not Tom. I can't blame him really. If I were confined to the apartment in solitude with nothing good to eat or fun to do and were a neutered virgin, I would probably be pissed and ungrateful, too.

It's a tough life being a cat.

I lean down to fill his bowl and give Tom a scratch behind his ear when he approaches to nudge me in the leg with a purr.

"Yeah, we're cool." I get up and leave him to his food as the microwave beeps, taking my own dinner into my room to eat while I grab my gym gear.

Chapter 3

AELA

MY LUNGS AND legs start to burn with exhaustion, but I ignore it as I push to finish my last couple of kilometres on the treadmill. So I turn the music up that's already blaring in my headphones for motivation.

I recheck the reflection in the window in vain and try to ignore the pang of disappointment when the view of the weight room is still the same—which is ridiculous. How can you miss someone you don't even know?

There's sudden movement beside me, and I startle, stumble and barely manage to save myself from face planting onto the treadmill. I glare at Kara, who had just appeared out of nowhere on my left.

"What the hell are you trying to do, kill me?" I gasp as I rip my headphones from my head. She laughs hysterically, bent over clutching her stomach, which draws the attention of everyone around us.

"Your face… priceless. Oh, my God. I can't breathe," Kara gasps through her laughter while I turn off the now life-threatening machine as I wait for her to stop.

I deepen my glare.

"You're a total bitch. What are you even doing down here?" I ask when she finally straightens, her laugh turning into a quiet giggle as she tries to control it.

"I thought I'd take advantage of the resident's discount and come see what you were doing. You've been gone over an hour. I got bored and lonely up there," Kara explains as she eyes the room expectantly, and then nudges me with a mischievous grin. "So, where is he?"

I don't bother trying to play dumb. "No show." I shrug, trying to be nonchalant as I grab my towel to wipe my face then collect my water bottle.

"Bummer. I was hoping you were taking so long because you had finally grown some lady balls and were at least talking to him."

I give her a 'shut up, you idiot' look before turning to head out. I stall not three steps away when I look at the stairs leading to the reception and change rooms.

"What the hell?" Kara complains when she runs into the back of me, and I can feel her follow my gaze.

He is coming up the last step, putting his earphones into place as he heads toward the warm up area. "Oh, yum. Is that who I think it is?" Kara whispers in my ear.

I pull away from her realising she's still against my back. I nod and tear my eyes away from him before I get caught. Kara lets out a little sigh and then smirks before latching onto my arm and dragging me after him. My heart rate spikes like I'm running again, and I panic as I try to stop us, pulling on Kara's arm.

"What are you doing? Stop. I'm not going over there." I felt flushed and embarrassed already and really just want to get away before our little scene draws his attention like it has the handful of other people we pass.

Kara continues on her course, determined, collecting two yoga mats in one hand to drop on the floor, positioning them with her foot while still holding me in a vice-like grip with her other hand.

11

"Stop it. Now sit and stretch like you're supposed to do after a run," Kara demands quietly. Then she peeks at him from her peripheral vision as she tugs me to the floor. I stretch my legs in front of me while I take a deep breath to calm my nerves and blatantly watch him stretch in the mirror. He looks a little tired today but still gorgeous enough to make my breath hitch when he reaches his arms up to grip two of the bars above him in the stretching station. The motion lifts his loose white singlet enough to reveal a good amount of bare skin around his navel and pelvic region, including his hipbones that start that very delicious 'V'— which makes me want to crawl over and lick it. My face flushes more, and I have to force my eyes away from him. I focus on Kara instead, who licks her lips and grins knowingly at me.

Several torturous minutes later, he bends down to grab his things—giving me a great view of his arse—then heads to the weights around the corner. I let out a relieved breath when he disappears, happy Kara didn't do anything. I gather myself mentally as I get up to return the yoga mat where it belongs before facing Kara.

"All right, you've had your fun teasing me. Now let's get some dinner." I offer her a hand up, but she continues to sit and look at me thoughtfully as she bites her lip. Crap. Nothing good ever comes from that look.

"Nope. You're going to talk to him. It's about time, and I'm not leaving until you do," Kara demands. I shake my head at her then start to walk away, but she stops me short when she calls out, "Either you do it, or I'll talk to him, and you know you don't want me to do that. Who knows what might come out of my mouth?"

I turn to glare at my so called best friend.

"Don't. Just drop it and let's go," I plead, but Kara folds her arms stubbornly.

"I'll invite him home and show him what you keep in the top

bedside drawer to the left of your bed." She continues her threat, and my hands start sweating as I turn to where I can see him on the bench press before looking back to her.

"You wouldn't. How do you even know?" I question, and she shrugs nonchalantly.

"I was looking for your phone charger because I couldn't find mine. By the way, I'm a little surprised you have one. I always figured if you bought sex toys, it would be in the butterfly department, but yours... it's pretty boss." Kara looks impressed, and I feel my face and neck inflame with embarrassment as I hit her arm and shush her, looking around to check no one's listening to our conversation. Thankfully, no one is within earshot.

"We are not having this conversation here, if ever. Can we go now? I'm embarrassed enough and starving."

Kara shakes her head then gestures towards the weight room. "You've got one minute, or I'm going in," she warns, looking at her watch.

"This is blackmail. You can't do this to your best friend. I'm pretty sure it's in the rulebook or something." I look back to the weight room in vain hope that he has given up early and left, though I know it's asking too much.

There he is, sitting on a bench, gulping from his drink bottle between sets. I try to calm my breathing that's coming too fast, then look back to Kara, wide-eyed and pleading, but she continues to ignore my protests, staring at her watch as the seconds tick by.

I panic, knowing full well Kara will go up and embarrass me deliberately if I don't do something and fast. I check my workout clothes and cringe. At least I'm wearing all black so you can't see the sweat I feel clinging to the fabric, but I bet my hair is an absolute disaster.

I can't believe, after all the fantasies I've had of us finally talking, I would be forced into it when I look like a crazy hot mess.

I smooth down my hair with clammy hands and take a breath that doesn't feel like it reaches my lungs and then straighten my spine. Fine. If I'm going to be embarrassed either way, at least I can keep it to a minimum..

I storm away from Kara, determined to just get it over with and try to come up with something to say while I watch him finish another set on the bench press. He racks the bar with a loud clang and then sits up on the bench breathing hard.

I pause my momentum not two steps away from him, my mind coming up blank with anything to say or how to approach this.

I look around desperately for inspiration. Maybe if I wasn't already worked to exhaustion, I could ask him to spot me or show me how to use one of the other machines, but just holding my water is making my arm shake. I can't do this.

I panic and turn to go back to Kara and plead for mercy, but suddenly, I get the breath knocked out of me by a hard wall of muscle that had come up behind me. The force I put into my turn bounces me off another man's chest and knocks me backward, projecting me right into *him* to my absolute horror.

He and I both go tumbling over the other side of the bench he was seated on, crashing to the floor with me sprawled over the top of him as he lands half on his side. One hand is trying to catch himself to avoid hitting his head while the other manages to grip around my waist as my back smashes into his chest. I close my eyes wanting to die in the moment of shocked silence that follows.

"Whoa. Shit, are you guys okay?" I open my eyes to see the wall of beefcake I'd just run into leaned over the bench, offering a hand to help me up. I realise I'm still reclined against the tattooed guy from the bench. I jump to my feet so fast, it makes my head spin, and I almost fall again because my left leg had become entangled with his.

Beefcake grabs my arms to steady me. I then turn to look down in horror at poor tattoo guy sprawled at my feet. "I'm okay. Oh, my God. I'm so sorry! That's embarrassing. I'm…I… Are you all right?" I ask when he doesn't make a move to get off the floor while he untangles his right earbud that fell from his ear in the crash.

A charming smile transforms his face as he watches me stuttering in a rush and then says, "I'm good, babe. But if you're going to throw yourself at a guy, at least give him a warning so he can prepare to catch you before you both go down," he jokes in a deliciously deep voice. He then slowly lifts himself up from the floor while I cover my face in embarrassment. *Hey, Death, any moment now would be good to come collect me.*

Beefcake speaks up and jokes, "Technically, it was me who threw her into you. Sorry, I didn't expect this little miss to ram into me, chest first. Wish I had been ready for it." I separate my fingers to glare up at his overly tanned, overly bulked, six foot self with greasy dark hair, a lecherous gleam in his brown eyes and thin-lipped smirk.

I take a deep breath to give him an earful, but the hot tattooed guy playfully adds, "That makes two of us." My breath leaves me in a rush, and I drop my hands to see his teasing grin as he removes his cap, running his left hand through his dark blond hair. I catch my first glimpse of amazing sky blue eyes with a dark outer ring before he pulls the cap back in place and shadows them.

My eyes stray to his tatted biceps that bulge and shift with the movement, and I'm rendered speechless.

"Everyone okay?" I hear Kara hesitantly ask as she approaches, and I turn to glare at her. *This is all your fault.*

Kara smiles sheepishly at me before looking over my

15

shoulder, her smile turning pleased. "Hi, I'm Kara, and this little missile here is Aela," she says to tattoo guy, making my glare become murderous. *Little? I'm only four centimetres shorter than her five foot eight*—although I do feel small next to him, who is easily over six feet tall.

"Dec," he introduces himself, and my outrage at Kara dies a little. *I have a name!* I could kiss Kara now, I'm so giddy. I'm smiling as I turn to face Kara and Dec. Beefcake says something that gets ignored while Dec looks at me curiously. His mouth twitches and the overhead lights glint off his lip ring as Kara looks at him, and I look back and forth between the two. Then I remember the humiliation I just lived through and my smile dims.

"Well, I would say it's nice to meet you, Dec. Really, I would, but that was so embarrassing, I may have to change gyms to live it down, which really sucks because I like this one and live only a few floors up… and now I'm rambling to make it worse. Great. We're going now. Sorry again. Bye." I grab Kara's arm as she continues standing there smiling at him adoringly when he starts to chuckle at my word vomit.

"Well, I may have a bruised butt cheek, but I will still say it was a pleasure to meet you, ladies. And don't change gyms. I promise I will try not to tease you about it." Dec makes a cross over his heart with a playful glint in his eyes.

I roll my own as he smiles gently, and Kara's smile grows, which didn't seem possible until I watched it happen.

"I like you. And we know Aela likes you after her display of affection there. If you're ever in the neighbourhood, we live on the tenth floor, apartment eight. Feel free to stop by and ram into her anytime in return." She winks. I feel my cheeks burn at what I hope wasn't a deliberate double entendre.

"Kara!" I scold, but she shrugs me off unapologetically as Dec chuckles.

"I'll keep that in mind." His voice dropped low and gravelly, causing my body to tingle in places that have no business getting tingly in public. I have to physically shake myself and tug Kara's arm again as I begin to drag her away.

"So… how much do you love me right now?" Kara murmurs once we're in the reception area waiting for the lift, and I turn to look at her like she's crazy.

"Love you? I level ten hate you right now. That was the single most humiliating moment of my entire life," I whisper harshly as I jab the up button repeatedly, trying to get out of there before she can find another way to embarrass me.

"But you sort of had an actual conversation with him, got a name to go with that delicious body, and got to feel it up," Kara argues with a nudge to my left arm.

"All of which would have been nice if not for the fact I practically assaulted him," I grumble as the doors finally open.

I drag her in with a burst of speed, and she snorts as the doors shut. "Focus on the negatives, why don't you. I think it was a success. Proud of you, girlie." Kara wraps her arms around me, squeezing. Trying to struggle out of her arms, I let out a huff and grudgingly accept it.

Chapter 4

DECLAN

'TIMES LIKE THESE' by the Foo Fighters blares in my ears as I finish my last set on the bench press. I sit up to gulp down some water and catch my breath before I move to the cables.

I wipe off my mouth as I lift my head to check the clock, but before I can get a glimpse, a soft, warm, yet hard body rams into me from my right, knocking the breath out of me and sends me sliding right off the bench.

A blur of brunette hair comes into my vision at the same time I get a whiff of coffee and vanilla. I reflexively put my hand out to stop myself from eating carpet, my other arm automatically wrapping protectively around the curvy little thing that crashed into me.

I get a hard elbow to the chest when we land, and I gasp for breath painfully. I look down to see just who exactly I have partially sprawled in my lap and grin when the first thing catching my eye beyond the mass of silky locks is a decent amount of cleavage. I have the perfect view from over her shoulder.

Her form-fitting workout gear leaves no curve on her tiny frame to the imagination. I have to fight the urge to trail my hand down the curve of her waist to her hip.

A guy, with too much upper body muscle to be natural, leans

over the bench I had been forced from with a look of shock as he extends a hand to the girl and asks if we're okay.

I tense as an irrational part of my brain that sounds very caveman-like shouts 'mine' and signals my body to hold onto her, but she suddenly shoots up off me like a little pop-up toy. She stumbles when she is almost standing due to her left foot somehow getting under my right leg in the fall. I prepare to catch her, but that arsehole grabs hold of her arms, steadying her. She turns to look down at me with a horrified look on her cute, heart-shaped face as she looks me over, searching for an injury.

Meanwhile, the douchebag that put his greasy hands on her shifts, catching my attention as he blatantly stares at her arse.

I have to grit my teeth and look away before I do something stupid, so I focus on detangling my earpiece from my singlet.

She sputters in a sweet, melodic voice while her cheeks turn an adorable shade of pink. This girl is too freaking cute.

I assure her I'm fine, but I can't help but tease a little as I climb to my feet, ignoring the pain in my chest where her tiny elbow hit me and watch as she tries to hide her face in her hands. She flushes darker in embarrassment. I want to take her hands away so I can look at the colour burn beautifully on her cheeks, but I restrain by shoving my hands in the pockets of my loosely fit shorts.

Apparently not wanting to be left out from her attention, Douchebag clears his throat and makes a smart arse remark about him being the one who threw her into me and how he wished he'd been ready for it. He looks her up and down suggestively.

I clench my fists in my pockets but grin when she spreads her fingers over her face to reveal her beautiful greenish-blue eyes that are apparently glaring at him. I watch her back stiffen while she takes a deep breath, no doubt intending to use it to put his stupid arse in his place. I speak up to distract her, not because I don't want to see him taken down a notch by this feisty little kitten, but because I don't trust him to be stable enough not to get offended and do something stupid. I've seen steroid users throw down for less.

"That makes two of us."

Thankfully, she exhales in a rush as she turns to me, dropping her hands from her face. The look on her face makes my dick twitch in my pants. *Shit. I do not need that guy to be responding right now.*

I take my hat off to run my hand through my hair as I breathe in to try to calm myself. I catch a gleam of heat in her eyes as she watches my arms as I put it back on, not helping matters.

Crap. Dead puppies. Old nuns. Grandma Lyn in her bikini... I struggle to think unsexy thoughts, which is pointless while I continue looking at her and fight to keep my grin in place.

It's then a blonde hesitantly approaches and asks if everyone is okay. I reply with a nod of my head while inside I'm screaming no!

I take a deep breath and find the new chick giving me a huge smile. *Weird.* She introduces them both to me, and I watch as Aela's back stiffens and wonder what caused it, wishing I could see her expressive face, but she hasn't turned back to face me since Kara approached us.

"Dec." I introduce myself using my nickname and then watch Aela turn to smile brilliantly at me like I've just given her the winning lottery ticket, not just my name. Douchebag introduces himself but goes unacknowledged, and after a moment's hesitation, he curses under his breath and walks.

I'm feeling like a bug under a microscope with the way Kara's looking at me, which makes me nervously rock back on my heels before directing my attention solely to Aela—not like that's very hard. Especially when her big smile suddenly dims as the blush returns to her cheeks.

Aela stammers adorably, and I chuckle, wanting to hug her to me. These urges to touch her are getting harder to control, which is crazy. I think I might be coming down with something or maybe walloped my head in the fall without noticing. Whatever it is, I will deal with it as long as Aela's around. I don't know why, but this accidental meeting has me feeling lighter than I've felt in a long time.

I tease her about possibly having a bruised butt cheek when I lie about never teasing her again after she complains about having to change gyms, which causes Aela to roll her eyes as Kara smiles. Her smile reminds me of the Cheshire cat from *Alice in Wonderland.*

Kara then says something about dropping by their apartment to 'ram into' Aela anytime. *Say what?* Kara winks suggestively, which makes me chuckle as Aela's blush creeps down her neck and to her cute little ears.

Since when are ears cute? I don't know, but hers definitely are.

Aela yells at Kara who just shrugs her off. These two are entertaining as hell.

"I'll keep that in mind," I reply to Kara as images of ramming into Aela run through my mind, and I shift to hide my growing hard on. Aela seems to pause for a moment and then she's off toward the stairs, dragging Kara behind her, who waves with an unapologetic grin. I salute Kara and watch their departure until they are out of sight. I chuckle to myself as I replace my earphones then go back to my workout with less enthusiasm than before.

Chapter 5

AELA

"GOOD MORNING," I sing as I bounce giddily into the kitchen to which Kara replies with a glare and a "humph" from her perch on one of the stools at the breakfast bar.

"Why are you so chipper? Did you get yourself some fun from your B.O.B. this morning?" she asks before taking a gulp of coffee, and it's my turn to glare as I set the ingredients for my microwave oats down on the bench.

"No. I moved that thing, by the way, so no more blackmail out of you. I'm just excited for everything that's happening today. I'm looking forward to my new classes and the labs. Then there's my appointment this afternoon to finally get my tattoo." I do a small excited bounce as I fill my bowl, put it in the microwave, and then push the quick start button until it gets to ninety seconds—since it's the only button that seems to work for me on the damn thing.

"How do you feel about that last one? You know you missed the deadline for a teenage rebellion if you're doing it just to spite your parents?" Kara muses over the mug she's holding in both hands like her only lifeline, and I shake my head immediately.

"No, you know I've wanted this for ages. I only waited to keep the peace since Dad totally flipped when he heard I wanted one, demanding it wouldn't happen while I was under his roof.

I'm a little nervous, but I can't wait." I quickly extract my bowl from the microwave when it has one second left, like it's a bomb going to detonate if it reaches zero. Stupid, I know. But I started doing it when I was little and old habits die hard. Plus, the loud beeping really annoys me.

"I can't decide what I'm more eager to see, the ink when it's done or the look on Nate's face when he sees it." Kara smiles devilishly which makes me grin. For as long as I can remember, Kara has taken delight in making my older brother squirm. They used to tease and torment each other pretty evenly until Nate suddenly decided three years ago he was too cool or too old for games and started calling her a bad influence on me. Of course, no one listened to him, and now he just puts up with whatever she does without reacting.

"That narc can kiss my butt," I state around a spoonful of porridge, which makes Kara wrinkle her nose at me before she looks to the clock and scrambles to gather her bag.

"Mine first. I've got to go. Text me if you wimp out. Otherwise, I will see you at Ink Fix at six." Kara giggles at her rhyme while giving me a quick one-armed squeeze and then rushes out the door.

I contemplate stretching out on the couch to watch some television since I don't have to be at Uni until ten, but then realise, with my appointment this afternoon, I won't be able to fit in any gym time tonight. So I get my bag packed for class, throwing my gym stuff in too so I can leave from downstairs after my workout. Probably a good thing since I know Dec won't be there this early on a Tuesday.

I feel equal measures of relief and disappointment over that thought but shove it aside to be ignored as I leave the apartment.

23

Chapter 6

DECLAN

I JOLT AWAKE to music suddenly blaring from the shop and curse as Tom jumps up onto the bed with a drawn out meow of complaint.

"I know, bud. Don't worry. I'll kick her arse." I scratch behind Tom's ear as I sit up with a yawn then drag myself out of bed. I step into a pair of shorts from the floor and collect a shirt as I head for the stairs, plotting murderous thoughts involving Kit, my receptionist slash piercer slash shop manager extraordinaire and my sister-from-another-fucked-up-mister. She looks like a punked up porcelain doll with her creamy skin, big green eyes and bright pink streaks through her white-blonde hair, with lip, nose and brow piercings as well as twenty-millimetre steel tunnels through her ears.

I find her perched on her stool before the Mac, grinning behind a cup of coffee as I glare at her.

"About time you got up. This shop won't run itself, you know," she quips as I reach around her to turn the music down to an appropriate level before Sonya from the real estate office next door complains.

"You run it so much better than me anyway. That was an arsehole move. We don't even open until ten, and my first appointment is at eleven." I grumble, which makes her laugh

24

while she hands over the coffee in the holder hidden beside her bag under the desk.

"Here. Have your coffee, Grump. And it was done by an arsehole, by the way, but not me." Kit gestures with a nod behind me so I turn to see Alex sitting on one of the benches. I glare at him as he raises his hands in supplication.

"Kit suggested it. You know I totally would have come up to snuggle and spoon you, wake you up real nice-like, but I'm exhausted. Really, it's your own fault anyway for not answering your phone." Alex has the nerve to glare at me like I'm the one who did him wrong as Kit throws a pen at him. I rub my hair in frustration.

"You try to spoon me, brother, and I will castrate you. Since when do you even get up before lunch, douchebag, and what the hell are you talking about? I was sleeping," I grumble, placing my coffee down to put my shirt on. I catch Alex looking at my chest in alarm.

"I accidentally crashed at Laney's last night after a marathon round of hot-as-fuck monkey sex and woke up to a stage five clinger so I had to bail asap. I walked here from Runaway Bay when your sleeps-like-the-dead arse failed to answer any of my S.O.S texts or calls, only to find my keys must have fallen out of my pocket at her place. I couldn't get into my car and again, you wouldn't wake up to let me in to get my spare keys. I sat on the front step for two hours until our little Kitty came to save me but refused me coffee even though she had two fresh ones from Zarraffas—which is just cruel. It's been a hard morning, bro." Alex pitifully eyes my cup. I yank down my shirt and snatch up my coffee before he can even try for it.

"What happened to your chest, by the way? That's a nasty looking bruise you're sporting there." Alex changes the subject as Kit hisses at him for calling her Kitty, and I shrug but can't contain the grin that lifts one side of my mouth at the memory of the little accident that caused the ache in my chest that's still a little tender.

"Accident at the gym yesterday," I vaguely explain as they both stop bickering to look at me curiously.

"Okay, Mr Vague. What are you hiding?" Kit asks with her pierced left brow arched in question while Alex starts grinning like a fool.

"Did you face plant lifting weights or something? That's fucking funny. Do tell." He rubs his hands eagerly for details, so I raise an eyebrow of my own at him smugly.

"No. A chick fell on me, and her elbow got me a good one when we crashed to the floor." He raises both brows sceptically at my explanation and Kit scoffs.

"Serious? Was she hot?" Alex asks, looking more interested when I nod.

"Deadly and an easy tenner." I grin, recalling the memory of Aela, all rosy cheeked and smiling up at me.

"Who is she? Did you get her number or bring her back here? Wait! Is she upstairs all gloriously sexed up and wrapped in your sheets?" Alex looks expectantly down the hall to the stairs leading to my apartment. I laugh as Kit calls him a pig then collects her cigarette pack as an excuse to get away from him.

"Aela. No. And I wouldn't tell you because you wouldn't be able to keep yourself from trying to get up there for a peek." I answer all his giddy questions at once, and he frowns suspiciously.

"You pretty much just said there is a possibility she is up there, but you won't say for sure. I don't know what to trust right now."

I shrug and bite off a laugh. He's too much fun to mess with.

"I should go get ready and grab some breakfast. I'll bring your keys back down." I turn to head back for the stairs, and Alex jumps up from his lounging position on the bench.

"Oh, I don't think so. I'm coming up there to check things out." Alex follows me down the hall, and I grin over my shoulder at him as he scowls.

"Suit yourself. Don't be too disappointed though when the only nakedness up there will be me in the shower."

After checking every corner of my tiny two bedroom apartment, Alex disappointedly leaves with his keys and a promise to drop in before his bartending shift at the local strip club, Ruby's.

I shower then dress in a clean pair of jeans and a Sullen singlet before feeding myself and Tom, who follows me around complaining loudly until I do.

When I get back downstairs, I find Kit leaning over the appointment book, mumbling a string of curses as she looks it over with her arms folded in agitation. Not good.

"What's the problem?"

Kit jumps as I come up behind her and then swivels in her chair to look at me as she takes a deep breath. "Skunk called, said he has the hangover from hell and can't come in. He has five clients today, one of which he has already rescheduled on twice. I tried calling BJ, but he's not answering his phone, and Josie said she can't be here until six because her kid is sick. So it's just you and me manning the shop for the day, and only you can ink," Kit explains, all in one breath.

I feel winded for her after all that and take a deep breath myself.

"I'll make a call. It's cool," I assure Kit with a pat on her shoulder. I go to get my cell, knowing there's only one person who could and would help out right now.

The one person I was hoping I wouldn't have to ask for help with my shop, but having been open only four months, we can't afford to turn away any possible walk-ins or have any dissatisfied clients.

One hour later, the front door of the shop slides open but fails to draw my attention from the backroom where I'm trying to finish the draw up for this afternoon's client—that is until a loud, booming voice calls out, "Where's my boy at?"

I smile as I rise from my desk and head out to the front. There's a young guy leaning over Kit's counter talking to her quietly, but my attention goes straight to Buzz.

The guy who taught me everything I know about tattooing manages to take up most of the room in the waiting area, which is no small feat, but Buzz is a big mountain of a man with an even bigger personality and presence. He looks like a retired bikie in all his leather, with a dark head of hair and beard, and tatts with his sunnies covering his eyes because that's exactly what he is.

Despite being in his late fifties, Buzz still manages to give off that badarse vibe, but behind it all, he's a big softie and would give a stranger in need the shirt off his back. Or in my case, step up to the plate to be a fatherly figure to a seventeen-year-old boy he didn't know, who was struggling with anger issues after his father bailed when things got too hard.

"Here he is. Geez, boy, you still growing? I swear you look bigger each time I see you." Buzz engulfs me in a 'bloke hug' which is basically getting pulled into him and three hard beatings to your back. I still haven't decided whether he doesn't realise his own strength or it's a deliberate manly test—or just proving he still has his brawn.

"Nah, old man. You're just shrinking as you age," I joke and receive a warning jab to my kidney that makes me laugh.

"I may be old, but I can still put you on your arse, son." Buzz removes his sunglasses, and I have to clear my throat around the lump that forms there from the look of pride in his eyes as he grins at me before taking in the shop.

Damn it. He's the only person who can affect me like this, especially with just a look. But his opinion has always mattered

28

to me. I may not like how he had to run his business thanks to his affiliation with the Blood Brothers motorcycle club, but Buzz is a good man, and he's been there for me when no one else was.

"Nice setup you've got," Buzz compliments as he steps up to get a closer look at one of my metal works propped up in the corner by Kit's desk, keeping his hands clasped behind his back as he leans over to inspect it.

I quietly chuckle, recalling last time he touched one of my pieces and according to him, "nearly took his index finger off." Though he only needed two stitches.

"How's it all going?" Buzz turns to look at me questioningly. I shrug nonchalantly but can't keep the content smile from my face.

"Apart from the mishap today, it's been good. Business has steadily picked up, especially with the news spreading of Kit's low piercing prices, and I've had a few good clients dropping my name around. I've even sold a few canvas and metal works," I explain, and he nods, beaming with pride again.

"Good to hear. We'll have to catch up for a beer when you're free. I got too used to seeing your ugly mug around my shop, and I kind of miss it." I catch the sincerity in Buzz's eyes before he claps his hands loudly and his business face slides back into place. "Right. I gotta roll. This here is, Jai. Came over from Cali and has been working with me for two months. Haven't seen a style he can't do yet so you should have no problems. Also, he's already on my payroll so he comes to you free for the day. Think of it as an apartment warming present." Buzz winks and crosses his arms so I know there will be no arguments allowed. I nod my acceptance, fighting to not roll my eyes, knowing it will only earn me a clap to the ear as I look to the guy he brought over to help us out.

Jai looks about my age, rocking a hippy/surfer style with his blond mop of hair, deep tan, blue eyes and a flannel shirt over a singlet and baggy, holey jeans.

"Thanks, Buzz. I owe you one," I reply as he turns to head out the door, stopping halfway out to look back.

"No problem, son. Just come over for dinner sometime soon. Mae misses you too," Buzz replies gruffly like there's something caught in his throat, and I smile at the mention of his wife.

"Done. See you soon," I promise. Buzz nods before turning to look at the other two still huddled at the counter.

"Later, Kitty. If these guys give you too hard a time, you let me know." Kit laughs and gives him a thumbs-up, which makes Buzz and I grin because we all know she can hand us our arses any day despite how little she is. Buzz walks out with a wave over his shoulder as I shake Jai's hand.

"Did Kit get you filled in on what's happening?" I ask and he nods, "All right. If anyone needs me, I'll be in my room. Kit, let me know when my guy shows up."

Kit salutes me then takes Jai to set up his gear in Skunk's workspace. I watch them from across the corridor for a second before getting back to my sketch.

Chapter 7

AELA

I TAKE A deep, relieved breath of fresh air when I step out of the science unit for the last time for the day as the sun is just starting to dip behind the buildings before me. The excitement of the first day back at campus quickly died off once my first math class started. I don't understand why the first day of classes is mostly wasted on talking about what you're going to learn over the semester. Just hand out a damn syllabus and get on with it.

I check my phone on my way to the parking lot to find three missed calls, a voicemail, and a text from Kara.

"Cold feet yet? Hope not because I'm on my way there. Xx"

I smile excitedly and text back a quick negative before stuffing my phone back into my bag so I can jog to my car.

I pull up in front of the black and white tattoo parlour that's only a couple of streets away from our apartment to find Kara sitting on the bench out front of the complex of shops.

Nerves start making an appearance now that I'm here, and I fidget, running my hands through my hair as I check my reflection in the rearview mirror. I try to take a calming breath when Kara opens my door, leaning in to inspect my face.

"You still have a few minutes. Want a shake or anything before we go in?" She smirks playfully, and I kick at her shin as I get out of the car.

"Yeah, I'm sure they'll love me in there when my nerves bring it back up all over their floor," I reply sarcastically and lead the way into the tattoo parlour with the neon sign that says Ink Fix and is casting an eerie blue glow over everything. The skin of my arms looks pale and alien-like in the light, which amuses me as I hold them out in front of me before Kara nudges me with a weird look.

I refocus, straighten my spine, and slide the glass door open to step inside. I look from the reception desk to the black leather seating area, finding it empty, but I can overhear a couple of people laughing and talking down the hall behind the counter.

I give Kara a questioning look, but she's distracted by a complicated looking metal sculpture until she feels me looking and turns to shrug at me before approaching the desk. Kara looks it over then presses what looks like a punk, rubber duck that lets out a loud squeak which makes me jump and then giggle.

"Hello…?"

Kara leans over the counter to call down the hall. A girl around our age comes out of a back room and heads our way, drawing my attention away from all the artwork around the shop. Not just because she's the person approaching, but because she's like a living artwork herself. From her white blonde hair that's streaked bright pink, matching pink lips, blushed cheekbones and shadowing around her eyes with dark lashes that all enhances her perfectly porcelain skin tone. She's wearing a pair of designer faded and torn jeans with a soft looking, but plain black, off the shoulder top, and her feet are rocking an awesome pair of lime green Chucks covered in studs and graffiti.

"Hi, ladies. What can I do for you?"

My gaze is drawn to the piercings that decorate her left eyebrow to the right of her top lip and the tunnels in her ears. Not many people could pull it all off without looking sketchy, but this girl still manages to look cute, in a bad arse sort of way. I don't realise I have been silently staring at her, smiling like some crazy person, until Kara clears her throat.

"Hi. Aela has an appointment at six."

The girl looks down to a schedule book in front of her that is covered in pencilled markings and smudges as though there had been a lot of rewrites. When I catch a look of confusion on her face, I hope I haven't been taken off.

"Which artist are you looking for, hon?" She looks up to me, and a stab of disappointment hits me in the stomach.

"Uh, Steve," I reply then look back to the book with her, hoping my name will suddenly appear.

"Skunk had an appointment written in for a Kaila that I've been trying to call. Is this your number?" she turns the book so I can see it easier, her finger held to a number. It's mine.

"That's me." I smile happily until the rest of what she said registers. "You said you tried to call?" I ask as she mutters something about a useless skunk which is odd, but I don't question her. She looks like she could kick my arse so she can be as crazy as she likes so long as it's a nice crazy.

"Wait, did you say your name was Aela?"

She pauses to look up at me questioningly so I nod. She leans over to rest her forearms on the counter top, looking me up and down in my lime green summer dress and flip-flops with a curious expression before continuing.

"This isn't the first time I've heard your name today and I don't believe in coincidences. Anyway, the dick you booked with has bailed today with a hangover, so I have a few choices for you. You can either reschedule, hoping he gets his arse in next time, or we have a fill in for today who can handle it for you. Or... I could get my boss out here to talk to you and see if he will do it. Now, he's still with a client for at least another fifteen minutes and thinks it will be his last for the day, but if you are who I've heard about—which will be off the charts serendipitous—I think he will be happy to make the exception. I can guarantee he does the best work on the coast if not the country, and I'm not just saying that because he's my boss."

She winks, leaning back onto her elbows to clasp her hands together under her chin while looking at me expectantly.

I turn to look at Kara for her opinion, but she misses it because she's too intrigued by the display case of body piercing jewellery. She must feel my look again, though because she shrugs.

"Whatever you want, Aela. I have nowhere I need to be anytime soon," Kara says without looking up then asks about a piece in the case.

What do I want to do? Well, I don't think I will stick with Steve. I don't want to wait any longer, and he sounds unreliable. What she said was a little cryptic and has me wondering what she was talking about, just who has she heard about, and what she has heard? It seemed that her boss was the option she was recommending, though and it sounds good. "If your boss is willing to do it tonight, that would be awesome," I reply, and the girl pulls away from Kara who was checking out the tragus piercing in her left ear.

"Sweet. Take a seat. I'll see if I can steal him away for a quick sec. Can I get you anything to drink while I'm back that way?" She's practically bouncing on her feet with excitement over my choice, which heightens my curiosity.

"No thanks…" I pause awkwardly because I don't know her name yet.

"Oh, right. I'm Kit. Sorry, it's been a really long day." Kit flutters her hands around her head in a crazy sort of gesture, and I smile as she walks back down the hall.

"I don't know what you're playing at, Kit, but this had better be good. I want to finish up so I can go have a shower and chill. It's been a long arse day." I hear a low rumbling voice and two sets of footfalls—one distinctly heavier than the other, heading this way less than a minute later. Something about the irritated voice makes my skin tingle with anticipation.

"I promise you, I really think this is worth it. Just give me a sec," Kit pleads as she bounces around the corner and into view. "Boss man, this is Aela, and she's hoping you will take over her booking tonight with Skunk." Kit gestures to me with her arms like I'm a prize on a game show. I try not to laugh until an all too familiar man is revealed, and my urge to laugh dies a sudden death.

No. Freaking. Way.

I blink my tired eyes hard, hoping I'm seeing things. But when I look back up, Dec is still standing there with a somewhat dumbfounded expression that I'm sure mirrors my own.

"Dec. No way. You work here?" Kara asks loudly, drawing our attention to where she is sitting with a huge grin on her face. Dec seems to recover first as his lips lift up into a tempting, self-satisfied smirk.

"I own here. What are you girls doing here? Assaulting me wasn't enough, so now you're stepping up to stalking?" Dec's gaze slides back to me with a hint of mischief, and I feel my cheeks flush as he folds his arms over his chest, making me swallow hard as I eye off the bulging muscles now on display.

I shake my head as I force my eyes up to meet his all too knowing gaze. "Arse. You promised you wouldn't tease me about that again. And I'm not here for you. I'm here for ink," I reply haughtily, which makes him grin as I smile reluctantly. "I promised I would try not to. What do you want done?" Dec steps over to sit on the edge of the glass-topped coffee table in front of me, so close that our knees touch, and I squirm at the heated look in his eyes as I picture the things I would like him to do to me. In this room. On this couch. If we were alone.

Mind out of the gutter, Aela.

I take a deep breath as I turn to pull my phone out of my bag to show him the design. Dec holds my hand longer than necessary in his when I lean forward to hand it to him. I jerk back when I catch his cheeky view of my cleavage, and he chuckles before looking at my phone's screen. "I gave the original drawing to the guy who said he would draw it up, who also said his name was Steve, but you all seem to know him as Skunk." I ramble and can't help the wrinkling of my nose at the name Kit keeps mentioning. *What kind of nickname is Skunk?*

Dec catches the look and chuckles again before returning my phone. "How big and where do you want it?" he asks, and I struggle to not think of him referring to what's in his pants. Obviously, Kara has the same issue because she snorts before covering her mouth to smother her laugh, pretending to be coughing.

Dec's gaze shifts between the two of us with an arched brow as I try to ignore the heat spreading from my cheeks and down my neck. I really need to get a grip.

"I want it on the back of my right shoulder and as big as it needs to be with all the detail in it. Steve already explained it would at least take up my shoulder blade. I'm fine with that," I explain while he nods approvingly.

"Kit says you're really determined to get it done now. But we won't be able to finish tonight. There are a few hours to that piece. If you're dead set on it, we can at least smash out the outline tonight then fill it in with colour when it's healed, or we can book in for another day and get it done in one long sitting?"

I really struggle to pay attention to the words coming out of his mouth while I look into his eyes. They are such captivating shades of blue-grey and black, but I somehow manage it and eagerly jump at his offer to start tonight, which makes him smile.

"Okay, I'll get Kit to print off your pic while I finish with my current client, and then I'll take a better look at it, draw it up and get the stencil ready. It'll take a while, though, so if you have anything to do for an hour or so, you may want to go do it, and we can call you in when I'm ready. Do I have your number—in the book, I mean?"

Dec smiles with what I think is an overdone innocence as Kit smacks him on the back.

"Cool it, Casanova. Her number's in the book. Skunk got it," she teases, and Dec frowns at the mention of Skunk as he gets to his feet.

"Right. I better get back to it then." Dec walks away somewhat abruptly, and once he's out of sight, Kit grins while taking my phone from me.

"Oh, this is going to be so much fun." She practically skips to the printer, which she connects with a USB cable to my phone and has it printing in seconds.

"What do you want to do for an hour?" Kara asks, sounding unsure.

"We can go get some food?" I suggest as Kit returns through the little swinging door to join us.

"If you have nothing better to do, I could get us some pizza, and we can turn the music or TV up and chill since you've been messed around?" Kit offers. It sounds good to me, but I turn to see what Kara thinks.

"As long as I don't have to cook, anything sounds great to me," Kara concedes, and Kit jumps up excitedly.

"Sweet. I'll make it Dec's shout since he will no doubt take half of what we get anyway. Any requests?" Kit asks as she grabs the cordless phone then looks over expectantly.

"Anything chicken, no onions and extra jalapenos?" I ask which makes Kit grin.

"That is my kind of pizza." She dials as Kara says she'll have anything.

An order for three extra-large pizzas, one meat lovers, and

two chicken pizzas—and then what I'm sure is a rather embarrassed or amused pizza guy later, Kit joins us on the comfy leather couch.

We settle in to watch *Mr. T's World's Craziest Fools*, which is absolutely hilarious. I don't know which is funnier—the video clips or his running commentary throughout them.

Chapter 8

DECLAN

WHAT THE HELL is wrong with me?

I forcefully push my way through the door to my workspace where the guy who was supposed to be my last client for the day is waiting for me to finish his tribal shoulder piece.

I take a seat on my stool and adjust it again to try to relieve the ache in my back and neck. "You still good, man?" I ask as I don a new pair of gloves then wipe his arm clear of blood while he gives a thumbs-up.

"I'm sweet, bro. All good out there?" He nods to the door, and I can't help grinning as I think of who is out there.

"Hell, yeah it is. Now let's get this shading done so you can get home to your missus before you're late for dinner." I restart my machine as he chuckles.

Twenty minutes later, I've wrapped the big man's arm, and I'm leading him down the hall as he thanks me profusely. We both suddenly halt in the reception area at the sight before us.

Kara, Aela, and Kit are spread out in the lounge area, having made themselves at home drinking beer and eating pizza. Well, two of them are drinking beer. Aela's gone for a tall, whipped cream monstrosity of a chick's coffee.

What made us stop, though was the sight of Kit feeling up Kara's boobs with a curious look. "I don't know what's going on here, but please, please don't let us interrupt unless I can join in," I call out, and all three girls turn to see us standing there gawking.

Aela laughs quietly while breaking down the whipped cream in her cup, and I happily indulge in naughty thoughts of what I could do with that whipped cream and her delicious little body. The guy next to me hands me the cash for his work then mumbles something before walking out the door.

Kit rolls her eyes at me as she gets up off the lounge and grabs a beer from the coffee table.

"Keep dreaming, Declan, and help yourself to some pizza since you paid for it." She gestures to the boxes on the coffee table, and I arch a brow in question at her.

"I did what now?" I move to inspect the boxes, finding my 'manly meat pizza,' as she likes to call it and grab a slice along with a beer out of the six pack sitting beside the pizzas.

"You heard me. Thanks for dinner, boss." Kit winks and smacks my arse as she passes on her way to the printer.

I take the open seat next to Aela and watch as a blush warms her cheeks. I fill with male pride over affecting her so easily but choose not to comment on it.

Instead, I lean into her more and whisper just low enough for her to hear, "What was with the boob grabbing?"

Aela smiles as I inhale the sweet vanilla and coffee scent that surrounds her. "Kit didn't believe they were real so Kara let her feel them to prove it." Aela shrugs like it's a regular occurrence.

"What about yours? Are they real?" I ask before I can even think to stop myself. I then bite my tongue, fighting off a grin when Aela turns to look up at me suspiciously.

"No one would mistake these things for fakes. Are you trying to cop a feel, Dec?" She fakes outrage, and I can't fight the grin lifting the left side of my mouth as I glance down at the beautiful handfuls we're discussing.

"I'm just saying if you have something to prove, then I am more than willing to test them for you." I try to look innocent as I take a gulp of my beer and she laughs, which makes something in my chest warm. It's a beautiful laugh. Just like her. Kit thrusts a piece of paper into my face so I stuff the last of my pizza slice into my mouth to take the paper.

It's the copy of Aela's tattoo, blown up to the size I would need which will cover her right shoulder blade. I look it over, admiring the colours and details of the lilies, roses, and butterflies, picturing the way it will move with her body.

It's beautiful—except for the quote in it that leaves a sinking feeling in the pit of my stomach.

Aela may be practically a stranger, but from what I do know about her, I can't imagine anyone wanting to change a thing about the woman and yet the fact she wants 'Love me for who I am, not what you want me to be' permanently etched on her skin suggests that some fool has somehow found her lacking, which makes me want to volunteer my fists to teach this douchebag a lesson.

I rein in the urge and settle back onto the lounge. When I feel Aela looking over my shoulder at it, I raise my left hand with the beer and stretch my arm out against the top of the lounge behind her head so she can see it better. *Well, that's the excuse I'm going with anyway.*

"Is this exactly how you want it?" I ask and Aela nods, sending some of her hair into her face, making me wish I wasn't holding my beer so I could move it for her to use the moment to justify my need to touch it, feel if it is as soft as it looks.

"Can I ask who the quote is for?" I keep my voice low so only she can hear and then watch as her mouth moves to speak but then pauses.

Aela takes a moment to think about it, biting on her bottom lip, which draws my attention to it before she turns to look up at me as though she only just realised.

"My family. Well, parents mostly. I swore to myself and Kara that getting this isn't a form of rebellion, but I've made it a statement to them." She sort of looks stunned at her confession, and a million miles away in thought, so I nudge her knee with mine and smile when she looks back to me. "They're kind of really controlling and strict. And pushy," Aela adds, and I drop the picture in my lap to place my right hand over hers that is now playing with the hem of her little green dress.

"You don't have to explain. Trust me, both Kit and I are experts in having messed up parents. I'm just glad it's not you pining after a guy you're better off without," I tell her and watch as her eyes light up before she laughs out loud.

"Wow. I hope I don't seem that sad. No, no douchebag guy for me. I haven't had time to spare for any type of guy actually, in a long time." Aela looks away, watching Kit as she fiddles with the television remote so Aela misses my ecstatic smile at her statement.

"No guy, huh?" I ask just to hear her confirm it, and she shakes her head without looking at me as her cheeks colour again, and my smile turns smug. "Well, no wonder you threw yourself into my lap," I joke and watch as she turns with her mouth hanging open before she backhands me in the chest with indignation, which makes me laugh. "Sorry. I couldn't help myself. I promise to try to be better from now on. I should get started on this sketch so we can get going. It'll be a long night for us as it is." I pull my arm back from around her reluctantly and finish off my beer.

"Yeah, okay. Thanks again for doing this, Dec. I know I'm probably irrationally stubborn about it, but I feel like I can't wait a second longer to have it as a part of me," Aela explains, and I wink as I stand.

"I totally get it. But since Kara is here for moral support, I guess this is your first time, so we'll see what you think once the pain starts." I smile when her look turns defiant.

She is just the cutest thing.

"I can handle pain. I won't wimp out," Aela states firmly, and I fight the urge to ruffle her hair.

"We'll see. I'll be back soon because there is no way I can focus out here with you all. But hey, do me a favour and call out if those two get frisky again." A bottle cap is hurled my way before I turn the corner to Aela's musical, heart-warming laughter.

It's almost impossible to concentrate when all I can hear is the hooting and giggling from the girls in the front room. I've got no idea what they are doing, but I resist the urge to find out, forcing myself to remain in my seat to finish this sketch.

Jai bursts through my door around twenty minutes later, grinning like a fool when I turn to look at him.

"Dude, are you aware there are three smokin' hot chicks partying it up out front?" Jai asks excitedly which I arch a brow at.

"It's hard to miss with all the noise. What are they doing?" I ask though I'm afraid to know. Especially when his grin widens.

"Kit's talking to one of them about nipple piercing as they play some card game with shots, and the really cute one is laid out on the couch, tapping her little feet to the music and watching them." Jai leans against the doorframe, giving me a confused look as he takes in my surroundings. Well, what he can see of it since the only illumination in the room is my desk lamp that's focused on the picture I'm working on to cut out distractions. Not that it's really working with all the noise the girls are making.

"So if you know they're out there, why the hell have you secluded yourself in the dark in here?" Jai looks at me as though I'm crazy so I gesture to the picture I'm replicating in front of me. He moves into the room to look over my shoulder, hair falling into his eyes as he tilts his head before smiling at me. "Which one is getting it?" Jai asks curiously with a scheming gleam in his eyes that I don't like one bit.

"Aela, in the green dress," I reply, a clear warning tone in my voice to discourage whatever he may be thinking.

I don't know if he picks up on it or not, but he straightens up as he says, "That will look hot when it's finished. Well, I'm going to chill with them while I wait for a walk-in until closing time."

I grit my teeth at the thought of this pretty surfer boy putting moves on Aela while I'm stuck in here for the next few minutes. It may not be good for business, but I do the only thing I can think of that's the least detrimental to my sanity. "Actually, man, I think you can finish for the day. If we have any walk-ins now, Kit can schedule them an appointment." I stand from my chair and hold out my hand, "Thanks for the help today, bro. You did some great work. I really appreciate it," I add as he slaps his hand into mine. He moves in for a 'bro shake' and I slap his back as he does mine, and then Jai pulls away with a knowing smirk.

"I get it, man, and it's cool. I don't want to encroach on your territory. If you ever need help again, just let me know. I had fun today. Kit's a really cool chick." Jai hands me his business card before leaving with a peace sign over his shoulder which makes me chuckle as I return to finishing the last touches to Aela's stencil.

"All right, Aela. We're good to go," I call out as I turn the corner to where the three girls are in the waiting area.

My eyes immediately zero in on the miles of legs Aela has on display, stretched out across the three seater sofa, her little green dress not even covering half of her smooth, luscious thighs that have my hands twitching with the need to run up them. For such a small girl, she sure manages to have a lot of leg, and the image of those lovely pins wrapped around me clouds my brain for a moment. That is until I realise the room is silent, and I'm just staring at her like a creeper. I clear my throat and tear my gaze away from all that gorgeous skin with what feels like the greatest self-control known to man.

"You ready for me?" I ask when I meet Aela's gaze, unsure if I'm asking about the tattoo or suggesting otherwise. Judging by the blush that warms her cheeks and the heat in her eyes, I'm sure she gets the suggestion I may or may not be giving.

Who am I kidding? I totally am.

Every muscle in my body is hard and straining, and I have to remember to breathe, to relax as I flex my hands to calm down and rein in the over-reaction my body is having to this beautiful little creature who is quickly overriding my normal brain functions.

Aela slides her feet to the floor with a small smile and brushes down her cute little dress as she stands.

"I'm more than ready," she replies with a daring look while making her way around the coffee table to my side. I swallow hard and take a deep, stuttering breath as I try to remind myself I can't just take her right now.

Not only is she here as a client, but we're not alone, for crying out loud, which reminds me—

"You want me to set up a bench to do this out here so you can have the girls around?" I ask since the room I use in the back isn't big enough to comfortably fit four people in and the whole reason Kara's here is for morale support. However, Aela shakes her head.

"No, I don't want Kara watching if I wince. She becomes mean after a few drinks, and she'll give me hell."

Ah, shit. This is going to be impossible.

My dick twitches at the thought of her alone in the back room with me. My mind is conjuring up images to encourage it, of Aela propped up on the bench, the dim light from my lamp turned on her, revealing all her smooth skin for me to freely run my hands over, to caress and kiss.

I'm thankfully yet regrettably pulled out of the fantasy as Kit announces loudly, "We may as well not be here with the way they are looking at each other. Don't worry. We can amuse ourselves out here." I turn to see Kit's grin as she waves us away.

"Just take it easy on my girl, Dec. Remember, it's her first time." Kara giggles, making Aela cover her face in mortification which has me fighting a chuckle as I turn, wrapping my left arm around Aela to guide her down the hall.

"I'll do my best," I call over my shoulder and am rewarded with Kit and Kara bursting into laughter and catcalls as I lean over to lightly kiss the top of Aela's head, unable to stop myself.

Her hands fall from her face as she looks up at me inquisitively. I grin sheepishly at her as I come to a stop at my room and open the door, gesturing for her to enter ahead of me.

Chapter 9

AELA

I FORCE MY lungs to inhale a deep breath as Dec flicks the light switch on the wall, revealing a small room with aquamarine walls covered in all manners of art consisting of charcoal sketches to colourful canvas paintings with their subjects consisting of anything from animals, cars, people, plants and skulls.

The room smells of antiseptic like the rest of the shop. It is meticulously clean, but manages to feel warmer than the front room even if the only furniture is a desk covered in papers with drawings on them, a black leather desk chair, a twenty-six inch LCD wall mount television, a small stool on wheels, a black leather bench, and a stand filled with equipment.

Dec moves ahead of me and starts adjusting the leather bench, turning it so its back faces the door and TV, before patting the seat to indicate I should climb on.

"Straddle it facing the backrest so you have something to lean on and get comfortable," Dec directs as he fiddles with his equipment. I do as instructed and try to breathe through the nerves that are hammering my stomach and making my heart try to beat its way out of my chest. I think it is more from being in this small room with Dec alone than the anticipation of the tattoo.

What was I thinking? I should have agreed to stay out where we had company, open space, and other distractions, rather than come in here where the air seems to be simultaneously warming and disappearing around me by the second and is filled with his earthy scent.

I force another deep, controlled breath into my lungs, hoping I'm not about to do something embarrassing while Dec moves behind me. I swear I can feel his body heat on my back but refuse to check just how close he is. Dec's hand appears to my right, and I look to see him offering a remote, so I take it automatically.

"Get comfortable and watch whatever you like. You want some water before we start?" Dec asks when he rolls the stool he is sitting on to face me, and I realise my face must betray how I feel right now.

I nod. "Please." Then I watch Dec lean down to a mini fridge under his desk before returning with a water bottle. I take it and break the seal while he watches me as though concerned I'm about to pass out or vomit on him.

I take a couple of gulps which helps cool me down then put the cap back on before propping it up between my legs.

Dec clears his throat and slides himself back out of view so I turn the TV on in hopes of finding a distraction.

"Can you remove the straps from your shoulder for me please?" His voice is low, causing goose bumps to break out down my arms at the sound. I move the straps of my dress and bra off my right shoulder as I resolutely stare at the TV, trying to act like I'm cool and that it's no big deal. Which it technically isn't, but my body seems to think it is as it heats up again. I can feel my blush spread down my throat.

This is crazy. I feel a nice chill as Dec presses against the skin of my shoulder with a wipe before running a razor over the skin to prepare it.

Whoa, wait. I have hairy shoulders?

I'll have to check this out. Images of the backs of hairy old

48

men fill my head through another swipe of the cool cloth, and then I feel him pressing the stencil paper carefully onto my back. Dec softly but firmly runs his hand over it to smooth it out, which I again try to ignore, before he peels the paper off and then leans over so I can see him. "Check that out in the mirror and tell me what you think." I get up on slightly trembling legs and smooth the bottom of my dress nervously as I make my way over to the full-length mirror behind the door. I turn so I can see my back in the reflection and instantly get a huge, excited smile.

It's only the black outline of the piece, but I can already picture how it's going to look when complete. "It's perfect." I turn to see Dec smiling.

When I slide my way back over the bench, Dec tucks a towel into the back of my dress to protect it from any excess ink or blood and then takes a deep inhale before blowing it out hard.

"Okay. Here we go… tell me if you're okay with this." He starts the machine. Loud buzzing fills the room, getting louder as it moves closer, and I feel like I'm about to jump out of my skin.

I feel a sharp, warm, itching sensation, but it's not unbearable, and I tell him so when Dec pulls away.

"Sweet. Let me know if you need a break or anything, okay?" Then he presses it against me once more, and I barely feel it while his other hand smooths over my skin to pull it taut where the needle is pressing.

***

"That's it. Are you still with me?" Dec's voice draws me out of the daze I've fallen into, and I look over my shoulder at him as the buzzing stops.

"Really? Already?" I ask and try to look at what he's done as he chuckles and wipes it off before covering it with antiseptic ointment.

49

"Already. Aela, it's been four hours. You okay?" Dec looks at me like I'm crazy, and I feel like an idiot. I stretch my back, feeling the stiffness in my spine from sitting still for so long as well as a slight burn in the skin of my shoulder and my arse is numb.

"You did amazing, by the way. I didn't get a single flinch out of you." I smile at Dec's praise as he covers my freshly inked skin in a piece of cling wrap, using tape to make it stick.

"It feels a bit like I have a sunburn. Nothing I can't manage," I assure him as I hear the snap of his gloves being removed.

"You seriously spaced out. I've never had anyone do that. I had to keep checking the mirror to make sure you hadn't passed out on me. I couldn't even get you talking when usually that's how people distract themselves from the pain. You kind of freaked me out, champ," Dec admits as I feel the warmth of his bare hands run along the edges of the tape, pressing it more securely to my skin. The feel of his calloused hands on me is nice.

It takes a moment for me to realise I should comment. "Sorry, I don't know what happened. I think I'm just really tired." *And you were touching me, but I won't admit that part out loud.*

"So, we'll book your next appointment in about three weeks when it should be nicely healed. I'll give you some antiseptic cream to apply when necessary. You'll have to rinse this with warm, soapy water in an hour or so. Keep it clean, don't get it sunburnt and no swimming or scratching."

Dec stands and then offers a hand to help me slide over the bench, which I take appreciatively since my butt is sore and my left foot has pins and needles. I lean onto my right foot to find it also lacking blood flow which causes me to stumble into Dec who grins as he catches me, holding me to his chest for a moment before I pull away in embarrassment.

"You have got to stop falling for me, Aela. It's really becoming a problem," he says jokingly, which causes me glare at him as I playfully backhand him in the chest.

Dec fakes being hurt with a wounded expression. "You have to stop the abuse as well, you mean little thing. People will start to talk when they see the bruises. Domestic violence is a crime," he adds.

I roll my eyes then he reaches out to gingerly put my bra and dress strap back into place. The back of his fingers gently sliding up my arm makes me shiver.

I hope he didn't notice, but when his eyes meet mine, I know he caught my shiver when I see the heated look in his gaze. My next breath stutters and my heart picks up in pace until Dec steps back, moving to open the door wider from its almost shut position. He then hands me a tube of cream from the desk beside it and aftercare instructions on a business card.

"So, I guess I'll see you tomorrow evening at the gym?" I ask in my rush to cover the moment we just had, and I then mentally kick myself when he gives me a quizzical look.

Way to show your stalker tendencies, Aela.

"Um, yeah. If I don't get held back here like tonight," Dec replies before moving to start down the hall.

I follow, unable to keep my gaze from wandering down to rest on his perfectly sculpted arse that makes me want to take a bite out of those jeans he wears so well.

"You're finally done? Spin around, girl. Let us see!" Kara demands as soon as we come into view to where her and Kit are sitting on the couch.

I smile as they bounce up out of their slouched positions to get a look at Dec's work. I turn around and receive appreciative noises. "How was it? We didn't hear any screaming out here, and we were listening hard for it," Kara asks as I turn back to see her eyebrows lift suggestively.

I shake my head while Declan chuckles.

"It was fine. I barely felt a thing." Both of them boo in mock disappointment before Kit looks to Dec, snorting derisively.

"I guess your reputation is made up of lies after all. Did you pay the girls to say good things after you were done?" she jokes and I wave my hands in front of my face to stop them from continuing.

"Enough of the innuendos. It's almost midnight. I have to be up early for school and I'm sure Dec is exhausted. Let's call it a night," I order and both girls groan in disapproval.

I guess Kara has found a kindred spirit here. These girls are too alike already.

"We were going to see if you two wanted to grab a drink across the road," Kit complains, and I shake my head as Dec holds up a hand to get our attention.

"Hold up. You mentioned school. How old are you, Aela?" He suddenly looks worried and very pale. I realise what he's thinking as he looks me up and down. I fight off a grin, deciding to mess with him.

"Not old enough to leave home according to my parents." I skirt outright answering him and watch as Dec blanches before turning to Kit, covering his mouth with his hand as he rubs it with agitation.

"Did we seriously not check her ID? Did I just give a pretty big tattoo to a minor without an adult's permission?" Dec is seriously starting to freak out, and I can't help but laugh. He looks so cute.

"Relax. I'm a second year University student and almost twenty-one," I assure him and watch the relief cross his face as the girls laugh and then his look turns devilish.

"You little minx. And here I thought you were the sweetest and innocent of the three of you. You know, payback is a bitch, and I still have to finish your tattoo," Dec warns suggestively, and I grin as I pull out the envelope in my bag with the money I was going to pay Steve. I give it to him as I reply, "I trust you."

Dec inspects the envelope before looking up to frown at me. "If this is for tonight it's too—" I cut him off before he can finish his protest, pushing his hands back when he tries to return the envelope.

"That's how much Steve estimated the tattoo would cost and you've done a better job than I could even imagine, so I'm paying for the rest of it up front," I state then cross my arms to show I mean business.

The man proves he is sexy as hell and smart by biting his tongue before grudgingly moving to the desk. Dec flips through the appointment book like a man on a mission then scribbles before practically stomping his way back and handing me another of the shop's business cards with an appointment time and mobile number scrawled on the back.

"If that time's no good, call and let me know," Dec says so I nod as I put it into my bag before I start to reluctantly make my way to the exit where Kara is waiting.

"Well, I guess I'll see you when I see you." I smile and Kit hugs me goodbye as Dec grins.

"See you tomorrow at the gym," he corrects, crossing his arms over his chest while leaning back against the glass display case.

My body seems to go into meltdown as I stop to look at him resting there with his legs stretched out and crossed in front of him—looking so delicious and self-assured. I get the urge to jump him right there, but Kara grabs hold of my elbow, obviously noticing what's happening, and drags me out the door behind her.

I turn away to watch where Kara's leading me as I trip over my own feet and regain some control of myself by the time we reach my driver's side door.

"Holy hot sauce, girl. The heatwaves between the two of you are combustible. I had to get you out of there before something caught fire." I lean against my car and grin as Kara fans herself emphatically.

"So, it's not just me who felt that?" I ask and watch Kara give a hard laugh before shaking her head.

"You need to do us all a favour and jump that guy soon. I was only a witness to the sparks, and I feel like I need a cold shower. I can't even imagine how you feel." Kara smirks.

I laugh as I sweep the hair back behind my ear when a breeze sends it into my face then look back to the shop before I can stop myself. Dec is still in the same spot, watching me with a look in his eyes that warms my lower stomach and other parts of my body. I inhale a deep breath.

"Let's get out of here before I do something crazy," I urge Kara in a low voice and quickly turn to get into my car.

I have to put a lot more focus into buckling my seatbelt and starting my car than necessary, and then I watch as Kara climbs into her own. Fighting the urge to look back into Ink Fix the entire time, I put the car in reverse and pull out of the car park, Kara following behind me.

Chapter 10

DECLAN

I WATCH AS Aela leaves my shop and don't even try to tamp down the surge of want that thrums through my body.

I stare transfixed as she leans against a car I assume belongs to her while a breeze plays with her dress, making it dance around her delicious stretch of legs. I emit a soft curse and try to relax the tightness of every muscle in my body by stretching out then lean my arms back against the counter.

It doesn't really help, though, as I can't take my eyes off Aela.

She laughs at something Kara says, and my eyes settle on her smiling face which makes that warmth in my chest reappear. I want to be the one to make her laugh and smile. I also need to feel her lips and body pressed against mine, explore her with my hands and mouth, and have her wrapped around me in any way I can get her.

As though Aela can hear my dirty thoughts, she turns to look my way, and our eyes lock. I figure her cheeks instantly blush, though I can't make it out from this distance before she looks away. I can only imagine the sheer need written all over my face that she witnessed.

It's not just need of the sexual variety, though. I want to get to know her, to be able to hold her in my arms just because I feel like it, to hear her talk about anything just to watch her expressions, and to take care of her.

I also seem to have grown a damn vagina since I met this girl. Who the hell have I become? I don't do relationships—especially with good girls like Aela.

Kit starts giggling, which stops my internal musings as I turn to find her watching me with a knowing smirk that I ignore. I try to subtly adjust my jeans that have felt at least one size too small since I first found Aela on my couch.

"I like those girls. I think I'll keep them. That means, whatever you are planning to do in that talented little mind of yours, you better not mess up. Or I will pierce your balls while you sleep," Kit threatens in a happy voice, but I catch the warning in her eyes and swear my balls slide up into my stomach with fear. I don't doubt her for a second.

When my ability to speak fails to return for at least a full minute, Kit smiles and pats me on the shoulder.

"Good. Now I'm off to get my beauty sleep. Don't forget to lock up." She kisses my cheek then leaves with a spring in her step.

I mechanically flick the lock after her car is out of sight, turn the lights out, and slowly make my way upstairs.

Shit. So help me God, I need more of Aela. Even with the risk of my balls being skewered like a shish kebab.

***

The next day of work seems to drag by incredibly slow, the clock changing only ten minutes every time I check.

At two in the afternoon, I'm fiddling with the appointment book during a quiet moment, and Kit laughs when she catches me looking at the clock again.

"Why don't you call Aela and see if she wants to go for

56

coffee or something before the gym? You don't have another appointment, and I can schedule any walk-ins," Kit suggests, and I turn to where she is leaning against the counter beside me, looking bored with her chin on her fist.

"Brilliant idea, only I don't have her number," I point out, jumping when Kit slams her hand down on top of the book I'm fiddling with.

"You do in here, dumb arse. Honestly, I swear sometimes it's like all your brain power goes only to your artistic side," Kit complains as she flips a page in the appointment book back to yesterday before underlining a number with her finger.

"I don't know if I want to kiss or kick you right now," I tell her, and she smiles, patting my cheek with a hard edge to it.

"The feeling's mutual. Now get the girl. I'll be in the back room checking stock if you need me." Kit hands me the shop phone before walking off down the hall.

I fiddle with the phone for a moment then put in the number and press call before I can talk myself out of it. It rings twice before cutting to voicemail, and I smile as I listen to her awkward greeting and can practically see her squirming self-consciously as she made it. I end the call before the beep, though. I hate leaving voicemails. My words always become stilted, and I find the whole recording thing as awkward as Aela obviously does.

I pull my phone out of my jeans to send her a quick text instead.

"Hey, little Miss Trouble. Are you free for coffee before the gym? Dec"

I flip my phone around in my hands for ten minutes before I receive her reply.

"Hey! First, you really have to stop calling me little. You're going to give me a complex. And trouble? I am the furthest from trouble a girl can get. Sorry, I'm in class right now. Won't be free until 5 and have already exceeded the healthy level of caffeine a human should consume by at least double today a la University student style. Raincheck? A. x"

I chuckle at her little admonition before replying.

"You are the epitome of trouble. Ever since you tackled me at the gym, there has been nothing but disorder and unrest in my life. My thought process is all disrupted because of you, and I have a rebelling employee threatening to cause bodily harm if I'm not nice enough to you. It has made working difficult. And you are tiny. Deal with it. The raincheck is accepted, but be sure to drink enough water before the gym. Your over consumption of caffeine will not mix well with cardio. :)"

I hit send then instantly regret it. Was that too much? What if she thinks I'm turning into some kind of crazy, obsessed stalker?

Why the hell am I worrying like a chick?

I drop my phone onto the counter with a clatter then grab my balls to make sure they are still there and try to get a grip on myself, literally.

I stand up straighter and run my hands over my head. To hell with what she thinks if she doesn't like it. But girls are supposed to dig all that feely crap so whatever.

Before I have a complete nutcase meltdown, my phone dings with a text, and I scoop it up to read her reply,

"I refuse to argue about your inaccurate rendition of our first meeting at the gym. I am curious, however, about your trouble at work. My thoughts seem to also be preoccupied today. That is to say, I have been thinking about you too. I will not accept your 'tiny' measurement. I am in the average height range for my age thank you very much, Gigantor. I'm also flattered you care about my water intake. Never fear. I've had plenty. I have to get back to notetaking. See you soon. A x"

Kit sticks her head around the corner from the hallway to find me grinning down at my phone.

"I haven't heard you talking on the phone like I usually can all through the shop. Don't tell me you bitched out and have just stood there trying to grow a pair," Kit accuses as she steps fully out of the hallway. I laugh as I put my phone away.

"Aela's in class so we texted. Coffee's also on raincheck, Miss Matchmaker," I reply before leaning back over the counter to glance at the clock.

I need something to distract me before I go stir-crazy. I jack up the volume on the music until Amity Affliction blares just under the allowed limit. I scoop up my sketchpad and pencil from under the counter then make my way over to the couch.

I slump in my seat and close my eyes, take a deep breath to clear my mind before I flip to a blank page and start doodling, letting my hand flow wherever it wants to go, just to see what comes from it.

An hour later, I'm torn from my trance-like state by Kit greeting someone who enters the shop.

I watch as the young girl talks to her about a navel piercing before looking back down to the sketch pad in my lap. I mutter a soft curse before shutting the notebook on a replica of innocent, warm eyes that have started to become very familiar to me in such a short amount of time.

Yeah, I have it bad.

Chapter 11

AELA

I ARRIVE AT the gym later than expected and shamelessly jog up the stairs to the main floor in search of Dec. A stab of disappointment hits me when I don't see him anywhere.

I'm too tired from a long day at school to do a full workout so I skip right to cardio, hopping onto my favourite treadmill that's closest to the big bay window at the end of the room. In my hurry to get to the gym, I'd left my phone on my bed when I'd gone up to get changed, so I plug my earphones into the gym's music channel as I start the machine at a low level to warm up. As soon as I hit the minute mark, I turn it up to eleven and up the gradient to match.

Just as I hit my stride, I get the feeling someone is behind me, watching. I'm about to look over my shoulder when the machine jolts unexpectedly as a set of arms come from behind me, hands lowering to grip the side railings.

I jump in surprise which throws off my stride and sends me backwards into a hard body with enough force to throw us both to the floor. I rub the pain in my ear from having my earphones yanked out while I turn to look at the gasping idiot beneath me.

"What the hell, Dec?" I pull myself up off him then watch as he struggles to catch his breath, sprawled out on the floor, holding his chest.

60

"I really... didn't think that through. Stupid... Sorry," Dec gasps out through deep intakes of air. I crouch down beside him, feeling a little bad but start laughing. Dec lifts his head to look at me before grinning mischievously and pushing on my left knee to send me over onto my butt.

"This makes us even now. No more picking on me," I tell him as he starts trying to sit up but stops to look at me incredulously.

"Ah, no way. You rammed into me again. It may have been my fault, but you winded the hell out of me. I think you may have collapsed a lung with your lethal little elbow," Dec argues.

I shake my head as I stand again before offering him a hand. "If you can talk crap, your lungs are fine."

Dec accepts my hand, and a thrill goes through me at the feel of his warm, calloused skin against mine. Instead of using the hold to stand, though, he tugs so I fall ungracefully into his lap and against his chest. I should have seen that coming.

I tilt my head to glare at him but can't manage it when I see his devilish smirk and the light in his eyes as he props himself up on his right hand, his other tightly gripping my hip.

"You fell for me again," Dec murmurs, his voice low and gravelly, sending heat flowing through my body that I try to fight while I laugh at his words.

"Only because you made me," I argue as I use my hand that landed against his chest to push away from him.

Dec shrugs, his grin widening as he tightens his grip on me, trapping me in place where I sit on his groin.

"What can I say? I have that effect on women. But to be fair, you took my breath away." I laugh out loud at his cheesiness and knowing grin, but it quickly dies off as his eyes lock onto my lips. Heat igniting in his eyes while he leans toward me, the air around us practically crackles with the electricity building between us when he stops just a breath away from our lips meeting.

Dec pauses there, his eyes flitting between my lips and my own gaze. He sucks in the ring on his plump bottom lip, making me want to lean in and bite it.

I'm about to give in when a loud and obvious cough sounds from above us, breaking the spell.

I look up to find James, the Asian guy from reception who has become a sort-of friend of mine, looking down at us with amusement, crossing his arms over his chest.

"Sorry to interrupt, guys, but it looked like you needed a reminder of where you are and that you're not alone." James tilts his head to a couple of guys beside him who are cycling on the bikes slowly while clearly watching us, and a few other people standing around gawking.

I blush and hide my face in Dec's chest as he chuckles. I pull back once his hand loosens on my hip then scramble to my feet as he slowly climbs to his, slapping hands with James with an unapologetic grin.

"Sorry, man. But you have the worst timing ever," Dec complains, making James laugh while my face burns so hot in embarrassment it feels as if it could catch fire when I put my hands on my cheeks. Dec wraps his left arm around me, chuckling when he gets a look at me.

"Don't be embarrassed. We weren't doing anything. Yet," he teases, and then the two guys share a grin.

James turns to me, gentling his smile. "Don't worry, Aela. Just keep it PG, guys." James winks and then heads towards the stairs.

I duck out from under Dec's arm before levelling a hard glare on him. "That was so embarrassing."

"Why are you glaring at me. How is it only my fault?" Dec complains but continues smiling unabashedly.

"All of it was your fault. You know it was," I argue with my fists propped up on my hips.

Dec looks me up and down with an amused smirk before leaning over to wrap his arms around me, pulling me flush against him.

"Maybe. But everything I did was your fault. I told you, you've messed up my thought process. By the way, you are sexy as hell when you act mad," Dec murmurs in my ear. His warm breath down my neck causes me to shiver delightfully, and I lean into him with weak knees. Dec leads me back a couple of steps until I find myself pressed against a pillar that separates the treadmills and bikes.

He presses into me until our bodies meet from chest to hip then lowers his head a little more to trail light kisses up my neck. I have to fight against my body's urge to get lost in him as I remember where we are.

I push against Dec's chest until he's forced to step back, putting a little breathing space between us.

"Not here. I'm not interested in putting on a show for these pervs." I gesture to the guys sitting back on the benches across the room from us and to the guys on the bikes. Dec sighs before playing with his lip ring with his teeth and releases me to run his hands through his hair.

"You're right. Are you finished working out?"

I nod even though he had interrupted before I could really start. I'm more than ready to get out of here.

"Sweet. I'll go get my stuff and meet you at the lift." He leans in and presses a kiss against my hairline then walks away, leaving me grasping behind me for the wall to keep me upright.

It isn't until I'm grabbing my towel and water from the treadmill that the nerves hit.

What does Dec think I just agreed to?

Sure, I want to jump his bones seven ways to Sunday but I can't. I'm not a virgin by any means and don't need some long term commitment, but I'm also not the type of girl who can do one night stands.

Or sleep with someone I don't know and despite having a crush on him for what feels like forever, I've barely learnt enough about him in the couple of days since we 'met' to feel comfortable enough.

Heck, I haven't even asked if he is single. Though going by his actions, I really hope so, or I'd have to hurt him. How do I tell him?

I gather myself mentally along with my stuff and force my feet towards the stairs, knowing I've taken long enough for Dec to probably be waiting for me by now.

I find him leaning beside the lift talking to Sophie, the bubbly blonde from reception who is swivelling back and forth on her stool behind the desk.

Dec looks over as I step off the last step and smiles brilliantly before pushing off the wall to meet me halfway, taking my hand in his. "Have a good night, Soph." Dec smiles at her as he leads me to the lift and I turn to see her smile and wave.

"Bye. Have a great night, you two." Sophie playfully winks at me. I try not to think too much of it.

"Have you had dinner yet?" Dec asks as the lift opens with a couple of guys stepping out, and I shake my head as we step aside to let them pass. "You probably want to go upstairs to get out of those clothes, right?" Dec assumes, making my nerves spike with panic as we step inside.

"I can't have sex with you tonight," I blurt then feel my cheeks instantly heat in embarrassment when his eyes widen in shock while he clearly tries to fight back a grin.

"I'm sorry, what?" Dec asks, and I shrug stubbornly because I know he heard. "Okay. I think you got the wrong idea so I'll just clear things up. I'm taking you out for food, and I figured since you're a chick, you would want some time to change out of your workout gear before we go out." Dec raises an eyebrow in question before I look away from him shyly, focusing on a scuff mark on the plain beige wall of the elevator.

"Aela…"

I ignore Dec's plea for my attention until I feel his warm, strong hand grasp my chin, gently forcing me to turn his way. I look up into his soft blue eyes as he draws me closer until he can wrap his free arm around my waist.

"Hey, I'm sorry. I didn't mean to embarrass you. But don't hide from me and don't be scared to tell me how you feel. I want to get to know you, Aela. Every way I can." His words make me melt a little, along with the tender look in his gaze as he keeps his eyes sincerely locked on mine.

I stare back, speechless until the elevator announces its arrival on my floor. Dec gestures for me to go first, and I have to forcibly shake myself out of my stupor before moving into the hallway.

"You need to be warned before I let you in—the place is still mostly a disaster. We've only been here three days and haven't had much time, so there's stuff everywhere, and Kara is a bit of a mess." Dec stops me from rambling by wrapping his arm around my shoulders and pulling me to him.

"I can handle a mess, Aela. Take a breath."

I unlock the door to my apartment and cringe expectantly as I enter, but it's not as bad as it was. The pile of empty boxes has been removed from beside the door and all of Kara's boxes that had been in the lounge room just this morning are gone.

Everything seems to be in place, apart from the smell of something burning coming from the kitchen.

I rush around the corner to check, and I hear Kara's muttered curses as something clatters loudly.

"Hey, what's going on?" Kara startles at my voice and curses again as she dumps a baking pan into the sink that has something charcoaled and lumpy caked to it.

"I got home early so I thought I could get this place in order and make something special for dinner, and we could enjoy our first proper dinner here." She runs her hands over her frazzled hair then sighs, turning to switch on the kettle and pulls out a cup of instant noodles.

"The stupid chicken moulded itself to the pan, and I'm over it so it's now 'fend for yourself' night, and I'm taking this to bed with me to sulk over my failure," Kara complains. Then she is distracted when Dec's phone begins to ring as he comes to stand behind me while I guiltily look at the murdered dinner she made—which is totally sweet while I had other plans without even thinking about her.

"Hey, what's up?" Dec answers his phone with a worried tone then gives me a questioning look, clearly asking where he can take his call. I point to the hall then turn my finger to the right so he knows to go into my room or any room on that side. Dec holds up two fingers before giving me a wink to let me know all is ok before walking away.

I turn back to see Kara glaring at me. "You could have warned me I was making an idiot of myself," she complains.

I try not to smile as I reply, "You were on a roll. Who was I to interrupt?"

Kara opens her mouth, ready with a retort but cuts off when we hear Dec clearly complain to whoever's on the phone.

"Are you serious? I'm a guy. What the hell am I supposed to know about baking? Unless she'll let me buy some from the bakery and decorate them. They'll never know." He pauses for a moment and then groans.

Kara and I share a puzzled look before he emerges from the hallway, looking at us pleadingly as he covers the receiver on the phone. "Either of you ladies know how to bake?" Dec asks looking desperate, and Kara snorts before holding up her baking tray of disaster and then points to me suggestively.

Dec's eyes turn to me with hope as he stops before me. "Cookies?" he prods, and I shrug uncertainly.

"I've done basic cakes. I can try cookies?" My answer turns into a question. Dec leans in to gratefully kiss my forehead before returning the phone back to his mouth looking annoyed at something that has been said over the line.

"I'm with some friends... No, not like that. Do you really believe I would bring that around Hope? Stop it. Problem solved. We'll be there soon." He ends the call abruptly before sliding the phone into his pocket with an apologetic look. Kara folds her arms, giving him an expectant stare.

"Explain yourself," she demands, and Dec grins as he wraps his arms around me from behind.

"That was my mum. She's getting ready for work and my five-year-old sister just let her know she's supposed to be bringing cookies for some school bake sale tomorrow. Mum asked for help because Hope is adamant they have to be baked at home and not store bought which is ridiculous but whatever," Dec explains then leans down to nuzzle into my hair before tilting me to the side so I can see him better.

"If you don't mind changing our plans to help me out and keep us from burning the house down, I will owe you big time," he pleads, and I melt at how cute he is.

Who would have thought a guy who looks like him would be willing to do something like this at the drop of a hat for his baby sister? Of course, I want to see this.

"I'd love to help but don't blame me if the house does burn down. Like I said, I've only ever baked a couple of sponge cakes before." Dec lifts me off my feet happily, squeezing me to him as I revel in the warmth of being surrounded by him.

"You're awesome. We need to get some stuff from Coles before they close, and I still need to feed you, so get a move on."

Dec puts me down and swats my butt, which makes me playfully glare at him before heading to my room to quickly change into plain jeans and a blue singlet knowing I'll get messy.

We take my car since Dec walked to the gym from his shop, but he drives—after adjusting the seat back as far as it will go which makes me laugh—while I google an easy yet fun cookie recipe. "What about gingerbread men. It looks easy to bake, and we can have fun decorating them." I look up from my phone to see Dec smile.

"That's perfect. Hope will love it," he decides as he pulls into the parking lot.

We rush into the supermarket, Dec grabbing the first employee we come across to ask for the baking isle while I get a basket, and then we practically power walk where he's directed. "You get the ingredients, and I'll get the topping stuff," Dec suggests before taking stuff off the shelves.

I check the recipe then start loading the basket while watching in amusement as Dec continues filling his arms.

"How many are we making here? Enough to feed an army or just enough that Hope can carry to school?" I call out as I pick up a steel cookie cutter before looking back over to see Dec grinning like a little boy in a candy store.

"I'm making sure we have everything to make the most kickarse gingerbread people ever," he states, walking over to dump his armload into the basket then takes it from me.

"Okay, we need eggs and then we're good to go," I inform him as I double check the recipe then follow as Dec leads the way again .

We take a detour through the nearest drive-thru to grab a couple of wraps, and I pick at my food while feeding him his chips as he drives when he complains he's starving. Both of us grin and laugh like fools when I deliberately miss his mouth and make him work for it. Dec pulls to a stop in front of a charming little cottage-like one storey house painted white with deep blue details and surrounded in a rainbow of flowers from the pots hanging from the balcony and the flower beds that take up most of the yard.

"Ready?" Dec asks after a moment of me sitting there staring, and I turn to see he has one foot out the door with an expectant look. I nod then slide out and wait for Dec to join me.

"Is this where you grew up?" I look around the front of the home and can picture a little Dec running around, up to no good, but he shakes his head.

"Mum and I moved here after—well, after I graduated high school." I watch him look away awkwardly and decide not to pry into the obvious change of what he was going to say. For now.

"Good lord, what are you planning to bake Declan Lewis?" A woman I'm guessing is his mother, calls out to us when she steps out onto the porch and notices the three bags we're carrying.

I assess her as we approach, admiring her long, honey blonde hair styled into a braid that sits over her left shoulder. She stands only a little taller than me and is about my size in her ill-fitting black uniform. Her skin is practically wrinkle-free until she smiles. She could pass for Dec's slightly older sister. I start thinking maybe she is until Dec jumps up the stairs to greet her with a kiss on her cheek.

"Hi, Mum. Aela's going to school us on how to make gingerbread cookies," he says happily before shuffling the bags he is carrying into his left hand to hold out his right to me. I take it as I join them on the porch and smile at his mother self-consciously when her eyes follow his gesture, landing on me.

"Mum, this is my friend, Aela. Aela, my mum, Nicola." I move to offer to shake her hand, but with Dec holding one hand and a bag in the other, my hands are full. So I make my smile bigger and awkwardly lift the hand holding the bag and sort of shake it at her which is just embarrassing.

"Hi, Mrs Lewis. It's nice to meet you. You have a lovely home." She looks me up and down before looking back and forth from me to Dec, smiling widely.

"Well, aren't you a sweetheart? Thank you, but call me Nic or Mum like everyone else does. I stopped being Mrs Lewis years ago."

I want to kick myself, but Nicola looks unfazed as she opens the door, gesturing for us to go inside. Dec is barely over the threshold before there's a little blonde running at him, wrapping herself around his legs like a monkey.

"Dec, you're here. We're going to make cookies!" she yells exuberantly though the last bit is muffled when she buries her face into his side. Dec chuckles, releasing my hand as he struggles to move out of the way.

"Easy, Bug. Let me put this stuff in the kitchen first." Dec awkwardly shuffles them both down the hall as I appreciate the hominess of the inside styling, spotting a ton of family pictures I intend to get a closer look at later.

Dec rests the bags on the kitchen bench before scooping the little girl up into his arms. She gives him a kiss on the cheek which he returns with a squeeze before gesturing to me. This makes her look my way.

I smile when I notice she has Dec's eyes and hair colour, a cute little button nose, flushed cheeks and a perfect little pink pout. She's adorable, and I can tell by the look in her eyes that she knows how to use it to get anything she wants.

"Bug, this is Aela." Her curious look turns into a bright smile which shows dimples on one side just like her brother has and before he can finish introducing us, she leans over to kiss my cheek.

"I'm Hope. You're pretty." She turns to look back at Dec. "Really pretty. Is this your girlfriend?"

Her bluntness makes me smile as Dec sits her on the bench and taps her nose in admonishment.

"Aela's my friend. Who is going to help us make gingerbread men," he announces the last part excitedly, and Hope grins before leaning around him to look at me.

"It's because he's smelly, right? That's why you're not his girlfriend?" Hope asks which makes me laugh and turn to consider the man in question as he looks at her in mock outrage.

"I do not smell," Dec argues with a poke to her belly which makes her giggle and nod her head vigorously,

"Oh, yes you do. All boys are smelly, like farts." Hope cackles at her own joke which gets a chuckle from the rest of us.

"Aela, help me prove I don't smell."

Before I know what's happening, Dec pulls me into him until my cheek lands against his pec. I inhale in a gasp at the unexpected move and get a whiff of clean, masculine... warmth. If warmth had a smell, this is what it would be. I may emit a sigh without noticing before breathing him in again then notice the shaking of his chest as he chuckles before squeezing me in his arms.

"He smells pretty good to me," I admit when I pull back from Dec's embrace, and he lets me break his hold, hands sliding down then away but not before he gives my left butt cheek a hard pat.

Dec leans over until he's eye to eye with Hope. "But you are right about boys smelling. Remember that and stay away from them until you're at least twenty, okay?" Hope makes a face at him as Nicola and I laugh.

"Good luck with that, Declan. Your 'cooties' phase didn't last too long. I've gotta go now. I'll be home around midnight. If that's too late, just let Sam next door know when you're leaving, and she will take over. Thank you both so much for doing this." Nicola moves over to kiss all three of us on the cheek in a rush.

71

"We're fine, Ma. We can stay until you get back. Have a good night. Don't work too hard," Dec replies then dodges when she goes to ruffle his hair.

"Be good for them, baby," Nicola gives Hope another kiss then grabs her bag and is out the door yelling, "Love, love, love."

Chapter 12

DECLAN

"LET'S GET THIS party started." I clap my hands then start to unpack the bags.

Aela checks the recipe she bookmarked on her phone then fiddles with the gauges on the oven while Hope turns Mum's stereo on that sits on the side bench. She switches it to the second pre-set radio channel so it's on Triple J, knowing it's the only one I can stand as it doesn't play the same poppy crap on repeat.

I watch in a mix of fascination and awe as Aela confidently starts combining all the ingredients in the mixing bowl which Hope pulled from the cupboard for her without needing to be asked.

They get to know each other by trading questions back and forth, and I space out, admiring the way Aela pays attention and seems genuinely interested in Hope while she works.

I hadn't had any girls around Hope since I moved away from home when I was nineteen—apart from a couple who turned up while I was babysitting which I'm embarrassed to admit she had seen quite a few when I lived here.

None of them had treated her like this. They either treated her like an inconvenience that was taking my attention from them, or talked to her in a really annoying baby voice like she was an idiot, or just flat out ignored her presence.

That warm, liquid feeling spreads in my chest again as I watch them interact, and a crazy image fills my mind of Aela doing this with a little girl that looks like Hope but with Aela's beautiful dark hair and pert little nose. My heart rate picks up, and I begin to sweat.

What the hell? I am so not ready for that.

Totally oblivious to my mental freak out, Aela looks over to me with a smirk before playfully glaring at me.

"Don't think you're getting away with just standing there looking pretty while we do all the work, mister," she warns. I grin as I step closer, unable to stop myself from leaning over so I can wrap my right arm around that tiny waist and then press a soft kiss to her cheek.

"I was waiting to be put to work while admiring your baking skills," I say close to her ear, watching with satisfaction as Aela shivers before I pull back. "And I'm too manly to be called pretty," I complain which makes them laugh.

"You have colourful pictures of roses and angels on your arms. They're pretty," Hope chimes in looking smug.

Aela adds, "Not to mention your ridiculously long eyelashes and pretty blue eyes." She flutters her own pair at me, and I can't help but smile at her teasing.

"I can't believe you two are ganging up to emasculate me after knowing each other for less than thirty minutes. Too bad for you, I'm content in my overabundance of masculinity." I puff out my chest during my declaration as Aela starts rolling out the mixture, laughing again at my words.

I love her laugh. I love it even more when I'm the one making it happen, even if she is mocking me.

Aela gives Hope the cookie cutter to press into the sheet of dough then presses it firmer, before lining the little people up on the two trays covered with baking paper—while I continue standing there uselessly.

The cookies are put into the oven then Hope asks if we can watch *The Beauty and the Beast*, her favourite Disney movie, while we wait for them to bake.

I try to talk her into something cooler but ultimately, give in because it's damn hard to deny that girl anything, even a movie she's watched a trillion times.

I microwave a bowl of popcorn then head into the lounge room as Hope is putting in the disc. I settle onto the three-seater couch close enough to Aela that our legs touch. I offer her some popcorn when she looks at me, doing my best to look innocent.

Hope skips over to us, and I move the bowl over so she can climb in my lap like she usually does when we're watching something together—except she pauses in front of us hesitantly looking at Aela.

"Can I sit on your lap?" she asks. I try not feel rejected when Aela smiles then wordlessly lifts her legs to curl between us before lifting Hope up to snuggle her in the little space it leaves between Aela and the arm of the couch with Hope's legs draped over hers.

I watch as Aela smooths Hope's hair affectionately, making her smile contently—and cue that warmth in my chest again.

I force myself to look at the television before pressing play on the remote and lower my arm to rest between us, looking down when Aela reaches out to squeeze my hand in hers. I let go of the remote and turn my hand to entwine our fingers and squeeze back.

I can't remember being this stoked to just hold a girls hand since I was twelve, but hell if I can wipe the grin off my face as our hands relax into the couch, fingers intertwined.

"Belle is my favourite princess," Hope announces during a part where she is singing in the village. I turn to see Hope looking up at Aela, running her little fingers through the hair lying over Aela's shoulder. Hope has a thoughtful expression.

"Really? Why is that?" Aela asks as she peers down at Hope.

"Because she is smart and nice and brave and pretty... like you." I watch with a grin as Aela blushes while Hope turns back to watch the movie.

Aela continues looking down at Hope for a moment before leaning down to kiss her hair and snuggles her a little tighter. I smile happily knowing Hope has now got her wrapped around her little finger just like she's done to the rest of us since the moment she was born.

Ten minutes later, the timer rings, and Hope excitedly jumps off Aela's lap to run into the kitchen, followed closely by Aela. This makes me chuckle as I pause the movie before getting up to follow.

By the time I turn the corner, Aela has the cookies out on the bench for inspection. "They look perfect to me," Aela announces so I begin to tear open the packets of smarties and other goodies for decoration, but she gathers the trays and takes them to the fridge, "They need to cool before we can decorate them," Aela explains when she turns back to find Hope and I watching her with confusion.

Oh. I stop breaking out the goodies, mainly because Hope shoots me a reprimanding look and starts sliding the packets to the side, out of my reach. Not before I get a handful of smarties into my mouth first, though, which she catches and smacks my arm, and that makes me grin.

Aela inspects the pile of stuff I bought then starts laughing as she turns to me.

"You went overboard here. What were you planning on doing with the mini marshmallows?" she asks, and I shrug, stalling to come up with an idea.

"They can have puffy coats. Or albino afros?" I offer which gets an indulgent shake of her head.

"Come on. Let's get back to the movie. We're almost at the

part where Belle gets to see the library which is one of my favourite parts." Aela takes Hope's hand to help her jump down from the stool she's perched on.

"Seriously? The library scene?" I ask doubtfully because I'm pretty sure every girl's favourite part would be the dance at the end with the happily ever after.

Aela looks over her shoulder with a saucy grin. "Smart chicks dig libraries. If a guy kidnapped me and had that library, I probably wouldn't try to escape."

I'm grinning when she turns away and hurry my steps until I'm right behind her.

"Remind me to show you the bookshelf at my place," I murmur and get her beautiful laugh in return as we settle back into the couch.

Chapter 13

AELA

"OH, MY GOD. What are you doing?" I ask through a laugh as I take in the gingerbread man Dec is working on.

At least, I assume there's a cookie under there, it's hard to tell since I can't see anything under the pile of icing, marshmallows, choc chips and two kinds of sprinkles he is messing with.

Dec looks up from his 'decorating' to look at me before looking back down. "What? It looks delicious," he says defensively when even Hope wrinkles her nose with distaste at his work. "It's meant to look like a kid made it anyway, right?" Dec continues. I open my mouth to argue, but Hope beats me to it

"I'm not taking that to school with me. I am a kid, and none of mine look like that. Gross, Declan," she complains haughtily. I bite my lip to keep from laughing.

Dec looks over to the collection we've finished then shrugs as he looks back to his. "Fine. I'll eat it. You don't know what you're missing. These babies would have sold out fast." He picks it up and manages to fit half of the cookie into his mouth in one bite, leaving a smear of blue icing and sprinkles on his lips, grinning at our identical looks of disbelief. Dec closes his eyes, moaning indulgently which sends tingles in places that shouldn't tingle around children. I have to fight to keep my mind out of the gutter.

"Sho's good," he mutters through his mouthful which makes Hope shake her head in disappointment.

"Mum would smack you for talking with your mouth full. That's yuck," she complains before giving me an apologetic look. Then she continues covering the body of her gingerbread person in rainbow sprinkles. I smile in amusement looking back at Dec, who has stuffed the remainder of the gingerbread monstrosity in his mouth and is trying to lick the gunk off his lips.

"You missed a spot," I point to the top left of his mouth.

Dec reaches up and wipes at his lips with his thumb but barely scrapes the icing. I lean over and reach to get it myself without much thought, cupping his strong jaw in my palm as I wipe the mess off with my thumb. I then go to step back as I lower my hand, but Dec catches my wrist in a firm grip. His eyes are dark and hooded when I look into them as they stare back at me.

He slowly lifts my hand back to his mouth, wrapping his lips around my thumb, his mouth warm and moist. I feel his hot tongue slide gently over the pad of my thumb as he sucks hard which makes my knees go weak, and a whimper gets trapped in my throat as I stop breathing.

Dec draws my thumb slowly back out of his mouth and playfully bites the tip before lowering our hands between us, his eyes never leaving mine.

"So sweet… And all mine," he murmurs. His voice low and gravelly causes goose bumps to rise on my arms, and I get the feeling he isn't just talking about the icing. I force myself to take a shuddering breath when I start to feel dizzy. I'm trapped in his heated gaze, which makes everything around us blur, leaving just the two us as he steps closer before snaking his arm around my lower back.

"Declan, you're too old to be sucking thumbs," Hope points out, popping the intense little bubble we had going on. I grin as I turn to see her sitting primly. Her arms are folded as she frowns at her big brother. "I finished my boys and girls. Can I have my bath now?" she asks Dec who nods as he steps away from me while grabbing a handful of smarties.

"I'll get the water going for you, Bug." He walks down the hall while tossing the chocolate into his mouth with Hope following behind him.

I take a deep breath to calm down enough to focus on finishing the gingerbread people. Nothing could wipe the wide smile from my face, though.

Dec returns just as I'm putting the lid on the container of biscuits looking sheepish as he watches me pack up.

"I'm so sorry. I really didn't intend for you to do all the work. I owe you something really big now." Dec apologises as he approaches, and I grin to let him know I'm okay.

"Hey, you bankrolled this project, and it was fun. I'm just glad I didn't mess them up." I try not to be affected when he steps up close enough for me to feel the body heat radiating from him without him actually touching me.

"You still bought too much decoration stuff, though," I point out, gesturing to all the bags of confectionary and the still half full containers of pink and white icing on the bench. I'm trying to break up the tension building between us again.

"It won't go to waste. I can think of a few ways I'd like to use it," Dec replies without looking away from me, his voice gone all low and growly again which calls to something deep inside of me.

I grin and wonder how far he's willing to take his teasing—which is all it is, right? I mean, his little sister is just down the hall. I get a wicked urge to push and see.

"Sounds intriguing." I turn to scoop my finger in the pink icing before looking back up to him as I slowly lift my finger to my mouth. I take a small testing lick before taking it in my mouth. Then I emit a moan low in my throat and pull it out clean and then bite my lip innocently.

"It is intriguing. I'm sure you would love it all," Dec assures, his voice dripping with sinful promises which cause my body to tingle delightfully. He suddenly pulls me into him with his palm pressed flat against my lower spine.

"I really like this icing." I reach over to scoop some more onto my finger and look up at Dec wickedly as I fight off my nerves. "But it's missing something," I add, reaching up to wipe some onto his neck just under his jaw which is as high as I can get my mouth on him without his cooperation.

I lean up on my tiptoes and tilt my head back until I'm close enough to extend my tongue and swipe at the icing. His stubble scratches against my tongue, and his skin has a salty hint to it that mixes deliciously with the sweet icing.

Dec growls. Yes, growls. As his hand presses more firmly against my back and his other clutches my hip, I sink back down to my feet to find the blue of his eyes has turned darker. I can't contain my grin. I thought that whole eye-colour-changing-thing only happened in romance novels, having never seen it happen before. I'm delighted to know I was wrong.

"You read my mind, babe," Dec murmurs then releases my hip to swipe some of the white icing and then smears it over my bottom lip.

I fight the urge to lick it off and wait expectantly as I watch him slowly lean down, his eyes never leaving mine until our lips are a hairsbreadth apart. His gaze dips to my lips as his hand lifts to tilt my chin up more before his tongue snakes out to flick against my lips, removing the sticky icing in one warm, wet sweep. He then presses his lips to mine in a soft, sweet caress.

He pulls back and then swoops in again, his lips harder, more insistent against mine before his tongue slips out, prodding for entrance which I eagerly give.

Holy. Hot. Kisses.

I've had some pretty memorable kisses, but Dec blows them out of my mind. His skilful tongue hot and demanding, as it becomes familiar with the inside of my mouth is claiming every dark corner as its own. The cool press and glide of his lip ring adds an extra thrilling sensation as his hands grip me tightly to him before the left slides up into my hair.

I wrap my hands around his neck to run my fingers through the soft hair at his nape as I press even more against him. Dec groans, sending flutters low in my stomach. He tilts his head to sink deeper into my mouth like he can't get enough as he angles mine back more by his firm grip on my hair.

Everything around us ceases to exist but my need for more of him. The kiss feels like it goes on forever yet not long enough, when he finally pulls back from me, gasping for breath as I do the same.

I lean in to lick at the steel ring in his lip because it's something I've been dying to do after watching him do it for so long. When I pull back, Dec's eyes are darker than I've ever seen them as he stares at me with a look that promises he has many more things in mind to do to me.

After that a-freaking-mazing kiss, I am more than willing to sign up for anything. I feel like I'm floating on air. Then my senses return, and I look down to realise I practically am.

I was so caught up in his kiss, I hadn't even noticed Dec lifting me off my feet, and he's now holding me effortlessly against him, one hand under my butt while the other still clutches my hair.

"Wow. Way to sweep a girl off her feet," I say through heavy breaths, and Dec grins devilishly before giving me another light, innocent peck.

"That was a kiss, Aela. I haven't even got my broom out." I smile at his innuendo and boyish charm before giggling.

Dec slowly lowers me to my feet in a way that has me sliding down the length of his lean, hard body, brushing against a part that is very hard and eager in his pants. My eyes are drawn to his groin where I can clearly see an outline that makes my breath hitch and my palms twitch with the need to inspect it.

I look up to see his proud grin and giggle as I pick up a small handful of chocolate sprinkles to throw at him.

"You keep that broomstick where it is, thank you. Your little sister could walk out here any second now," I warn with a playful glare, watching as Dec raises a brow at me.

"I know you want my broomstick," he replies smugly then throws a marshmallow at me.

"You really want to start this? Because I will finish it," I threaten, throwing more sprinkles at him just as he picks up the bowl of white icing.

"You started it. I was just retaliating, but if you're willing to throw down... bring it on." Dec's voice is an enticing low growl as he scoops two fingers through the bowl, and though I know this is silly and will more than likely not end victoriously for me, it's too tempting. I throw another handful of marshmallows at him before scooping up the bowl of pink icing as he lunges for me, and I let out a squeal.

"What is wrong with you two? You're supposed to be the grown-ups. I'm not helping clean this. I just got in my jammies," Hope yells from where she stands at the end of the bench with hands on her hips.

She's glaring at us where we sit leaning against the cupboard underneath the sink, our legs entwined while I struggle to keep Dec's hands back that are covered in a mixture of sprinkles and icing.

We pause to look over at her while giggling breathlessly, and then I look around us at the mess we've made of the kitchen floor. I guiltily bite my lip, looking back to Dec, who turns to me and starts laughing as he looks me over. Then he leans in and licks some of the mess off my cheek which makes me squirm underneath him and squeal in protest again.

"Is it just me or does she look so cute, you have the urge to mess her up a little too?" Dec whispers loudly, looking back to Hope who glares at him warningly. I laugh as I push him away. I sit up when he finally pulls back and look down at myself and laugh again.

"Grow up, idiot. You better clean up before Mum comes home. I'm going to finish watching the movie until bedtime." Hope walks away, and Dec leans back with a chuckle.

"We got told off by a five-year-old," Dec needlessly points out while scooping some icing off his neck then licks it off his hand. I scrunch my nose and giggle again at the sight of him with icing splattered all over his shirt, in his hair, and some smears on his shorts.

"You got told to grow up by a kid in princess jammies," I point out, and he chuckles again before standing up and leaning over to hold a hand out to help me up.

"We may have gotten carried away." Dec looks around the floor which is a slippery mess. I nod my agreement when he turns back to face me then removes a bit of gunk from my hair with a chuckle. "Come on. I'll let you have the first shower and find you one of my old shirts while I clean this up." Dec carefully leads me to the hallway.

"I helped make the mess. I can help clean it up too," I protest, but Dec shakes his head while flicking the light switch in the all-white bathroom.

"You did all the baking. I can handle the cleaning." He walks into the next room, returning a second later to offer me a black t-shirt. I go to argue again, but he covers my lips with his hand.

"I need something to distract me from the thought of you in here wet and naked anyway. Don't fight me. Just get in there before I join you and forget about Hope being here." Dec effectively shuts me up, and I step back to shut the door between us.

I have the fastest shower known to man, and yet when I come out, the kitchen floor is spotless, and a now clean Dec stands at the sink doing the dishes. I get the urge to go up and hug him from behind but ignore it, sitting on the bench beside him instead.

Dec looks up from the dishes to smile at me before his gaze travels down my torso then back up. "You look good in my shirt," he murmurs.

"How did you get clean without a shower?" I ask curiously, and he nods to a door beside the glass backdoor.

"I used the tub in the laundry. I needed to try to cool off. I think I might need to again." Dec smirks before flicking some suds at me. I jump off the bench in protest and shove him in his side.

"Don't start again. You only just got the kitchen clean." I warn him with a playful glare while he just grins.

"You can go watch the movie with Hope if you think that's safer." I nod at his gesture to the lounge room.

"I think I will. It is my favourite Disney movie, after all." I grin as I take the cold bottle of water he offers me.

"Let me guess, the whole taming the beast thing appeals to you?" Dec grins cheekily. I laugh and shake my head.

"No. I told you, it's all about the library. I've wanted it ever since I first watched the movie when I was little. And Chip— gotta love the little guy." Dec smiles and is about to comment when Hope calls out to me. I smile and then go to join her.

85

I walk in to find Hope curled up on the couch in a tiny ball, her eyes glued to the screen, and I smile again when she turns to look at me. "Will you lay behind me and rub my back like Mummy does while we watch the movie?" she asks sweetly, and of course, I go over and slip behind her.

"Sure, sweetie." I prop my head up on the arm of the lounge and gently rub her back once I'm comfy. Within moments, my eyes start to feel heavy so I close them just to rest them for a minute.

I startle awake to find Dec trying to gently pry Hope from my arms while the movie credits roll up the screen.

Dec shushes to calm me then lifts the sweet little bundle effortlessly into his arms, expertly curling her to his chest like he's done it a million times. I watch as he walks out of the room then take a moment to yawn and stretch before I sit up and realise I need to pee. I go to the hallway and pause at Hope's door which is half open, the room dimly lit by a cute pink and purple princess castle lamp that sits on her bedside table—I would have gone crazy over it when I was little.

I watch as Dec lovingly pulls the blankets up over her as she stirs, curling up again on her side.

"Duckie?" Hope calls out quietly, and Dec sits beside her to rub her back.

"Right here, Bug. Go back to sleep," he assures her, and she rolls over to see him.

"I like Aela. Can she come to my birthday party?" she asks. He smiles while stroking her hair.

The scene before me melts my heart. There's something about a big strong guy that's capable of looking after a child like this that just hits the right spot in any woman. I'm pretty sure it's encoded in our DNA.

"I'll ask her," Dec promises. She reaches up to touch his cheek.

"You should make her your girlfriend. I like the way she makes you smile. She thinks you smell nice when you're gross, and she doesn't care that you keep licking her, which is just weird." She giggles at the last part, and he squeezes her nose as he laughs quietly too.

"I'll do my best. Now go to sleep, Bug. I love you." He leans down lower to give her a kiss, and she makes a loud lip smacking noise before yawning.

"Love you too, smelly duck." She smiles then snuggles up to her blanket.

I continue to the bathroom before Dec can bust me lurking.

When I re-enter the lounge room, Dec is slouched in the three-seater, legs stretched out in front of him with the news on but clearly not paying attention. He stares off into space while playing with his lip ring, so I take the moment to really look around the room and inspect the family pictures all over the place. I smile when I spot a few shots of a little Declan, his cheeky grin effortlessly charming even back then. There's a girl that looks to be the same age and almost identical to him in a number of the pics I look at. There's a rather cute one of the two of them covered in mud and grinning at the camera which makes me chuckle. I turn to see Dec watching me.

"You have a twin?" I ask happily, unprepared for Dec's sudden reaction as he climbs to his feet, walking over to take me in his arms. His body is stiff as he drags me back to the couch to sit beside him.

"I did," he confirms then offers me the remote. "Want to see if there's anything you like on or pick another movie?" Dec asks. Though it may be rude of me since he's clearly trying to distract me and put a stop to the subject, I'm confused by his answer so I prod.

"Did?" I scrunch my brow as I watch his jaw clench. Then it dawns on me that something horrible happened for it to be past tense. I cover my mouth as I look at him apologetically speechless. Damn it. Way to go, Aela.

"She died from leukaemia our senior year of high school," he finishes bluntly while fiddling with the remote.

I take it from him and squeeze his hand in mine in silent support, not knowing what to say and afraid if I open my mouth, I'll say the wrong thing again.

"It's okay. Grace had been fighting it for years before she gave up on all the treatments and decided to go out on her own terms. She was brave," Dec says to me, sounding robotic. I clear my throat, trying to clear the emotional lump forming there.

"You don't sound like you're okay, and you don't have to be. Hell, Dec, no one really recovers from losing a loved one." I release his hand to wrap my arms around him, curling into him with an overwhelming need to comfort Declan as he stares ahead rigidly.

"It was her choice. We all had to accept it and support her. Sometimes, though, I wish I could have stopped her which is selfish of me, right? I mean, there's my twin sister who is like the other half of me, dying slowly and painfully, and here I wish she would have continued to live with it a few more years so our family might not have been torn apart. So our father wouldn't have decided everything was too hard to deal with, leaving our pregnant, grieving mother and me to fend for ourselves. And of course, Hope was the perfect match that I failed to be. Crazy, right? I was Grace's twin, practically an exact copy of her, but not a match in the way she needed." Dec stops his heartbreaking declaration deep with self-hatred, inhaling a deep breath.

He pulls out of his staring at the wall to rub his hands over his face, distorting the skin as he pulls it before looking at me wearily. He reaches out to stroke my hair back then lets out a tired sigh. "Sorry. I haven't had to explain about her to anyone before, and I think I'm just really tired." Dec smiles carefully,

88

and I lean over to kiss his cheek.

"Don't apologise and don't feel ashamed of the way you feel. I didn't know her, but I'm sure Grace wouldn't blame you for feeling like that after what you went through." I gently hold his face between my palms then press another kiss to his lips as headlights flash through the front window followed by the sounds of a car pulling up in the driveway.

Dec wraps his arms around me tightly for a moment then gives me a tender kiss in return. Then he rises to go open the door for his mum as I hear footfalls on the porch steps. They talk quietly in the hall for a moment before Nicola pops her blonde head around the corner, smiling as she steps into the room.

"Thanks for helping out at such short notice, Aela. I hope those two didn't give you too much trouble." The way she says it with a smile as she removes her shoes makes me feel as if I had been babysitting for her.

"No trouble at all. Hope is a total sweetheart. Declan is a handful, though." I joke as he appears in my line of sight, leaning against the entrance to the room with his arms folded, and Nicola laughs quietly.

"You don't know the half of it. Next time you come, I'll pull out the photo albums and tell you the stories of my little hell raiser." She winks playfully as Dec groans then Nicola smiles warmly. "I'm mostly kidding. He's a good guy, my sweet boy," Nicola assures me as though she's letting me in on a secret. I look over at the man in question who fidgets uncomfortably.

"I know," I reply without taking my eyes off Declan.

"Right. Well, we'll leave you to it, Mum. Aela has to be up early." Dec starts motioning it's time to go, and I decide to let him off the hook and not point out that I actually don't.

Nicola stands back up to hug us both, whispering in my ear, "Don't let him run you off," before moving to Dec and telling him she loves him.

I smile at Dec's, "Love you too," before he kisses her hair adoringly.

I wave to Nicola who stands out on the porch watching us leave as Dec drives away. I then turn to watch him with a smile and stretch out stiff muscles in my back. His eyes flick away from the road momentarily to watch me before returning, and I watch as he tightens his grip on the steering wheel.

"I'm sorry again for getting heavy on you back there," Dec apologises, but I shake my head.

"You can get heavy on me anytime. I don't mind at all." I realise after it's out that it could have a dirtier meaning than intended, and I snort as Dec quietly chuckles.

"I'll be sure to remember that." His voice is low and full of dark promise.

I bite my lip and fight not to shift uncomfortably in my seat as I continue looking at him daringly. "You do that." My voice has gone throaty with need. I grin when it gets a reaction from Dec as his fingers twitch on the steering wheel.

Dec goes quiet for the rest of the ride to my place, and it isn't until we get there that I remember he doesn't have his car.

"You can continue on to your place. I'll drive myself back," I offer, but Dec continues to turn into my underground parking.

"This is fine. I could use the fresh air, and it's only a short walk," he says stubbornly, smoothly manoeuvring his way into my parking spot.

"But it's late. And Southport—" I argue. Uselessly, I might add, if his arched eyebrow and smirk is anything to go by, and yeah, I know it's stupid. This is Dec I'm worrying about. I'm pretty sure he could handle any trouble that may come his way and who's stupid enough to try him.

"You think I can't handle anything that goes bump in the night? I'll have you know, I've been sticking it to the bogeyman since I was five." I roll my eyes at his insulted tone, and he flicks my ear making me jump. I glare at him as I rub the slight sting away.

"Never doubt my arse-kicking awesomeness. Also, Southport isn't the ghetto. Close, but still not." Dec ignores my glare as he grabs his gym bag from the backseat and slides out of the car to make his way over to my side. He opens my door while I gather my bag, phone and flip-flops I had kicked off as soon as I got in the car.

Dec continues to ignore the glare I struggle to keep as he whistles on our way to the lift. Only after he pushes the buttons inside the contraption for the lobby and then to my floor does he turn to raise his brow at me again, this time in question.

"You flicked my ear. Not cool."

"You doubted me then rolled your eyes. Suck it up," Dec counters then presses into my personal space until I'm backed up against the wall of the elevator.

"You're sexy when you're mad. Even if it's fake mad, it's still hot as hell." Dec nuzzles into the hair on my neck, taking a deep inhale that gives me goose bumps as he slides his arms around me.

"Good night, Aela," he murmurs into my ear as I clutch his shirt. The elevator dings and the doors start to open. He takes a step back, and says, "Oh, if you're not doing anything, Saturday a month from now, you may want to get yourself a princess outfit or tiara if you don't already have one. Hope wants you at her birthday party." I smile up at his grin as he releases me reluctantly, stepping backwards out of the elevator.

"Will you be my Prince Charming if I do?" I flutter my lashes at him as I joke, but instead of laughing, his look turns heated as he plays with his lip ring with his teeth.

"I'll be whatever you want me to be, baby. I'd even go as a frog so you have to kiss me. Speak to you soon," Dec promises as the doors start to close. I fight the urge to stop them and follow him.

Once I'm in the apartment, I lean heavily against the door and take a deep breath. I am so in trouble. That guy is giving me feelings that have no business being in my life right now. I need to focus on my classes and labs. I have no time to even entertain the idea of having a relationship.

"Wow. Look at you, all starry eyed and flushed. Good night?" I startle, turning to find Kara curled up in the corner of the couch against the wall, eating chocolate. I give her a smile so big it hurts my cheeks, but I couldn't contain it if I tried.

"Great night," I correct, walking over to join her when she silently gestures for me to sit and spill the details. I take a line of chocolate from her bar as she notices my shirt.

"The guy can kiss… and he is so sweet with his baby sister that it makes me want to tie him down and have his babies," I tell her. I watch as her eyes go wide, and she pretends to choke on the chocolate in her mouth.

"Details. Now," Kara demands. I grin as I get comfortable, knowing she will keep me here until she's satisfied.

So I tell her because she's my sister, and we have shared everything. Even things I wish I could take back. Kara coos happily for me when I finish catching her up. I laugh as my back pocket vibrates with a text. I pull it out to read it, grinning as Kara tries to look over my shoulder.

"Is it too soon to be speaking again? If it is, I don't care. Just letting you know I arrived home without a problem in case you still worried. Told you the night fears me. I'm like Batman only without the lisp, tights, and cool weapons. X"

Kara and I laugh then I tell her goodnight before heading to my room. Once I'm changed and curled up in my blankets, I re-read his text and smile as I send a quick reply,

"It's never too soon. Glad to know you and your ego are safe. What about the cape and abs of steel? You're not a real hero without them." I snuggle with my phone in my hand but barely begin to drift off before I get a reply,

"Have you never seen *The Incredibles*? No capes! I will show you my steel abs next time. You will be both assured and impressed. X"

"That's right. I forgot capes kill. Looking forward to inspecting this steel you speak of. I hope it's hard ;) Goodnight. Xx"

I hear my phone buzz shortly after my reply, and though my eyelids feel like lead, I force them open to read Dec's text.

"Oh, I'm hard all right. Sweet dreams, beautiful. And by sweet dreams, I mean of me. Naked in bed as I am right now. X"

I warm at the image he puts in my mind, and I end up dreaming of just that. Damn him.

Chapter 14

DECLAN

IT'S BEEN OVER two weeks and some days since Aela and I have really hung out.

I would think she was avoiding me if it weren't for our run-ins at the gym the days she can make it at the same time as I'm there. Oh, and our late night texts while she's working at the university café.

The woman takes multitasking to extremes. I don't know how she does it. I feel exhausted for her just thinking of all she does between classes, shifts at the café, and the lab work Aela's attempted to explain to me the many times she's had to decline my invitations to meet up. It sounds tiring to me, but it doesn't seem to affect her. Whenever I see Aela at the gym, her smile when she sees me is stunning enough to knock me off my feet.

Tonight, though, I am guaranteed to get her to myself for several hours, because tonight is the appointment to finish off her back piece. I confirmed with her this morning to make sure she remembered and can't believe how much I'm looking forward to it.

If Alex knew, he would demand I hand in my man card. I don't care. They—whoever 'they' are—can take my non-existent member card and label me a pussy for life. I miss her. The two hours every other day at the gym and nightly texts have only made it worse, which is weird since I haven't had her in my life long enough to miss her when she isn't there—but damn it, I do.

So here I am, after impatiently waiting all day, sitting at the front counter with an obligatory Corona Alex shoved at me from the carton he brought in since it's his day off. Half listening as he and Skunk talk up the fun they had last night that I bailed on while Kit mumbles about them being pigs and other less complimentary names.

"Dude, have you come down with something that sucks the fun out of you as it turns you into an old man or what? You need to come out tonight," Alex demands then glares at the warm, barely touched beer I've been nursing for half an hour.

"Dec is just smarter than you two dickweeds and is no longer interested in trashy barflies," Kit pipes in, making both of the guys give me inquisitive looks. I restrain myself from squirming in my seat by gulping down a few mouthfuls of beer.

"Seriously, Dec. It's been months. Has your dick shrivelled up and fallen off or what? I'm worried, bro." Alex's eyes widen in alarm. "Did you catch something from that last chick? Man, she looked a little…" He trails off with a grimace, and I choke on my mouthful of piss tasting beer.

"Hell no! My junk is perfectly fucking fine, arsehole. I'm a little disturbed that you're keeping track of my sex life, though," I yell at him once my coughing subsides, making Kit and Skunk laugh. "I'm busy tonight. I have an appointment shortly," I explain, ignoring Kit's smug smile.

"So we'll head out after. We have plenty of beer to tide us over until then," Alex argues with a shrug. I balk at the idea. I don't want him here when Aela arrives. Not because I'm worried he'll try to cut my grass, but because he is an attention whore when it comes to women. Before I can think up an excuse to get them out of here, though, Kit opens her big mouth.

"His girl is the appointment coming in, and considering how

strung out he's been all week, I'm pretty sure he's hoping he will be busy with her afterwards too." Kit sounds so smug. For a moment, I think it's because she knows she just threw me to the wolves, but when I send a glare her way, I see her sights set on Alex who is sporting an overly exaggerated pained expression. I sigh in resignation knowing he's going to continue to bitch me out. I don't know why, but those two are forever competing over anything, their favourite topic being 'I'm Dec's number one best friend because...' It's stupid, and I refuse to be dragged into it, but that doesn't stop them.

"What the hell, bro? You went and got yourself hooked on a girl and didn't tell your best friend?" Alex complains while crossing his arms over his chest.

"She's just a friend, and I have told you about her. It's Aela from the gym." I correct the both of them with my own arms crossed then get smacked in the back of the head with a magazine by Kit. I question her with a silent look while she continues looking smug.

"More than a friend from what Hope told me when she hung here while Nicola got some stuff done the other day. Yeah, your sister wasn't impressed with your licking and sucking. By the way, if that's your A-game, you really need some lessons in seduction." She starts laughing while the guys look at me like I've just grown a third eye, their faces so funny I start chuckling too.

"Hey, you weren't there so you can't judge. My game was in top form that night, thank you very much," I assure Kit as she looks behind me to the front door. My entire back goes warm with a prickling sensation that I've come to accept only happens when Aela is watching me. The sensation is weird, but I've stopped questioning it.

"Here's the only person who can really confirm that." Kit smiles widely, completely ignoring my warning look.

"Hey, doll, how's things?" Kit calls out as I turn to catch my first glimpse of Aela in too damn long, and it steals my breath.

She stands there looking nervous but gives me a big, sweet smile while blocking Kara from entering. My eyes travel her body from her hair that's down and curling over her shoulders, her little pink and white sundress that reveals a little swell of cleavage and all that leg again, all the way to her little toes painted in pearl polish.

My God, she looks so sweet and innocent. My mind instantly pictures ways to corrupt her, once I get her alone, with that dress bunched up around her hips. I try to stop by focusing on her face, her lips as she replies to Kit, but again, my thoughts go X-rated, and I'm struggling with all my blood flowing south. I need to kiss those lips. I tear my eyes away before I'm sporting some serious wood for all to see, refocusing on her eyes that haven't left mine at all, and I adore the softness in them.

"Oh, damn. You've gone and got yourself a real girl. Are you crazy?" Alex asks like he expects me to know what the hell he means by that. I watch Aela's forehead scrunch in confusion and her lips jut out sexily in a pout to match as she glances at Alex whose gaze shifts back and forth between the two of us.

"As opposed to what? A blow-up doll? Sorry to disappoint you," Aela comments, making Kit and Skunk laugh out loud with applause. Even I grin proudly as I turn to wrap my arm around her shoulders and draw her further into the room so Kara can get in behind her.

"Just ignore him, trouble. Ready for another round with me?" Okay, despite the way my voice went low, I really didn't mean for it to sound like the proposition it came out as. It doesn't help with my situation, especially when I watch the interest spark to life in her eyes as she blushes. Damn. I feel like the dirty snake in the Garden of Eden right now, yet it also feels like she is the apple, and I'm being tempted. Either way, I'm sure I'd be going to hell for the thoughts running through my head.

"Ready when you are," Aela replies in a low, sultry tone. I bite the inside of my mouth in an attempt to regain some control. I haven't felt this out of control over my own body since I was fourteen. I gesture with a nod to the back room, and Aela starts to move before Alex steps in.

"You're not getting rid of me that easily, bro." He frowns at me before holding his hand out to Aela. "Hello, beautiful lady. I'll introduce myself since these arseholes won't. I'm Alex, the awesome best friend who is currently questioning why I put up with this and don't just find a better bro."

He then turns back to glare at me before Kit calls out, "You stick around for the free tattoos and because no one else will put up with your shit." I bite off a laugh, nudging Alex with the toe of my Converse because he still has a hold of Aela's hand, and she's starting to look uncomfortable. Instead of releasing Aela, he raises her hand to his lips to kiss the back of it. I'm pretty sure we all roll our eyes at him.

"I guess you're the mysterious Aela, who has turned my bro into a teen girl." He grins at her dubious look before I smack him in the head as I take her hand from him with a glare his way.

"You're full of shit, and you know who she is because I just told you." I tug Aela to my side then look down at her cute little grin. "Like I said—ignore him. I don't know the guy. Whatever you do, don't feed him, or he'll follow you around like a stray too," I warn mockingly which makes the girls laugh as Alex shakes his head sadly.

"Whatever, fucktard. I was your first Facebook friend," he points out self-righteously so I turn to him with a grin.

"Only because you made my account. I would have deleted you, but your trolling amuses me," I quip and then watch as he turns a sad look on Aela.

"Don't fall for this jerks crap, Aela. Can you imagine how he

98

treats his women when he treats his best friend like this?" Alex points to himself then wipes away an imaginary tear.

Aela giggles and pats his arm in fake sympathy. "Thanks for the warning. I'll keep it in mind."

I shake my head then start her down the corridor, away from the attention sponge with a firm look his way so he knows not to follow.

"You coming in this time, Kara?" I call out, looking back over Aela's head as I reach the door.

Kara waves me off with a smile from where she leans over the glass counter before Kit. "I'll be in soon. I want to catch up with Kit for a bit." I notice she has Alex's attention, or at least, her cleavage that's propped up by her forearms does.

I pull Aela into my room, leaving the door open while I gesture for her to get comfy on the bench I already set into position for her.

"And who is this beauty? Hey, I'm Alex, but you can call me Mr Licks. It's what the ladies call me round here." I hear what I assume is Alex putting his move on Kara followed by the laughter of his audience, including Aela.

I shake my head as the girls out there swiftly cut him down before I turn the music on to drown them out.

"Sorry about him. I'm pretty sure he ran headfirst into too many walls as a kid." I take a seat on my stool and listen to her amused laugh. Once she is settled on the bench, I lean in sliding the straps of her dress and bra down her right shoulder, and Aela's laughter dies off. I appreciate the slice of skin I've revealed, in particular, the skin I've permanently marked. I have to run my hand down it, feeling the soft, smooth warmth of her skin against mine.

"It's healed beautifully," I announce into the thick silence before snapping on my gloves so I don't get carried away. I prep her skin, pretending to ignore the goose bumps that appear along her arms. Then I start my machine and begin with shading in the top butterfly.

Ten minutes in, I have to pause when Aela starts giggling so hard, her back shakes.

"What's so funny?" I ask as I peer over her shoulder. Aela's head turns at my question, putting our lips only inches apart. I zone out while watching those perfect lips as Aela continues to giggle.

"Are you doing it right because it's kind of tickling. I thought tattoos are supposed to hurt?" Her left brow arches in question while I work to look affronted.

"There you go, doubting my awesomeness again. I'm really going to have to teach you a lesson, miss." I drop my voice threateningly and watch as her look turns devious. I love the challenging spark that enters her gaze.

"Oh, how are you going to teach me, sir?" Aela playfully prods then sinks her teeth into her bottom lip.

It makes me want to bite, suck, kiss and lick it for her. The little minx knows exactly what she's doing to me too. Her fake innocent look can't hide the gleam in her eyes.

Bring. It. On.

I lean closer to her ear, keeping my voice to a low whisper, "I'll bend you over this bench and spank that delicious little arse of yours to a sweet shade of pink until you promise to never doubt me again." I watch as she shivers, and then I lean back to catch the blush rising in her cheeks and the lust in her eyes before she turns away to lean forward against the bench again.

"Kinky," Aela replies, trying to sound unaffected, but her voice comes out breathy, and I can't stop my winning smirk.

I get back to work without further commentary, noticing her grip tighten on the sides of the bench where she's wrapped her arms around it in a bear hug. If it tickles afterwards, she controls herself.

I let her relax with just the buzz of my machine, the music on low and the noise our friends are making in the front room to break our easy silence as I focus on the colour I'm packing into her skin. But after a while, I find myself missing her attention. Another first for me.

"So, how's school going?" I pick a safe topic I know will get her talking, knowing how excited she gets about her lab work, even though I can barely follow when she's on a roll.

I know she does stuff with yeast.

Aela tilts her head to see me, resting her forehead on her hands on top of the bench as she smiles.

"I'm keeping up so far. It's challenging, and I'm a bit scared since it's only the third week, but I'm positive I won't have a mental breakdown before the end of the year. Statistics is kicking my butt, though. I hate numbers, and it all just seems random." Her cute rambling is cut off when Kara interrupts. She is leaning against the door where she's smiling at us like we're cute puppies or something equally adorable.

"Don't let her uncertainty fool you. My girl is a science genius. She's going to cure cancer and shit."

I grin as I catch Aela's eye roll before she turns to look at her best friend. "Sorry to interrupt. I just came to see if you cuties want anything from Zarraffas. Kit and I are making a coffee run."

Aela gives her an order for one of those ridiculous girly coffee drinks then I nod my acceptance. "Kit knows my usual. But tell her no sugar this time. It won't sweeten me up. It will just piss me off and then I'll make her drink it."

Kara salutes me then turns back down the hall only to be replaced a moment later by Alex.

He stands there silently looking the way he came. I assume he's looking at Kara, as I hear the girls leaving before he turns to watch us with a calculating expression which is never good. I choose to ignore him and go back to my work.

101

"Aela, have you got any plans after this, honey?" Alex asks finally, making me look up to glower at him in warning.

"Absolutely none. For the first time in too long, my schedule is free until Sunday, and I'm going to enjoy doing nothing. Why?" Aela questions warily which makes me smile.

My girl is smart.

"No way. It's Friday night. You're giving all uni students out there a bad name if you don't come out with us, have a few drinks and get a little crazy. It's an essential part of student life."

Aela shakes her head at Alex's protest.

"Sorry. That may be what all the cool kids do, but not me. I'm not big on alcohol. Give me a great book, chocolate and my bed, and I'm set. I just want to relax," Aela explains, leaving Alex with an incredulous look as he turns to me for help which makes me smile smugly.

"Don't look at me. I told you, I'm not going out." I turn back to continue with the lilac ink. Seeing he isn't going to get any help from me, Alex tries again.

"We can chill. We'll go to a quiet bar, have a couple drinks, nothing crazy. I promise. Your friend and Kit are coming… and so is Dec. He's playing hard to get now, but he'll give in by go-time. Don't make me beg. I will if I have to, though. My knee hurts, but I will get on it if it makes you agree."

Aela turns to look at me questioningly which makes me look up from her tattoo, and I sigh after a moment.

"For Christ's sake. He's like a dog with a bone. He won't let it go so we may as well give in now to get some peace," I concede, ignoring Alex fist pumping the air like an idiot as I watch Aela make up her mind.

She's fascinating. I can practically read her thoughts from her slight expressions. Finally, she turns to smile at Alex with a nod.

"Fine. I guess a couple of drinks and a night out won't hurt."

Alex laughs victoriously as I look up at him.

"You got what you want, now get out so I can concentrate, or we'll never get out of here," I order then go back to work but not before I catch his teasing grin.

"You've never made me leave while you work before. But then, you've never had an Aela distracting you. I'll go, for the sake of the art, a great night, and for Aela to put in a good word for me with her friend with the legs."

I pause for Aela's giggling and catch Alex waggling his eyebrows at her. I throw my water bottle at him, but he ducks out of the doorway, chuckling.

***

Seven hours, one beautifully finished tattoo, and three rounds of drinks with at least a dozen shots later, I'm leaning against a wall at The Beer Garden.

We're at the pool tables where our group takes turns playing 'losing team buys next round.' To make it fair and because despite what we look like, we are gentlemen enough to refuse to let the girls pay, we coupled up. Aela teaming up with me, which was a blessing because the woman is a total pool shark. She also demanded I look at her arse when she leans over to shoot.

I kid you not.

Aela is self-conscious about her dress being too short to lean over the table without showing her butt and demanded I tell her if it does. I take my job seriously and make sure not to miss a second every time she leans over, even though the dress is just long enough to not reveal anything but more leg which both disappoints and relieves me at the same time. Although I'm dying to see what's under that cute little dress, I would have to introduce my fist to the other fuckers I keep catching watching her if they see it, instead of just the glares I've been doling out practically since we got here.

"Shots!" Alex announces, placing a tray holding ten shot glasses on the table beside me before handing two to Kara, his teammate. He then takes two for himself, singing the LMFAO song as they clink glasses and throws back their first shots as the rest of us pick a glass.

"Hold up," Alex makes us pause with our shots in hand as he replaces his empty for a full glass, looking around at us all with his free hand held up as he takes a breath.

"To great friends, great sex, and the awesome possibilities of combining them both!" Alex toasts, making the girls laugh as we all throw back our shots. I smile when I look down to see Aela licking her empty glass experimentally and then grinning playfully when she finds my gaze.

"I liked that one. It was really sweet. What was it?" Aela asks as she leans into me.

I smirk as I slide my arm around her back, gripping her waist as I lean down closer so she can hear me over the music. "Wet pussy. You're right, it is real sweet," I murmur against her ear and then watch the blush bloom on her cheeks as she turns to look up at me sceptically. I shrug. "It's Alex's favourite shot to order. He enjoys the reaction around him when he calls out for a bunch of them," I explain which makes Aela laugh. She then snuggles into my side while looking over to watch Alex and Kara messing around at the pool table.

I gather her close, enjoying the feel of her warmth against me as I lower my chin to rest on her head. I marvel at how perfectly she fits me, like a missing piece of the puzzle I didn't know was missing until she was placed there.

"I think those drinks have snuck up on me all at once." I barely hear Aela over the music so I move to peer at her face over her shoulder while she turns more my way.

I catch the glaze in her eyes and the flush in her cheeks and smile as she bites her bottom lip. "I really don't drink much. By much I mean, like the last time I had a drink was so long ago, I'm having trouble remembering it." Aela frowns adorably as her eyes wander to the side in thought. I chuckle as I move us over to the barstool Kit vacated to play.

I lift Aela effortlessly up onto the stool then stand in front of her, my hands remaining on her waist as she leans back to rest against the wall.

"You've drunk quite a bit, pretty quickly. You want some water?" I ask as I lean in to kiss the tip of her nose when I get the urge.

"Hell no. Another shot is what our girl wants." Alex appears beside me, holding a shot out between us. I'm about to protest when Aela takes it and throws it back, hitting her head on the wall in the process.

I laugh as I pull away with a shake of my head when Aela turns to glare at the wall like it appeared out of nowhere to deliberately hurt her. I accept the cold beer and extra shot from a tray that's been brought over for Alex, who is watching Aela with an impressed look as she rubs the back of her head.

I nudge him to steal his attention, and he looks over with a smirk. "Skunk has racked and is ready for you guys," Alex gestures to the pool table, explaining his interruption so I nod as I turn back to Aela.

"You up for another game?" I ask. She slides fluidly off the stool onto her feet, not caring that it lifted her dress a little high as she did it. I bite off a smile as I follow. She is just so damn cute.

"Why do they call you Skunk, Steve?" Aela asks as she takes the cue from beside him. He grins before taking a swig of his beer.

"Because his farts will bring tears to your eyes," I answer for him, laughing as her nose wrinkles adorably when she turns to check if I'm serious.

"You guys are gross," Aela complains with a laugh as Skunk shrugs shamelessly.

"Kit, you're up," Skunk calls out to where she is leaning against the other end of the table, giving a hard time to the guy who had the balls to approach her. Kit turns to face us with a flick of her colourful hair and a cheeky smirk that flashes a dimple.

"I'm out for a smoke break," Kit declines as she fishes a cigarette from the small case in her bra. I glare at the guy with her when his eyes bug out watching.

"Come on, Kitty. You can wait one more game," Alex taunts, which makes her send him a glare as she slides her lighter from her pocket.

"I will claw your eyes out. You can be Skunk's bitch for a round. Aela will own you anyway," Kit retaliates then turns, pushing the guy in front of her out of her way as she struts to the smoker's area on the balcony with Kara not far behind to keep her company.

"You heard the woman. Take your shot, bitch," Skunk taunts Alex who gives him the finger in reply as he takes up a cue. Alex breaks, sinking a small and then misses his second shot but is smiling when he stands back up while Aela approaches the table for her turn.

"Hold up, miss. Thank you, Janie-baby." I follow the direction he's looking to see another round of shots being delivered to the table. Alex smacks the waitress's arse as she turns to leave then he hands Aela a glass, "A shot before your shot," he orders.

Aela smirks knowingly as she takes it. "You're trying to get me drunk so you win," Aela accuses. Alex shrugs unapologetically as he takes a glass himself then offers the tray to Skunk and me.

"Whatever it takes, baby girl," Alex admits.

Aela glowers at him. "That's dirty play. And just so you know, alcohol has never affected my game before."

She smiles and turns to take her shot, sinking two balls one after another until Alex steps up behind Aela as she lines up her third shot. He leans over, his chest against her back and his hands resting on the table beside her hips, making me grip my beer tighter and take a step to break them up, but Skunk holds me back knowingly.

"I like dirty. I happen to be real good at it." I barely make out what Alex says before Aela misses her shot and collapses to the table in a fit of laughter as she hits him away with her cue.

"You're a dick," Aela complains when she collects herself, pulling back off the table then backhands his chest on her way to stand next to me.

"I have one. You wanna see it?" Alex jokes with an eyebrow waggle, making Aela shake her head as she leans into me. I can't help but wrap my arm around her possessively as I glare at him to cut it out, which is kind of ruined when Aela's cute giggle makes me smile.

"Can I take your photo?" A worker from the bar approaches with his camera and is a little uncertain.

Aela immediately turns into me, throwing her arms around me as she presses her chest against my torso and cuddles in with a smile and nod to the photographer. The flash goes off, blinding me, and Aela leans up to press a kiss to my lips, and there's another flash. My brain finally catches up, and my arms tighten around her when she starts to pull back. I keep her there a moment longer, so I can gently nip at her bottom lip before stealing a real kiss. I slide my tongue against the seam of her lips until they open invitingly then her tongue meets mine, hesitant and sweet at first, but she quickly turns heated and greedy. I love getting this reaction from her.

107

Aela pulls me closer with fistfuls of my shirt and dominates my mouth with hers. I know how she feels because I want more, too. I want to see just how riled up I can get her, and yes, I am fully aware of the caveman side of me, screaming to make sure every guy in this damn place knows she is mine with this kiss. I blame Alex. I wrap my hands in her soft, silky hair, tilt her head back a little more and take over, plunging my tongue into the depths of her sweet mouth that tastes like peach schnapps.

Aela emits a low moan in the back of her throat which has my dick twitching to life. She slides her left foot up the outside of my leg until her knee hooks over my hip and then begins gently grinding herself against my growing hard on.

Everything and everyone around us ceases to exist. I slide my right hand out of her hair and glide it down over her gorgeous curves until it meets her arse over her dress. I lift Aela tighter against me, eliciting a gasp from my girl as her hands move into my hair and tug it roughly. I don't think I've ever been harder in my life.

I need to get us to a bed. Now.

"Ho-ly shit, dude." Alex's voice penetrates the moment like a bucket of ice cold water thrown on me as I slam back to the reality of where we are. Shit.

I pull away from Aela slowly, opening my eyes to see her staring back at me with the same recognition in her gaze. She blushes then pulls away to bury her face into my chest with embarrassment. I chuckle as I wrap my arms around her protectively. I finally look away from her to see the photographer gone and Skunk and Alex with identical impressed looks on their faces. They sip their beers like they need the cooling off.

"Dude. If a camera can get you two that hot, you have to make a sex tape. Fuck, it would make us millions," Alex suggests with a look of awe. I arch a brow silently in reply as Aela tries to bury herself into me more.

"I don't know about you guys, but I need a refill after that. To hell with the game. This round's on me." Skunk slaps me on the back then makes his way through the crowd to the bar. I ignore Alex's continuing look as I lean down to kiss the top of Aela's hair.

"Hey, you coming out of there?" I whisper near her ear. She shakes her head in reply, her nose skimming against my breastbone as her grip on the sides of my shirt tightens. I smile and have to forcefully pull her back to see her face which is entirely bright red.

"There's nothing to be embarrassed about. I'm sure there are couples getting hot and heavy in the corners doing a lot more than making out around here. No one's judging you," I assure her as I cup the sides of her face, kissing the tip of her little button nose.

Just then, Alex cuts in, and says, "I'm judging. I'm scoring you a hundred out of ten. You should be proud as hell, girl. That was the hottest kiss I've ever seen" He got a small laugh out of her. I give him a thankful half smile as she turns to look at him. "You're such a lucky bastard," he mutters when Aela gets distracted by the girls arriving back to our side.

"You all interested in coming to see Kit's friend and his band play in Coolie?" Kara asks while Kit frantically types away on her phone.

"I'm down if you're going." Alex shrugs and I give an internal groan knowing which friend it is. The band was bad enough to make my ears bleed the last time Kit dragged me along, and I have zero interest in enduring that again. Aela shakes her head as she pulls away from me which gives me hope that I won't have to.

"Sorry, guys. I'm not feeling too good, and I'm tired, so I think I'll just head home. Have fun," Aela apologises as she slings the strap of her little bag over her shoulder.

Kara looks her over like a mother hen with a frown. "Do you want me to come home with you?" she asks, but Aela waves her away before Kara can finish the sentence.

"Don't be silly. Go, have fun," Aela urges, but Kara doesn't look convinced.

"I'll take her home," I offer. I wrap my arm around Aela's waist, and Kara turns to me where she pauses silently, contemplating.

"I'm trusting you to get my girl home safely. Keep in mind, I know where you live and will mess you up if you don't treat her right," Kara warns, making me bite off a smile as I nod solemnly.

"I'll look after her," I promise. Then Aela mutters about us talking about her like she's not there, making me hide my grin in her hair.

Kara nods her acceptance. Alex fights his way through the crowd to get Skunk as we make our way to the exit.

It isn't until we're outside in the blissfully cool air that I notice how heated Aela has become. She's flushed with a slight sheen of sweat and fanning herself as she stumbles, and I realise just how drunk she really is.

I pull her closer to me as we head to the taxi bay following the others at a small distance. "Let's get you some water." I steer us into the seven-eleven as Aela looks up at me gratefully.

"When was the last time you ate?" I grab a water from the fridge and watch as she bites her lip, looking sheepish.

"I had a wrap at lunchtime." I shake my head and lead the way to the hot food section, but after looking at the selection, I don't trust any of it to not make her sick.

I pay for the lone water then we walk out to find our group looking for us. I wordlessly lead Aela into the next shop which is an American pizza joint and her eyes light up. Aela sips on her water as she eyes her choices hungrily. She chooses a barbeque chicken slice and makes sure the guy behind the counter picks

110

the biggest piece which makes him smile in amusement as I pay. I wrap my arm around her as we step back out, and she shoves the water into the crook of her elbow, immediately stuffing her face with pizza and moaning at the taste.

"There you are," Kara notices us approaching then nods her approval when she sees what we disappeared for.

"Thank you. That was the best pizza I've ever had," Aela slurs after inhaling her slice, leaning heavier into my side.

"Feeling better?" I ask quietly, and she nods while yawning.

Twenty minutes later, our group is finally at the front of the cab line. We say our goodbyes as the other four climb into a van.

Skunk pauses to slap me on the back in farewell. "Man, you owe me big for missing her appointment." He shakes his head as he looks at Aela wistfully. He then smiles at me before Kit tugs him inside, slamming the door on Kara's threat to be good.

On the short ride to Aela's, I enjoy having her curled up against me as she dozes off while clutching my waist.

I'm reluctant to wake the gorgeous woman when the taxi pulls up to the curb in front of her apartment building. I look down at what I can see of her face that looks completely relaxed and secure in my arms. I run my thumb over her little pout which makes her try to squirm into me more with a slight frown. I smile until the driver clears his throat, making me meet his eyes in the rearview mirror.

"Sorry." I lean towards Aela to retrieve my wallet from my back pocket, handing him a fifty dollar note which is over double our fair, but I let him keep the change.

"She's a precious little thing. You take good care of that one," the old man murmurs as he turns back to take the money I offer. I look away from him as I open the door and watch as the light that comes on shines in her glossy hair and illuminates the space.

"I want to. If she lets me," I confess as I run my hand

through her silky hair which makes him chuckle.

"If there's anything I've learnt about women from my wife of forty years, it's that the good ones are stubborn. They make you fight for them and will put you through the ringer, but they're worth it all."

I smile and nod my acceptance of his advice. I run my hand up and down Aela's arm before patting then shaking it when I fail to get a response.

"Come on, Sleeping Beauty. Time to get out of the cab and get you upstairs," I murmur as she starts to stir.

Beautiful sea green eyes blink up at me sleepily as she lifts her hand to shade them from the light. I help Aela out then guide her to the glass doors where she stumbles while searching inside her bag.

"Crap," I hear her mumble before suddenly pulling from my grip to crouch down, dropping her bag on the ground to search every corner of it.

"What's wrong?" I ask when Aela tilts her head up with a frustrated sigh.

"Kara has my keys," she explains with a defeated look on her face, leaning back to sit on her butt on the cold ground with the bag in her lap. She looks so miserable it makes me smile as I lean over to scoop her up into my arms, making her squeal. "What are you doing?" Aela demands as I start walking away determinedly.

"Taking you back to my place," I answer matter-of-factly. I look down to see her eyes widen in surprise as her hands wrap around the back of my neck to make it easier on me to carry her, her bag hitting me in the shoulder.

"And why are you carrying me?" Aela continues, a cute frown wrinkling her forehead.

"To get there faster. You looked ready to fall asleep on your feet so I'm going to get you to bed before that happens." I try to reason but really, I just couldn't handle her looking upset and wanted to hold her again.

"I can walk. I'm wide awake now. Besides, this rocking isn't doing good things for my stomach," Aela quietly protests so I instantly, but carefully, lower her legs to the ground. I still keep her pressed against me once she's on her feet, though.

I look up at the sound of a car horn and shake my head in amusement at the carload of idiots hanging out of their windows. They are hollering for us to get it on. Aela pulls away to start walking so I take her hand and walk beside her.

By the time we get to the back of the shop where the outer entrance to my apartment is, Aela is leaning heavily against me. I guide her with my arm around her waist. She stumbles then trips over the bottom stair, emitting a little squeal, but I tighten my grip before she can really fall which makes her laugh. I lean down to scoop her legs out from under her since she has barely any weight on them anyway. I grin when she makes a loud noise of protest as I carry her up the stairs. I'm able to successfully rearrange my arms around her, fumbling with my keys to unlock the door.

I elbow the light switch a couple of times until I get it on then take Aela to my room, dodging Tom, who comes out to weave in and out of my legs trying to trip me up.

I place her sitting up on the edge of my bed then tilt her head up with a finger under her chin to check how she's holding up. Her glassy and bloodshot eyes are heavy lidded, and she blinks slowly up at me before her eyes can focus.

"How you feeling?" I murmur as I wipe her fringe away from her face then cup her cheek.

"I'm sleepy. My eyes hurt," Aela complains adorably then leans back to crawl up my bed. I turn my head, standing up quickly when I inadvertently cop a view of her luscious arse in a dark pair of lace panties. This certainly has my dick awakening from its slumber against my will.

Aela settles against the headboard then strips off her jacket and starts slipping the straps of her dress down in agitation, making my eyes go wide.

"What are you doing?" I ask as she reaches behind her. She tugs her bra out the front of her dress, sighing in relief when she throws it my way.

"Hot. Uncomfortable," Aela explains like she has a limited vocabulary. She starts struggling to pull her dress off while sitting on it. I watch in amusement as she groans and curses before taking pity on her.

I retrieve a singlet from my drawers then move over to stand beside her. "Here, let me help you, little fool. Lift your hands in the air." I make an 'up' gesture with my hands in front of her, and she laughs as she complies.

"And wave 'em like you just don't care," Aela sings, waving her arms and laughing uncontrollably which gets me chuckling too as I tug her dress out from beneath her. I'm determined to keep my eyes above her neck as I remove her dress, tossing it onto the chair in the corner before pushing the singlet over her head, but she starts fighting me on it when I get her covered. "No, Dec. It's hot," Aela complains, stretching her arms out from under the singlet so I can't put them through the holes.

"Babe, if you're going to sleep in here, I need you to wear it," I tell her as I manage to wrangle one arm through the right hole. Aela looks up at me pitifully with a pout which begs to be bitten, but I refrain. Barely.

"You don't want me naked in your bed?" she asks, sounding hurt. I give a harsh laugh at the ridiculous question.

"I've been anticipating and dreaming of it for the last few weeks. But not like this, not while you're drunk. I have a hard enough time with self-control when it comes to you. Having you naked in my bed will be impossible to keep away from. But I

114

won't take advantage of you like this. I'm not arsehole enough to do that as much as it kills me, so I need you in this poor excuse of a barrier for the sake of my sanity." I stare into her eyes with my hands clenched on the bed beside her hips to keep me up in front of her at eye level.

She stares at the determination in my gaze then emits a huff of breath before complying, sliding her other arm into place.

I can't help looking down her body appreciatively once it's no longer exposed. Taking in the swell of her breasts, I bite back a groan when my gaze travels down and is held where the singlet pools in her lap, exposing some of her underwear.

I bring my gaze back to meet hers, my lips quirking mischievously. "But if you still want to get naked when you sober up, just let me know." I wink, pulling back when Tom jumps up to rub against my arm. "Make yourself comfy. I'll be back in a sec." I exit the room to her delighted crooning at Tom as he snuggles her. I set out fresh food for the fat guy, grab a water and some Panadol before turning the light off and return to the bedroom.

Aela's illuminated by the dim light from the street outside as she scratches Tom's head lovingly. He's pressed himself up against her breasts, purring like a motorboat while nudging her affectionately with his head.

"Okay, buddy. Stop putting your moves on my girl. Out." I clap to get his attention as Aela giggles. I wait while he grudgingly passes me with his tail in the air all snotty like. I shut the door on him and hand Aela the pills and water. "You'll feel better in the morning if you have some Panadol now before you really need it," I explain, and she takes them gratefully. I slip out of my jeans and shirt, leaving my boxer briefs on and slide into my side of the bed. I lay on my side, watching Aela swallow the pills with some water, somehow finding even her swallowing erotic. I shake it off as she leans away, placing the water bottle on the bedside table before shifting to curl up facing me. She tucks her hands under her cheek on the pillow with just the sheet over her. *Goddamn, she's beautiful.* I continue to watch her eyelids flutter as she slowly sinks into sleep. I appreciate the view of the way the shadows dance over the delectable curves and dips of her body. My jealous fingers twitch with the need to do the same dance over her skin. I get the urge to sketch her, exactly how she is right now but don't want to disturb her. Instead, I slowly commit every nuance to memory so I can sketch it at a later date if I still want.

"I can feel you staring, Dec. Stop it and go to sleep," Aela murmurs, making me smile. I wriggle closer, wrapping my left arm over her so my hand rests in the dip of her spine. She adjusts to snuggle in, and I have to bite back a groan, feeling her breasts pressed up against my chest. I release a heavy breath then force my eyes to close and my muscles to relax one by one. Despite the fact I'm used to sleeping alone to the point I've never been able to sleep beside anyone except Hope, it isn't long before sleep takes me.

Chapter 15

AELA

I WAKE UP to sun blaring in my eyes, a bladder threatening to burst, and a very warm, heavy weight pressed up against my back and over my legs.

For a disorientated moment, I don't know where I am, but as I turn to see the weight spooning me is a shirtless Dec, the night before starts to come back to me.

I admire Dec's sleeping face for a moment because he looks so peaceful and handsome, but my bladder is screaming urgently so I have to turn away before I can get my fill of him. I carefully slide out of bed until my left knee reaches the floor and let out a sigh of relief. But as I tug my right leg out from between his, Dec makes a deep noise of protest low in his throat, reaching for me with his now empty arm. A frown forms on his face when he fails to find me and then his eyes open, immediately meeting mine.

"You know, people usually wait until after getting laid to do the whole bail-while-they-sleep thing," His voice is deliciously low and throaty with sleep which gives me tingles before his words register—then I extricate myself from beneath him with a huff.

"I'm not sneaking out. I need to pee," I argue, squirming where I stand until he points to a closed door off to his side of the room with a lazy grin. I shuffle as fast as I can while clenching my pelvic muscles tight and sigh in relief when I open the door to find a spotlessly clean bathroom.

After I relieve my bladder with a sigh of bliss and wash my hands, I groan when I catch my reflection in the mirror, all crazy haired and racoon-eyed. I clean up as best I can, washing my face, finger combing my hair, and then rub some toothpaste over my teeth with my finger before helping myself to some mouthwash before going back out to the bedroom.

Dec is stretched out on his back, hands folded under his head, the sheet draped over his hips leaving his bare upper body on display. His hunter-like eyes track me as I make my way around the room.

"How are you feeling?" he inquires as I sit and carefully leaning against the headboard of his bed.

"I'm a little queasy and my head hurts, but not like it should after all those drinks. Thanks for looking after me." I blush, recalling he had to carry me up the stairs and help me change.

Dec chuckles before reaching over to pull me down closer, pressing a tender kiss to my forehead. I snuggle against him, enjoying the warmth emanating from his body. We silently enjoy the peace of the moment as he lazily skims his hand up and down my back.

"Tom will be waiting for me to get his breakfast out there, probably tearing my stuff up. Are you up for some bacon and eggs?" Dec asks a while later.

I look up at him curiously. "Tom?" I ask, watching as he slides out of bed, stretching his arms above his head. I admire all the lean muscle that's on display since he's only wearing a tight pair of grey boxer-briefs.

There's so much mouth-watering skin on display that my eyes don't know where to go first. There are his bunched muscles in his back and tattooed arms, the side peek of an eight-pack and those delicious pelvic muscles that form an arrow to a part of his body I really want to see. His perfectly round butt I want to sink my teeth into, his clearly defined legs and calves. Heck, even his feet are sexy which is weird because I usually hate feet—they are the weirdest, creepiest part of the human body—but his are big and perfectly shaped.

When I make my way back to his gorgeous face, I find his eyes on me as he smirks knowingly. Instead of looking away in embarrassment like I usually would, I smile playfully which makes him chuckle.

"Yeah, Tom. My housemate. He'll probably barge in as soon as I open the door to complain about being locked out all night. Stay right there. I think it's a breakfast in bed day." Dec pulls a singlet over his head then opens the door. Before he can take a step out, a large grey blur shoots between his legs and jumps onto the bed. I smile when the biggest cat I've ever seen—and vaguely remember from last night—walks up to nudge me with a loud meow that makes Dec huff in obviously fake annoyance.

"Tom, I told you last night, Aela's mine so get off her." I laugh as I scratch the cat's chin, and it purrs loudly, totally ignoring Dec.

"This is your housemate? I wouldn't have picked you for a cat guy." I look up to grin at Dec who shakes his head adamantly.

"I'm not. Their fur gets everywhere, and their shitty, snobby attitudes suck. But Hope found this guy when she was four, and he was a tiny thing, only a few weeks old. She smuggled him into her room because Mum is allergic. Two days later, I get a call from her begging me to take him because Mum went in to clean up and found him in the wardrobe with a bowl of milk and some leftover lasagne. Because, you know, that's what Garfield eats so all cats must love it. Anyway, I can't deny that girl anything, so I went to collect this pathetic little ball of fur and have had him since." Dec shrugs when he finishes his explanation which makes me melt a little more as I picture it.

"Why'd she name him Tom?" I ask curiously which makes Dec laugh.

"She called him Princess which just wasn't right. I renamed him because he goes after all the ladies like a total tomcat." I laugh at Dec's story until he points to Tom with a straight face.

"Laugh all you want but look who has his head pressed between your tits without you really noticing."

I look down and giggle when I see Tom's eyes shut in bliss where his head is squished between my boobs as I run my hand down his back. "Smooth bastard," Dec grumbles, then exits the room.

"If you're that jealous of the kitty, I don't have a problem with you replacing him," I call out daringly over the noise he starts making in the kitchen.

"I'll hold you to that invitation after breakfast," Dec yells back, which makes me smile. I curl into the covers on my side with Tom in front of me, taking a deep inhale that's saturated with the delicious smell of Declan. I use the alone time to properly take in his impeccably clean room which is decorated in shades of blue and beige. The prerequisite poster of a naked, tattooed pin-up girl on the back of his door is the only thing that gives the room away as belonging to a guy. I admire the chick with long blonde locks, long, lean figure, and overly fake boobs. I hope she isn't a sign of Dec's type because I'm about as opposite as you can get which makes me cringe and look away. My eyes catch on the bedside lamp that's a tangled looking ball of chrome strips. I turn it on experimentally and notice how the light reflects off the chrome that casts shadows from certain angles. It's unique and pretty cool. I bet it would look awesome at night.

"How do you like your eggs?" I hear Dec ask, just before he appears at the door and I flick the lamp back off. Dec notices and gives me a questioning look then looks to the window as though checking that daylight is still spilling in.

"Sorry. I was curious how the lamp would look turned on. Sunny side up is good," I reply to both his voiced and silent questions.

Dec smiles as he looks to the lamp then back at me. "You like it?"

I nod. "It's awesome. Where did you get it?" I go back to admiring the lamp that's more like a piece of art.

"I made it, actually," Dec states like it's no big deal. He is then gone from the door before I can turn to look at him in bewilderment. I jump out of bed, Tom complaining when he's jostled. I find Dec casually breaking eggs over a frying pan.

"You made that?" I question then watch as he nods while giving the eggs more focus than really necessary.

"I like to mess around with metal and other stuff in my downtime," Dec adds cagily. I don't understand his weird mood, but I force my way in between his hard, warm body and the stove to get his attention, cupping his cheeks to make his eyes meet mine.

"You're ridiculously talented." His lips twitch in a small smile at my compliment. I lean up to press a kiss to them before pulling away. Trailing my hands down his arms, I continue, "Seriously. Is there anything these hands of yours can't do?" His eyes glint playfully as he smirks, wrapping his arms around my waist. His hands slide to rest on my lower back where he presses me against him until my braless chest meets his.

"Babe, you haven't even seen how talented these hands are yet." Dec's voice drops suggestively low and growly, making what he says sound like a sinful promise that sends a warm tingle throughout my body.

As I try to come up with a reply, the bacon starts spitting loudly. My arm gets splattered with fat which makes me jump away with a yelp, reflexively pushing out of Dec's embrace. He turns the heat down on the pan and pulls my arm up to press a kiss near where I got burned.

I smile at the sweet gesture then grab the glasses of juice from the bench to follow when Dec leads the way back to his bedroom with the plates. I take in his apartment on the way. The big, black leather lounge suite and artwork on the walls as well as some metal pieces on display that I hope to get a better to look at later.

I flinch when I try to settle back on the bed and bump my bandaged tattoo against the headboard as I wriggle to get comfy, Dec noticing when I gasp.

"We should take that bandage off and give the skin a wash after this, and then I'll put some cream on the tattoo for you," Dec suggests before taking a forkful into his mouth. I nod my acceptance as I take a bite of my own and groan at the flavours bursting in my mouth. It's so good my eyes close in bliss. Dec is watching me with avid interest when I open my eyes, which makes me blush and look down at my plate self-consciously before I force myself to look back up and smile. *Yes, I love good food. Sue me.*

"I know you said you were happy to be doing nothing today, but do you want to chill with me until I have to go downstairs at one?" Dec asks between bites. I smile tight-lipped before swallowing a mouthful.

"Sounds great," I reply and am relieved he brought it up before I could start stressing about overstaying my welcome.

"You have to stay in what you're wearing now, though. No extra clothes allowed until we leave," he adds mischievously which has me rolling my eyes.

Dec finishes inhaling his food long before me and sets his empty plate on the bedside table on his way to the bathroom. He comes out with a washcloth and swipes a jar from his dresser as he returns. He sits in the middle of the bed where he gestures for me to turn my back to him. I shuffle my way around on my butt before Dec's hands grip my waist to place me where he wants me between his legs. I gulp then force myself to focus on my food as I feel the bandage slowly and gently separate from my skin.

Dec places the bandage on its back beside me when it's free which makes me turn to look at it. I gasp both from the sight of all the ink and blood on the bandage as well as the feel of the warm cloth pressed against my tender skin. "That's a lot more blood than last time. Is it ok?" I try to look over my shoulder but can't see much.

Dec glides his free hand up and down my left arm soothingly as his eyes meet mine. "It's a little red and angry looking but okay. The excess blood will just be from last night's alcohol thinning your blood," Dec assures me as he applies the antibacterial cream. The movement of his fingertips takes my attention as the cream puts the fire out of the burn in my healing skin and his touch gives me butterflies.

"Done," Dec leans in to murmur below my ear a few minutes later. He presses a light kiss to the sensitive spot on my neck, causing my breath to catch. He takes my empty plate to stack on top of his before wrapping me in his arms so I'm encased in him. It feels cosy and safe. I laugh when he nuzzles into my neck, his day old stubble scratching slightly as he lets out a pleased sigh that gives me goose bumps and tingles.

"This is nice. But I was promised booby snuggles, so get comfy, woman." Dec leans us to the side towards the pillows where I happily follow his order until he swats at my butt.

"Hey!" I try to reprimand him sternly, failing when I giggle which makes him smirk. I settle on my side facing Dec, my head propped up on my hand as I dig my elbow into the pillow. Dec moves, leaning over to grab a remote from his bedside table before snuggling in. He forces his right arm underneath my pillow and his left leg between mine. The right side of his face presses to my chest, and he lets out a very male groan of pleasure.

"There are well over four thousand songs on this thing so you should be able to find something you like, or I'll have to kick you out because that would mean you have bad taste in music. That's a real deal breaker for me." Dec hits the button on the remote to turn on the speaker system his phone is connected to before handing me the remote and settling.

I squint at the display on his phone as I scroll through playlists, looking for something to match the tone of our morning. I'm impressed with the wide range he has, from jazz to death metal, old school to current chart toppers and everything in between. I select some Jack Johnson then snuggle into Dec who nods approvingly.

I find myself trailing my fingers up and down the tattoos covering Dec's arm around me, smiling at the content look on his face. "Will you tell me the stories behind some of your tattoos?" I ask quietly as I trace the weeping angel that covers his upper arm.

"My mentor did that one on the first anniversary of Grace's death," Dec explains without looking at the tattoo I'm tracing. He tilts his head back to look at me when I stop.

"I already had one for her that I got before she passed away." He lifts his leg to show me the colourful sugar skull/owl on his left calf. "Grace was crazy about owls and sugar skulls. She collected anything with them on it and planned to get a similar tattoo on our eighteenth birthday, but when the time came, she was too sick. So I got it done for her. I'll never forget the look on her face when she saw it." Dec smiles fondly as he looks across the room, clearly reminiscing. "It was the most animated I had seen her in months, she was so happy and excited." Dec pauses as he looks down to the tattoo. "I had the pocket watch added after she died which is a replica of the one she bought me, set to the time she passed away. Kind of morbid, but I felt like I needed it at the time." Dec turns quietly introspective.

In hindsight, I should have known a crying angel wouldn't represent a happy memory. I point to the tattoo on the inside of his elbow that looks a lot like a teal green Care Bear with a glass of whiskey as the picture on its belly. Alcoholic Bear?

Dec follows my gesture then cracks a smile and chuckles.

"I passed out at Skunk's twenty-first and woke up with that from the bastard." He chuckles again, his eyes meeting mine with a tender look as if silently thanking me for the distraction.

Dec runs his fingers through the hair on my forehead as he pulls his arm back from underneath me to prop himself up. "You are so damn beautiful," Dec states quietly and seriously, leaving me speechless so I do what I always do when I get nervous. I resort to humour.

"You already have me in your bed. You don't need to sweet talk me into it," I point out, but he just smiles. He places a kiss to the tip of my nose before moving suddenly so that I'm caught with him straddling me, his hands pinning both of mine above my head.

Our eyes lock. The look he gives me warms me in places that seem to react to him like calcium chloride to water. Dec slowly lowers himself to me, his eyes never leaving mine until closing when our lips are a breath apart. He slowly presses a soft, delicate kiss on my lips then another, before trailing light kisses down to my jaw, over my neck to my ear, nuzzling my hair out of the way and eliciting a gasp from me when he grazes a sensitive spot.

"You're also sexy as hell. Seeing you in my shirt, in my bed and making those noises... damn, baby. Makes me want to do a lot of things that would make you blush," Dec murmurs in my ear before taking the lobe between his teeth. He nips it hard enough to make me gasp in pleasurable pain before he sucks the abused skin into his mouth, flicking his tongue over it, making me squirm with need as he eases the pain. There seems to be a direct line from my ear to my core that clenches with everything he does.

"I'm good with that. More than good." I gasp, clenching my hands under his unbreakable grip on my wrists as he continues with his maddening kisses down my neck before chuckling.

"Tempting. But I need you at optimal health when I finally take you. I've waited too long for you to wear out on me quickly." Dec pulls back to meet my gaze as he tells me this. I release a shaky breath as I watch the determined self-control lock down his need for me. Damn. Resolved. Dec leans back, slowly sliding to lie beside me while I struggle to find words.

"You are a mean, cruel man. This is the second time you've turned me down after getting me worked up now," I point out with a huff.

Dec's gorgeous, playful grin appears, never failing to make me smile in return though I try to fight it.

"The wait might feel like torture, but it won't kill you." Dec mocks me with a squeeze of my nose that makes me glare at his stupid, sexy face.

"Fine. If we're not going to have sex, then what are we going to do for the rest of the morning? Stare at each other stupidly while we listen to music?" I huff again as I shift to face him with a petulant look.

Dec laughs loudly, his hand resting in the dip of my waist squeezing playfully. "You want to play twenty questions, smart arse... or we can watch something?" Dec offers.

I look around the room for a television then give him a curious look when I fail to find one.

Understanding me, Dec stretches up to tug on the bottom of the large painting above his bedhead which starts pulling away from the wall on its own in slow motion to reveal a thirty-two inch LCD screen on a hydraulic actuator. I'm impressed yet nervous at the same time.

"Is it safe to have it hanging in mid-air over your head like that? What if it falls?" I ask nervously, then slide my way out of the danger zone beneath it.

"I will either die a tragic death or be horribly disfigured," Dec states matter-of-factly, laughing at my wide-eyed look. "It won't fall. I promise." He tries to assure me, tugging me to move back to him, but I resist.

"Put it away. I'd rather play twenty-freaking-questions than have my face flattened." I tell him, and though Dec rolls his eyes, he pushes a button on another remote and the screen slowly lowers back to the wall before he pulls me into his side.

And that's how we spend the rest of our time, laying entwined on his bed as we throw any typical, inconsequential question we can think of at each other until he has to get ready for work.

"Are you coming to Grace's birthday next Saturday?" Dec asks, holding me back from descending the stairs by my arm, and I turn with a wide smile.

"I already have my costume," I confirm then watch as he takes the step down to where I am.

With a pleased grin, he asks, "When are you free next? I want to take you out before then." He slides his fingers through my hair to move it away from my face, and I try not to melt at the tender move.

"I'm free Thursday after six," I offer before he leans in, pressing his lips to mine softly.

"It's a date. I'll pick you up," Dec promises against my lips before pulling back, taking my hand as he leads the way down the steps backward, refusing to take his eyes off me. Dec reaches the floor and forces me to stop three steps up, conveniently at eye level. He moves in close, hands going to my waist and kisses me again, making me laugh against his mouth.

"Keep this up, and I will drag you back upstairs," I warn, then gasp when Dec lifts me by my waist, holding me against him.

"Promises, promises," he murmurs before nipping my bottom lip. He then lets me slide slowly down his body to the floor. "I don't want to let you leave yet. But I have to get to work," Dec murmurs, opening the door to the shop. He pulls me into his chest again, his mouth hard on mine, tongue seeking access to my mouth before I know it. I eagerly let him in and meet his tongue with my own, hands cupping the back of his neck to regain my balance as his rest at my lower back.

"Dec... is that you?" I hear Kit hesitantly call from the front room. Declan ignores her, clutching me closer and tilting his head the other way like he can't get enough.

"Dec, your—*oh*. Hey, guys... sorry." I force my eyes to open just in time to see Kit ducking back out of sight up the hall. I giggle into Dec's mouth which effectively breaks the kiss. Dec smiles and leans his forehead against mine as he takes a deep breath through his nose.

"Hello, Kit," Dec calls out before taking my hands from around his neck, keeping hold of one to lead me down the hall.

"Sorry, I didn't realise..." Kit gestures between Dec and me, her sentence trailing off before she tucks her hands under her elbows that are propped up on the side counter.

"Kara obviously did though because she gave me these to give to you. She said I'd see you first." Kit moves to dig around in her bag before throwing me my car keys.

"It's fine, Kit. Thanks," Dec assures her while snaking his arm around my waist. Kit catches the move and smiles before looking back up to us.

"Your client is here when you're ready." She nods to the waiting room. I lean over to see a middle-aged guy slouched on the leather couch, reading a tattoo magazine.

"Hey, Sonny. Come on back and make yourself comfy. Let me just see my little lady out," Dec greets the guy who drags himself up off the couch while giving me a once over.

"Always with the 'little' comments," I complain, making Dec chuckle as he leads me out the door. I wave to Kit who winks.

Dec gallantly opens my car door when I press the remote to unlock it. "I'll speak to you soon, babe," he promises, leaning down and pulling me into him. I lean up to kiss him goodbye but pull away before we can get carried away again.

"If we'd had sex, this is where I'm supposed to smile sweetly and say 'call me' but we haven't, so I refuse to use that lame arse line. I'll see you tomorrow in the gym?"

Dec laughs at my playful barb and nods, cupping my face in his hands to swiftly kiss me again.

"See you later, trouble." Dec finally releases me then steps away from the car so I reluctantly slip into my seat. I watch him in my rearview mirror as I pull out into the road. I smile when he stops at the shop door to look back.

This morning was perfect despite the sexual tension I can't get rid of. I feel like a giddy teenager, and just when I think nothing could wipe the smile from my face, my phone rings through the car's automatic Bluetooth connection.

I sigh as 'Dad' flashes across the display screen on the stereo faceplate. I press the silver dial to answer, and before I can utter a greeting, my father's gruff voice surrounds me in my tiny car.

"Aela. We haven't seen you since you left, and you haven't returned any of my calls. We gave you a few weeks to settle in, but if you're available tonight, I want you here for dinner." I let out another quiet sigh of resignation.

"Hi, Dad. I'm sorry everything has been a little crazy, but I can be there at seven," I promise, knowing it is easiest to just agree. Otherwise, I'll never hear the end of it, and it's not like I had plans anyway.

"Thanks, sweetheart. I'll see you then. Love you," he replies tenderly. My dad, the master guilt tripper without even knowing it.

"I love you too," I reply before he ends the call, and my music resumes.

Chapter 16

DECLAN

"I NEED YOU to reschedule any clients I have after five on Thursday," I tell Kit with a grin as I step back in the shop after I reluctantly watched Aela leave.

Kit frowns as she flips through the appointment book and then growls a curse at me.

"You're booked out for the next two months, Dec. Where do you expect me to fit them in?" she asks, exasperated, which fails to affect my good mood.

"Whatever works for them, if I have to start earlier or stay later a few days so be it, but I'm taking Aela out that night so I need it free," I explain, shrugging nonchalantly.

Kit's eyes light up as she smiles exuberantly.

"You know I hate making these calls, but okay. If you're willing to lose sleep or gym time— I know how much you need the two since you get really grumpy without them—and since it's for Aela, then I'll do it for you two." Kit starts making moves to get to work on it but pauses when I lean toward her on the display case.

"Can you help me with where I should take her, too?" I implore, giving her a hopeful look. "You know I don't do this. I don't have a clue where you take a woman like Aela to impress her," I add which makes Kit laugh.

"I think Aela's pretty impressed with you already. But you're right. The places you normally go leave a lot to be desired in the romance setting department. Let me call around, and I'll get back to you." I lean over a little more until I can reach to smack a kiss to her cheek. Kit laughs, pushing me back to my feet.

"Thanks, Kit. You really are the most awesome best friend a guy can have." I lay it on thick with gratitude which makes her laugh again.

"One day, I'll record you saying that so I can shove it in Alex's face. Now get to work so I can get this mess sorted." She points me down the hall. I happily go with a big smile.

About four hours into Sonny's piece, a commotion out front breaks my concentration. I lower my machine to the trolley as heavy footfalls make their way up the hallway. I look to the door to see a large, dark shadow approaching.

"Declan. You're an extremely hard guy to get a hold of considering you live and work at the same address." Joe, the president of the Blood Brother motorcycle club, is standing in my doorway. Joe is an intimidating S.O.B.—not that I'd ever admit that out loud. Easily six foot tall, almost as wide as my doorframe, and his forty-something-year-old body is covered in tattoos and scars that represent the tough as nails life he's lived. From his shaved head to his toes—not that you can see his feet through his boots right now, but I was there when he was getting some ink on his feet so I know. He has a small scruff of beard covering his jaw, and his eyes are dark, almost black that have never failed to make whomever he stares down take a step back.

"I'm a busy guy. What can I do for you, Joe?" I ask as I wipe down the excess ink and blood from Sonny's arm.

"We need to have a chat. I'll keep the Kitten out there company until you've finished." Joe returns down the hall. I utter a curse under my breath. Kit isn't going to hide her dislike of

Joe's presence, and things will go bad if I leave them alone for long. Luckily, I only have a few minutes until Sonny's koi piece is complete.

"Who the hell was that?" Sonny asks quietly as I take up my machine.

"No one you ever want to know," I reply then get back to work, though I fail to get back into my zone. Whatever Joe wants can't be good. Worry about what it can be, and Kit sitting out there alone with him, is a lump of dread in my stomach I can't shake.

When I walk Sonny out, the air feels thick with tension in the main room, although I find Joe sitting completely relaxed on the sofa, watching a gangster movie on the classics channel. I fight back a derisive snort at the sight.

Kit's sitting on her stool behind the counter, her back against the wall while she glares at Joe as though she could incinerate him with her mind alone if she just focused enough.

Sonny wisely keeps his head down as he pays up with Kit while Joe turns to give me a pleased smile that doesn't reach his cold, calculating eyes.

"What are you doing here, Joe?" I get right to it as soon as Sonny scurries out the door. "I mean no disrespect, but I doubt you have any skin left to ink or want a piercing, and that's all we do here," I prod impatiently and somewhat sarcastically as Joe pulls himself up to stand, his eyes flicking to Kit before meeting mine.

"Like I said earlier, I've been trying to get a hold of you. Your lovely little Kitten however, has had every man I've sent return with their tail between their legs without having seen you. You know the old saying, 'you want something done right, do it yourself.' So here I am," Joe explains.

I turn a questioning look to Kit, which she answers with an unrepentant shrug before looking down to brush something invisible from her top.

Joe laughs harshly as I turn back with trepidation.

"Buzz mentioned proudly at our last poker night how successful your shop has become and it got me thinking. Now you see, you had protection by default thanks to Buzz, and I really didn't think you would do much business here in Southport since it isn't really a tourist hotspot, but you're close to the university and students with their busy lifestyles are our number one clientele for the pick me ups we trade. So I'm here to make you an offer. Let us set up shop here, and unlike every other parlour in Australia, you won't have to pay a percentage from your own profit to have protection. We'll even give you a decent cut from what we make here," Joe finishes as he stuffs his hands into the pockets of his leather jacket. I can do nothing but blink at him several times in disbelief before I finally find words.

"You know that I left Buzz in the first place because I didn't like the drug dealing, right?"

Joe nods solemnly before continuing, "And I respect the guts you have to do that. But, well... this is just business. Nothing personal. We could use the money and whether you like it or not, you need our protection. There isn't a parlour in Australia not affiliated with a club and right here you are on the outskirts of our turf but close to the Knights of Chaos, who will have you paying out your arse and dealing more than just drugs. My sources tell me you've captured their interest also. With us, you just have to turn a blind eye. You won't even have to touch the stuff," Joe adds, which makes every muscle in my body tense.

I don't like feeling backed into a corner or threatened. I've never stepped down from a fight, now here I am being told everything I fought to get off the ground was pointless because I'm going to be forced to go the same way as Buzz whether I like it or not. My mind starts going a million miles an hour, picturing different ways to show Joe exactly what he can do with his offer.

My hands shake from being clenched so hard. Joe notices it before giving me a warning look.

"I'll give you some time to calm down. Be smart and think about this before you make any hasty decisions." Joe tosses a card onto the coffee table before walking by me, murmuring a silky goodbye to Kit that had to have made her skin crawl because it did mine.

I'm so mad, I can't move until the sound of at least three bikes fade out into the distance. In the resounding silence something snaps inside of me, and without much thought, I flip the coffee table as hard as I can into the wall across the room where it crashes loudly, the glass top shattering, glittering shards raining down to the floor.

I stalk after it determinedly, gripping the leg that's in reach to haul it over my shoulder to slam onto the floor as I release my frustration in a loud shout, the table breaking apart with the force and leaving just the leg in my grip.

"Dec!" Kit yells before coming to stand before me with her hands out pleadingly, her eyes filled with worry.

"Come on, big guy. I know he's a creepy arsehole and what he said is complete bullshit, but don't take it out on the shop. I'm hung over and had to put up with him making me feel all kinds of McStabby as it is. I don't have the energy to clean up after you go all 'Hulk Smash' on the place."

I stop, breathing harshly, my chest rising and falling rapidly and my heart racing hard as I drop the table leg to the floor. Kit wraps her arms around me to try comfort me. It's only when I press my hands to her back, I notice her trembling and instantly feel guilty for my outburst, knowing how much any acts of violence scare the crap out of her thanks to her messed up childhood.

I kiss the top of her head in apology as I give her a squeeze in my arms. I hold her until she stops shaking then pat her back so she will let me go.

"I'm sorry, baby girl. I'll clean up my mess." I silently curse when I turn to see the huge hole the table made in the wall. I gather all the wooden pieces of the table and haul it out to the side of the complex where the dumpster is as Kit collects the dustpan and bin to thoroughly sweep up all the little shards of glass. I carefully collect the big pieces then take all of it out. When I come back in, Kit's sitting on the couch with her legs pulled up to her chest, arms wrapped tightly around them. She looks lost in thought but turns to look at me when I sit next to her with a loud exhale.

"What are we going to do?" she asks in a small voice as I rub my hands over my head, pulling harshly on a chunk of my hair.

"Buy a new coffee table," I offer tiredly, receiving a small smile for my effort that quickly falls as her eyes turn serious and scared. This makes me reach out to pull her into my side, unable to stand it. I've made it my mission to protect her from the world since we became friends in the second year of primary school. It was when she offered to share her cobbers and strawberry milk after I punched a boy from third grade who had freaked her out by aggressively trying to kiss her and made her cry when he pulled her hair.

I took that mission seriously. From scaring off other boys to beating up the ones who broke her heart in high school, and her deadbeat father when I finally found the bruises he gave her when we were seventeen.

Kit is the other sister I never had. She's always there for me and is such a good person that for me, nothing is right in the world if she isn't happy—or at least her grumbly, bitchy self that we all love.

"I don't know, Kit. At the moment, all I can come up with is to avoid Joe, buy some time and pray for a miracle," I tell her honestly, coming back to the here and now.

The front door slides open, and we both turn to see a chick I recognise as my next appointment walk in with a big smile. Kit jumps up to welcome her while I rub my hands over my face feeling overwhelmingly tired as though it's already been a long day, especially when I think back to how happy my morning was with Aela.

I force a smile and struggle to turn on the charm before leading the client down the hall. Kit gives me an encouraging smile as I pass her which is like a little ray of sun behind dark clouds.

I nudge her playfully and smile as her little laugh follows me.

Chapter 17

AELA

THURSDAY NIGHT COMES around way too quick for my liking with how busy I was after my day off, and it catches me unprepared.

My room looks like a hurricane rolled through it. Clothes cover every surface while the hangers in my walk-in are practically bare, and all my drawers are open and overflowing while I sit on the floor in the thick of it moping. And this is how Kara finds me when she gets home.

"What the hell is going on?" Kara asks as she takes in the devastation. I pull my head up off my knees to see her at my door.

"I ran out of time. I haven't got a single thing I can wear tonight. I wanted the perfect sexy outfit so Dec couldn't turn me down again tonight if he tried, but all I have is cute girly clothes. I have the wardrobe of a freaking twelve-year-old. I'm a grown arse woman. What the hell is wrong with me? Why have you let me dress like this?" My voice is shrill as I rant until Kara walks in to grab my shoulders, shaking me hard to knock me out of it. Then she squats down to be at eye-level with me.

"Firstly, there is nothing wrong with your clothes. You always look beautifully lady-like which is never a bad thing. Secondly, I've seen the way Dec and other guys look at you.

Trust me when I say you're all woman to them, and Dec had admirable reason to turn you down last time. Finally, you have my permission to call me 'the-most-awesome-bestie-in-the-universe.' Why? Because I have you covered. Come with me." Kara pulls me to my feet before guiding me out of the room with her.

I watch curiously before following to the lounge room where she throws a shopping bag at me. "I know you've been run ragged the last few days. We didn't get a chance to fit in that shopping trip we planned. I had to go to the shopping centre on my break, and this caught my eye in a window so I thought I'd get it in case. You're welcome."

I lower my eyes to the bag and reach in. I extract a pile of black fabric and unfold it while letting the bag fall to the floor. My eyes water in my overly emotional state when I find myself holding up a figure-hugging halter dress with a lace coverlet that reaches mid-thigh.

I crush it to me as I fling myself at Kara who laughs as I wrap my arms around her in gratitude.

"You're like my fairy-freaking- godmother. I love you," I tell her between repeatedly kissing her cheek.

"Bitch, please. I'm better than that. This dress will still exist well after midnight whether you're still in it or lose it on a bedroom floor. I love you, too. Go get ready," she replies, shoving me away firmly but carefully, and I laugh as I rush to my room.

I hear the intercom buzz just as I'm applying my mascara and am assaulted by nerves that seem to spread all over my body. I pause so I can take a calming breath when my hand starts shaking. I hear Kara answer it, followed by her running through my room before I see her at the door to my bathroom through the mirror, smiling excitedly.

"Your Prince Charming is here, my *Sin*-derella—with a

capital *S*." I laugh as I lean over to slide on my sapphire blue satin stilettos Kara gave me last Christmas. I haven't had a reason to wear them until now. I stand back up and straighten out my dress and then consider my reflection. The dress fits like a dream. My hair is cascading over my shoulders in loose curls, and I chose to go a little dramatic with my makeup—smoky eyes and bright red lips. It's the most grown up I think I've ever looked.

Kara jumps when we hear the knock at the front door then runs back the way she came.

"Hey, bad boy. You sure scrub up well. Come on in before the cougars in the building sniff you out." I shake my head as I listen to Kara and put in my dangly earrings. I hear Dec's gravelly voice reply, too low for me to make out the words but Kara laughs.

I find them at the kitchen counter when I walk out. Dec is sitting on a stool with his back to me listening to Kara talk about the characters we've met that share the building with us as she is making herself a sundae.

Dec laughs, and Kara looks up, her eyes meeting mine over his shoulder. She gives me a conspiratorial wink which makes Dec turn in his seat to see me.

"Hey—oh… *Whoa*." I get a thrill out of watching his mouth fall open with eyes wide, slowly taking me in from head to toe as I approach.

I appreciate Dec right back, of course, loving the dark blue button up shirt that makes his eyes stand out even more. He wears his shirt with the sleeves rolled up to his elbows and the first few buttons undone, showing a hint of his chest tattoo. He even has the longer part of his hair at the top of his head smoothed back perfectly.

"Sweetheart, you take my breath away," Dec murmurs, sliding from the stool to greet me as though I'm not walking to him fast enough for his liking.

I force myself to not fidget under his gaze that refuses to leave me, roaming all over my body, seeming unable to settle. He stops when we're toe to toe, and I notice even in my heels I only reach shoulder height on him.

"How pissed will you be if I ruined your lipstick right now because I really need to kiss you?" Dec asks, reaching up to smooth his hand over my hair. I hear Kara laugh as I smile up at him.

"It's smudge-proof... so knock yourself out—" I murmur, his lips crashing into mine before I can finish the last word. Dec's kiss is intense and scorching with need as he grips my waist in his big hands, tugging me against him and trapping my arms between us. I grasp his shirt to stabilise myself when I'm left feeling unsteady. Though with his arms like a vice around me, I know he wouldn't let me drop.

Of course, Kara only allows us a moment before coughing loudly to get our attention which makes Dec extract his mouth from mine only enough to speak.

His lips move against mine still with every word, "Kara, how much would it take if I offer to pay you to go out right now for a couple of hours?" he asks without looking away from me, his voice thick with need, which sends a deliciously warm tingle down my spine.

Kara snorts in amusement as she passes us to get comfy on the couch resolutely. "More than you have, bad boy. I have me a couch date with my huge-arse bowl of ice cream and Jacob Palmer, also known as Ryan Gosling's abs in *Crazy Stupid Love*. And you two have a date to get to. Aela didn't get all dolled up for you to just mess it up here. Go. Now." She makes shooing motions to the door which makes me laugh. Dec sighs heavily but is grinning when he pulls back, taking hold of my hand.

"Kara's right. You look amazing, and I need to take you out. But I'm looking forward to messing you all up later." Dec promises the last part low for my ears only which makes me squirm before he leads the way to the door. I stumble along behind him and turn to speechlessly wave goodbye to Kara, who smirks before shoving a spoonful of ice cream into her mouth.

Our ride in the elevator is quiet as Dec runs his free hand down the curve of my waist and hip while still seeming unable to look away from me.

Outside, he pulls me to a stop beside a gorgeous sky blue, old school muscle car that glitters under the streetlights.

"Aela, meet the second most sexy thing in my life," Dec gestures to the car. I raise my brow sceptically as I turn to him.

"The first being you?" I ask mockingly which makes Dec's grin widen as he flicks my nose.

"No. You," he corrects. I shake my head in amusement as I lean up to kiss his chin.

"Your flattery never ends, does it?" I whisper while Dec lowers his head to kiss me on the lips.

"Get used to it. You're beautiful and amazing. I plan to tell you every day you continue to let me hang around." Dec pulls away to open my door then heads to the driver's side of the beautiful car.

"Okay, this may be a really stupid question, but I only know cars by their emblems on the back, so what is this beast?" I ask as I stroke the supple, black leather seat as Dec closes his door.

"A 1966 Pontiac GTO," he replies absently like he's had to answer the question before. At least, that makes me feel not so stupid.

"She's beautiful," I state as I catch the cars shimmery reflection in the glass doors of a building we pass.

"She wasn't when I first found her in the back of a shed at my grandmother's home. My pop owned her until he passed away way before I was born. Then she stored it in the shed because Nan couldn't bear to sell it on him. She passed when I was fifteen. I had to help Dad go through all her stuff. As you can imagine, I wasn't happy to do it until I stumbled upon this old thing covered in a tarp underneath piles of junk. I talked Dad into letting me keep it even though I wasn't old enough to drive yet. For a while, she became our 'bonding project' until everything fell apart. I eventually picked it back up by myself until my old boss, Buzz, came over one day. When he realised he couldn't convince me to cut my losses and sell her to the junkyard, he started helping out. Everything had to be replaced, and I may be a sentimental idiot because she's shit on petrol, but I could never get rid of her. It's not like I take her out much since I live within walking distance of everything I need, so I don't care."

His sweet story makes me smile as he goes quiet, focusing on driving while I watch where we're heading since he refuses to tell me where we are going. Lucero croons quietly about his guitar in the background from the sound system. I'm confused when he pulls into the parking lot at Burleigh Headlands since I thought we were going to dinner, but Dec just smiles as he gets out so I follow his lead. Dec comes to my side, takes my hand in his then walks us to the footpath heading back down towards the town.

"Stop over-thinking, brainiac. Just enjoy the walk," Dec orders with a chuckle, and I turn to look at him curiously.

"What makes you say I'm over-thinking?" I ask as I enjoy the view of the beach. Dec pulls me against his side, tapping my forehead with the index finger of his free hand with a grin.

"The adorable crease you get here. Plus, I can practically feel the heat radiating off your head from the energy your brain is burning. Stop. You don't need to know everything," Dec explains playfully. I fail to come up with a decent comeback so I resort to being childish and stick my tongue out. Suddenly—before I realise what he's doing—Dec turns so he's in front of me and leans in, taking my tongue into the heat of his mouth. He sucks it hard once and then runs his own around it. My core throbs like my tongue has a direct line to it before he playfully bites on my tongue then releases it with a pop—and a challenging glint in his eyes.

"Eww, you're so gross," I complain and laugh, though really, the move was unexpectedly hot and left me wet and throbbing.

"You loved it," Dec assures confidently like he knows exactly what he did to me. He slides his arm around my shoulders and squeezes me to his side. We continue to walk as he leans into me to nuzzle my ear which gives me goose bumps.

Could my body be any more responsive to him?

I have to focus on making sure my legs don't buckle as Dec straightens then steers us to the right. We're approaching the big white building on the beachside which is a beautiful upscale restaurant. I turn to look at Dec questioningly so he nods for me to ascend the stairs. His arm lowers until his hand is pressed to my lower back, right in the dip where the back of the dress starts, so his warm palm is half on bare skin.

I smile in approval then turn to watch my step.

Dec has a candlelit table reserved for us on the outdoor deck with a stunning view of the rainbow-coloured sunset spread over the beach as the sun dips behind the mountains inland. We sip our drinks—beer for Dec, while I try one of their specialty vodka cocktails our waitress, Tess, recommends. I continue to stare at Dec which makes me smile knowingly.

"Would you like oysters to start, seeing as how they're an aphrodisiac and all?" Dec asks, peering over his menu at me. I scrunch my nose as I meet his gaze.

"I've never seen the appeal myself. They're slimy, salty and gross so, no thanks. Don't let me stop you if you want them, though. I'll try to keep my gagging to myself," I reply and watch him laugh as he lowers his menu.

"Hell no. I tried one when I was twelve and spat it across the room, hitting my grandma's friend with it," Dec shares and we laugh.

We both choose prawn appetisers. His are tiger prawns with chorizo, baby roquette, grapes and mint chutney while I have deep fried Oskar prawns with coconut, macadamia nuts and curry mayonnaise—which is to die for. We follow with our main courses of Moreton bay bug with a buttery sauce, parmesan herb gratin, and Asian salad for Dec—which I try not to curl my nose at. I stick with the eye fillet steak with sweet potato puree, fennel slaw and red wine jus, which is so good, I emit a moan on the first bite without meaning to and then watch as Dec chokes on his mouthful.

"Wow. I picked the wrong meal if it's that good," he remarks with a raised brow and amused smirk as he beat on his chest to clear his airway.

"This is orgasmic. You're missing out," I reply while cutting another forkful. I peek up at him suggestively which makes him chuckle, shaking his head like he doesn't know what to do with me.

Dec is the perfect dinner date. The conversation flows easily throughout the meal, and he mostly remains on his best behaviour apart from a few cheeky innuendos. He doesn't react at all to Tess's overt attempts to get his attention, which is impressive because I'm not half gay, but I'll admit I admired the red-headed bombshell, but Dec treated her respectfully like any other server.

I whimper pitifully when I arrive back at the table after excusing myself to use the bathroom to find Dec has ordered a dessert plate to share. The plate has three different mouthwatering chocolate desserts. Dec smiles. The flickering candle light reflects in his eyes, giving him a devilish look. He then leans toward me as I take my seat.

"I'm so full I could burst if I have another bite, but that looks too good to turn down," I complain while picking up the spoon in front of me to take a small sample of the mousse. It is divine, of course. I close my eyes and emit a sigh and then hear the bang of something landing on the table.

I open my eyes in alarm to see Dec has dropped his spoon and is gesturing for Tess impatiently.

"We need to get this to go. Now. It's an emergency," he informs her as soon as she is within hearing. All of this before I can ask what's wrong. Tess pouts but nods and quickly takes the dish away.

I try to remain straight-faced when Dec's eyes turn my way. I notice they look much darker than normal—the dark ring normally circling his iris is no longer distinguishable.

"Emergency?" I ask while I prop my chin up on my hand, leaning my elbow on the table. I'm pretty sure that's a growl that comes from Dec's throat as he leans in precariously close to the candle.

"I have a problem we need to urgently take care of and you, trouble, are lucky I know you weren't doing all that deliberately, or you would be getting the spanking of your life. I am so goddamn hard right now," Dec murmurs low enough so I can just hear him then he leans back when Tess approaches with a container and the bill. Dec barely glances at the slip in the black folder, before placing a couple hundred dollar notes into it which is a hefty tip. He then hands it back, swiftly taking the container while wishing her a goodnight without taking his eyes from me. He gestures for me to walk ahead of him. I smile as look back to see Dec walking with one hand in his pocket trying to look casual with the stiffest shoulders I've ever seen which makes me giggle. *Stiff, get it?*

Dec levels me with a glare so I quickly turn back and watch my way down the stairs. "Eek." I give an undignified squeal when I'm unexpectedly scooped up over Dec's shoulder fireman style as I reach the bottom of the stairs. He strides determinedly towards the car which makes me laugh breathlessly until the bouncing starts not being so good on my full stomach.

"Dec, put me down unless you want vomit down your back. I'm still so full, but if you keep going, I won't be." He immediately stops to lower me, keeping his arm around my waist.

"You okay?" he asks patiently. I smile as I take a steadying breath and nod. Dec looks up, and I watch him grin before leaving me abruptly, heading over to the grassy area where a lady in a long maxi dress is walking around the couples cozied up.

I watch curiously for a moment as they talk. I then shake my head when I notice her basket and the flower she hands to Dec. He hands her some money before she gives him more flowers with a laugh. It looks like he emptied her basket because she starts swinging it happily as he makes his way back to me with a pile of cellophane-wrapped roses.

"Honestly, you're over doing it now, you crazy man," I state as he stops before me to offer the sweet smelling roses with a huge grin and a shrug.

"I haven't done a first date before. I want this to be the first date to end all other first dates," Dec explains sweetly while reaching up to smooth my hair. He then pulls me in for a tender kiss. I lean back in when he pulls back so I can press another kiss to his lips.

"You blow me away with how charming you are. Thank you for the roses, the amazing food… and the unforgettable date," I say in between kisses, which makes Dec chuckle.

"You said something about blowing?"

I roll my eyes as I pull back, but he leans over me, face turning serious. "You're welcome, but the night's not over yet." Dec presses a kiss to my forehead and then I grin playfully before biting my bottom lip.

"That's right." I continue up the walkway, my pace picking up when the car comes into sight.

"What time do you have to be up in the morning?" Dec asks, looking pensive as he opens the car door for me.

"Whenever I want. I'm free until my Coffee House shift at one," I answer, watching Dec smile brilliantly, flashing his dimple.

"So we can have a sleepover?" Dec bites his bottom lip a little, showing he likes this idea which makes me grin back with a nod. "I should warn you, though. I don't plan on much sleeping getting done." Dec chuckles darkly as he shuts my door. It gives me butterflies in the pit of my stomach.

"I'm looking forward to it," I murmur as he slides into his seat. I lick my lips that suddenly feel dry. Dec catches me doing so as he looks over while turning his key in the ignition. I can just make out his growl over the engine rumbling to life that sends vibrations through the car. This makes me clench my legs in an attempt to curb my throbbing need for him.

"We have to get home, quick. I don't want you or the ice cream melting all over the car. I'm dying for a taste." Dec's gaze drops to my lap as he plays with his lip ring, letting me know just what he means. It makes me squirm as he forces his focus on getting us to his place as fast as possible without breaking any laws.

I'm out of the car before Dec can extract his keys from the ignition and hear him chuckling as I juggle my roses and our dessert container. I shut the car door then start for his apartment.

"Where's the fire, babe?" Dec mocks as I hear him climb the stairs behind me. I turn to face him when I reach the top to wait for the door to be unlocked.

"In my panties, and I need you to put it out now so I need you to hurry up," I daringly reply then watch his brow quirk over his dark eyes that slowly peruse my body as he approaches. His hands reach out to lightly grasp behind my knees when he's still a few stairs below, trailing up as he continues to ascend, the fingers of his right hand boldly slipping under the hem of my dress to continue their caress up my thigh. His left hand stops on my hip. I gasp as his chest meets mine at the same time his fingertips come in contact with the saturated lace between my legs.

Dec curses.

"You're soaked," His voice is low and gravelly in the crook of my neck, and the combination of that and his fingers caressing over the lace has me trembling against him in need.

"Declan," I plead, unsure what I'm pleading for.

His hand leaves my hip before I hear the door unlock behind me with a loud click and then swing open.

I step back feeling breathless, overheated and like my heart is about to beat out of my chest I'm so worked up.

"Give me a moment." I pant, thrusting the roses and dessert into his arms before stumbling my way in haste to the bathroom off his bedroom, quietly shutting the door behind me. I grip the cold, porcelain basin tightly as I lean over it to take in my flushed, glassy and wild-eyed reflection in the mirror. I try to catch my breath. I've never been this worked up before, and I'm a little overwhelmed.

The two guys that make up my sexual history—one, my fumbling high school boyfriend and the other, a biology classmate last year who really needed to study the female anatomy more—really don't compare to Dec. I fan myself with a tattoo magazine from off the bench and force myself to get a grip.

I don't hear Dec moving around the apartment so once I'm calm, I open the door to go in search but find him sitting on the end of his bed facing me. His hands are clasped between his knees as he watches me with concern, which I can easily see despite him sitting in the shadows, the only light filtering in from the living area.

"Are you all right? You know we don't have to do anything you don't want—" I cut him off by pressing my lips to his.

"I'm great," I assure when I pull back to force my way between his legs which makes him sit back while looking up at me. I cup Dec's face, enjoying the scrape of his facial stubble against my fingers then lean down to kiss him. It takes him a moment to react but when I slide the tip of my tongue against the seam of his lips, they open, and his hands lift to grip my hips as his tongue meets mine.

It isn't long before Dec takes control, his tongue dominating my mouth but keeping it slow and sensual as he pulls me closer. I'm forced to straddle him with my knees on either side of his hips on the bed while his hands move to grip my arse underneath my dress. I wrap my arms around his shoulders, running my hands through the back of his silky hair where there is just enough length to grab and tug it to tilt his head back so I can deepen the kiss.

Dec pulls me hard against his chest then thrusts his denim clad groin, making me gasp against his mouth when his hard length rubs against where I'm most desperate for him.

He throws his head back with a groan that sounds like he's in agony. I trail kisses down his neck then take the lobe of his ear into my mouth to nibble and suck which gets a gasp and another groan out of him. His hands tighten on my hips while he thrusts against me again with a curse.

I struggle with the buttons of his shirt impatiently until Dec helpfully lifts it over his head by the back of the collar, tossing it behind me. I return the favour and reach back to untie the knot at my nape then let the silky ties fall from my hands and down my body, exposing my breasts since I'm braless.

"You're so damn perfect," Dec murmurs before cupping my breasts with his hands. He rubs his thumbs over my nipples making me whimper. He leans in and takes the left into his mouth which makes me shudder with an overwhelming warmth building in my core. I swear the guy could get me off just by doing this, but I want more.

"Dec, please. Now... more." I pant, unable to form a coherent sentence as I lean back to pull my dress over my head. I'm in too much of a rush to be naked to deal with the zipper.

Dec wraps his arms around me then flips us so I'm on my back. My head sinks into the pillows as he hovers above me, his hands propping him up from beside my shoulders as his eyes slowly trail down my body appreciatively.

"Off." I tug demandingly at the button of his jeans. This makes him chuckle, but he complies, the zipper sounding loud and erotic at the moment. He shuffles the jeans down his legs, kicking them off once they're below his knees and then reaches over to his nightstand to retrieve a condom. He pauses again to stare at me, balancing on one arm so he can push my hair away from my face.

"Beautiful, I planned on taking this slow and savouring you, but I've waited so long that I can't go another second. You are driving me crazy. It's going to be hard and fast, but I'll make it up to you later." Dec's voice is gruff as he leans back onto his knees then tears open the condom wrapper with his teeth. Rolling the condom down his shaft, I watch and gulp at the size of him.

Oh hell. He's huge.

Dec grins when he sees the look on my face. He then lifts my feet one at a time to take off my heels, and then smoothly removes my panties.

He groans when he's hovering above me again, and I feel his cock rub against my wetness. This has me gasping before he tilts his hips away. I whimper in protest, but then his fingers are there, testing my readiness as he slides first one then another finger into me, hissing a curse at the tight fit when my inner muscles squeeze against the invasion.

I cry out, clutching the pillows in a death-grip when Dec curls his talented thrusting fingers up to rub against my g-spot while his thumb circles my clit. I shudder and close my eyes at the overwhelming pressure it causes.

"Fuck. Me." Dec curses again and then his fingers disappear to be replaced with the head of his erection stretching my entrance as he slowly forces his way in, the initial stretch stealing my breath. Dec is shuddering when he pauses once fully sheathed, letting the both of us adjust to the feel of him filling me while I slide my hands up to grip his back, pressing my fingertips into the tense muscles there.

"God, you feel amazing. So tight." Dec pants while dropping to his elbows so we're pressed skin to skin from the chest down, then he skims his right hand down my body to grip my arse, lifting so we're pressed together at a different angle. I've never felt so full in my life, and I relish the feeling, but I need more. I need him to move.

I reach to grasp his arse then pull to make him rock with me. Thankfully, Dec gets the hint and gives me what I want, forcing my breath out with each thrust as my spine arches and my head tilts back. I am revelling in the sensations the friction of his movement is causing within me. I gasp his name which has him picking up the pace with a growl of approval in my ear. He nibbles and sucks my neck right on the spot that seems to have a direct line to my core as his free hand clutches my hair, tugging it lightly—which almost sends me over the edge but not quite.

"Dec, more... harder... oh please," I beg but don't care as long as I get what I need to climax.

"You need more? I'll give you more."

Dec groans then grasps my left ankle to place it over his

shoulder while continuing his thrusting that gets harder and impossibly faster. He switches the arm he's leaning on then his thumb of his left hand brushes my clit before rubbing it in a circular motion.

"Come for me, Aela. Come on, baby." Dec pants in between ramming into me just as the pressure inside of me finally bursts and sends me over into the most intense orgasm I've ever had that ignites my whole body and causes me to see stars. I call out his name and cling to him as though I will be torn from this universe without him to anchor me. I hear Dec calling my name, but it seems like it comes from far away. Then his thrusting slows before he finally collapses on top of me.

When I come back to earth, I force my languid body to move, wrapping my arms and legs around Dec in a bear hug while ignoring our sweaty, overheated state. This makes him chuckle before lifting his head to grace me with a smile as he presses a kiss to my lips. He then groans as he moves so his arms are propping him up on either side of my head.

"I don't think I've ever come so hard in my life. I hope you're comfy because even thinking about moving is too much right now. You're amazing," Dec murmurs. With a lazy grin, he drops to rest his chin in my cleavage. I giggle as I run my hand through his hair in an attempt to repair the mess I made.

"That was all you, hot stuff. I just greatly appreciated your effort," I reply, feeling the vibrations of his quiet chuckle on my stomach before he shakes his head in amusement then turns down to press kisses to my breasts. I squirm then emit an excited gasp when it causes his dick to twitch inside of me since he still hasn't pulled out and Dec groans.

"You're trying to kill me."

I laugh at the complaint as I push his shoulder to roll him off of me, making him groan again in protest.

"I'll give you a breather because I need to pee and that

dessert is calling my name." I feel a chill in the absence of his body heat so I search the floor for something to throw on when I get up, grabbing his shirt since it's in reach and put it on as I walk across the room. I can feel Dec's eyes on me the whole time and grin at his appreciative growl.

On my way out of the bathroom, I check my reflection and can't help the amused chuckle at the very satisfied, well-screwed look I'm rocking with the bed hair, stubble rash on my neck, bright eyes, and rosy complexion, not to mention the rumpled men's shirt I'm wearing.

I comb my fingers through my hair as I open the door to see a still deliciously naked Dec prowling my way with a very sated look on his face. He playfully smacks my arse as he passes me to enter the bathroom which makes me jump and causes him to chuckle.

"Bring the dessert back here, and we'll have it in bed, but you have to lose the shirt," Dec suggests before turning to shut the door. I stop it to playfully pout at him.

"You don't like it? I thought I looked hot in this," I jokingly complain. And then I get a warm tingling low in my belly as he slowly looks me up and down before his eyes meet mine, letting me see the heat that is banked there.

"I love you in my shirts, but I want you naked for dessert," Dec replies, his smoky voice filled with promise. He winks as he shuts the door.

I scramble excitedly to the kitchen to grab the container from the fridge along with two spoons and a bottle of water before making my way back to the room, skilfully dodging Tom when he tries to slip in with me.

Dec comes out just as I drop the shirt, and we slide under the blanket together then he reaches over to seize our dessert, wincing when he removes the lid.

"We lost the ice cream, and the mousse isn't too pretty, but the rest is good. I probably should have separated the ice cream to freeze, but I was distracted." Dec looks sheepish as I hand him a spoon before eyeing the disaster myself.

"Chocolate is always good, even when it's a melted mess. Especially after sex. Nothing beats chocolate after sex," I state before taking a spoonful of slop and cake.

Yep. Still tastes like heaven.

I close my eyes in enjoyment while slowly removing the spoon from my lips, making sure to lick it clean. I may release an indulgent sigh because, when I open my eyes, I see Dec watching intently, his breathing a little heavy like I'd just performed a sexual act on him.

"What about chocolate with sex?" Dec murmurs before leaning over with an offering of mousse on his spoon but tips the spoon before it reaches my mouth. The mousse slides off to land on my chest, trickling down as I make a sound of protest. That is until Dec lowers his head to collect it with his tongue, starting from the bottom and working his way up between my breasts.

I'm breathing heavily when he pulls back. He then feeds me a spoonful of cake, his eyes glued to my lips until I swallow the mouthful and then he swoops in to kiss me.

"I can be down for that," I finally reply when he pulls back with a wicked, anticipating grin.

Chapter 18

DECLAN

I'VE LOST MY mind.

I'm sure of it because I get so turned on watching Aela eat that it hurts. Seriously, since when is eating sexy? Maybe it's just the way she eats. The little moans in the back of her throat as she leans her head back and closes her eyes. It's like she's having sex with her meal and makes me irrationally jealous of her food. I want to be the only one to get that response out of her. All through dinner, she drove me crazy, and now she sits naked in my bed while eating dessert. This is a million times worse.

Despite coming the hardest I ever had in my life just a few minutes ago, my dick is rock hard and begging for her mouth to give it the attention the spoon is receiving as she sucks it clean when I feed her another bite. I run my finger through the icing on the cake then wipe the lump of chocolate over Aela's pert nipple while she's stretched back in bliss, grinning when I hear her gasp. I tug her down the bed with an arm beneath her knees then move to straddle them as she watches with an excited gleam in her pretty, sea-coloured eyes that I could lose myself in. I swipe the excess chocolate from my finger down her stomach before leaning down to press my tongue flat to her left nipple, flicking up so I remove the chocolate in one hard swipe. Then I switch to repeat the move on the other nipple. Aela fists my hair, panting breathlessly as I cup her tits to nibble, lick and suck the perfect handfuls.

When I have her writhing underneath me and wrapping her legs around my waist, I move lower to lick the traces of icing from her stomach that lead to the sweet juncture between her thighs. Aela calls my name then whimpers as I flick her clit with the barest touch of the tip of my tongue, making me feel like beating my chest proudly all caveman-like. I chuckle before diving in to lick over her folds and use my thumbs to open them while the rest of my hands pin her legs in place. I lick over her opening from bottom to top, savouring her wetness on my tongue and wanting more. I don't know what I enjoy most—the taste of her or the feel of being inside of her. I'm going to have to get as much of both as I can tonight to decide. I grin at the thought as I plunge my tongue inside, thrusting it in an imitation of what we did earlier that I can't wait to repeat after I taste every inch of her body. Aela tenses, tilting her pelvis up as though needing more so I replace my tongue with two fingers and move my mouth back to her clit, flicking my tongue over the nerve bundle before sucking her nub into my mouth.

"Oh, shit, Dec... Don't stop... I'm..." Aela gasps and writhes underneath me as her inner muscles start pulsing tightly around my fingers, and I look up to watch as she comes apart. *Hot damn.*

Her body is so readily responsive to my touch. There is nothing sexier than watching her panting and writhing in ecstasy. I gentle the movements of my tongue and fingers as Aela sinks languidly into the mattress, breathing deeply. I grin when her eyes open lazily to meet mine, and then happily lick her folds clean of the sweet, slightly tangy fluid she gushed. Then I crawl up her body to kiss her tenderly and reach for another spoonful of dessert.

Aela mewls against my mouth when I pull away but giggles

as I press the spoon to her lips.

"You're right. Chocolate with sex wins, hands down," Aela states after eating the spoonful.

I chuckle while trailing kisses across her left collarbone then down over her breast where I nip playfully at her nipple before continuing down.

"Don't you want some chocolate?" Aela whimpers when I nuzzle her hipbone.

"You taste sweet enough. I don't want to ruin it with chocolate." I murmur my refusal in the dip of her hip which causes her to laugh and try to push me away. I kiss across to the other hip then down the length of her leg to her ankle. I nip hard enough to elicit a gasp out of her, and then rub my thumb up the instep of her tiny foot. She moans so I continue the massage, appreciating just how tiny her feet look swallowed up in my big hands. I want to continue to kiss and nibble on them—which is weird. Feet are weird and smelly, but as with everything else about her, Aela's feet are an exception and cute as hell. I treat her left foot to the same treatment then trail my kisses back up to her lips that kiss me back lazily as though she is about to fall asleep any second if I don't do something about it. I fully intend to do just that despite how gorgeous and relaxed she looks right now.

I apply another condom then slide right into her tight heat which makes Aela gasp, opening those pretty eyes that are filled with passion when they meet mine. I take her slow and deep this time, caressing and kissing any skin I can reach. Our first time blew my mind with its intensity, but this time, it rocks me to my core. The tenderness and connection when our eyes lock—it's as though our souls recognise each other. It feels like for the first time in forever I'm exactly where I'm supposed to be. It's crazy, overwhelming and scares the shit out of me.

It seems like we last a lifetime before we come simultaneously with loud cries of bliss. I use the last of the strength in my trembling body to roll us so I'm on my back, Aela lying half on top of me as I grip her to me tightly. I fight to catch my breath as I remove the condom then toss it into the bin in the corner. I know we should clean up, but I can't will myself to move or release Aela.

I smile when I feel her lips press against my chest and tighten my hold on her as I drift off to sleep.

***

I wake to Tom wailing and scratching at the bedroom door and groan, but smile when I'm distracted by the warm, silkiness of Aela's naked arse grinding into my groin as she stirs.

Best. Wake up. Ever.

I release her tit from the claim my hand made during my sleep, then gently slide out of bed though it's the last thing I want to do. I pull on a pair of sweats on my way out the door then scoop up the grumbling fur ball before he wakes Aela. I ignore Tom's glares as I put him down at his empty bowl then fill it after getting the coffee brewing.

On my way back into the room with two cups of morning elixir, I pause at the doorway to enjoy the view of Aela partially wrapped in my bed covers, one bare shoulder and bent leg peeking out, tempting me. She sleeps on her side, hair fanned out over the pillow, shining in the morning light filtering through the blinds. She's so damn beautiful it hurts.

I place the mugs on the bedside drawers before getting back under the covers. I lean against the headboard beside Aela, relishing the warmth of her body against mine and the little sigh that escapes her lips as she snuggles into me. I watch her sleeping for a moment before collecting my coffee to sip while I push the hair out of her face and reminisce on how incredible our night was.

"There better be some of that for me to make up for waking me up after wearing me out last night," Aela grumbles throatily without opening her eyes. I chuckle as I lower my cup under her nose so she can breathe in the scent.

"I have another mug here, but you have to sit up for it," I tease. Aela groans in reply while burying her face into my ribs.

"Next time, bring a straw," she complains, dragging herself up. Aela grins when our eyes meet while I extend the mug to her which she takes then turns to lean back against my chest in the crook of my arm. Hell if she doesn't fit perfectly there as I rest my hand just above her hip.

The morning escapes us as we lay there and talk. Aela seems just as reluctant as I am to leave our little bubble that seems to be keeping reality and the stresses of our lives at bay. Or it could be just me feeling this. Having Aela in my arms distracts me from worrying about my myriad of problems.

"We should stay in bed forever. I'm pretty sure I could teach Tom to fetch us food before we starve to death or at least open the door for deliveries." Aela laughs at my suggestion as we look to where Tom is stretched out flat in a sliver of sunlight on the floor, looking like a lumpy animal rug.

"If you could, we'd become obese and end up like those people on TV who need the fire brigade to extract them through the window with a crane. No thank you." Aela fakes a shudder at the thought and then sighs as she checks the time on her phone.

"We should get up. You need to be downstairs soon," she adds which has me tightening my grip on her in protest. I bury my face into her vanilla coffee scented hair. Aela pats my arm understandingly, and I sigh in defeat.

"Yeah. I need to have a shower and get ready. Want to join me?" I raise an eyebrow at her while trying to look innocent but am pretty sure Aela sees right through it, judging by her smirk.

"That would be nice, but I don't like the idea of getting clean when I have to slip back into last night's clothes. It defeats the purpose." She tries to turn me down, but now I've got the image in my head of having her in my shower. I'm not about to let her get away that easily.

"You can wear one of my shirts home. It'll cover more than that little dress of yours anyway," I argue then lean in to whisper deeply in her ear, "and no one said anything about getting clean in there, baby. I plan on getting very, very dirty."

I watch as goose bumps run down Aela's arm before she turns with an amused grin. "You're incorrigible." She laughs when I scoop her up into my arms, heading for the bathroom.

"That wasn't a *no*." I point out playfully then set her on the vanity to start the shower, kicking the door closed before Tom tries to sneak in and watch.

We're running late and have to bustle once we get out of the shower that was hot as hell, even when the water ran cold. Meaning the breakfast I planned to cook is reduced to just a couple slices of toast as we hastily dress, but it was so worth it.

Aela buttons herself into one of my navy blue dress shirts that covers her to mid-thigh. She cinches in the waist with a thin leather belt that I don't remember seeing before, but is from my collection. I blink in awe as she folds up the sleeves and turns my shirt into a sexy little dress. I've never liked chicks I've slept with trying to wear my clothes before, but watching as she judges her reflection in the mirror, I would gladly hand over all my shirts to fill Aela's closet. Seeing her in my stuff wells me with a strong male pride as though the shirt is labelling her mine for all to see, and I love it. It also makes me want to drag her back to bed and make us even later but I refrain.

"Do I look okay, or is it too obviously a walk of shame look?" Aela asks as her eyes meet mine in the mirror. I shake my head as I wrap my arms around her waist.

"Stride of pride, baby. You look fucking fantastic. You

161

should wear my shirts all the time." She giggles as I nuzzle into her hair that curls freely down her back.

"Cut it out, caveman. We haven't got time for another round," Aela scolds with a laugh as she steps away from my wandering hands to slip her heels on. I sigh and sulk which makes her laugh more.

My eyes are glued to the seductive sway of Aela's hips as I follow her down the stairs to the shop. I'm so focused on her movements, I fail to notice we are at the front door and there are people around us until Aela turns to wrap her arms around my waist.

"I'll speak to you later. Thanks again for last night," Aela murmurs so only I can hear then tilts her face up, silently requesting a kiss. I lean down to grant her one as my hands rest at the top of her arse, my tongue delving into her mouth until she emits a little whimper of need. I grin as I release her and step back.

"My, my, Declan. You need to share your secret on where you find 'em. What's your name, sweet cheeks?" A rough male voice interrupts, and I turn to the waiting area to see one of Joe's greasy lap dogs sprawled on the couch, looking Aela up and down suggestively while another sits on the other seat looking bored.

"It's easy if you don't have a face even a mother can't love. What do you want, Snake?" I step in front of Aela to take his attention off her. He grins knowingly, showing his rotting, yellow teeth, and I try not to cringe.

"Now, is that any way to speak to an old friend after I've waited over an hour for you to show? I see what had you so busy though so I don't mind. In fact, I wouldn't mind doing the same thing for just a few minutes."

I feel Aela stiffen where she's pressed against my back while Snake's eyes keep dipping to the side to get a glimpse of her.

"Sorry, Dec. I was hoping he'd get bored and leave after I told him you weren't in. He also scared off your client," Kit apologises from behind me where she's sitting on her stool glaring at Snake like the piece of trash he is as he winks back.

"Enough bullshit. Why are you here?" I ask, ignoring his attempt to piss me off and work on relaxing my jaw as it ticks from being clenched so hard.

"Joe sent us to see if you've thought about his offer yet," Snake drawls while cleaning his nails with a pocketknife in a way that would look casual and bored if not for the menacing promise in his eyes as he meets my gaze. He looks just like his namesake, waiting for an excuse to strike. It has the back of my neck tingling in warning, but I'm not afraid of Snake and his pissy little knife. I know I could take him, but I have the girls behind me, and I don't know what his mate is packing.

"He gave me his number and no deadline, so I'll call when I have my answer. Dropping in to fuck with my business is not appreciated so get your arse out of my shop before I show you where to shove that little knife of yours." Threatening Snake probably isn't the best idea I've had. But despite his act, I don't think he could really do anything when they still want something from me, and certainly not in the middle of the day on a busy street with plenty of witnesses passing.

I watch Snakes eyes flair with anger, but he controls it almost instantly before smiling darkly.

"Before the week is out, tough guy. That's your deadline. If Joe doesn't get the answer he wants by then, we'll be back to show how we can really fuck with your little setup here." They stand simultaneously then start for the door. The other guy that has so far been silent, passes us with barely a glance, but Snake slows as he deliberately walks around us to the door, perusing Aela who watches him with a confused yet bold expression, clearly stating while she may not know who he is or what he wants, she knows he's bad news yet he doesn't scare her.

"And I don't just mean the shop. If I see this sweet little thing around, I may not be able to stop myself from giving her the fuck of her life." Snake leans in close to threaten quietly. His rank breath blows strands of Aela's hair before she pushes him back with a disgusted look on her face.

"Get the hell away from me. It's never going to happen, you disgusting pig."

I pull Aela behind me, ready for him to retaliate, but Snake just smiles with a look that resembles a hunter who's just sighted his next big trophy kill.

"Leave. Now." The clear warning in my voice when it comes out deep and gravelly draws Snake's attention back to me.

"Never say never, sweet cheeks—especially when you don't get a say in the matter. You lot have a good day now. I'm off to get laid so I know I will." With that, Snake makes his exit with a casual gait.

The shop is silent as we listen to the rumbles of the motorbikes come to life then fade away. My anger level has way surpassed the coffee table incident which, at the time, didn't seem possible, but I'm shaking with the need for violence and destruction.

Instead, I turn to wrap Aela in my arms as she trembles slightly in the breeze from the air conditioner and seems to be in shock.

"Did he really just hint at raping me? Arsehole. I should have kicked him in the balls instead of pushing him away, but I didn't want to get anywhere near his junk." Aela's the first to break the silence with her incredulous statement. I tighten my hold on her and kissing her hair as Kit snorts.

"You all right, trouble?" I murmur near Aela's ear as I look over to check on Kit to find her looking pissed as hell and contemplative—which is never a good thing.

"I'm okay. Confused. I have a billion questions swimming through my head for you, but I don't have time to sort through them. I have to get moving or I'll be late," Aela looks to the clock in frustration as I pull her against me tighter, the alpha male in me wanting to keep her safe beside me and not let her go. But I know I can't stop her from leaving.

"I'll explain later, sweetheart. Just know you have nothing to worry about. I'll sort it out," I force more confidence in my assertion than I feel, hoping Aela believes it. The girl has enough on her plate without worrying about my problems, and I know she will if she doesn't believe I have it handled. She's just that caring.

"I'll walk with you, babe. I need a coffee break after all that," Kit calls out as she grabs her bag then comes around the counter with an understanding look my way, knowing my protective instincts are on high and I need an intervention.

I smile appreciatively at Kit over Aela's head before burying my nose into Aela's hair to breathe in as much of her scent as I can before she leaves. I think I'm addicted to her smell.

"Your client should be back any minute now. I delayed him to get him out of the shop and let Snake happily think he ran him off, so you have work to set up for," Kit informs while sliding on her sunnies. I give her a nod as I reluctantly release Aela.

"Thanks. I'll set up in the space behind the counter for today so I can keep an eye on things."

I look back down at Aela and raise my left hand to tilt her chin so she faces me. "Later, Trouble. I miss you already," I admit, not caring if I sound like a pussy. I press a kiss to her lips and watch her eyelids flutter closed. I release her before I cave to the temptation to deepen the kiss because that will lead to me carrying her back upstairs.

"I swear that nickname suits you more." Aela protests and then leans up to press her lips to mine again. "Bye, hot stuff," she adds then quickly turns to link her arm with Kit's and walks out the door as though she can't trust herself to stay a second longer, either. I'm grinning from ear to ear, still watching the girls out the window as Alex walks in. His head turns to watch them as he lowers his sunnies with a curious expression.

"Was that Aela leaving, wearing your shirt from our senior formal as a dress?" he asks, watching the girl's retreating forms. I turn to him in shock.

"How the hell do you remember a shirt I wore seven years ago, yet have trouble every other Monday finding your car after a weekend bender?" I ask incredulously, and Alex shrugs nonchalantly.

"I remember everything from that night," he answers, turning to face me, but his eyes focus on a point above me as though he can't meet my eyes or maybe he's just lost in memory.

I have an idea what it may be about but choose not to comment as I make my way behind the counter to set up my gear.

"So, the chick's wearing your clothes and you're grinning like a fool. I guess you finally wet your self-imposed drought?" Alex smirks as he leans against the glass counter with a teasing grin I pointedly ignore as I turn the music on.

"Okay, I'm not going to give you shit for it, man. I'm happy for you. You've changed, and I may not understand the why's of it, but you seem happier than you have in years—which is good to see. You deserve it, and now I'm going to change the subject before it gets all emotional, touchy-feely up in here, and we start doing each other's hair and talking about feelings. So, how was it?" Alex wags his eyebrows expectantly which makes me laugh hard.

"Out of this world. Totally worth the wait," I reply as I smile at a guy walking through the door with a wary look around the room. I recognise him as my first client for the day. Alex looks like he has something to add to the subject, but I give him a warning look before turning to the guy who visibly relaxes when he sees the bikers are gone.

"Hey, man. Sorry about the delay. Come on through and we'll get rolling." I pull out the stencil of a lion's head mid roar that's for his shoulder. Just as I sit on my stool after getting all the prep done, my phone signals I have a text. I turn to look at Alex who grabs it for me wordlessly, knowing I won't touch it once I'm gloved. I watch him read for a moment before his head lifts to look at me with a confused but amused look and a wide grin.

"What?" I ask impatiently.

"Aela says, 'Miss you too, really should have stayed in bed and started Tom's training.' She also added a couple kisses on the end. Do I want to ask what you two freaks are planning on doing to that cat? Will I need to call the RSPCA?" Alex inquires, looking unsure which makes me laugh.

"Get your mind out of the gutter. I suggested teaching him to open the door for food deliveries so we could stay in bed," I explain then frown as I watch him scrolling up the page. "Get out of it, arse-licker," I grumble, but he ignores me as he continues with a shit-eating grin.

"You two are so sweet, my teeth hurt just reading this. And not a single sext? You disappoint me," Alex mocks but puts the phone back on the bench as my client chuckles.

"Is there a reason you dropped in or are you here just to be a pain in my arse?" I pause what I'm doing to give Alex my full attention and watch as he tries to look affronted.

"That hurts, bro. I wanted to see if you were up for lunch at Dukes. They're having a two for one happy hour, and I feel like we haven't hung out much since you got all boring," Alex complains then glares at me. "And don't you dare point out how much of a clingy bitch I just sounded like. I heard it, but I'm not taking it back. It's true." He crosses his arms over his chest with a look, just daring me to comment, but I don't because he's right. We haven't hung out much since I quit the one-nighters and it wasn't from lack of trying on his part.

"You're right, but I'm booked out today. How about a boy's night tonight anywhere you want?" I offer, and he grins excitedly.

"I have work 'til ten so we'll start there. That is if Aela doesn't mind you going to a strip club," Alex mocks and I snort as I start up my machine.

"Aela's not a ball and chain," I argue as he raises a brow in disbelief.

"We'll see. I'm out to get a feed. Catch you later." He throws out a peace sign as he strolls out.

Chapter 19

AELA

I DUMP MY purse on the lounge and toe off my heels in a rush as soon as I'm in my apartment, barely managing to kick the door shut on my way to my room.

"Good morning," Kara greets me while she leans against the doorframe and sips her coffee, taking in my cursing and manic rush with a grin. I don't have time to do a full change, but I tug on a pair of tights and slip on a pair of black flats to make the ensemble suitable for work.

"Is this too 'I was running late after amazing sex and had to borrow his shirt because I didn't have any clean clothes'?" I ask Kara as I turn to her with my arms held out to my sides awkwardly. My question makes her choke on a sip of coffee, and she splutters while thumping her chest with blurry eyes as she looks me up and down.

"Only because I know it's true. You actually make it look cute," Kara replies once her throat clears. She then grins wickedly. "So… amazing, huh? Tell me all about both the date and the sex," she demands. I roll my eyes as I apply gloss to my lips in the mirror and wince because I don't have time to apply more than that. Good thing I'm having a good skin day for once.

"You'll have to settle for a quick rundown because I'm running late. We had the most amazing dinner on the deck at

169

Oskars, sunset and all. Then he gave me an armful of roses and multiple orgasms. The guy is a sex god."

I grin at her impressed face through the mirror as I force my hair into a ponytail then collect my apron before rushing by her.

"I'll let it go for now but tonight, you can forget about studying. We're having a couple of drinks, and you're going to spill all the deets, my dear," Kara demands as she follows which makes me laugh as I grab my keys and bag.

"We'll see. Gotta go. Love you," I call as I rush out the door.

"Love you back, bitch," I hear her yell through the door, and I smile.

After all that, I manage to make it to work right on time. Malcolm, my giant of a manager, is watching with a quirked brow and crossed arms as I shoulder my way through the door while tying my apron around my waist.

"Stoner Johnny turns up for work a whole day early while Miss Always-Early-and-Organised cuts it close. Is today backwards day?" he asks as I shove my bag into the cubbyhole, and I huff a laugh as I nudge him out of the way.

"Still not late so my title remains," I point out as I peek over the counter to look over the seating area which is half full. Most of the students are sipping their caffeine fix behind laptops; apart from a group of twelve huddled in the lounge corner with their books out and in deep discussion.

Malcolm turns to continue watching me curiously which has me feeling like a bug under a microscope since he towers over me at his ridiculous six foot eight height. The guy is a formidable sight for people who don't know him. Built thick with muscle and tall, arms covered in tattoos, eyes so light blue they are like ice, with a Mohawk that changes colour every month and a ring through his left eyebrow. Malcolm also knows how to use it well, rocking a mean scowl and a take-no-shit attitude when needed, but he's quietly a teddy bear. He makes sure the girls who work the night shift are walked to their cars every night and puts the cocky male customers in their place when we get hassled and genuinely cares about everyone. He's also brilliantly smart, as a fourth-year bachelor of engineering student with honours in electronic and biomedical engineering. All while being a single dad to his five-year-old daughter at just twenty-three.

"There's something different about you today," Malcolm observes as I wipe down the coffee machine, more for something to do than because it is necessary.

My cheeks flush instantly at his words as the tender muscles twinging between my legs whenever I move remind me of what's different. I silently curse myself to get a grip. It's not like I have a neon sign or anything declaring 'I got laid.' You can't tell these things just by looking at someone.

"Either you got laid really well, or you received another high distinction mark on your assignment. Since I know those papers haven't been graded, I'm going with the first. Am I right?" Malcolm pushes, oblivious to my internal dialogue which has me turning to him reproachfully.

"I'm going to ignore that question." I move towards the counter as I notice a couple of students approaching.

"Yeah, you got some. You're all glowing and smiley with a spring in your step even though you were late. Do I know the lucky guy?"

I blush when it's clear the customers heard him as they look me over, and I turn to give him a glare of embarrassment.

"I'm pretty sure I could slap your arse with a sexual harassment charge for this, Mal," I warn but Malcolm just grins boyishly because he knows I wouldn't.

"Sweetheart, you can slap my arse with anything you like. You don't need to make up an excuse to do it." He winks, and I hear the girls giggle at the counter which has him sharing his grin with them.

171

I roll my eyes as I turn back to serve them.

"I'm finishing my law degree if you want some help with your harassment case," The pretty redhead of the two offers playfully, which has me also grinning as I turn to raise my brows at Malcolm, who chooses to ignore it as he mans the machine and looks expectantly to the customers.

"What'll it be, ladies?" He acts all business-like as though nothing just happened which has us laughing.

"Two large mochas. One with cream," the blonde orders as I put them into the register as Mal makes their drinks.

My feet are hurting four hours later when there is finally a lull in the rush of incoming students, and I get my break.

I make myself an iced mocha and take it to a table out front with my physics book to get some much-needed studying done, but I become distracted before even opening it, watching campus life out the window as I think of Dec.

I'm worried about the bikers that were waiting for him this morning and what he might be involved in. I'm also annoyed that Kit refused to spill anything when I tried to grill her when we left and just told me to wait for him to explain, but I'm also happy he has a friend who has his back like that. I pull my phone out from my bag and smile when I see a text from Dec timed an hour ago.

"You forgot something when you left which gives me an excuse to come see you without looking needy. What time is your break?"

I start to reply but receive another text from him before I can finish.

"I hope you're not planning on having only coffee for lunch. Extraordinary brains need more than that to sustain them. Good thing I have you covered."

I look up as a shadow converges on the window beside me and feel my face split into a huge smile when I see a grinning Dec. He's rocking a pair of reflective aviators as he holds up a

Subway bag with my roses from last night in his other arm.

He's still looking all mouth-wateringly dishevelled in his loose, white V-neck shirt that shows the top of his chest piece and displays his inked arms. The sun catches the natural highlights in his messily styled hair. His holey black jeans that I know from this morning hug his arse perfectly. I watch, awestruck, as he makes his way inside to my table then leans over from the opposite side to press a kiss to my lips. He places his armload on the table and takes a seat, sliding off his aviators to hook them in the neck of his shirt.

"This is a pleasant surprise," I finally speak when my brain re-loads as he hands me a sub from the bag.

"I hope I got your order right. I took it upon myself to get Kara's number from Kit to ask her what you like when you didn't reply to me earlier," Dec explains. His low, gruff voice makes my stomach quiver which has me blushing.

My goodness, I really need to get control of my body.

"Sorry, I only just now saw it. We've been flat out," I apologise then become enraptured when Dec smiles brilliantly, dimples and all.

"It's okay. I'm glad, actually. I thought I had scared you with my text. I was a little nervous I'd come in here to have you send me away like some crazy stalker," Dec jokes. I laugh at the absurdity of the thought.

"If you bring me sweets, you can stalk me anytime," I point knowingly to the Subway cookies paper bag and get him laughing.

"Keep it down, you two. You're disturbing the customers," Mal complains beside us, and I smile. I knew it wouldn't be long until he came over like the nosey old lady he is.

"Hey, man, how's it going?" Dec greets him, and they do that guy hand slap/shake thing guys do.

"Can't complain, Declan. How's things?" Mal replies then I

look between the two, who clearly know each other, in surprise as they chat. "I'll come by the shop once I have some free time again. I have a bare spot on my calf for you to fill," Mal tells Dec with a grin. His smile softens a little when his eyes flick to me before returning to Dec. "You be good to my girl here, yeah? She's not like the others."

I pick up on the warning tone in his voice and almost choke on my mouthful of food. Before I can safely swallow to tell him to butt out, Dec answers with a soft look my way that has warmth spreading through my chest.

"I know. My woman's one of a kind."

Mal studies Dec for a silent moment before his eyebrows raise and he nods, looking satisfied as he walks away.

"Not that I don't enjoy your company but shouldn't you be at work right now?" I ask Dec, choosing to not comment on his claim, and he shakes his head.

"I have an hour to spare and thought I'd come over for our talk if you were free, and since I've been guilt tripped into a guy's night so we probably won't be able to talk tonight," Dec explains. I feel a little disappointed that we will miss our nightly chat, but I have him now so I can't feel too sorry for myself.

"Must be nice to be your own boss and take off whenever you want," I comment, and Dec tosses his head back with a laugh.

"I may pay for it all, but Kit is the one in charge of that place. She handles all the bookings and everything else. I just turn up when I'm told to," he insists which has me grinning with him.

I finish the last of my sub, sip my coffee, and then look up to Dec who looks serious and a little reluctant to have this conversation he came for, but he takes a deep breath then resolutely meets my gaze.

"I'm sorry for what you got dragged into this morning. I

want to brush it off and assure you all is fine, but I don't want to lie to you. Especially if you still want to hang around, because I don't know what's going to happen yet, and it may get dangerous. The club those guys are with want to use my shop to sell stuff they know I don't agree with, so at the moment, we're at an impasse that will come to a head this weekend. I don't know what to do. I guess I'm just avoiding thinking about it and hoping for a miracle which is stupid, but I haven't got a better idea so far. I won't let anything happen to you, though. I don't want you to worry. I will handle this mess and make sure Snake stays away from you." Dec's expression is a mixture of sadness, determination, and hope as he explains.

I take his clenched fists that rest on the table, wrapping them in my hands when he's finished.

"I wasn't worried about me, only you. Thanks for telling me, though you really don't owe me an explanation. It's your business, but know if you need to talk or anything, I'm here," I promise before adding, "I've been told I have this extraordinary brain, and I don't mind lending it to you."

Dec smiles gratefully then tugs our combined hands to him until I'm leaning over the table so he can lean in and kiss me. The kiss is tender and sweet which melts my insides as his tongue slips into my mouth to caress mine. His hands move from between my hands to cup my face gently.

"Aela, you're paid to serve coffee not suck face with your boyfriend. Breaks over, girl," Malcolm calls out, not one to pass up a chance to embarrass the hell out of me. Dec holds me to him when I try to pull back, continuing his tongue's caresses for a moment longer, before drawing back and sucking on my bottom lip. Then he rests back in his chair to look at me. The passion in his eyes is clear as he grins cockily.

"I'll give you a free hour on your next session if you let us continue, Mal," Dec counters. I slap his arm as my cheeks burn with embarrassment while the few people around us openly gawk. I try to ignore them as I rise from my chair, gathering everything I have on the table while the guys chuckle proudly.

"Enjoy your guy's night." I dismiss Dec with a glare as he slowly stands while looking me over, clearly liking that I'm still in his shirt.

"I can think of anything more enjoyable right now," Dec replies, his voice suggestively huskier than normal. I hide my shiver by nudging him towards the door.

"Get out. You've made enough of a scene thank you very much," I complain but smile as he swoops in to kiss me once more.

"Bye, baby," Dec murmurs then leaves as I shake my head then make my way back behind the counter with my armload of books, cookies, and roses with a big, goofy grin.

When I get home at eight, Kara is busy making a mess in the kitchen while booty-shaking and singing at the top of her lungs with *Sway* by Savage pumping so loud she doesn't hear me enter.

I lean against the breakfast bar to watch in amusement for several moments before she spins and finally notices my presence which makes her smile widely before continuing to grab a chopping board.

"You should show Alex your moves. I bet he could get you a job at the strip club with him, and you could get paid big money to do that." I laugh, and she stops slicing the mushroom she's holding to turn to me with a hand on her hip.

"Puh-lease, girl. My moves are too hot for public display. They would give those lecherous creeps a heart attack," Kara states then turns her back on me and continues to shimmy while I laugh.

I watch as Kara dumps the mushroom in with the sizzling chicken then turns to the fridge, removing a jug containing a lime coloured concoction with a flourish.

"I made Illusions for our girl's night, and I'm making creamy mushroom chicken for dinner. I was going to invite all the girls and make it a big catch, up but it's a weeknight, and I want you all to myself to hear about your date. Especially after he called me while I was at work to ask what you like from Subway, sounding all nervous and sweet." She watches me expectantly while pouring a glass then offers it to me.

I smile as I raise the glass and take a few slow mouthfuls of the sweet, creamy drink just to torture her a little, but I have to lower it before I choke on it through my laugh when she groans impatiently. So I tell Kara about my surprise lunch while she flits between me and the stove.

Kara's shaking her head with a small smile when I finish. "Boyfriend seriously has it bad for you, babe," she states while turning to stir the sauce in the pan. I shake my head at her back.

"We're just hanging out and having fun getting to know each other. I don't have time for anything serious. Boyfriends expect time, attention and effort which, right now, I have none to spare, no matter how perfect he is," I argue, which has Kara turning fast to face me, spoon still in her hand that flicks sauce across the bench.

"You seemed to be doing an all right job of it these past few weeks. Yeah, I've heard your late night chats." She smirks as I wave my arms in the air as if I can physically clear it of her words.

"I'm not arguing with you about what we are or aren't. I'm going to change into my pyjamas if you don't want any help here," I offer, but Kara waves me off with a flick of a hand over her shoulder.

"I've got this, and I'll pull out our new vase for your roses. Go get comfy," she urges so I slide off my stool, taking my drink with me to my room.

A few hours, more drinks, and a yummy dinner later, we're

curled up in opposite corners of the couch, giggling as I recount the night before.

The drinks have the effect Kara no doubt desired as I spill more details than I ever planned to share.

My laugh is cut off with a squeal as I jump off the lounge when my butt starts vibrating. We both laugh even louder when I see I'd been sitting on my phone which is still on silent from work and a picture of Dec he'd taken of himself this morning pulling a face fills up my screen with an incoming call.

"Hello?" I giggle through my greeting and then strain to hear him over the background noise.

"Hey, trouble. What are you up to?" I hear Dec's deep voice as I take my seat back, smiling up at Kara as she blatantly watches me.

"Having cocktails at home with Kara. How's guy's night?" I ask with a raised brow and a slight stab of jealousy when I hear a couple of female giggles close in the background, but I ignore it. It's not like I have a claim on him.

"Well... I'm sitting at a pub, nursing a beer while trying to ignore Alex entertaining a couple of Brazilian backpackers beside me and missing your voice. I've become accustomed to hearing it every night now."

I melt at his slightly slurred confession as Kara teasingly points at what I imagine is my goofy grin with an indulgent shake of her head then whispers, "You two are disgustingly cute."

"Sounds like fun," I joke then enjoy listening to him chuckle. I hear Alex's voice but can't make out his words before scuffling noises are all I can hear, and then Alex becomes clear, obviously having taken the phone.

"Is this the beautiful Aela, who has my boy all tied in knots?" he purrs over the phone, and I give a bark of laughter.

"Hi, Alex," I greet and then he laughs.

"You owe me, bro. I knew you wouldn't be able to help

yourself," he yells, sounding distant and slurring also.

"What are you wearing, beautiful?" Alex teases smoothly, which has me laughing as I hear Dec's indignant yell. There's a slapping sound, and Alex curses, and then Dec's devilish voice comes back on the line.

"Ignore him. He's a dick."

"Don't hate on me just 'cos I'm not afraid to ask the questions you are too pussy to ask," Alex calls out, making Dec sigh which crackles over the line.

"I'm not afraid to ask that. I just don't want to get a hard-on in public when I get the picture in my head, cos it'll be sexy. Aela's always sexy, even first thing in the morning—"

"Declan!" I cut off his rambling to regain his attention then bite my lip to hold in the laughter when there's a pregnant pause.

"Yeah?" he sheepishly replies. I have to press my hand to my mouth to contain a laugh at Dec's wary tone.

"As much fun as it is to hear you two like this, I'm going to go to bed and let you get back to your guy time, okay?"

His ensuing sigh is equal parts relief and disappointment.

"Okay, baby. Goodnight," He concedes, which I repeat before ending the call with a smile.

"Yep. Absolutely, disgustingly adorable," Kara mockingly complains, and I chuckle as I finish my drink.

"On that note, I am going to bed since I have to be up in roughly six hours and didn't get enough sleep last night as it is." I take my glass to the kitchen and rinse it before going back for my phone.

"Night, hon." I start towards my room as Kara turns the television on and music off.

"Sweet dreams, Aela. And by sweet, I mean I don't want any moaning waking me up." She's smiling wickedly when I turn to flip her off with a sarcastic laugh.

***

I groan as my alarm rips me from my sleep and sigh in defeat because I can't hit snooze a fourth time. I force one eye open to turn it off properly, rolling onto my back with a huff and hold my phone above my face to check it when I notice I received a text from Dec at three a.m.

"Ae you awle? You ruined my bed. I can't slepp cos tyre not in it. Come ocer?"

I blink to clear my vision, thinking I don't see it clearly but laugh when I re-read the text and then reply.

"I just learnt I'm fluent in drunken auto-correct texting. I'm sorry I missed it at the time, but it put a smile on my face when I wasn't happy to be awake just now. Hope you got some sleep and aren't feeling too bad when you wake up. X"

I force myself out of bed to get ready, but as I'm sliding on a pair of jeans, my phone draws me back to my bed when it vibrates.

I smile as I slide my thumb over Dec sticking his tongue out on my screen.

"Morning. How are you feeling?" I receive a groan in reply which has me cringing in sympathy.

"I don't suppose we can pretend all contact last night never happened?" Dec asks though you can tell by his tone he knows it's not going to work.

"No can do. You gave me crap about how we first met for ages, so I'm going to cling to anything that embarrasses you," I state smugly while trying not to laugh.

"I'm so sorry, Aela. I had too much alcohol so you can't hold anything I said against me. I was trashed. I swear I'm not turning into a needy, crazy stalker guy," Dec declares then starts coughing which ends in a painful moan.

"You sound like hell," I comment, and he groans again in

agreement.

"I feel it," Dec's voice is huskier as he complains, which sends a delightful shiver down my spine that I instantly berate myself for because he's sick.

I spot the time and cringe.

"Shit. I have to get to class, but if you need anything, let me know, okay?" I offer as I struggle into a shirt using one hand.

"Will you come be my naughty nurse and look after me?" Dec asks in that deep voice which causes me to whimper, and he clearly hears it because he chuckles.

"If you can still think dirty, you're going to be fine," I state, shaking my head as he laughs then hisses.

"I could be on my deathbed and still want to do dirty things to you, trouble. Have a good day," Dec corrects me cheekily which I ignore.

"Hope you feel better, bye." I end the call, running out to get the coffee brewing then back to my bathroom to get ready. When I make my way back into the kitchen, Kara has beaten me to the coffee and hands me a mug.

"What idiot signed me up for early classes?" she complains through a yawn, and I laugh as I grab my things to go.

"That'd be you," I point out.

"Exactly, I'm an idiot," Kara mutters as I blow her a kiss, rushing out the door.

Chapter 20

DECLAN

SATURDAY ROLLS AROUND in what feels like a blink of an eye while I've been flat out, and I wake up to my phone blaring Mum's ringtone.

"Hello?" I cough to clear my throat when my voice is rough and then wince when Hope squeals in outrage.

"Are you still asleep? It's my birthday, Declan. You promised you would be here before my party starts when the little hand is on the twelve, and it's already on the nine!" Her voice becomes more high-pitched the longer she talks which has me holding the phone out in front of me away from my ear. I groan and use my free hand to rub my face.

"Well, I'm not asleep anymore, so just chill out. I know it doesn't look like much on the clock, but there is still heaps of time before the party, Bug. I will be there soon."

I hear Mum in the background and smile as I hear her scolding Hope for sneaking out with the phone to call me after she was told no. I listen to Hope argue with her in vain before Mum demands the phone.

"Hey, honey. Sorry if the little sneak woke you. I left her for a minute while I brought in the washing, but she is jacked up on sugar from her 'Birthday donut breakfast' and has been asking to call you since sunrise." Mum laughs good-naturedly as I haul myself up into a sitting position on the edge of my bed.

"It's fine, Mum. I have a bit to do first so I should be up anyway," I reply as I dodge Tom on my way to the kitchen.

"I can't wait to see you dressed up. I'm going to take loads of pictures of you guys." I groan at her teasing and then we say our goodbyes. Tom makes a long, loud complaint because I'm taking too long to serve his bowl as I put my phone down. I then turn to match his glare.

"Oh, no, buddy. You don't get to complain today. You're not the one who has to spend the day dressed like a tool surrounded by an army of little pink covered demons high on sugar. You complain again, and I'll bring you too, give you a cute little bow to match them," I threaten as I place down his full bowl. I grab myself some cereal before heading back to my room while texting Aela to make sure she isn't bailing on me.

***

"Come in." Aela calls, sounding breathless and far away when I pause to knock at their door although they know it's me because I just spoke to Kara over the intercom to let me in the building.

I enter and watch Kara spill her spoonful of cereal down her chin as her eyes bug out at me from her spot on the couch. "Good morning, Kara." I try to act normal as she drops her spoon into her bowl to wipe her chin.

"Holy hotness," she says in a long breath and then seems to snap out of it while lowering her bowl to the coffee table, meeting my gaze with a sheepish smile. "Aela, your Prince Charming is here. You need to come see this," Kara calls out. I cringe as I tug on my collar.

"I'm coming. I just can't find my other glove. You— Holy shit!" Aela gasps when she sees me as she rounds the corner while tugging a long, gold glove up her left arm. Her eyes slowly travel my body, but I don't notice because I'm too busy doing the same to her.

Aela is dressed as a Disney princess. Not just any Disney princess, but Belle. She's eight-year-old Dec's fantasy come to life. I take in her curls that are half pinned up while the rest sit over her left shoulder, her rosy cheeks and innocently pink lips, just a hint of cleavage in the fitted gold bodice that accentuates her tiny waist before the skirt flows out to sweep the tips of her toes that are decked in gold, glittery slippers.

Aela looks so sweet and innocent, yet my mind is a catalogue of dirty things I want to do to her. I'm itching to get under that skirt and find out what Belle wears under that thing.

"I could cut the sexual tension in here with a knife," Kara exclaims, dragging me out of my thoughts as I turn to see her grinning back and forth between Aela and myself. I smirk as I turn back to Aela who's blushing with a huge grin.

"You should live in a suit. Seriously, you look so edible. I just want to tear you out of it," Aela insists. Her eyes wander down my tailored grey suit with a blue vest, a gift from my mum for my last birthday that I've only worn once, but I am willing to consider Aela's suggestion if it will keep her looking at me the way she is right now.

"You're more than welcome to do just that. I'm sweating my balls off under all these layers," I admit humorously to lighten the mood because as much as I'd love to take Aela to bed, Hope would kill me for being late. Not just by being upset with me but for the fact I'd let her down, and I can't ever do that to her. The girls laugh, Aela's nose wrinkling adorably as she shakes her head.

"And then he ruins it by talking about his sweaty balls," Aela complains, smiling brilliantly at Kara when she throws over the missing glove that was tucked into the lounge beside her.

184

"Just keeping it real," I state before adding, "You look amazing. Hope is going to lose her mind when she sees you," I murmur as Aela moves closer until I can pull her into my arms to press a kiss to her forehead.

"She isn't Belle too, is she? I don't want her mad at me," Aela asks, and I shake my head with a laugh.

"Are you kidding? Princess Hope is herself today," I correct as I help her into the glove.

"All right, you two kids give me a big smile then go have fun." We turn to see Kara holding up her camera to get a pic so I pull Aela in and smack a kiss on her cheek that has her giggling as I hear the shutter sound a couple times.

"Okay, Belle. We've gotta get going before the bakery shuts, or I will have one pissed off princess on my hands."

We say goodbye to Kara, and I take hold of the present Aela moves to collect that has an explosion of pink ribbons on top.

Aela waits in the car as I run inside the bakery to pick up the cake. Which I'm thankful for, when I find a familiar blonde behind the counter, and it isn't because I ordered with her, but because she was one of my last hook ups.

"Declan... Uh, what... I mean, hey." She stutters in shock when she looks up to see me while I contain a sigh of relief when I see her name tag because I can't recall her name—if I ever even got it in the first place.

God, I was a dick.

"Hi, Jade. I'm here to pick up a cake order," I tell her, shoving my hands deep into my pockets self-consciously as she takes in my stupid suit.

I'm starting to really regret cheating out of getting a costume. Then again, I'd take this over tights any day.

"There must be a mix-up. The only order left for today is for a six-year-old girl." Jade's brow scrunches in confusion then she starts searching through papers before I step up to stop her.

185

"That's the one. It's my sister's birthday," I inform her, though I shouldn't have to since the order clearly has my name on it.

Jade looks back up to me with a flirty smile as she flicks her hair over her shoulder.

"That's so sweet. If you need someone to keep it safe on the ride over, I can close up here and be ready to go in five minutes?" She offers with a calculated lean over the counter, so I have an unobstructed view down her shirt of her breasts. I contain my cringe while faking a polite smile as I lock eyes with her deliberately.

"Thanks. But my girlfriend's in the car so the cake will be fine." I get a little thrill at calling Aela my girlfriend and watch Jade's eyes narrow as she straightens in a flash before going to the fridge to bring out the cake. Her rough handling of it makes me worry the cake won't survive before I even get it to the car.

Jade throws back the lid of the huge white box, revealing a three-tiered pink and purple glittery castle fit for my princess with, 'Happy 6th Birthday, Hope' written in chocolate on the silver base. Jade looks at me expectantly with a haughty expression on her face. I smile and nod my acceptance as I retrieve my wallet from my jacket, and she forces the lid back down.

"Tell Cherie, she's amazing for me," I express as I hand over the cash for the cake, ignoring Jade's caustic look and whatever she mutters under her breath. I take the box gently into my arms then get the hell out of there.

"Friend of yours?" Aela asks, sounding amused as I take my seat once she has a hold of the cake, and I cringe, knowing she witnessed all that.

"Definitely not," I assure as I carefully pull out into traffic.

***

As soon as I pull up into the driveway, Hope bursts out through the front door, practically flying to the car with a squeal. I laugh while I get out and scoop her up into my arms, patting down the layers of pink netting and satin of her dress until I can see her face as she giggles.

"Happy birthday, Bug." I squeeze her in my arms and then kiss her cheek as I make our way to the front of the car to open Aela's door.

"Guess what? I have a pink jumping castle, and it's awesome." Hope squeals excitedly as she wraps her arms around my neck, pulling until her face is all I can see so she has my full attention. She continues to ramble about the surprises I organised for her.

"Is that my cake?" Hope asks suddenly as she looks over to greet Aela and spots the box on her lap with the familiar bakery sticker on it. I chuckle as I put Hope down before reaching in to take the box and sneak a quick kiss from Aela before pulling back.

"It is. But you can't see it until later because it's a surprise," I explain to Hope as she bounces in front of me, her hands clasped to her chest.

"Just a little peek, please?" Hope begs as I shift the box to one arm to help Aela from the car, and I grin.

"No way. You have to wait until everyone gets here," I tell her. Then I watch Hope's little eyes bug out as she stares at Aela for a silent moment, the cake momentarily forgotten.

"Oh. My. God. You look like the real Belle! You're so pretty..." Hope continues to explode with compliments for Aela, ordering her to spin around before dragging her inside as I watch on with amusement.

Just as I'm stepping onto the porch, I hear the rumbling of motorbikes and stiffen in horror before swinging around to survey the street, expecting trouble, but whoever it is drives the opposite way. I release I sharp breath in relief just as reality hits. Fuck. What am I doing?

I still haven't contacted Joe. I haven't even got a definite answer for him apart from 'I don't want to do this.' It's the weekend. I don't know if my time is up now or tomorrow so I could be putting my family and a bunch of kids in danger by being here.

"You okay?" Aela asks from behind me.

I turn to see her standing inside the door with a look of concern.

"Fine," I tell her with a forced smile then make my way inside, gesturing for Aela to walk ahead of me.

"Well, look at you. Doesn't my son scrub up well?" Mum asks as we walk into the kitchen. She rushes over, cupping my chin in one hand. She shakes my head side to side affectionately before leaning up to kiss my cheek as I smile down at her.

"Hey, Mum." I kiss her back then move to rest the cake on the bench so I can make room in the fridge for it. Aela offers to help with anything my mum might need help with.

"You need to put your prince stuff on," Hope demands around a lollipop in her mouth, bouncing on her toes beside me with a plastic sheathed sword and crown in her arms. I smile as I take them with a kiss on her head then look to Mum.

"She's going to be a diabetic before the day is out at this rate," I state, which makes Mum towel whip me along with an eye roll.

Chapter 21

AELA

HOPE'S PARTY IS a big success. That adorable little girl's ear to ear smile fails to dim all day as she skips from pony rides to the jumping castle, party games, then to the food table to stock up on the vast supply of pink sweets with her tribe of little followers.

Everyone seems to be having a good time, both the kids and the parents who decided to stick around, and I'm enjoying getting to know Nicola more, in between visits from Hope who introduces me to all her friends as she climbs in and out of my lap.

The only person who doesn't seem to be having fun is Dec. I don't know what happened, but his mood plummeted before he walked through the door and hasn't changed.

He's sitting back in the chair beside me, silently watching the chaos around us warily while absently playing with my curls. I've tried to get him talking, but his short answers are starting to wear thin on me. For a moment, I thought maybe he had changed his mind and no longer wanted me here. I offered to leave, but he just snapped that I was being ridiculous so I left him to stew in silence.

"The king is here, now where is my princess?" I hear a familiar voice yell from the back door and look to see Alex in

189

normal clothes, walking out with his hands raised high as he searches the crowd of little people.

"Alexei!" Hope calls from the jumping castle with one hand held out while the other holds down her tiara. He dodges his way over to swing her up in his arms, which causes her to squeal.

"King of shit," Kit mumbles as she takes the seat to my left. I snicker as she turns to face Dec and me, looking us over as I appreciate her costume that consists of a pink tutu, black singlet and tights, biker boots and a little silver tiara with spiked, leather bracelets around her wrists.

"Damn. I didn't realise we could dress up," Kit complains which has me laughing before I realise she's serious. "Aren't you two adorable, though?" Kit adds with a smirk before Dec slowly ascends from his chair.

"I'll be back in a sec," he murmurs near my ear before he straightens and heads over to Alex.

"Wow. Who rained on his parade?" Kit asks as we watch Dec go, and I shrug in reply.

"Beats me. He's been weird pretty much since we got here," I reply, smiling as Hope comes over to kiss Kit before sitting on my lap again. Her happy face turns thoughtful as she searches my face for a moment with her hands holding my cheeks.

"What did my dumb arse brother do?" Hope asks quietly which has Kit laughing as I swallow mine so I don't encourage the little terror.

"Hope, I don't think you're allowed to say that word. It's not nice," I try to carefully reprimand her, but she shrugs her little shoulders.

"Mum says it's not a bad word, but I can only call Declan and Alexei it when they are being dumb. They are always being dumb," Hope explains. I can't stop the laugh this time as Kit laughs harder.

"Fair enough. But Declan didn't do anything," I assure her

then watch as Hope's eyes search both of mine back and forth before she huffs and climbs off my lap. I watch as she walks determinedly around the side of the house where I'd seen the guys disappear not long ago.

I look questioningly to Kit who just shrugs with a smirk, letting me know she doesn't know what Hope's doing either, but she finds it amusing as hell.

"We need a pile of sweet, sugary, carbs and some fun. I'll be right back." Kit skips off to the food table. I watch her until I hear squealing laughter and turn to see Hope flung over the shoulder of a burly, older man covered in tattoos with dark scruffy hair and a beard that reaches his chest, wearing dark sunnies, a leather vest over a white singlet and faded jeans. He's chuckling with a deep rumble as he jogs to the jumping castle which he dives into, making the kids inside scramble out of his way. It makes me smile, although I am concerned. He's clearly a biker and Dec is having a problem with bikies.

"This is the best thing about kid's parties." Kit offers me a small paper plate piled with fairy bread, mini donuts, cake pops and an assortment of pink lollies. I take it gratefully and Kit holds out a cake pop from her own plate. "To our sugar high," she toasts. I laugh as I tap her cake pop with my own before I catch sight of the guys rounding the corner.

Dec's smiling genuinely again, and I smile in relief as they head over, Dec's eyes never leaving mine as he dodges little, sugar-fuelled missiles that pass him.

"Carb loading, are we?" Dec asks as he steals a cake pop from my plate.

"It's a party so they don't count. Plus, you can maybe help me burn them off later," I reply with a wicked look his way as I bring the cake pop to my mouth and slowly lick the icing off suggestively. Dec groans before leaning over and seizing hold of the hand holding the stick to shove the whole cake into his mouth.

"Don't start something we can't finish right now," Dec warns with a low growl in my ear that sends shivers of anticipation across my neck and down my spine. I pull back to look at him, taking in the desire burning in his eyes before his look turns soft. "I'm sorry about before. I didn't mean to take things out on you," Declan apologises quietly, running his hand over my left cheek and I lean into his touch.

"It's okay," I say and then turn to kiss the palm of his hand.

"It's not. But I'll make it up to you later," Dec promises before leaning in to kiss me gently. The seduction in his tone causes me to smile against his lips. When he leans back, he drags me into his side, under his arm, and when we turn to look around, we're met with identical starry-eyed looks from Kit, Nicola, and Hope while Alex shakes his head which gets Dec laughing.

Chapter 22

DECLAN

I FEEL LIKE I'm sitting on a grenade with the pin pulled.

Like my next move could destroy everyone around me.

I'm twitchy, sweating bullets in this stupid monkey suit, and just waiting for an explosion.

I'm freaking out, but I try to not let it show. I don't want to diminish the happiness that radiates from Mum and Hope by making them worry.

Aela can feel it, which means I'm failing, and when she tries to get me to open up, I desperately push her away even though a part of me cringes, knowing it upsets her.

Alex and Kit show up, and I'm so lost in my head, I don't hear a word Kit says as I watch Alex mess around with Hope. I'm at the breaking point under the pressure and feel like if I don't talk it out, I'll lose my mind. I tell the girls I'll be back and make my way to Alex as fast as I can without drawing attention.

Hope is laughing as Alex throws her up in the air, but my approach distracts him. He pauses with her held out before him, looking me up and down with a grin.

"Nice getup, pimp," Alex jokes, but when his eyes meet mine, he knowingly sees my inner turmoil and lowers her to his hip. "You good, bro?" Alex asks curiously, and I have so much I need to say that the words catch in my throat as I struggle to keep them in and shake my head in reply.

"Okay, baby girl. You go have fun so I can talk to your knuckleheaded brother." Alex immediately puts Hope on her feet where she looks back and forth between us for a moment before taking off. Alex gestures towards the side of the house where no one is congregating so we can have a little privacy. We amble over there. As soon as I've decided we've walked down enough so no one can overhear us, the words spill in a rush without pause from my mouth as I tell Alex everything. I'm breathless when I finish as Alex stares at me silently with wide eyes and eyebrows making a run for his hairline.

"Shit, man. Why am I only hearing of this now?" he asks. I shrug, drained of words. Alex begins to pace in front of me thoughtfully for a few moments before turning to face me. "Have you talked to—" He's interrupted by the side gate slamming open with a loud bang, which causes us to jump and turn defensively to see Buzz striding through like he owns the place. Mae trails behind him.

"What trouble are you two up to now?" Buzz demands before coming over to slap us on the back in his usual rough greeting. "We've gotta talk later, son," he says quietly so Mae can't hear.

Before I can reply, Hope pushes her way between us with a scowl, her hands on her hips as she targets me with a death glare.

"Declan, go say sorry to your girlfriend right now. I don't know what you did, but you have to fix it." Hope imitates Mum's stern voice, and I try not to laugh at how cute it is.

"She's not my girlfriend," I correct, just to rile her up as I silently add a *yet* onto the end. Hope steps closer as she squints even more so that I doubt she can even see me at all.

"Whatever. Go apologise even if you think you didn't do anything wrong because her eyes are sad, and she isn't smiling normal, and it's making me sad."

Hope's demand turns pleading and instantly kills all amusement I found in her little rant. I knew I was messing up with Aela earlier, and it makes me sick to know that I hurt her even a little bit. Hope is right. I have to make it right. I drop into a crouch until I'm eye level with Hope and give her a small smile.

"You're right, Bug. When did you become so much smarter than me?" I ask her, only slightly kidding which gets a smug grin out of her with a shrug of those little shoulders.

"At birth, duh," Hope replies haughtily then Buzz leans down to scoop her up, making her squeal.

"All right, little Miss Attitude. That's enough cheek out of you," Buzz tells Hope then swings her over his shoulder before jogging for the jumping castle, jostling Hope while she squeals with laughter as they go.

"Hello, my sweethearts," Mae greets Alex and me with tight hugs and a kiss on our cheeks, leaving behind a smear of red lipstick that she smudges off with her thumb when she leans away. "Did I hear right? You have yourself a girl?" Mae's eyes sparkle happily which makes me smile.

Mae has worried about my lack of a serious relationship for as long as I can remember. She's always badgering me about it or trying to fix me up with any chick in my age bracket she comes across, most of which are her friend's granddaughters.

Sadly, Mae wasn't able to bear a child when she was younger. It's a shame because the woman has the biggest, caring heart I know and has taken us all in as her 'babies'—which is what she loves to call us. I love the woman like a second mother, and she's always been there when I've needed her, along with the goodies she's constantly baking which has her smelling like sugar.

"You did. I do, and I'll introduce you. But first, I've been ordered to do some apologising. Excuse me for a moment," I reply, which has her smiling exuberantly as she tucks some white hair behind her ear that got caught in the breeze.

"Excellent. I'll go see your mum." Mae spots her through the glass sliding door behind us and with a pat to my shoulder, makes her way inside.

I turn to head back to the party, and Alex joins me, grinning with a rub of his hands which has me looking at him questioningly.

"I don't think I've ever seen you grovel before. I'm not missing this. I hope Aela makes you work for it."

I shake my head at his explanation. "Arsehole," I mutter before turning the corner, my eyes instantly seeking Aela. It's like a physical punch to the gut when her eyes meet mine. Although she is smiling, I see the worry there that Hope had picked up on. Aela deserves better. I have to fix it.

Aela forgives me way too easily which makes me feel like even more of an undeserving ass while I also thank my lucky stars that she did.

An hour later, the frilly army from hell has dwindled down to a handful of stragglers who have moved on to sitting in the corner, drawing on balloons with sharpies.

Aela and Kit have taken over the jumping castle where laughter and curious noises abound as the walls dip to the ground every now and again. Mum has pulled out the alcohol for the adults and started dinner to celebrate now that the kid's party is over. I'm supposed to be supervising the permanent marker art to make sure it only goes on the balloons, but the jumping castle keeps stealing my attention as I roll my beer bottle back and forth in my hands. Buzz takes a seat beside me with a chuckle, and I turn to see him sipping his beer with a spark of amusement in his eyes as he watches me.

"You have it bad for the girl," Buzz ribs me. I shrug as I take a gulp of beer, not bothering to deny it.

"She's a good one. It makes an old man happy, and now Mae can stop worrying you'll be a bachelor to the end. But if you think she's done bugging you, you're wrong. She'll be pushing for wedding bells and babies next." Buzz laughs loudly with amusement, and I fight the mental images his words have caused.

Aela in white, looking even more like a princess. Aela round with my baby. A little girl that is a mix of the both of us being held in her arms.

"Mae shouldn't get her hopes up. Aela's too good to get mixed up in my mess. I should let her go before it gets too serious, but I'm selfish and can't do it. I don't want her hurt, though, and this shit with the club is just heating up. I don't know what to do about anything right now," I reply quietly, running my free hand through my hair and tugging on the strands in frustration.

I watch the light dim in Buzz's eyes as his expression turns grave. "I'm so sorry, son. I wish I had never opened my mouth that night, but I'd had a few drinks and was so proud after coming to see you. I forgot who I was with," Buzz apologises before taking another gulp of beer as I nod my acceptance. "I'm trying to fix it. I've been looking into moving the business into Surfers to get the clientele Joe wants, but that takes time you don't have right now thanks to Snake," he adds and looks like he's going to say more but Alex interrupts.

"Dude, why the hell are you over here instead of watching that? Do you even know what you're missing right now?" Alex points over his shoulder to the jumping castle which peaks my curiosity so I stand to go see, the other two following.

"Holy shit." I choke when I catch sight of Aela and Kit rolling around, playfully wrestling through breathless laughter.

"Is there any jelly cups left that we can add to this?" Alex asks excitedly, which has us laughing before he yells out for Mum, but not loud enough for her to hear.

"I thought we were going to work off your carbs later, babe?" I call out, drawing Aela's attention from where she's straddling Kit to look at me. Kit uses the distraction to roll so they switch places before pushing off to go to the side while Aela crawl-bounces to the opposite side.

"Oh, we are. This is freaking fun, though," Aela explains as she pulls herself up to stand. Then they breathlessly count to three before bouncing at each other, laughing the whole time.

Buzz carries over a stack of chairs that he separates before taking one with a grin as he gets comfy to watch the show. I shake my head at their ridiculousness before taking a seat beside him, sipping my beer.

"You need to remove some layers, girls. Especially that skirt, Aela. There's so much of it, it could be a choking hazard or trip you. For safety reasons, of course." Alex adds the safety part to the end of his comment when I glare at him. I grin at his reproachful look as I slap the back of his head from behind our seats.

"Look, I have pretty tattoos like Ducky," Hope exclaims as she comes to stand in front of us so I look down to see her proudly holding out her arms that are covered in permanent marker scribbles.

Oh shit.

"That's beautiful, darling. What is this one?" Buzz asks, trying to smother a laugh as he points to her forearm that has what looks like a smiling penis on it.

Mum is going to kill me.

"That's Adrian's space ship. See, it's going into the stars." Hope points out, and I see red. I'm going to wring the boy's neck for putting his penis on my baby sister. But first I have to get it all off her.

"Bug, I told you to draw only on the balloons. We have to get it off before Mum sees." I scoop her up into my arms then look to the guys who are laughing their arses off. "I need you to check the other brats for any ink while I try to remove this," I tell them then jog to the back door.

Mum is busy talking to Mae at the sink so I slip inside, bunching Hope's dress for some cover as I wrap my arm around hers for good measure and make my way to the hallway.

"Dec, did you—" Mum calls out just as I'm turning out of sight and I cut her off.

"Be right back," I call out before running into the bathroom, locking the door behind me before I sit Hope on the vanity. I get the water running warm then drown her arm in liquid soap before getting her princess shower pouf, dip it into the water, and then begin scrubbing her arm vigorously. Hope watches it foam up curiously. I scrub until the skin starts turning pink then get Hope to lean so I can rinse her arm off. The ink is barely faded.

"Shit."

"That's a bad word, Duckie," Hope reprimands me in a whisper. I look to her with my brow raised.

"So is doing this to yourself. At least my bad word was an accident," I quip before adding more soap to scrub again.

"It's starting to hurt." Hope complains after a moment. I rinse again which reveals little change so I move her to the opposite side of the sink to try the other arm.

Three rinses later, there's a knock at the door, and I'm pretty sure I match Hope's wide eyes as we look at each other.

"Just a sec," I call out then rub Hope's arms down with a towel and hope the faded ink will just magically disappear. Not a minute later, the door clicks open to reveal Mum standing there with a green bottle of rubbing alcohol in her hands and a knowing smirk. *Busted.*

"Nice try, but I haven't been a mother as long as I have without learning when my kids are up to something." She walks in to inspect Hope's arms, shaking her head in amusement.

"Well, at least you didn't put any on your face like Adrian's moustache," Mum says as she wets a cloth with the alcohol rub, which reminds me of the little penis boy. Now I know which one to look for.

I'm distracted when my phone starts ringing, and I pull it from my pocket to see an alert from my app for the shop's security system, saying there's been a disturbance and the police have been notified. Dread settles like lead in my stomach as I shove my phone back into my pocket with a curse and meet Mum's questioning gaze in the mirror.

"I have to go. Something's happened at the shop."

I kiss them both on the head then rush out as Mum calls my name with concern, but I don't have time to waste.

"Whoa, where's the fire?" Buzz complains when I run into him at the end of the hall, which makes me stop as I look around at everyone who's now inside.

"The alarm's been triggered at the shop. I've gotta go," I explain and his face hardens.

"I'm coming with you."

We rush out the door, the others yelling to each other indecipherably behind us as I jog to my car while pressing the fob to unlock it. The passenger door opens as I take my seat, a flash of gold fabric catching my attention, and I turn in shock to see Aela buckling up.

"Aela, I don't know it's safe to come—"

"Drive," she demands, so I give up and turn the key, the car rumbling to life angrily.

Alex's jeep follows us with Buzz in the passenger seat, which would make me laugh any other day because Buzz has always refused to ride shotgun to anyone. But I'm too focused on getting to the shop immediately.

A cop car is already there by the time we pull up.

I see that the glass sliding door to the shop has shattered, the top half is obliterated, and a fist size object has broken the glass of my bedroom window. I climb out of the car and two officers turn from inspecting the destruction to eye me warily as I approach.

"Evening, officers. I'm Declan, the shop's owner." I introduce myself to calm them down and hand the larger officer my keys when he asks for them so they can enter the premises.

I impatiently wait outside while they go through the place top to bottom before coming back to where I'm leaning against the hood of my car with the others around me.

"There doesn't seem to be any sign of disturbance inside, but we'll get you to go through and check that nothing is missing," the younger, scrawny officer says when he stops a couple feet away from me, and I nod before following him back inside.

They're right. Everything is untouched apart from the mess of glass. They question me about anyone I think would be responsible for it, and I decide not to inform them of the bikies since it wouldn't do any good. The door is dusted for fingerprints, and the officers leave when they don't find any evidence except for the large rock that was resting on Aela's pillow on my bed. The four of us stand there looking around quietly, not knowing what to do or say as the police drive away.

Aela's the first to break out of it, walking over to wrap her arms around me from behind and buries her head in between my shoulder blades.

"You okay?" she murmurs quietly then starts rubbing her hands over my biceps. It isn't until then that I realise my hands are shaking from the anger building up in me now that the shock is fading.

"I'm struggling to convince myself the bastard knew we weren't home. Because if we were in bed where we usually are when you're over, you would have been brained by that fucking rock. I want the son of a bitch who did this," I demand that last part at Buzz, who shakes his head as he ditches his e-cig that Mae is making him use to quit, producing the real thing from his vest pocket as Alex hands him a lighter.

"Let me handle it, son. This was a message. They knew you weren't home, but I have a message of my own for the bastard because I know Joe wouldn't have ordered that bedroom shot. Not his style."

Buzz takes a long draw then holds the smoke in his lungs for a moment before exhaling. A black van unexpectedly pulls up behind Alex's jeep and my body tenses as I turn, prepared for an altercation, but Buzz moves forward, slamming his arm into my chest to hold me back. "Park it, son. I called a guy to replace the glass." I relax with a loud exhale into Aela's embrace.

"You kids go down to the pub and have some drinks. I'll call when it's done," Buzz orders then walks over to the guy hopping out of the van.

I turn in Aela's arms to wrap mine around her and pull her into my side as I start for the pub down the street—until Alex draws my attention to him, laughing.

"Uh, Dec. You may want to ditch the sword. They won't let you in with a weapon," Alex mocks and I look down to see I still have the prop from the party attached to my belt.

"I wouldn't mind a minute to get changed, too," Aela adds.

I look down at her in dismay because I had big plans for the slow removal of that dress. Aela catches my look and smiles knowingly before patting my chest reassuringly. "I'll wear it again for you later," she promises, and Alex pretends to gag.

"All right, I don't need to hear about your role-playing. Just hurry up. Now I really need a drink," he complains, which makes Aela laugh before she gets her bag out of the car.

We hurry to my room in the shop so she can have some privacy, and I can watch, because finding out what she's wearing under that skirt is a better distraction than a beer will ever be.

"Why are you just standing there? Get your sword thingy off," Aela demands, noticing I've propped myself against my desk to watch. I smirk salaciously at her words.

"I'd like to sheath my sword inside of you and get it off, but we don't have time for that. Now, strip for me, woman. I've been dying to see what's under that skirt all damn day," I reply. I watch as she smiles with a wicked gleam in her eyes while her hands slowly bunch up her skirt.

"What, you mean this little thing?" Aela reveals the small scrap of beige lace that's between her legs then turns her back to me so I see it's a G-string.

Her delicious arse cheeks I want to sink my teeth into are begging for my attention. I immediately drop to my knees and shuffle towards her. I wrap my hands around the front of her knees as I lean in to press feather-light kisses across that perfect arse then sink my teeth in, eliciting a gasp from Aela as I trail my hands up her thighs until I reach the soaked lace covering her.

I groan in appreciation of how saturated it is as I continue my kisses and nibbling.

"Dec, Please?" Aela gasps and moans wantonly, which makes me grin against her luscious flesh as I slide the tips of my fingers under the fabric to caress her heated, silky flesh. My mouth waters for a taste.

A loud banging from outside draws my attention, reminding me we're not alone, and the guys would be able to hear any noise we make. I refuse to take her with them here despite how much my dick is screaming because those sexy little sounds and screams Aela makes are all mine and no one else's. Plus, I know if we keep Alex waiting much longer, he won't have a problem barging in.

I pull back with a pained groan which only gets deeper when I see the pinkness of the flesh of her butt cheeks from where my five o'clock shadow has irritated the smooth skin. I force myself to stand and back up a step with a playful slap to her arse that causes her to jump with a yelp as I retreat to a safe distance.

"Get changed quick, babe. Before my dick convinces me that I don't really care that we have company, and I take you so hard, the whole neighbourhood will hear how much you like it." My voice is low and growly with need.

I curse as Aela strips off her skirt in a sudden tug, before bending down at the waist to retrieve a pair of jeans from the bag she dropped to the floor beside her. The little minx pauses there to look at me around her legs, giggling at the sight of her effect on me.

Two can play at that game.

I walk back over and snap the elastic of her G-string against her arse with a quick tug then hook my thumbs in it to drag it slowly down her legs. I tap her feet so she'll lift them in order to free her of the tiny fabric, which I ball in my hand before standing then step back to the desk as though unaffected by her nakedness. I shove the scrap of lace into my pants pocket, and then remove the toy sword from my belt.

My rock hard cock hates me so much right now and screaming for relief. I wince as I try to adjust my pants, but it's pointless—my guy isn't going to calm down while in the vicinity of an almost naked Aela.

I force my eyes closed then turn to the door. "I'll be outside when you're ready," I call out as I practically run from the room. I stop at the front counter in the shop, where I remove my jacket, vest and tie to leave on the glass top before I carefully pass Buzz and the repair guy to find Alex sitting on the car park curb with a cigarette in his hands and a raised brow at my appearance.

"This is disappointingly quick if you messed around like I expected you to," Alex states coolly. I smack the back of his head in reply, which makes him lean away with a glare as he rubs at it with annoyance as though it stung.

A couple moments later, Aela makes her way outside to us in a snug black sweater and skin-tight jeans with a glower my way that has Alex choking on his exhale of smoke.

"Couldn't even get her over the finish line first, bro. What is wrong with you?" he questions then jumps up out of range of my repeat slap with a chuckle as I groan in annoyance. "Looks like you could use a stiff drink, baby girl. Let's go get you one," Alex suggests to Aela, sweeping her in under his arm and begins to lead her down the road.

I growl behind them before Aela turns to look over his shoulder at me.

"I could use a stiff something," she complains, which has Alex barking out a laugh, squeezing her to his side approvingly.

"Alex," I growl in warning, but he brushes me off with a peace sign over his shoulder with the hand holding his cigarette away from Aela.

The pub is pretty dead when we get there, but for a handful of patrons around the bar that pays our entrance no notice.

Alex and Aela take a table, sitting side by side as they chat and laugh like old friends.

I go to the bar for our first round from the balding, overweight barman who barely manages a grunt in greeting before moving away to make our drinks.

Great customer service. No wonder the place is so busy.

"Hey, handsome, want some company?" A middle-aged, bottled blonde sidles up beside me. I automatically look her over, though I'm not even slightly interested. Her face could be pretty if it weren't caked in makeup in an attempt to cover her wrinkles. She's wearing a halter top that leaves very little of her fake breasts to the imagination, the smallest skirt you can get before it's called a belt, and heels so high she's almost on the tips of her toes. The whole look is sad rather than sexy. She catches my look and takes it as a green light to run her hand over the crotch of my pants that thankfully softened on the way here, and is staying that way as she fondles me. I remove her hand and return it to her side with a shake of my head.

"No thanks. I have my girl here with me," I tell her, smiling at my claim on Aela.

"Too bad. Have this in case you change your mind." She pouts and shoves a napkin in my pocket that I guess has her number on it, and then whispers in my ear, "I'm up for anything. Anytime."

She winks then struts away as the bartender slams the three bourbon and cokes onto the bar before me, snatching up my money like it will disappear if he's not quick enough. I roll my eyes as I remove the paper from my pocket but smile when I feel the damp lace still there. I drop the napkin on the bar, gather the drinks, and make my way to our table.

Aela is giving me a weird look filled with a mixture of emotions as Alex fights to contain a smirk that widens as his gaze meets mine. Aela takes her drink and gulps it down as soon as I set them on the table, which has me quirking my brow at her questioningly.

"I'll go snag us a pool table." Alex takes his drink into the other room, clearly giving us a moment though I don't know why. I watch Aela curiously as she glares at Alex's retreating back, fidgeting in her seat before taking a deep breath like she's gathering courage then turns to face me.

"What are we doing?" She sounds frustrated.

"Going to play pool, apparently," I reply in confusion then watch her cheeks turn crimson as she closes her eyes and shakes her head.

"I mean this," Aela gestures with her index finger between the two of us before continuing. "We say we're just friends, who hang out a lot, but we don't kiss like friends and the sex sure as hell isn't just friendly. You get territorial when a guy speaks to me and just now, I wanted to scratch that grabby skank's eyes out so bad that Alex had to hold me in my seat, which isn't friend-like or even Aela-like. I don't do jealousy, but every chick I see flirt with you has me seeing red. That's not a healthy friendship. I just need you to set me straight," Aela explains in a rush then avoids my gaze as she swipes her fingertips through the condensation on her glass.

"You want to do this now, right here?" I question because this really isn't the ideal setting. Not at all romantic.

Aela nods with a hard swallow like she's waiting for a death sentence to be delivered. I reach out to take her hand in mine, pulling her closer to face me as I lean in.

"I'm not good boyfriend material, Aela." She tries to pull away, but I grip tighter to continue. "It's not that I want to sleep around because I don't. At all. It's because I don't have the time needed to make a relationship work between the shop and my family. I have too much going on to take time each day to coddle someone and assure them I love them. Just the thought of that is exhausting. And you, you deserve a guy who can give you all the time he can. To be romanced, showered with affection, and all that. But I want you. In my bed every night and around me all the time we can get. Our nightly chats are what I look forward to most every day. So I'm willing to try anything you want to do."

Aela's watery eyes meet mine when I finish, and I lift our hands to press a kiss to the back of hers.

"I just want you. I've said I don't have time for a boyfriend either, but I want to make time for you. We can figure this out. We've done okay so far," she replies.

It makes me so damn happy that I pull her onto my lap and slam my lips into hers before she knows what hits her. I cup her cheek in my right hand with my other arm wrapped around her tightly as I use my mouth to show her the feelings I can't put into words just yet.

"We should go play pool before I start undressing you right here and the police end up being called," Aela pulls back to murmur in my ear. I chuckle as I squeeze my hand that's gripped her arse by its own volition.

"Let's go then, trouble,"

I'm grinning like a fool as Aela leads me by the hand into the games room. Alex is chalking up a cue as we enter and smirks when he takes in our entwined hands and stupid grins.

"This sickeningly sweet thing you two have going is set to get worse now, isn't it?" he complains with a smile.

I grab a cue and Aela giggles then leans up to kiss his cheek as a reply. "Hey, now your girl is spreading love everywhere, dude. Control that shit if you don't plan on sharing," Alex calls out as he wraps an arm around Aela's shoulder, and I shake my head at him.

I let Aela kick Alex's ass in the first game followed by mine in the second—though the second game wasn't because I let her.

Damn adorable pool shark.

Kit shows up, looking indignant during my game with Alex. "So this is the big emergency you all ditched me at your mum's for?" she asks, stealing my drink I had just put down to take my shot.

"No. Ink Fix got smashed up. Buzz sent us here before Dec went Terminator on us and started his mission to kill the guy who did it. How did you get here?"

Kit turns her glare on Alex at his question.

"I know, dick. Mae gave me a ride when Buzz called her then he pointed me this way after filling me in. Said to tell you they finished and he's leaving. You all ditch me again, and I will mess you up," Kit threatens with a glare to all of us, which has me biting off a laugh.

I know Kit's serious, but it's hard to accept the threat when she's in a tutu and tiara, looking even more doll-like than usual.

Alex goes to get the next round as Kit joins Aela at the table. "I called Kara when I found out where you all were, and she's going to be here any sec. She was just out messing with her camera. And your mum sent me back with enough food to feed an army because you skipped out on dinner. I shoved it all in the shop's fridge," Kit says the last part to me, and at the mention of food, my stomach grumbles, reminding me I haven't eaten in hours.

"What's going on, bitches?" I turn at Kara's voice, doing a double take at the no longer blonde, but bright blue and black streaked longhaired Kara. She's almost unrecognisable in ripped, black jeans and layered singlets—very emo looking.

I turn to catch Aela's reaction, but she's smiling like it's nothing new as Kara sits beside her and they start talking.

"What's with the wig?" I blurt out tactfully.

Kara looks over with a shrug of her shoulders.

"I like to change it up when the mood strikes," she explains then we all turn when Alex comes to a standstill at the table, eyes glued to Kara as he slowly takes her in. She gives him an expectant look as though bracing for his reaction.

Alex sets down the drinks in his hand before leaning down beside her, "Hi, I'm Alex. You have a name, sweet thing, or can I call you mine?"

I shake my head at his lame line as I take my drink. Aela opens her mouth to reply, but Kara beats her to it with a huge smile, "Smooth, lover boy. I'm Kasey, Kara's twin. Can't you see the resemblance or do you not know her?" she replies.

I choke on a sip of my drink as Aela rolls her eyes with a grin behind her glass. Kara turns to glare at me in silent warning to not ruin her game, not realising how gullible the idiot is and will accept what he sees as truth.

"Twins. Seriously? Holy shit. Where is the snarky tease?" Alex looks around eagerly, turning back with a frown when he doesn't find the blonde he was expecting to see.

"Around. She was talking to some idiot not a second ago," Kara replies vaguely, which has the other three of us fighting to smother our laughter when it clearly goes right over his head.

I leave her to her fun and turn back to the pool table to figure out my shot even though Alex has probably forgotten all about the game. He approaches after I sink three of my balls, though, with the biggest shit-eating grin and excited gleam in his eyes as he leans in. "Twins, bro. Can you believe it?" he murmurs low so the girls won't overhear.

I shake my head at him. "No. I really can't." I reply seriously before he slaps my chest twice in excitement at what he takes as my agreement.

"Seriously. I haven't had twins since the two I bagged last year after you turned them down, and they weren't identical or half as hot. I need to find Kara and get this magic happening," Alex whispers, scoping out the place.

"Dude, you have to calm down. I don't think it'll happen. Kara hates you, remember?" I remind him, but he waves me away dismissively as he looks for his next play on the table.

"It's happening. Have a little faith. This one seems like she's up for a fun time, and Kara only plays at hating me. She wants me really," Alex swears so I give up and let him fantasize all he wants since that's all the happiness he'll get out of this.

We stay until closing then go our separate ways with Aela coming home with me while Kasey leaves Alex hanging with a kiss on the cheek before offering to drop Kit home.

Kara never did show up. *Funny that.*

Chapter 23

AELA

A WEEK AND a half drags by slowly and thankfully drama free. Or maybe it's just me dragging since I'm in bad need of catching up on sleep. Don't get me wrong, I would do that weekend over again anytime, apart from the drama. We didn't end up sleeping when we got back to Dec's place Saturday night.

We cleaned up the glass in his room, stripped and remade the bed because of it, and had to calm a skittish Tom who wouldn't come out from under the bed for ages. By the time we crawled into bed, Dec was still too wired, so he showered me with affection and orgasms until well past sunrise, and then talked me into a beachside buffet breakfast, followed by some shopping. We finally crashed for a couple of hours at my place until Dec needed to get to work, and I had to check on lab work and feed the mice.

Follow that up with late night calls and ten days packed with work, classes, and labs, and I'm proud to have made it to this Wednesday, but the hump day is kicking my arse.

I drop in for my shift at The Coffee House between classes and Mal is there, shaking his head as soon as I dump my bag in the cubby. "You're looking rough. Do I need to tell Dec to lay off the sex for a night and let you sleep?" He mocks so I whip him with a towel as I look over the quiet seating area.

"I wish too much sex was my problem," I counter and get a raised brow from Mal in return.

"You're going to burn out if you continue like this. I'm cutting your shift tomorrow. Get some sleep," he orders then moves to serve a customer as I smile appreciatively.

Three hours later, I'm strolling across campus to class as the sun goes down, taking in the atmosphere appreciatively as the day cools and relieved students take their leave. I sip on my large cappuccino with my hands wrapped around the cup to soak in the warmth.

When I'm halfway there, I get the feeling I'm being watched, which has me automatically looking around, but I don't notice anyone in sight, let alone looking at me. I shake it off dismissively, but the weird feeling is enough to make me wary and choose to take a detour through the art building rather than stay alone out in the open.

By the time I take my seat in class, I've shaken the weirdness off, and the coffee seems to have perked me up enough to be ready for the lecture. Just as the professor starts, my phone chirps, drawing everyone's attention. I give a sheepish look around the room as I pull it from my bag to turn it to silent and see the text is from Dec.

"I'm missing your face. When are you free tonight?"

I smile and quickly reply that I won't be home until nine, before sliding my phone into my pocket. I shouldn't have bothered, though, because a few minutes later, it vibrates. I try to ignore it, but it may as well be burning a hole in my jeans. I'm dying to get to it so badly. I force myself to ignore it and pay attention but cave not twenty minutes later.

"I'll bring dinner and meet you in your bed. Naked."

The image his words give me is so tempting, I start trying to convince myself I don't really need to put in some lab time but unfortunately—or maybe fortunately for my education, which is supposed to be the most important thing to me right now—it doesn't work.

So after the lecture, I head to the lab.

The whole time I'm there, I'm distracted, though. Unable to focus, I eventually come to the conclusion I'm not going to be any good here so I stop to feed the mice who, against the rules, I have started to name and become attached to.

Stupid, I know.

I end up leaving later than I originally wanted to with barely any progress, which just pisses me off as I eagerly race home.

I enter our apartment to find Kara on the lounge with a noodle box container in her lap that she digs into with her chopsticks before looking up to smile at me. "Boyfriend brought us dinner and is waiting in your room where you have my permission to sex him well with gratitude, you lucky bitch."

I laugh at her welcoming, dropping my keys into the key bowl near the door, and notice Dec's are in there also, which makes my chest feel warm as I dump my bags on the empty couch.

I take out my ponytail as I make my way to my room and then open the door to see Dec propped up in the middle of my bed by a pile of pillows, stretched out with only his boxer-briefs covering him as he eats, watching television.

"I read there'd be nakedness," I complain as Dec's eyes turn to me, and he grins while finishing his mouthful.

"You got a penalty for being late," he replies as I close the door behind me then make my way over to perch beside him so I can get a kiss.

"You might want to reheat your box before eating it. I was going to put it in the fridge if you weren't back before I finished mine," Dec tells me with a nod to my bedside drawers where a noodle container is.

"My box is toasty warm, thank you very much, but I'll go

heat this up." I grin playfully then get to my feet with the box just as I see him catch my innuendo.

"I'll check that when you get back." His voice dips deliciously deeper, and I wink before heading back out to the kitchen.

When I return, Dec is under the covers and has lit the candles on the bedside tables, which are the only light in the room apart from the television, and I smile at his attempt to make it romantic.

"How's your box now?" Dec asks playfully. I toe my shoes off with a mouthful of satay chicken and veg, trying not to choke on a giggle.

"Good to go. Are you finally naked under there?" I counter as I remove my jeans and then my bra using one hand. Then I slip in under the covers as Dec holds them up invitingly.

"You'll have to see for yourself," he murmurs in my ear as his arms wrap around me. He draws me in until my shoulder is pressed against his chest and his left leg is thrown over mine. I switch my noodles to one hand to trail the knuckles of my free hand down Dec's torso, enjoying the warm silkiness of his skin until I hit his bare hip and moan appreciatively as I straighten my hand and reach to squeeze his naked butt cheek.

"Eat your food first," Dec grumbles, so I withdraw my hand with a playful sigh to take another forkful and snuggle in.

"Your bed is insanely comfy. I hope you're up for a bed buddy every night because it's ruined me for all others including my own, much like its owner." I raise my brow at him in amused disbelief, and he turns to look at me, "I'm serious. What is this thing made out of, clouds wrapped in unicorn pelt?"

I laugh at him as he wriggles in his spot.

"It's just a pillow top," I explain then Dec pulls me even more into him, which didn't seem possible. I watch him for a moment after he turns back to the TV, noticing the purpling under his eyes that are a little bloodshot.

"You look as tired as I feel," I comment softly. I reach my right hand out to smooth under his left eye. Dec nuzzles my wrist appreciatively as his eyelids lower.

"It's been a long few days," he murmurs just as I think he won't comment. I stuff the last of my food into my mouth and then reach to put the empty box on top of my nightstand so I can snuggle properly.

"Maybe we should just curl up and crash. We could both use the sleep," I suggest, yawning at just the thought of sleep. Dec has other ideas though and swiftly rolls us until I'm flat on my back with him caging me in from above as he gathers my shirt to remove it.

"A little sleep deprivation isn't going to keep me from showing my girl how much I missed her," Dec murmurs as he dips down to kiss my cheek, and I melt at his sweet words.

He trails kisses down my neck, nipping at my collarbone before pulling back with a smirk. "Not to mention, the cardio will put us in a deep sleep when we're done," he adds before burying his head into the crook of my neck to nibble on my ticklish spot there. He is so proud he found even though he knows I hate it.

I squeal and scream for him to stop as my legs reflexively pull up to kick in the air, which places him between my legs. I arch my back, trying to get away from his tickling. I feel his hardness rub against me where I'm already wet and aching for him and let out a low, needy moan.

Dec curses as he grinds against me several times then pulls back, taking my underwear with him that he flings over his shoulder, then reaches to collect the condom from my nightstand and applies it, before leaning back down to slide inside me without pause.

Dec's first forceful thrust causes my breath to catch as I cling to his shoulders and revel in the feel. He pauses there to

215

rain tender kisses over my face, but I can't stand the stillness. I feel too full.

I lower my feet to his arse and force him to rock into me while pulling on his arms. He gets the hint and begins thrusting his hips against me as I lift my pelvis to meet him.

"Jeez, baby. You're so tight."

His pace becomes faster when I squeeze my inner muscles around his thickness, and he begins pounding into me deliciously. I'm clinging to his back when Dec suddenly tilts his angle of penetration, grinding against the nub of nerves in my clit, and I almost instantly shatter around him. I cry out his name as Dec thrusts even faster, his gasping breath matching the speed of his hips until he too finishes, his body locking up before collapsing onto me in a sweaty, panting, exhausted heap of hot flesh.

A sudden blast of rock music jolts me from a deep sleep, and it takes me a second to realise it's not my alarm before I hear Dec clear his throat and the music stops. I hear his sleep-roughened voice.

"Hello?"

I realise it's his phone. I relax back into my pillow until Dec flies up into a sitting position with a loud exclamation that has me jumping again.

"What... you mean right now?"

I turn to see him throwing his clothes on in a rush as I listen to his side of the conversation. "No, don't go out. Lock the door, and I'll be right there... No, Kit... Kit!" Dec pulls the phone away from his ear to look at the screen then curses, shoving it in his pocket.

"What's going on?" I ask as I get up to scramble into whatever clothes I can grab while Dec turns to me with wild eyes as he shoves his feet into his boots.

"Someone's smashing up the shop. Kit says she was alone,

cleaning in the backroom before it started and is going out there even though I said not to." Dec runs out the door with his shirt in his hands.

I curse at being a woman who needs more clothes on than he does in order to not get arrested in public for indecent exposure, because I'm not letting him run off to the rescue alone. I hurry after him as soon as I have a shirt over my head, forcing it down my waist as Kara comes out of her room curiously.

"Trouble," I explain to her questioning expression as I pass, then grab mine and Dec's keys from the bowl on my way out.

Dec is long gone by the time I reach the elevators. The shop is less than a five minute stroll from here and I know Dec will be on foot because he hardly ever drives if he can avoid it, so once the elevator arrives, I hit the ground floor button instead of the garage. The morning traffic will slow me down if I try to drive and I want to be there with him to make sure both he and Kit are safe.

I don't manage to catch up, but I do see Dec ahead of me once I start running through the pedestrian traffic of office workers walking to the neighbouring buildings.

I look around in shock when I step in front of Ink Fix that is void of people, but a complete mess.

Every bit of glass from the counter to the mounted television has been smashed to smithereens, the display cases and beautiful metal sculpture tipped over, lying on their sides.

I follow the sound of Kit's yelling down the hall to find her facing off with Dec in the storage area where the stairs to his apartment are, her arms crossed as he holds an aluminium baseball bat out away from her.

"This is not enough protection for you to be going after thugs who do this shit, Kit. When I say stay in here and lock the damn door, I mean it," Dec is shouting at Kit who looks just as mad as she glares back indignantly.

217

"I will not sit back like a damsel in distress while punks come in and tear this place up. No way in hell, Declan," she counters. They both glare at each other in silence until I distract them, cursing when I step on a large piece of glass that pierces through the thin sole of my ballet flats and lodges into my heel. They turn to see me attempting to balance on one foot while I pull the injured one up to inspect it.

"Honestly, you too?" Dec grumbles in frustration. "Did I not tell you to stay home, trouble?" He exhales in an irritated groan as Kit moves over to make sure I'm okay.

I wait until I've extracted the glass from the rubber sole and see that I'm only bleeding a little before looking up to glare at Declan.

"No, you didn't, and I wouldn't have anyway. You didn't know what you were running into. You needed someone to have your back," I argue. Dec grabs fistfuls of his hair as he swings away from us. With his arms stretched up like that, his shirt lifts to reveal a decent amount of skin, which I can't help admiring before his arms drop with a shake of his head as he turns back.

"What is it with you women? Why do you have to do the opposite of what I say and then do something stupid while I'm trying to keep you safe?" Dec complains which gets both our heads snapping up to glare at him.

Dec takes a step back like he knows he's just stepped into a shit storm, but the defiant look he returns says he's standing by his words.

"I don't know. We're just stupid women," Kit huffs.

"You didn't tell me to do anything, and I don't take being ordered around very well, anyway. So if I think it would be safer to follow you, then that's what I'll do. I wasn't being stupid. I had my phone ready to call triple zero," I inform him. I then watch his sheepish expression turn to relief when we hear footfalls crunch over the broken glass, clearly thankful for the distraction no matter who it may be.

Dec protectively forces his way in front of us at the door before we can turn to see who it is. Kit and I can't see a thing through his solid form taking up the doorway. But I know it's not a threat when his shoulders relax.

"The fuck happened in here?" I hear Alex exclaim then see his face as Kit impatiently pushes her way passed Dec with a broom. I grab the dustpan and begin to follow her, until Alex looks at me bug-eyed so Dec follows his look, cursing as he holds an arm out to stop me.

"Babe, it's cold. Go up and borrow one of the hoodies from my closet," Dec urges.

I scowl at him because I don't feel cold and don't like his bossiness. He looks meaningfully at my top so I look down and see I'd dressed in only yoga pants and a white workout top. No bra and my nipples are making themselves known. I laugh in embarrassment, crossing my arms over them as Alex, and now Skunk, try to catch a look over Dec's shoulder after he spreads his body in the doorway to stop them. I realise I'm not dying of embarrassment like I usually would and laugh even more. Seems getting dirty with Dec is a good cure for my out of control blushing. Dec growls warningly because I'm not moving so I smile at him before doing as he ordered and make my way upstairs.

I hear him shepherd them out with a muttered, "Fuck off, arseholes," when Alex and Skunk mockingly complain.

I grab a grey hoodie I find on the kitchen bench that smells like Dec—but not in a funky way—instead of getting a clean one, because I love his smell. Then I feed Tom when he rubs against my leg with a pitiful complaint, because I doubt Dec will make it up here anytime soon.

I notice an open sketchpad I can't help peeking at, and my breath catches as I take in a charcoal portrait of myself, asleep with my hands tucked under my head. It's beautiful. It makes me feel more beautiful than I've ever felt. Overwhelming warmth spreads in my chest where my hand is pressed over my thumping heart, and my eyes water as I flip through pages to find more of me. I recall every time my eyes meet Declan's and correct myself—I've felt beautiful every time I've been caught in his gaze. The way he looks at me, like I'm the Holy Grail, his own cherished miracle. The reverent way he touches me and holds me in his arms is also the only time I've felt accepted. It's like I don't have to try to be better or more because I am enough. I am exceptional just the way I am to him. Dec doesn't know how much that means to me after a lifetime of having my parents constantly push me to do better than my best. I'd do anything to keep that—to keep him.

I'm falling hard.

A burst of laughter escapes me as I correct myself again and force myself to admit it, at least in my head.

I've fallen for Dec.

I close the pad from my prying eyes then make my way back downstairs, feeling mind-blown from my revelations.

I feel like the world has shifted and everyone should be reeling from it, but as I stand back and watch for a moment when I return to the front of the shop, everyone is cleaning and carrying on, totally unaffected.

As though he feels my presence, Dec looks over his shoulder to meet my gaze from where he is lifting the metal sculpture back into place. He raises his brow questioningly in a silent check that I'm okay. I smile warmly in return and am sure my eyes reveal my feelings as he smiles gently before making his way over to wrap me in his arms.

"You look a little spooked. Are you okay?" Dec murmurs in my hair, and I nod as I burrow into him as much as I can.

"Don't worry. I'll sit down when I finish tonight and sort

this out before it escalates," Dec vows. I squeeze him tighter for his concern even though that's not what's got a lump in my throat right now, but the overwhelming emotions that are set to burst inside of me for him.

"I'm fine. But you can't tell me not to worry about you because I will. I care about you. I'm sorry I can't help clean up. I have a class in thirty minutes that I can't miss," I tell Dec after I gain enough control of myself to speak and look up to his beautiful, stormy ocean eyes.

"It's all right. We'll be cleaned up before we have to open, no problem. I'll have Alex walk you back. Don't fight me on this. I need to make sure you're safe but can't leave right now so just humour me, please," Dec pleads when he sees I'm about to argue. I melt into his arms, nodding my acceptance against his chest. "Be careful. Don't go anywhere alone, okay?" Dec adds as he kisses my hairline then leans back to press his lips to mine.

"There are always people around on campus. I'll be fine," I try to reassure him, but he doesn't look convinced.

I carefully move across the room to check Kit is okay before I leave, as Dec takes over sweeping for Alex, and they huddle for a quiet conversation.

"Babe, it takes more than a couple of young punks who run from a chick with a bat to scare me," Kit swears before Alex steps up to sling his arm around me. "I'd be more worried about you with this idiot," she adds which Alex blatantly ignores to smile brilliantly at me.

"You ready for me to escort you home, madam?" He tries to use a proper English accent that just doesn't work for him then drops it. "Just so you know, I'm taking my duty so seriously I'm willing to make you the Whitney Houston to my Kevin Costner. I'll carry you home while simultaneously kicking arse *The Bodyguard* style. Feel free to bust out in song about how much you will always love me. I'm down with that," Alex informs me in all seriousness, making me laugh out loud.

"Alex, she doesn't have time for your shit. Just get her home," Dec barks so I swallow my giggles to say goodbye to everyone, giving Dec a final, quick kiss on my way out.

Of course, our trip to my building is uneventful apart from Alex's amusing commentary on the people we pass. But he still insists on coming up to the apartment to 'check the premises are clear.' He then makes himself at home on the kitchen bench to bug Kara as I rush to my room to get ready.

Since I'm only going to classes today, I decide to throw Dec's hoodie back on over my black sundress I change into. It might not look fashionable, but I could do with the cosiness of being wrapped in his scent today.

"Alex told me what happened. You okay?" Kara asks from my bedroom door with worried eyes. I smile as I slip on my shimmery black flats, throw my other pair since there's a hole in the sole of one.

"Yeah. Worried about Dec, but I'm fine," I promise, heading for my bathroom to brush my hair and teeth with Kara following.

"I'm worried about you getting involved in all this. I don't want you getting hurt," Kara murmurs after a while of watching me brush my teeth so I turn to give her a hug.

"I'll be careful, promise," I try to get out through my mouthful of minty foam. This makes her laugh as I rush to spit it out in the sink before I swallow or choke on it when it threatens to make me laugh too.

"I love you, brat," Kara tells me when I finish.

"And you know I love you, too. I gotta get moving, but I don't have work tonight so we'll have a movie night in?" I offer and Kara smiles with a nod.

"I'll get the Ben and Jerry's," she states as Alex pops his head into the room, looking inquisitive and up to no good.

"You girls really shouldn't leave a guy alone in your

apartment to amuse himself for so long. I found some interesting things in the TV unit drawers," he warns which has Kara flushing and turning to smack him in the arm. I watch on curiously because I didn't think there was anything except some of her camera cables in there.

"Shut your mouth and get out, you perv," Kara yells, shoving him out of her way while he chuckles and stumbles back.

"I should have known they were yours. Great selection. Can I borrow *Wild and Raw* or maybe we can watch it together? Watching porn while snuggling is the best way to watch it."

I finally catch on and laugh out loud as Kara screeches in frustration, pushing him all the way out to the hallway.

"Never will I ever watch porn with you," Kara replies scathingly.

Alex pulls her into him by a firm grasp on her elbows, giving her a look that practically scorches. "Never say never, babe. One day I might get fed up with this little 'hard to get' game you have going on and give you what you really want." His voice is deep with promise. The usual playfulness he surrounds himself with is totally stripped away in all seriousness which shocks me—Kara too, if her silence is any indication.

Alex stares at her for a moment before looking up to me, his half smirk in place as though back to his usual teasing self.

"I'll get you to drop me off at the shop on your way if you're ready to go," he tells me as he releases Kara to turn and walk down the hall.

"Arrogant, hot-as-hell arsehole," Kara mutters and then storms into her room, slamming the door on Alex's chuckling.

I rush to grab my bags from the couch while looking at Alex thoughtfully as he stands by the door patiently. His hands are shoved into his jeans pockets as he stares back at me with a raised brow.

"You're a bit of an enigma," I tell him on the way to the

elevator. Alex chuckles, pressing the call button for the lift before shrugging.

"Chicks dig a little mystery so I'll take that as a compliment."

I watch him on the ride down which he ignores until the doors open to the underground parking where he shoots me a questioning look.

"Just don't hurt her. I know Kara acts like she has a thick skin, but it's only because she's been burned in the past. And don't tell her I told you that or she'll kill me," I warn.

Alex grits his teeth but doesn't reply until we're in the car.

"I may be a man-whore, but I don't lie or make promises I won't keep. The chicks I hook up with know the score beforehand. It's not my fault some are batshit crazy and delude themselves into thinking it can be more. I don't deliberately hurt anyone," Alex informs me as I reverse out of my park. I pause to look at him, but he's staring resolutely out the window.

I don't know what to say in reply so I drop it, and we make the short drive to the shop in silence, which is so unlike the Alex I've gotten to know. He jumps out as soon as I pull up with a barely muttered, "Thanks for the ride," before shutting the door and walking to the shop.

I pull back into traffic with a sigh and make my way on auto-pilot, contemplating this new side of Alex until my head hurts.

I make it to campus with just enough time to grab a coffee before class, which I'm thankful for since I didn't have breakfast and won't be free to eat after this until one. There's no way I'll survive that long without caffeine.

"I thought I made it clear I didn't want to see your face today," Mal yells grouchily over the line in front of me when he notices my entrance, which has every head in the place turning to look at me.

"Take it easy. I'm here as a customer. Now caffeinate these

people, before I take my business to the coffee cart that's closer to my block," I call back.

Malcolm grins proudly at using the opportunity to embarrass me as he gets back to work. The line moves quickly, and when I get to the counter to order, Mal slides over a tall cup with a grin.

"We both know the coffee cart doesn't have it as big, strong or hard as mine and can't make you happy as I can. But take this peace offering and get going before you're late."

He dismisses my money as I laugh at his double entendre, so I slide the money over the counter then grab a banana and honey muffin, holding it up so he knows I'm taking it, forcing him to put the cash into the register with a resigned sigh.

"You're right, Mal. Even I can't satisfy myself as good as you do," I play along with a wink before sipping my drink. I am sure he blushes a little. Johnny is choking on his laughter at our antics while wiping down the machine so I grin at him as I turn to leave before Mal barks at him to unload the dishwasher.

I'm smiling and swear I can feel the fog in my head clearing as I sip my coffee on my way across campus, dodging other students that are either dawdling like groups of zombies or running through, clearly late for class.

I get a tingling of awareness at the back of my neck as I'm approaching my building, but again, when I look around, I don't see any causes for alarm, so I ignore it while holding the door open for a professor approaching with an armload of papers before following her inside.

I greet the handful of classmates that are already in class before making my way to my usual seat in the back corner just as our professor arrives. I pull out my notebook and pen then open my muffin so I can tear pieces off to nibble. Although the morning didn't start off so well, I'm feeling upbeat and ready for the day. That could just be the coffee talking, though. Mal really is a wizard with the stuff.

By one in the afternoon, my peppiness has died a horrible death, which lets me know it was courtesy of the caffeine.

My head is pounding. My feet are dragging and my stomach is rumbling as I make my way to the secure parking building at the back of campus that my parents have dished out a pretty penny for my years of access.

I'm watching the path ahead as I plan out my afternoon now that I have a three thousand word essay to complete before tomorrow afternoon. Thankfully, no one is around to hear my groaning about not getting to take a nap and see Dec like I had planned.

I yank open the heavy door to the stairwell of the parking lot then start up the steel stairs, trying to recall if I'm parked on the second or third level. I'm rounding the first landing when I'm suddenly slammed into the wall from behind and pinned there, my wrists forced to the wall beside my head while a body presses against my back.

"Hello, wildcat," A gruff voice murmurs beside my ear, the stench of stale beer and cigarettes on his breath assaulting my senses as I try to pull away but even my face is pressed to the brick wall so hard that the rough surface abrades my cheek.

I suck in a lungful of air after getting it knocked out of me and prepare to scream when a hand covers my mouth knowingly.

"Don't go screaming out. I've finally got you alone so we don't want any disruptions now."

It's then I recognise the voice, and a chill trails down my spine as my heart threatens to beat its way out of my chest. Snake.

I try to break out of his grasp, but he presses against me harder, his hips grinding so I feel his hard-on against my arse, and I have to swallow against the urge to vomit as he groans appreciatively.

"Now, we're going to slowly make our way to your car. I'd

happily do you right here, but I don't want to be interrupted while taking this fine arse. Any sudden movements or noise, and I'll have to make you hurt, so just do as I say," Snake orders then cautiously removes his hand from my mouth, quickly bringing it back to press something cold and sharp to my side in warning.

"You feel me, wildcat?"

I nod my head against the brick because there's no way I can speak right now as I try in vain to control my breathing and keep the tears at bay as my body trembles.

"Let's go, easy now."

Snake pulls me from the wall with a firm grasp on my left wrist, forcing it down to my stomach and using his arm to hold me tightly to him as his right hand continues to hold the knife against my opposite side.

I may be an atheist, but I pray to whoever might be listening, begging for an escape as he guides me up the next flight of stairs.

"Open the door. Slowly," Snake orders when we reach the next landing. I reach out for the handle with my free hand that trembles.

I take a deep, steadying breath then pull it back with as much force as I can so my arm knocks his hand holding the knife away from me. I jab him hard in the ribcage with my elbow, making him release me as he stumbles back.

The second I'm free, I push my legs to run as fast as I can through the door, screaming at the top of my lungs while I gun it for my car. I hear Snake curse before the sound of his boots hitting the concrete echoes around me.

An engine starts from the level above, which is the most beautiful sound in the world as I run up the incline, my eyes blurring with tears. I feel Snake gain on me a second before my hair is yanked back painfully, forcing me to slam into his chest.

"You're going to pay for that, bitch," he snarls in my ear, struggling to haul me back between the cars and out of view. I drag my feet a few paces until I force my right leg up and back as hard and fast as I can so it connects with him, and he curses again as he drops me on my arse.

I drop my bag from my shoulder as I scramble up on hands and knees then run out, waving my arms frantically and screaming for help as a blue sedan rounds the corner with their headlights on. I need them to stop. I run straight for it so they'll have to stop or run me over. The car jerks to a halt, only inches before me, then the driver's door opens.

"Aela, what's wrong?" Seth—a guy from my statistics class whose bulk rivals Malcolm's—steps from the car, looking around cautiously as I continue to run towards him.

"He has a knife," I gasp breathlessly just before I barrel into Seth's chest, and he wraps his arms protectively around me as his eyes scan the parking lot.

"No one's here. Looks like they took off."

I pull my face out of his chest to look behind me, expecting Snake to pop out of the shadows but nothing moves except for the stairway door slamming shut with a bang that makes me jump like a gun shot.

"Are you okay?" Seth asks as he looks me over, noticing my grazed cheek, messed hair, and one remaining shoe on my foot. "Do you want me to call security?" he adds with concern when I struggle to take a deep breath to control the effects of the shock and adrenaline running through me.

"No. I'm okay, but can you wait until I'm in my car?" I ask shakily, stepping back to break from his arms as he frowns.

"Aela, if someone attacked you, they might go after another student on campus. People need to be warned," he replies disapprovingly, and I shake my head.

"He won't. It was personal. Please, I just want to get out of here," I plead then watch his eyes widen before he looks around us again.

"What the hell have you gotten yourself into?" Seth asks incredulously, but I just shake my head in reply. I can't talk. I just need to get out of here before I break down.

"Okay, I'll wait here and follow you out. So long as you can promise me you will be okay. Otherwise, you should call the police or... someone," Seth adds. We cautiously collect my missing shoe and everything that spilled out of my bag.

I take deep, even breaths to try to control myself as I sink into my driver's seat, trying to ignore the shaking of my hands as I insert the key and start the car.

Seth lets me overtake him, and then he follows as I drive through to the exit. I keep expecting Snake to jump out, but he never does. I expel a huge breath of relief once I'm out of there.

I wave gratefully as I look in my rearview mirror when Seth beeps his horn as he turns in the opposite direction. I'm too spooked to go home alone so I head to the only place I need to go to feel safe.

"Good afternoon, wel— What the hell happened to you?" Kit's usual greeting and welcoming smile changes when she looks up and notices me. Her jaw drops and eyes go wide at my appearance.

I try to fix my hair by running my fingers through it but doubt it helps at all when I feel the mass of tangled knots.

"Is, is Dec free?" I stutter as Kit rushes around the now glassless counter shelves and immediately inspects my sore cheek which is starting to feel swollen as well as scraped. It must be from being slammed into the wall.

"He should be just finishing up with a client. Let me clean that up and grab you some ice before it gets worse, and you can tell me what happened." Kit takes my hand, leading me down the hall that is filled with the buzzing of various machines. I look longingly at Dec's door which is shut as we pass, but we don't stop.

229

Kit orders me to sit on the bathroom toilet seat cover as she grabs a clean washcloth, wetting it before gently wiping my cheek. I grit my teeth at the stinging it causes, and Kit gives me an apologetic look before turning to rinse the cloth out. I'm shocked by how red the water turns. I refused to look at my reflection in the car mirror because I didn't want to see the damage, but I didn't think it was that bad.

"Spill," Kit gently orders while retrieving a first aid kit from the cupboard, so I talk. I numbly recount the attack as she cleans my cheek with alcohol wipes and presses a cold pack wrapped in another cloth to it that I take over holding when she borrows Dec's comb to brush my hair.

"Holy shit. Dec's going to go Terminator," Kit mutters when we're done. She pulls me up, wrapping her arms around me. "Thank god that guy was there to stop the bastard," Kit's whisper hitches as she tightens her grip around me, and I pat her back with my free hand.

"Kit, I need the key for the till. Where are you?" Dec calls out from downstairs, and she sighs, finishing tidying up our mess then turns to consider the state I'm in.

"Well, it doesn't look as bad now that it's clean, but you're going to have a nice shiner tomorrow. Now brace yourself for the shit storm." Kit takes my hand comfortingly as Dec calls for her again.

"Calm down, I'm here. I had to help Aela," Kit calls out as we descend the stairs. Dec marches through the door with a confused expression.

"What are you talking about, Aela's not here— Hey, baby." His face lights up when he sees me coming down behind Kit, that is until he notices the icepack I'm holding to my cheek. His face falls as he bounds up the stairs separating us, causing Kit to hug the wall to make room for him.

"What happened?" The concern in his eyes as he gently pulls

my hand away from my cheek gets to my already overwrought emotions, causing my eyes to start leaking uncontrollably. Dec looks even more alarmed, his wide eyes flicking back and forth between mine as he starts smoothing my hair in an attempt to calm me. The hastily built dam that kept it all at bay has broken now that I know I'm safe. I'm suddenly a hyperventilating, sobbing, mess.

"Snake jumped her in a car park at school," Kit answers for me when Dec asks again. His hands still in my hair. He turns to look at her incredulously before looking back at me with sorrow and guilt in his eyes. This kills me because it's not his fault. I shake my head then bury my face in his shirt as I cling to him.

Dec wraps me in his arms tightly while murmuring sweetly to try to calm my hysterics as Kit repeats everything I told her, even the part about me coming here to feel safe because I was too scared to be alone at home.

"Tell Skunk and BJ I need to speak to them when they're finished and then try to get a hold of Alex for me. You're not to leave here by yourself for anything and give Kara a heads up also. We don't know what this bastard has been up to, so better to be safe than sorry." Dec pauses to kiss my hair when I whimper at the thought of Kara getting attacked. "I'm going to take care of my girl then make some calls. Yell if you need me." He finishes his orders then my feet are scooped out from under me when he leans down, taking me into his arms to carry me back upstairs while continuing his gentle, soothing murmuring. Dec lays me on the couch then presses a kiss to my forehead as he brushes my hair from my face.

"I'll be right back, baby. Do you want anything?" he asks gently while spreading the blanket from the back of the lounge over me.

"Just you," I whisper pathetically but don't care. I just want the peace and security of being held in his arms for a little while.

231

Dec walks into the kitchen, and I hear him talking to Tom as he feeds him before coming back to offer me some water and two pills which I look at curiously for a moment before he kneels down.

"That cheekbone must hurt. These will make you feel a bit better," he explains, so I take his offer gratefully.

Dec takes the glass back to place on the coffee table before lowering himself gingerly to stretch out against me, taking over holding the icepack to my cheek with his right hand as he slides his left arm under my head.

"Just relax, baby. I'm not going anywhere," he murmurs, then leaves the icepack balancing itself on my cheek to run his hand soothingly up and down my back, breathing in deeply against my hair while I sniffle into his chest.

I soak in the warmth of his body against mine, and the strong, steady beat of his heart against my ear, and I fall asleep within minutes as whatever those pills were takes away the niggling pains all through my body, like magic.

***

It's much darker when I wake up with Tom snuggled up to me. For a blissful, confused second, I forget what happened and why I'm on Dec's couch, but then everything comes back, hitting me like a lead weight to my stomach. I lean up to check the clock that says I've been out for four hours.

I hear Dec murmuring quietly behind his closed bedroom door as I sit up and stretch. I feel a little better physically, despite a few pangs of pain and my left eye that struggles to open much from the swelling around it. I bet it looks as lovely as it feels. Emotionally, though, I feel raw and exposed. Like my nerves are frayed and are a shredded livewire.

I get up to use the bathroom, avoiding the mirror as I relieve myself and wash my hands before ducking back out. The noises of me moving around obviously gain Dec's attention because he opens his door to peek out, phone to his ear. I muster up a small smile for him before wrapping myself in the blanket from the couch.

"I've gotta go, man. See you soon." Dec ends his call while walking over to take me in his arms.

"Sorry. I was hoping to be done before you woke up. How are you feeling?" he asks between pressing kisses to my head. He leans back to see my face as I nod.

"I'm feeling better, thank you. I'm sorry about my freak out," I reply quietly as I pull my gaze away from his in embarrassment.

Dec gently turns my face back so I meet his gaze and observe the anger there that's barely contained.

"Hey, don't you dare apologise for anything. None of it was your fault but mine, and I'm going to take care of it tonight," Dec states gruffly then pulls me in against his chest, his hand bunching up the hair at the back of my head.

"I have to go out for a while, and you'll be staying with Alex until I'm finished. Kara brought over a bag of clothes and stuff for you so you can get changed, and we'll grab some dinner," Dec adds in a tone that says he is expecting an argument, but he won't hear it. Good thing I'm feeling compliant, though I'm worried about what he's going out for.

"Can I ask what you're going to do?" I ask quietly, leaning back to look up into Dec's face. He sighs, moving his hands to cup my face, his right thumb gently stroking under my left eye which hurts a little, but the tenderness of his touch makes it bearable.

"You can always ask me anything, babe. I'm going with Buzz to see the president of the Blood Brothers to sort this shit out and make it clear if anything else happens to you, I will let this place burn to the damn ground before I ever let them in here," Dec replies fiercely, and I cling to his shirt with concern.

"Are you sure you can trust Buzz to have your back? He is one of them after all."

Dec smiles wide and confidently, not a trace of doubt on his face. "Buzz is more than just my old boss. He pulled me out of a downward spiral after Grace died and my dad left. I had so much anger and grief, I didn't know what to do with it. I was fighting and drinking heavily among other things, anything to numb the pain. I got into a fight behind Buzz's shop where we knocked over his bike, and after chewing my arse out, he saw something in me that made him take me in instead of giving me a beating. I was cleaning his shop to work off the cost of fixing his bike while Buzz trained me in their boxing gym when he found my drawings and made me his apprentice. Buzz showed me how to control all the negativity in my head and has been like a second father to me. He even stopped me when I was thinking of patching into the club, telling me I was too good for that. So, yeah, I trust him with my life," Dec assures and my eyes water at the story of a lost and destroyed, younger Declan.

I tighten my arms around him and press a kiss to his shirt-covered chest as his hands rub my shoulder blades. I need to get a hold on my emotions. I need a little distance.

"Do I have time to shower? I feel coated in dirt."

And this isn't a lie. I could use a good scrub to get rid of the grimy feeling Snake left behind. And some comfy clothes. God, I hope Kara packed me comfy clothes and not some impractical, sexy getup.

"Go ahead. Take all the time you need. I'll order us some food. If I'm not here when you're finished, just come downstairs."

Dec kisses my head before releasing me so I scrounge up another smile for him and collect my bag from the coffee table on my way to his en suite.

After scrubbing every inch of skin within reach until it's pink while trying to keep my injured cheek dry, I step out of the shower into the steam-filled room and hesitantly open my bag that's perched on the toilet seat. I breathe a sigh of relief when I see my favourite over-stretched black sweater, tights, and Jack Skellington slippers. Kara knows me so well. I use my hairdryer I find in the bag, avoiding the fogged up mirror as I dry my hair, throwing it up in a messy bun and then apply some deodorant before leaving the room. I feel more like myself and more emotionally stable. I dig my phone out of my day bag to thank Kara, except I already have a text from her stating she is working late on a project with a friend so she'll stay there, and she hopes I'm okay. I text her a huge thank you, telling her I'm fine, and for her to be careful. Then I head downstairs.

I hear the guys talking in the room opposite Dec's and hesitate at the open door before looking in to find Dec with Skunk, BJ, and Kit, lounging around the small room that's decorated with grey walls with framed black and white sketches.

Kit notices me first and gestures for me to sit beside her on the small black leather loveseat against the back wall.

I get three steps into the room before Dec's hands grip my waist from behind and guide me backwards to perch between his legs on the desk he's sitting on beside the door. He leans me back until I'm resting against his chest, his chin tucked into the curve of my shoulder as his hands trail down my sides and over my tights. I'm nestled in his crotch and feel the hardening there when he groans appreciatively against my neck, which tickles and makes me flinch and lift my shoulder towards my ear to force him away.

"You feel amazing in these clothes. All soft and warm," Dec murmurs against the sensitive skin behind my ear. My stomach and pelvic muscles tighten as I giggle then lean away from his caresses, shifting in his lap, which makes him groan again, and his hands move to grip my hips tightly.

"Down boy," I whisper, sitting back and turning to drop a kiss to the tip of his nose before facing the others in the room that are watching us with amusement.

"Here, sweet stuff. After the day you've had, I imagine you could do with this," BJ turns to face the bench he was leaning against to pour a shot of Jack Daniel's before offering it to me. I go to take it, but Dec pulls me back with a protest.

"Beej, she's had strong painkillers that shouldn't be mixed with alcohol," he warns so BJ shrugs then toasts me before slamming back the shot himself as I roll my eyes but don't argue because I didn't really want it.

The bell over the front door chimes so Dec leans back where he can see through to it, before patting my legs for me to get up so he can walk out. I can't hear any talking out there over the music, but the bell rings a couple more times before he sticks his head back in the room.

"We've got food, and your guy's here, Skunk," he reveals the paper bag while informing Steve of his client's appearance. Steve pulls himself out of the black leather and chrome swivel chair he was leaning back in, clapping for everyone to clear out of the room before following to greet his client.

Dec takes my hand with his free one, leading the way back upstairs where we eat pasta from the cute Italian restaurant across the road. Then we gather our stuff to head out.

The nights are getting cooler now that autumn is here, and I'm extra thankful for my sweater as I wait for Dec to reverse his car from the small shed in the back of the shop that can just fit his car inside. Seriously, Dec has to shuffle sideways to get to his door and squeeze himself in.

I try to ignore the skittish feeling I get from being out in the open at night, but can't help flying into my seat as soon as the car is out enough.

Dec drives with one hand on the wheel to hold mine in the other over the gearshift. He is the epitome of calm and controlled as he changes gears with his fingers as my knee bounces nervously with my anxiety over his plans.

We pull up to a large, two-storey Spanish-styled home, sheltered by lush green foliage in a pricey neighbourhood. I turn to Dec in disbelief which makes him chuckle as he shuts off the engine.

"This is Alex's parents' house. He's watching it while they're away on holiday," Dec explains, climbing out of the car then collects my bags from the back seat as I get out and start up the stairs when he gestures for me to go first.

A sensor light turns on as I step onto the front porch then Dec reaches around me to bang on the large decorative wooden door with the side of his fist, not even bothering with the metal doorknock.

"Alex, open the damn door," he yells after a silent, expectant moment and then continues to pound on the wood until we finally hear fumbling on the other side of the thick door.

It swings open to reveal a shirtless Alex, who braces the door open with one arm, passionately kissing a blonde in a skimpy black dress that looks like it was sprayed on her it's so tight. She is holding a pair of ridiculously high stilettos.

They both look rumpled, and it's clear we've dragged them from bed though they weren't sleeping.

Alex finally releases the girl, and she stumbles back, her makeup totally messed up as she pointlessly rubs at the smudged lipstick on the side of her lips, winking back at Alex while he forces her out the door.

"Call me, Licks," she purrs over her shoulder before turning to face us, her eyes sparkling with arousal as she looks Dec over before Alex slaps her arse in dismissal to get her moving.

I yank an amused looking Declan out of her way impatiently before turning my glare on Alex who grins lazily, pushing his hair out of his eyes before he steps out to wrap me in his arms. He presses my face tightly into his chest which reeks so I struggle out of his grip.

"You smell of sex, cheap perfume, and smoke," I complain as I struggle, but Alex tightens around me as he breathes in deeply above me.

"Mm… you smell great too, like vanilla and coffee. Makes me want to lick you up," he murmurs playfully then releases me when I jab him hard under his ribcage with my fingertips, making him jump with an undignified yelp.

"What made you think it was safer for me to be here rather than at the shop again?" I complain to Dec, who stops glowering impatiently at Alex to turn to me.

"Because it's secure. No one in the MC knows about this place, so we'll be crashing here tonight no matter what, and despite his stupid mouth that's begging for my fist right now, Alex is the only person I absolutely trust to keep you safe while I'm gone," Dec explains.

Alex sticks his bare chest out while flexing his arms.

"It's my guns. Dec knows they're lethal," he jokes, but neither of us laugh before I sigh, giving in.

"Fine. But I won't be held accountable if you take too long, and I kill him," I warn Dec.

He grins before wrapping his free arm around me. "I'll take care of the body if you do," he promises. I laugh as I lean up to kiss his cheek.

"Oh, please. You two would be devastated to lose me," Alex objects while he takes my bags from Dec.

"I'll be back as soon as I can," Declan promises quietly, cupping my face in his hands. He then leans down to kiss me sweetly in a silent promise. His tongue teases mine for a moment before he pulls back, but I cling to him, reluctant to let him go for fear he might get hurt.

"Be careful," I whisper, and he nods before looking over to Alex.

"Look after my girl. But keep your hands and all other questionable body parts to yourself. Keep your phone by you, ears open and no alcohol until I'm back," Dec orders, which makes Alex chuckle as he playfully punches him in the arm.

"I've got her, bro. Crack some skulls for me while we have a sober slumber party," Alex encourages. Dec shakes his head before letting me go with a final kiss to my hair, turning away without another word.

"Come on, chicky. We'll put these bags away then see what's on the telly. Do you need something for your eye?" Alex asks, putting an arm around me to guide me inside while I fight the urge to run after Dec to stop him.

Chapter 24

DECLAN

I HATED HAVING to turn away and leave Aela. I knew she was safe with Alex but after seeing her all roughed up and breaking down on the stairs as Kit told me what happened, it physically hurts to not have her by my side where I can keep her protected. I have to keep reminding myself that having this meeting is the only way to make her safe. Plus, the more what happened sinks in, the harder it is to control my bloodlust for Snake.

I hope that piece of scum is at this meeting. I have to flex my hands from their death-grip on the steering wheel when it creaks in protest. I turn up Parkway Drive's *Cold Day in Hell* until I can feel the base vibrating in my chest.

I find the address Buzz gave me in the warehouse district in Ashmore and park in the first available spot a couple metres up. Dogs bark like crazy as I approach the high fence that's got barbed wire looped over the top. The fence is blacked out with dark plastic sheets. I'm sure it would be an intimidating scene to anyone else, but I'm so filled with adrenaline and fury, I couldn't care less that I'm about to go in there unarmed while they probably have a ton of guns and weapons that could kill me a hundred times over within seconds.

Buzz appears, rounding the opposite corner in front of me, a concerned frown darkening his face. "How's she doing, son?" he asks after his slap to the back greeting.

"Roughed up and scared shitless but putting on a brave face," I inform him, cracking my knuckles in aggravation.

Buzz nods and then punches a code into a side gate, which unlatches with a beep. He swings it open, walking through with me right behind him.

The dogs I heard barking are chained to a line that runs the length of the opposite side of the grounds, but that doesn't stop them from trying to rush us, barking loudly and snapping their mouths until Buzz raises his hand and yells for them to heel.

Suddenly, the large Rottweiler and German shepherd turn into a couple of innocent puppies, their tails wagging as they sit and beg for attention. Buzz ignores them, continuing to the two storey building's dark tinted, glass door entrance a few metres from the closed garage doors. He pulls the door open wide to step inside, looks the room over before turning back to me as I enter behind him, gesturing with a head tilt for me to follow as he starts for a set of stairs hidden in an alcove to the left.

"Hold up. We have to check him for weapons," a guy calls from the other side of the dim room at the bar setup.

Buzz looks at him in annoyance before turning to me, "You packing?" he asks so I shake my head.

"Nope," I confirm, recalling Buzz demands vocal responses to his questions.

"He's not stupid enough to lie to me, Prospect. So piss off." Buzz turns impatiently, continuing up the stairs so I do the same as the guy curses but doesn't come after us.

The stairs lead to a dull white hallway that has at least ten closed doors running down each side. I hear a mix of laughter, talking, moaning, music and obvious sex noises, as Buzz continues his march down the hall. We turn right before making another left then come to a halt at the single door where he knocks politely.

"Enter," I recognise Joe's voice calling out, then Buzz opens the door, and we step into a sleek office setup.

Joe is sitting in front of a large window behind an even larger mahogany desk. A barely-legal looking chick wearing only a pair of tiny denim shorts with half her arse hanging out faces him from her perch on the desk.

"Leave us, sugar," Joe demands without taking his eyes off us but stops her with a hand around her wrist when she bends to pick a scrap of fabric up off the floor. "As you are. Go find my room," he demands, and I look away as the girl turns to walk out, topless.

"Declan, you wanted a meeting. I hope it's to tell me you're ready to allow us access to your shop," Joe addresses me. I grit my teeth to control myself as Buzz takes a seat facing him.

"I'm here to tell you if you want my business, then you had better put your Snake on a tighter leash than those pups outside and leave Aela alone. She has nothing to do with this. Hurting the people I care about is a bad way to try get me to agree with you. All it does is piss me off," I ground out.

Joe leans back in his chair, looking to Buzz.

"I'm assuming Aela's the bitch Snake took a liking to?"

I step up to lean over his desk before Buzz can get a word out. "Do not call her a bitch, and he more than took a liking to her. He attacked her today at the university in the middle of the god damn day," I yell, feeling my control slipping by the second as Joe remains stoically expressionless.

"Snake has been AWOL since he was ordered to steer clear of your shop after the brick incident and was taught not to mess with the club's future business, so drop the attitude with me, boy. I haven't done anything against you and yours," Joe says in a warning tone as Buzz tugs me into the empty seat beside him.

"I assumed Snake took off to cool down and lick his wounds before coming back, but I'll put the word out for the guys to bring him in. We'll find him and make sure it sinks in this time. If—you let us set up in your shop," Joe's eyes gleam triumphantly.

"I want him myself, and I want him first," I state, but Joe shakes his head.

"I can't hand over a brother just because he scratched your ride. Unless you want to patch in?" Joe counters, and I slam my fists against his desk.

"He tried to rape her. She is battered and bruised, and I want his fucking blood spilled by my hands, or you get nothing. I don't care if you burn my fucking shop down to spite me, I will watch it burn knowing you didn't get what you wanted. The shop is just what pays the bills. Aela means more to me." I get a quirk of his brow in reply.

A couple of his guys quietly enter the room to stand behind us, waiting for me to lose my shit.

My mind catches up to my mouth. What I said about the shop and Aela sets me aback for a moment. Not because it wasn't true, but because I realise I meant every word.

"We'll put you in the ring with him. Make it an event and sell tickets even, but not until you let us in the shop. You don't get anything for nothing, Declan."

To hell with this. I burst out of my chair, knocking it back as I explode, "Fuck this bullshit. I'll find him my fucking self." The guy to my right grabs ahold of my shoulder. I throw him off as the other behind Buzz steps in to grab my other arm so I swing my right fist over until it connects with his face.

"Get the hell off me. I'm leaving," I yell, but a couple more guys burst through the door ready for a fight.

Before I know it, all hell breaks loose and not just because I've gone to that dark place I haven't been since I started fighting after Grace and Dad left. But because guys in black and blue gear that the back of my mind registers as police charge into the room and fight to get everyone on the floor with a lot of yelling that fails to register with me. I'm too far gone.

It takes a good tasering to drop me to the floor after everyone else has either surrendered or been taken down by force. I hit my head on the bottom shelf of a bookcase that was behind the door on my way down.

The pain is all consuming as I twitch uncontrollably before checking out as I sink into the endless darkness of unconsciousness.

Chapter 25

AELA

IT'S BEEN HOURS since I watched Dec leave, and I'm pretty sure Alex hasn't stopped talking for a second during that time. Except to drop some skittles into his mouth and even then, he resumes talking while chewing, which is just gross.

Within the first half hour, I retrieved my laptop from my bag after Alex situated himself on the couch with a bowl of candy and decided we'd watch a Fast and Furious marathon on one of the movie channels. I couldn't stand just sitting there longer than ten minutes, so I figured I'd try to be productive and distract myself by getting my assignment done.

Of course, that went to hell. I've barely written anything because I can't stop looking at the clock and worrying about Declan. Plus, I have Alex's mouth to contend with since I set myself up on the floor in the lounge room with the coffee table as my desk because I don't want to be alone.

I stare at the little blinking insertion point on my document but can't make sense of the words in my head because all I can hear is Alex's obnoxious chewing.

I turn to glare at him, wishing I could develop Jedi mind powers already to make him shut it and choke on his mouthful. Alex must feel my gaze because he turns, raising a brow questioningly when his eyes meet mine before looking down to his bowl and leaning over to offer me some.

"Want to taste the rainbow?" Alex asks, jiggling the bowl, but I shake my head.

"No. I want you to shut up so I can concentrate," I reply shortly, turning back to stare at my laptop screen.

"What are you working on?" Alex leans to see the screen over my shoulder before I push him away, my palm to his forehead.

"I have a three thousand word essay due tomorrow." I rub my fingers deep into my forehead to try to relieve the tension there, but it does little to help.

"What are you studying, anyway? Dec's never mentioned what you're doing. He just brags that you're as smart as you are gorgeous," Alex adds as I hit up google.

I really don't know how students survived pre-google days. Google knows all.

"I'm working on getting my Bachelors of Science, majoring in biochemistry and molecular biology," I answer distractedly, without taking my eyes from the screen.

I get a few moments of blissful silence with no further questions until Alex pauses the movie. He moves to face me while tapping my knee for attention.

"Okay, explain that using little words a senior year dropout can understand?" he demands, and I sigh as I turn to face him.

"I'm hoping to get my doctorate for studying the chemical processes and substances inside living things that make them living." I dumb it down as much as I can, and Alex still looks confused. "You had to have studied basic biology in high school science," I complain impatiently then he grins, leaning towards me.

"Yeah, but I studied that more physically out of class than I did theoretically in it." Alex wags his eyebrows suggestively. I bite off a laugh as I shake my head disapprovingly, turning back to my laptop.

"So what kind of doctor are you going to be when you finish? A surgeon, a paediatrician or what?" Alex continues with his questions, and I shake my head as I scroll through links blindly.

"Not that kind of doctor. I'll get the title before my name, but it'll be scientific, not medical."

Alex snorts indignantly, "I'm struggling to see the fun in all this. All that boring studying to be a doctor and you won't at least get the prescription pad to go with it?" he complains.

I bark out a laugh as I turn to see his pitying look.

"I think the stuff I learn is fun. I enjoy exploring what makes us tick," I explain a little defensively then turn back, resolved to shut him out.

"Wow... you are super smart. Wait. So you would be able to do like, Breaking Bad stuff in a lab if you wanted because I could totally be the Jesse to your hot chick version of Heisenberg," Alex asks excitedly, and I laugh out loud at his ridiculousness.

"That's illegal and lethal," I point out as I finally get a mental grasp on the words I want to put down on my paper.

"But you could if you really wanted to," Alex assumes which makes me giggle, but I refrain from commenting which he doesn't really need me to in order to continue his fantasy anyway. "Seriously, we could make millions. I know people through the club who could sell it for us. I bet we could even get Dec out of trouble with the Blood Brothers if we make a deal to supply..." Alex rambles on until I can't take it anymore and turn to him with incredulity.

"I can't focus with all this noise you're making. It's not going to happen. You're no drug dealer, and Dec would kick your arse for even thinking about it. Now will you take a breath and shut up?" I snap, and Alex finally quiets, looking properly scolded, which has me biting my tongue so I don't laugh.

"Sorry, I'll stop. Right after this, I won't say another thing. Not a single—"

"Alex!" I yell through a laugh, throwing my pen at him, which has him retaliating with a handful of skittles as he grins sheepishly.

"Sorry. I think I've had too much sugar. I'll try to be good," Alex apologises then makes a gesture of locking his lips.

I retrieve a skittle that managed to get down my shirt and lodge itself in my bra, looking up when Alex whimpers.

He presses his fisted hand to his mouth while watching me like he's trying to hold back his smartarse commentary.

I roll my eyes before throwing the lemon skittle at him which he catches, popping it into his mouth with a wink.

I get back to my paper with a shake of my head, and Alex remains silent, resuming watching his movie.

Too bad I barely put a dent in the word count before his phone rings. After a short, mostly one-sided conversation that I block out determinedly, Alex bolts out of his seat with a curse, gathering his shirt, wallet, and keys. This gets my attention just before he turns my way, looking worried.

"We have to go get Dec from the cop shop."

I immediately shut my laptop without bothering to save my work as I scramble to my feet, and we rush out the door.

Alex barely has his car in park, before I'm out and running for the stairs to the station. I grab the handles on the glass doors to push my way through before noticing the pull sign when they fail to move. I then yank them open.

I search the reception area anxiously until my gaze lands on Dec, slouched over in the corner on the small row of seats, his hands hanging between his knees and his chin against his chest. He looks up when I rush towards him and opens up immediately for me to curl into his lap with my arms wrapped around his shoulders as he squeezes me against him. Dec hears when my breath hitches as I bury my face into the side of his neck, and he gentles his hold to run a hand over my hair, trying to soothe me.

"Hey, I'm okay, sweetheart. Let's get out of here before they try to pin me for loitering," Dec tries to joke, but it sounds forced, then he stands with me still wrapped around him.

I release him when my feet touch the ground and then gasp when I get a look at his face.

"Will it help if I tell you the other guys look much worse?" Dec forces a grin, hissing when it tugs on his split lip.

He also has a bruise forming on his cheek that will match mine in few hours and a nasty looking bump on his forehead.

"Guys, plural?" I ask incredulously, tenderly gliding my fingers over his cheek before he captures my hand in his, drawing it down between us.

"It's okay. They had a medic look me over," Dec assures while rubbing my back, interrupted by Alex walking over to slap his shoulder.

"Whoa, dude. Looks like someone made you his bitch," Alex jokes.

I turn at the sound of a loud group of officers approaching from down the hall behind the front desk, meeting the surprised gaze of a familiar face. I smile politely at Senior Sergeant Kevin Lange. One of Dad's good friends.

He pauses, raising his brow questioningly as he looks at the guys joking amicably beside me. One of the officers calls his name from the side door they are exiting through, and Kevin gives me a disapproving look before following the others.

"Let's get out of here," Dec murmurs in my ear as he squeezes his arm around my shoulders to gain my attention. I nod my acceptance before Alex leads us out.

Alex drives us to collect the Pontiac. Dec holds me tight against him in the backseat while giving us a quick, and I'm sure edited, recount of what went down at the compound with the unfortunately timed raid and how he got so banged up.

Despite his insisting I stay in the jeep, I jump out to ride with him when we get to his car that's parked in a creepy vacant lot. I'm worried about him driving, though he promises he's fine, and Alex announces he'll follow us back to be sure we all get there safely.

When we get back to Alex's home, Dec leads me with his arm around my shoulders to sit on the couch, then leans down slowly to kiss my forehead.

"I'll be back. I need a shower," he murmurs then straightens stiffly before walking back down the hallway.

I don't know why, but I get a pang of unease in the pit of my stomach at the action. Usually, he'd ask if I wanted to join or just take me with him so I'm left feeling like he's trying to shut me out. I shake the thought out of my mind before it can really take hold. The poor guy took a beating and feels like crap no doubt. It has nothing to do with me.

I drag my laptop over from its spot across the coffee table to see if I can get a little more of my paper done.

Two hours later, Dec still hasn't returned, and I accept defeat because I'm struggling to focus and keep my eyes open. I save the document then shut the laptop with a sigh because I'm barely halfway through.

"I'm going to bed," I announce to Alex as I lean over to gather my mess of papers and books before standing with the armload.

"You want some company until Dec comes out, I'm a fantastic snuggle buddy?" Alex wags his brows with a grin, making me snort as I kick his denim-clad knee so his feet come unhooked, and his leg falls from where it's propped up on the coffee table.

"Goodnight, Alex," I say dryly. Stepping over his remaining leg stretched out to the table as he chuckles.

"Sweet dreams, Aela," he replies suggestively, running his hand down his abs like he thinks I'll dream of him.

I laugh as I turn away and head down the hallway. I open the door to the guestroom Alex put me in and hit the light switch to find Dec sprawled out on his back on the bed with an arm flung over his eyes, in only a loose pair of sweatpants that sit deliciously low on his hips. I think he's asleep, so I try to be quiet as I walk in, put my stuff down and change into some sleepwear. Then Dec moves his arm at his side to hold out in a gesture for me to go to him.

"You okay?" I ask quietly, gingerly sitting beside him after turning the light off. He silently pulls me to his side until my head is resting against his chest and our bodies are pressed together.

"I'd do anything for you, you know," Dec murmurs after a silent moment but doesn't reply to my question.

I lean up to press a kiss to his jaw, hoping he'll lift his head so I can get a proper kiss, but he remains still, his arm over his eyes. I frown as I run my hand down the silky, warm, unyielding flesh of his torso.

"I know. Just like I'd do anything for you," I reply, my breath a little shaky because he's acting so off, and it's making me nervous.

Finally, he lowers his arm to smooth his hand over my hair and lifts his head off the pillow to meet my gaze. His eyes look sad in the light of the moon peeking through the cracks in the blinds.

"What's wrong?" I croak. Then he leans down to press his lips to mine, softly and sweetly, as his hands cling to me somewhat desperately. I slide my tongue into his mouth to meet his, and Dec emits a groan, clutching me tighter.

One hand grips my hair as the other holds tightly to my arse which he uses to drag me up his body until I'm covering him. He

251

then delves deeper into my mouth, not caring about his split lip as his mouth presses hard against mine.

We're both panting for breath when Dec pulls back to sink into the pillow. I lean down to tenderly kiss his chin and then his swollen lips before we struggle to get under the blankets where I snuggle into him again once we're comfy.

Dec curls his left arm that's cushioning my head to stroke lazily up and down my back as the other rests on my hip. I sigh happily as I drift off to sleep.

I wake to my alarm blasting from where I left it in my bag across the room and stumble over to turn it off quickly before checking to see if I woke Dec, but he looks like he's been awake for a while if he even slept at all. He doesn't move. Just continues to stare at the ceiling with his head propped up by his right arm tucked beneath it.

He looks rough and pale, his left eye is blackened and swollen, and the right has a purple shadow. The cut in his lip looks sore and scabby, and he has a bruise on his jaw also.

"Morning." My voice comes out scratchy from sleep, so I clear it as I sit in my warm spot on the bed, smiling at him as I stretch my back and arms.

I wait a moment for a reply then move so I'm straddling his waist, leaning in to take up his view and gain his attention, but his eyes shift to the side, avoiding mine.

"I have time to make it a good morning," I murmur playfully, ignoring aches and pains and the fact that we're both battered and bruised, because he looks miserable, and I want to make him feel good. I run my hands down his chest, leaning up on my knees to continue the trail to his crotch, but before I pass his navel, Dec moves, depositing me on my butt on the mattress as he scrambles off the bed.

"We have to get back to the shop. I have to feed Tom, and you'll need your car to get to school or whatever," Dec insists while tugging a shirt down over his head.

"Okay," I choose not to comment on his weird mood but frown as I get up and prepare to leave.

"I'll go warm the car up," Dec explains, taking one of my bags I've finished packing on his way out.

I change into another sweater and tights, brush my hair and teeth then make sure I have everything before heading out, hearing Alex's loud snoring on my way.

Dec is sitting in the idling car, messing with his phone as *Asking Alexandria* blares from the speakers. I open my door, hauling my bag over the seat before sliding in and buckling up. Dec pulls out without so much as a glance my way and the air in the car feels thick with tension and silence even with the loud music the entire ride.

Both our phones start ringing almost simultaneously as Dec pulls up beside my car in front of the shop, killing the ignition. I barely register my dad's name flashing on my screen before I hit answer, muttering a greeting as I watch Dec answer his call.

"Mouse, we want to have a family dinner tonight. We will even wait until you're free if you are busy. We haven't seen you in too long." My dad greets me with his pet name for me with an attempted stern tone, and I smile as I watch Dec pinch his nose as though he's trying to ward off a headache as he listens to whoever is on the line.

"Sure, Dad. I finish work at six and will head right over." I accept easily because it's best to just appease them if I can, and really, I've kinda missed home these past few days.

"Mum, I'm not sure it's a good idea right now. There's a lot going on. No... Okay, yes. Bring her around, and I'll sort something out," Dec grumbles, which distracts me from whatever Dad says next.

Dec throws his phone onto the dash with a soft curse and then rests his head against the steering wheel.

"Yeah, uh… Dad, I have to go right now. See you tonight." I hang up then reach over to rub Dec's back. "What's wrong?" I doubt he'll answer me because he hasn't answered any other time I've asked, but I try anyway.

"Hope is sick. Mum's bringing her over so she can go to work because they're short-staffed," he grumbles after a moment, and I fail to see how it's so bad.

"I can watch her upstairs while I work on my paper before my class at two?" I offer, then Dec throws his door open with another curse as he gets out to start pacing while gripping his hair.

I watch him curiously as I climb out of the car, moving to stand by the driver's door before he finally turns to face me, still avoiding my eyes.

"You should go to The Coffee House where you're safe. I'll deal with Hope. I sorted a few things out while I couldn't sleep so you'll be protected," Dec suggests, and I look at him with disbelief.

"With everything that happened yesterday, I think it would be best if you're not around me so much. I lost my head last night, and if they're looking to retaliate, I pretty much put a bright red bullseye on you for the best way to hurt me. I couldn't live with myself if you get hurt again because of my shit," Dec's eyes finally meet mine through his rambling explanation and the mixture of fear, sadness, and determination in his eyes makes my heart stutter.

"Wait. Is this you breaking up with me?" I ask, my voice going pitchy at the end with incredulity, and Dec looks away again.

"You're better off without me," he states stubbornly then clenches his jaw.

I speechlessly watch him fidget as a biting cold forms in my chest, slowly spreading through my body while my mind is a whirlwind of different emotions and words I want to say but can't.

The sounds of an approaching car distracts me, and I turn to see Nicola pulling up in her silver Yaris.

"Hey, kids. I'm so sorry for this," she says as she climbs out, leaving the car idling while she runs around to the passenger side. She extracts a drowsy Hope, who is wrapped in a purple and pink blanket, from the passenger seat and then juggles her to grab a backpack from the floor space.

Dec rushes to unlock the door to the shop, instructing Nicola to lay Hope out on the leather sofa just inside. He drops a quick kiss to Hope's forehead as they pass him before looking back to where I stand awkwardly on the footpath.

"You're busy, and I don't want to argue with you right now, but can you call me later when you have a chance?" I ask quietly, silently willing the pressure of tears building behind my eyes to go away because this is stupid, and I will not cry.

He stands there watching me for a moment with sad eyes before Nicola calls out to him, which breaks him from whatever it was. He takes a step back with a nod to me before turning and rushing into the shop like his arse is on fire. Or he just can't get away from me fast enough. I turn and get in my car although it's the last thing I want to do. I start it up and shift into reverse then look back up to the shop, unable to stop myself, just as Nicola exits with a concerned look my way. I wave, forcing a smile then reverse before she chooses to come over. I decide to do as Dec suggested and head to The Coffee House.

Even though I don't want to be around people, I'm still not ready to go back to my place alone. I use the parking closer to the café even though I have to pay there. I then do my best to cover the damage on my face in the rearview mirror using makeup Kara packed me so I don't draw attention.

I use the employee back door because I can't be bothered to

walk the long way and figure Mal won't mind. Sure enough, as soon as he sees me, Mal charges over to wrap me in a bear hug that lifts me off my feet, leaving me awkwardly patting his back since he has me trapped around my elbows.

"You okay, babe?" Mal murmurs against my head before putting me back on my feet to search my face and winces.

"Thanks. Why don't you just tell me I look like shit?" I complain half-jokingly. He leans in to smack a kiss on my head before releasing me.

"You're just a little banged up. I'm sure any guy in here would still try to pick you up if they thought they had a chance," Mal states, and I give him my best cynical expression.

"Right. You mind if I make myself at home to get some stuff done until my classes?" I ask, and he gestures for me to go ahead before getting back to work.

I take the back corner table and set myself up with my laptop to knock out my paper, but I can't even focus enough to begin, which just pisses me off. I've never let a guy interfere with my studies. Plus, now that everything's had a chance to sink in, I'm ready to kick Declan in the shin for trying to break up with me like that. Breaking up with me to protect me? Seriously? When he is where I feel most safe? What a dick move. I get that he's freaked out by his troubles escalating, though, which is the only thing stopping me from confronting him.

"Whoa. Who are you plotting to kill?" Mal interrupts my thoughts, leaning over my table to place a toasted Turkish bread sandwich and my usual frappe beside me. I give him a questioning look because I didn't order anything.

"I just spoke to Dec, and he said you didn't get a chance to eat this morning," Mal explains.

I roll my eyes. "Did he also tell you he broke up with me? So he doesn't need to be checking up on me," I grumble but gratefully take the food.

Mal looks at me incredulously for a moment before shaking his head. "You two hurt my head. Holler if you need anything or when you're ready to leave 'cos I'm walking you to class. You can't be walking out there alone right now."

Mal walks away and despite myself, his confusion has me smiling as I pick at my sandwich then push myself to focus on my essay.

***

At seven that night, I grudgingly force myself up the three stairs to my parents' white-bricked, two-storey home. Though after the day I've had, I don't think I have the patience to put up with them. All I want is a bath, bed, and a tub of Ben and Jerry's cookie dough ice cream.

I pause at the front door to mentally gather myself, take a deep breath, and uselessly attempt to straighten out my oversized sweater, knowing Mum is going to hate it, but I'm too comfortable to feel a need to change.

"Hello…" I call out as I enter the all-white foyer, leaving my shoes tucked under the little glass table on the polished marble floor.

"In the dining room, Mouse," Dad calls, so I head straight down the hall to the kitchen then turn to the room on the left. My parents and brother are already seated and sipping on drinks, all looking perfectly presentable with the guys in crisp business shirts and Mum in a black boat-necked, fitted dress, her dark hair that matches mine, swept up into a sleek updo, which has me feeling like garbage.

Their greeting smiles drop almost instantaneously when they get a look at me, and Mum rushes over with a horrified gasp, placing her hands on my shoulders as she inspects me closer. I cringe when I realise it's because of my black eye that no amount of makeup can disguise.

"What in the world happened to you?" I wince at her shriek as her hands move to my cheeks so I cover them with mine.

"I'm okay. It was just an accident and isn't as bad as it looks." I try to reassure them all as Dad stands from his seat while Nate clenches his fists on the table with an irritated shake of his head.

My brother speaks next. "It's a black eye, Aela. You don't get them by accident unless you play sports, and we all know you stay away from them because you're bloody clumsy. If that criminal you're seeing has anything to do with this, I'll kill him."

My mouth drops in shock at Nate's words while Mum steps back looking aghast, clutching the gold heart-shaped locket with our photos in that hangs around her neck, which she's worn every day since we gave it to her for Mother's Day when I was twelve.

"What... how do you— Criminal?" I look between the three of them, hoping someone can fill me in on what I'm missing as Nate shoves his chair back to stand with fierce eyes.

"Kevin called me today asking if you were okay. When I asked why, he told me he'd seen you down at Southport station last night, looking beaten and were huddled up to a tattooed punk they'd arrested during a bikie-gang raid. Said he'd wanted to approach to make sure you were okay, but you smiled at him, and he was running late so he let it go, intending to check on you at home today, but he turned up to find another punk answering your door shirtless who tells him you're not home then slams the door. Care to explain?" Dad gives me his best disappointed look that never fails to make me feel nauseous. I silently curse myself for forgetting about Kevin. I should have known.

"First, Declan is a tattoo artist and a great person, not a bikie. He was just in the wrong place at the wrong time. My bruising is not from him. He would never do that, but I don't want to talk about the accident, and lastly, I won't be seeing him anymore since we broke up so it's a non-issue. Now, let's calm down and sit to have dinner without any badgering. Because I don't know about you lot, but I've had a long day, and I'm hungry," I state commandingly, leaving the two men wide-eyed because I've never been confident enough to stand up to them when they get going like this, except for when I pushed to move out. Even then, I was more pleading than demanding.

I hold my shoulders back and bite off a grin, rather proud of myself and hope this new me sticks around. I swear I catch a little grin from my mother before she turns to the kitchen compliantly.

Dad returns to his seat while needlessly smoothing his perfectly groomed salt and pepper hair while I ignore Nate's hovering over me, moving to the side bar to pour myself a nip of vodka over ice before returning to take my seat, designated by the only empty place setting.

"Since when do you drink?" Nate demands, grudgingly taking his seat across from me, and I give him a mocking grin.

"Since I've embraced the party life of a uni student," I retort, and then take a sip while I challengingly meet his glare until I place the glass down and Dad chuckles.

"Okay, you two. Enough or I'll have your mother pull out your old 'getting along' shirt. I'm pretty sure it'd be a tight squeeze but don't think I won't force you both into it," Dad threatens which has me grinning at the memories of that tattered shirt of his we used to be put in when we were younger and arguing. It never got us to stop, but we did learn to be quieter about it.

Mum comes back, expertly carrying all four plates as she does, serving them to each of us with a kiss to our heads, before taking the seat between Dad and me as we praise her for the roast chicken and vegetables that have my mouth watering at just its sight and smell.

After dinner, Mum brings out her popular cherry ripe slice for dessert, which I force my full stomach to accept because I can never turn it own.

She then talks Nate and myself into having coffee before we leave, and I joke she's trying to keep us there by fattening us up so much, we won't fit out the door.

At midnight, I have to force myself to leave because I'm reluctant to go home alone even though I know Kara is there. I had almost convinced myself it was a good idea when Mum suggested I stay the night in my old room, but I mentally kicked myself for being a chicken and declined before following Nate out the door.

I sing along to my radio that's turned up loud on the ride home in an attempt to ignore my irrational nerves, but I search every dark corner of our parking garage when I pull in.

I sit there once the engine is off, inspecting the silence for anything suspicious before warily getting out and briskly walking to the elevator, all my senses on high alert. I breathe a sigh of relief, and then shake my head at myself for being so edgy, once I'm safely inside the apartment, leaning against the locked door.

I drop my keys into the bowl and my bag on the lounge as I kick off my shoes and hear a door down the hall open. Kara bursts around the corner, and I'm wrapped in her arms before I can take two steps.

"Thank God you're okay. I was so worried. Alex filled me in on what happened when he met me here today to check everything was safe. I'm so sorry, Aela."

She's wrapped around me so hard I can barely breathe, but I return her hug until she pulls away to get a good look at me.

I wipe away the tear that spills from the well in her left eye, and she laughs self-deprecatingly.

"I'm supposed to be comforting you, not the other way around, damn it. How are you not crying?" Kara complains, before swiping at her own eyes impatiently.

"I think I did more than my fair share of ugly crying yesterday. My tear ducts probably need time to refill." I shrug like it's no big deal but, really, I'm just determined to not cry anymore. I hate crying in front of people. It makes me feel so weak and grates on me that I did it so much yesterday.

The hard stare and raised brow Kara gives me says she sees right through me. Thankfully, she decides to drop it and drags me to sit on the lounge, ordering me to 'stay' like an obedient pup, before disappearing down the hall, returning to march into the kitchen with her doona bunched up under one arm. I watch curiously though I can't really see her, but I can hear rifling in the cutlery drawer and then the fridge door slamming. She then makes her way back with two spoons and a tub of Ben and Jerry's.

Kara plops down beside me, drags the coffee table over to put her feet up, throwing the blanket over us and then turns on the television.

Kara selects the first season of New Girl that she recorded because we love that show before silently handing me a spoon.

I take it then wiggle around to get comfy. We watch the first three episodes before I'm out like a light with a belly full of ice cream that, while yummy, failed to ease the ache in my chest because Dec never calls or even texts like he agreed to do.

Chapter 26

DECLAN

QUITTING AELA COLD turkey is a million times harder than when I did it with smoking. I'm apparently just as hard to be around for the others, but I don't give a shit. I've been irritable and moody for two weeks, which worsened each day since I pushed Aela away.

I smashed my phone that first night. I threw it into the brick wall after staring at it for over three hours, fighting with myself over contacting her. I knew it was the best thing for her.

The night we stayed at Alex's, I thought about it long and hard as I stayed awake with her held tight in my arms. I wanted to attach her permanently to my side to keep her safe because I need her, but I love her enough to let her go after facing the fact that she won't be safe as long as she's around me.

I still don't know what's going to happen after what went down at the compound. I'm strung out, waiting for retaliation. I know most of the club has made bail, but it's been eerily quiet from them. Even Buzz has been too busy to return my calls.

I don't want Aela in their line of fire. Being in my life has done enough damage to her, and I can't stand the thought of her being hurt anymore because of me. I want her happy and focused on the degree she's worked so hard for.

I know breaking up likely hurt her, but she'll be able to heal and move on, unlike a bullet to the head or anything else the MC could do, which constantly invades my thoughts, giving me new nightmares that tear me from the little sleep I manage to get and running for the toilet to hurl.

For the last week, I've avoided the front of the shop, hiding in my room or upstairs. I can't stand the worried looks from everyone because I haven't been looking after myself, or Kit's heated glares as she calls me a different derogatory name each day, getting more inventive as she goes. Today, I'm "Sir Arsehole-a-lot." That's kind of weak for what she's been dishing out but gets her point across, nonetheless.

I drag my sorry arse into the backroom for a coffee refill and barely startle when the door slams open not a minute later. I look over my shoulder to see Kit in the doorway, glaring with her hands on her hips, reminding me of a pissed off Tinker Bell. It almost gets a ghost of a smile out of me.

"Enough of the god-damn zombie bullshit, Declan. I may not like you much right now, but we all love you and will not sit back and watch you waste away anymore. Go have a shower, shave off that hobo scruff growing on your face and find some clean clothes because you're taking me to The Vault for lunch. You will eat every bite of the largest steak they have."

I let her finish ranting then take a sip of coffee before commenting, "You haven't used my actual name for weeks. I was starting to think you forgot it and forgot that I was your boss who could fire you for the shit you were pulling."

Kit shrugs with her hands still propped on her hips as she looks to the ground before coming back to me.

"Yeah, well... you're still an arsehole. But it takes the fun out of thinking up names for you when you just take it like a bitch," Kit retorts huffily, gesturing for me to head upstairs as ordered.

"I have an appointment at one," I point out, and Kit shakes

her head.

"No, I rescheduled it. You need more than coffee in your stomach before you pass out over a client, and we get hit with a lawsuit. When was the last time you ate an actual meal?"

I struggle to recall my last proper meal that wasn't toast because I've had no interest in food and have to fight to get it down when I do try to eat.

"Exactly. Now get going. You have twenty minutes then I'm coming up there, and you won't like it if you're still like this," Kit warns in her best menacing act—which gets a lift of the corner of my mouth. I move to hug her, but she holds her hands out while taking a step back. "Not until after you shower. Seriously, you even smell homeless."

I give in and climb the stairs because I really don't have the energy to fight with her. Honestly, the climb is exhausting enough, which is a wake-up call.   Kit is right. I can't keep punishing myself because of my actions. I have people who rely on me and stuff going on I need to be alert for. I need to get my shit together. I feel like a blindfold has been removed when I enter my apartment, cringing in shame as I take in the mess.

There are holes in the far wall, and the lamps are broken. Empty bottles and cans, sketch pads, papers and dirty clothes litter the place. I head to my bathroom and wince at my pale, drawn reflection in the mirror over the sink. I turn the shower on and strip off my clothes, noticing my jeans hang looser than normal from my hips as they slide off effortlessly while still done up. I step into the shower, not bothered to fuss over the temperature and scrub from head to toe.

Images from the last time I was in here with Aela assault my mind. I have to squeeze my eyes shut and grit my teeth against the ache exploding in my chest as I fight to shut out the memories.

I stumble out still covered in suds and roughly dry off with the cleanest dirty towel available before taking my electric shaver to my 'hobo beard' because I can't be bothered with a proper shave.

All the drawers in my room are bare of clean clothes, but I find some in the dryer to wear and belt up the jeans to keep them from sliding down because while I look like a delinquent with my tats and piercings, I refuse to ever have my jeans hanging under my arse.

There's a line I'll never cross.

I hear Kit enter the apartment just as I finish brushing my teeth, so I walk out for her to judge.

Her perusal starts at my feet, and she's frowning when she gets to my face, "Better. But you could do with some concealer under those bruised eyes of yours."

I shake my head as I hunt down a pair of shades.

"You keep your makeup away from me, woman. My sunnies will do fine. This is as good as you're going to get out of me today," I tell her and she grins as I slide on my black Vans.

"I'll take it. Let's go," Kit concedes while I shove my wallet in my back pocket and automatically look for my phone before recalling it was broken. I make my way to where she waits by the door. Kit gives me a quick squeeze around my waist then bounces down the stairs before me.

Josie is manning the front desk, swivelling back and forth in the chair, dressed in her usual hippy attire of a long multi-patterned skirt and plain singlet with a scarf containing her long, russet coloured dreadlocks.

She smiles as we pass, heading for the door.

"Looking good, boss man."

She gives Kit two thumbs up, the stacks of bangles on her arms jingling as they slide on her arms. "Guess we can hold off the intervention for now." She giggles and I quirk a brow over my shades at Kit who ignores it as she calls out 'we'll be back' while stepping out into the perfectly sunny day.

My eyes hurt from the first glimpse of sun they've had in weeks, but I revel in the warmth on my skin as we head to the restaurant down the road.

I slide into the red leather bench against the wall of the elegant establishment with a nineteen twenties gangster vibe, with the charcoal, red and white colour scheme and fancy chandelier lighting.

Kit orders two steak meals for us, making mine a double and gets herself a pink lemonade and orange juice for me, deliberately ignoring my Jack and coke request.

My eyes get caught on the glass beading reflecting the light in the fixture above us as I feel Kit's gaze on me.

"I got the replacement for your phone. No throwing this one or you can deal with the paperwork."

Kit pulls the box from her bag, sliding it over the table where I let it sit as I lower my head to look at her.

"Thanks but you didn't have to. I can clean up my own messes," I tell her, and she shrugs.

"Oh, I know. Your disaster zone of an apartment is all yours to fix, but we need a way to contact you so I handled it."

Our meals are placed in front of us, and I look pleadingly to Kit over the excessively sized slab of meat before me, but she gestures with her knife for me to get started. It looks and smells delicious, though, so I don't need much prompting to dig in, and my taste buds rejoice, causing me to groan indulgently at my first mouthful.

Before I know it, my plate is scraped clean, and I'm leaning back with an overly stuffed stomach as Kit finishes her meal with a pleased grin.

"You want dessert too?" she asks with amusement, but I shake my head, groaning because my stomach is protesting the large amount of food after being deprived for so long.

"I warned you to slow down, or you would be sick, but you never listen. You really should've learned by now that I'm always right, and you should listen to my wise awesomeness," she emphasises, scrunching her nose when I burp rather loudly, my caveman manners showing their appreciation while my normal manners are still high on the onion and bacon gravy.

I sigh happily when it lessens the pain in my belly.

"Come on. We'll walk this off, and you can tell me what's going on with you," Kit suggests while sliding out of her side of the booth.

"I just have the flu. You'll probably catch it now too, which is why I was avoiding you all," I offer in a useless attempt to evade the feelings talk as I go to the counter to pay for our food where Kit pulls a face that says she knows I'm full of shit.

"It's not contagious. It's just heartbreak. The only cure I know is friends, time, and maybe rebound sex. But I don't want you to do that last thing because I want you two back together, so I suggest you talk it out with me. I think I know why you did it, but I want to hear it anyway so I can smack you in the head." Kit says her piece and then quietly waits for me to talk as she leads us to the parklands instead of Ink Fix.

I make her wait until we're stretched out on one of the double sized sunbeds in the park before I explain myself, both the reason I pushed Aela away and how I feel like a shell of a person, filled with only darkness and pain without her, almost similar to when Grace died, only without the anger.

When I'm done, I wait expectantly for Kit to hit me or say something, but after several moments of silence, I turn my head to find her sitting with her legs crossed as she wipes under her eyes.

I questioningly raise my brows, which has her forcing out a harsh laugh and smacking my chest as another tear slides down her cheek.

"Shut up. That was beautifully sad," Kit retorts before scrambling over to cuddle my side. "You know, Aela's not doing too well with this, either. You both look like hell and so damn sad it hurts, only she's trying to conceal it by keeping busy. Kara is really worried."

I rub my chest to try to ease the stabbing pain her words cause but refuse to dwell on it. I get up off the bench and say, "Enough talking. Let's get back. I have a home to restore, and it wouldn't hurt for you to do some work since you're on the clock."

Kit doesn't call me out on being evasive, but she does give me a knowing look as she slides off the bench.

"All right, Mr Man, but I'm still not helping you up there," Kit complies, linking her arm with mine as we head back.

At around nine that night, I've cleaned most of the apartment spotless and am transferring the second load of clothes from the washer to the dryer when there's loud, urgent banging on the door, and I hear Kit yelling for me.

I step out into the hallway just as she realises it's not locked and barges in with wide, frantic eyes.

"What's going on?" I listen expectantly for any sound of trouble in the shop but don't hear anything as Kit rushes my way, grabs my hand and then tugs me to the stairs.

"Kara just called. We have to go to the hospital. Aela's been attacked again."

My stomach drops, my knees give out, and I fall to the floor while my world comes crashing down around me as my nightmares become reality.

Alex appears in the doorway his eyes filled with sorrow as they meet mine, and shakes his head knowingly at what he sees there.

"No, man. Don't go there. She's alive, just badly beat up. Jesus, Kit. You can't just burst out with half the story," he yells the last part at Kit while pulling me to my feet. They then lead me to his jeep parked out in front of the shop.

My mind is going crazy as I sit silently in the seat beside Alex, my knee uncontrollably bouncing as I ignore Kit and Alex arguing over the back of his seat where she clings to the headrest from her seat behind him.

As soon as Alex slows in the parking lot, I jump out of the car, slamming my door against their protests as I run to the Emergency doors. I rush to the counter and am thankful there's no line as I peer through the safety glass to see a harried looking woman peer back at me expectantly, "I'm here to see Aela Montgomery. She was brought in by ambulance," I tell her. She turns to the computer to type in the name.

"Are you a relative?" she asks, peering over her small glasses at me while impatiently moving her blonde hair from her eyes.

"No, I'm her..." I stop because I was about to say boyfriend, but I can't claim that anymore. The receptionist watches me fumble with my words before sighing.

"Sorry, but due to her circumstances, we're only allowing immediate family to visit, apart from her boyfriend who rode in with her."

Boyfriend? I startle at the word and stumble back with fisted hands just as Kit rushes through the doors.

Chapter 27

AELA

I FINALLY CAVE and try to call Dec after two weeks of not hearing from him. I was tired of trying to act as if it wasn't a big deal.

I didn't want to be that clingy, annoying girl who couldn't take a hint, so I'm proud I made it two weeks. But I need to hear his voice and accept what is or isn't going on between us. I freak out about what to say, pacing the length of my bedroom for an hour. Before I realise what I'm doing, I get mad at myself and hit call.

I panic but stick to my guns until it goes straight to voicemail and I deflate. I listen to his message, relishing his deep, husky voice until it ends then I hang up. I sigh and get dressed for school though I really just want to climb back under the covers of my bed and never come back out.

I'm so tired. These past weeks, I've made it my mission to stay busy to keep my mind off Dec's dismissal. As a result, I've been lucky to get four hours of sleep a night which is taking a toll, and I'm getting sick of the concerned looks from Kara and Mal.

Once I'm ready to go, I make my way into the kitchen to microwave my oats and fill my travel mug with coffee.

"Good morning," I call out when I hear Kara's door open

and bare feet slapping against the tiles as she makes her way to the kitchen. I finish filling my cup then pour one for her as she takes a seat at the bar.

"What time did you get in last night?" Kara asks through a yawn then smiles appreciatively when I pass her a coffee.

"Around two. I had to stop by to feed the lab mice after work." I shrug then stuff my face with oats even though they are still too hot.

Kara gives me a look I've become too accustomed to these days as I shovel the last spoonful in my mouth. I dump my dishes in the sink since it's my turn to do them tonight anyway.

"Don't. It's too early for that look, Kara. I'll see you later." I lean over to kiss her cheek as I grab my coffee, scoop my bag up by the handle, and then rush out the door as she protests, calling for me to stop.

I'm early to campus as I have been lately, so I can get a ground floor spot in the so-called secure parking lot, and then warily walk the long way out to avoid the stairwell exit. I also walk through as many building as I can, instead of the quiet pathways, getting to my building just before my first class starts.

When I'm done with my three classes of the day, I make my way to The Coffee House to meet with the study group I joined last week, and we go over the latest physics work that I've already got a handle on, so I spend the hour assisting the others with help from Mal who stops by in between customers.

Once our time is up, I remain at the table for a couple of hours so I can get a head start on my Evolutionary Biology paper even though it isn't due for a week before starting my shift.

We're kept busy courtesy of the trivia night being held in the library next door, and before I know it, Sara taps me on the shoulder to let me know she's here to take over for me, and I sigh in relief.

"Johnny's still not here to cover for me yet, but I'll take my break to walk you to your car," Mal calls out as I grab my stuff, and I wave him off though I know he won't accept it.

"We're too busy, and I'm still parked across campus. I'll call Tim to drive me in his security kart," I argue, but Mal shakes his head, throwing his towel down on the bench.

"Tim will take his time getting here as usual, and you'll get fed up waiting and slip out on your own. Not happening on my watch, so let's go," Mal demands, taking my heavy bag from me to effortlessly swing it over one shoulder to carry before nudging me out the door.

"I would have waited," I protest, but Mal just ignores it because he knows he's right. I would have waited maybe fifteen minutes then snuck out.

"You ready for exams in ten days?" Mal asks as he keeps an alert eye on our surroundings, which I try to ignore so I don't get creeped out while I shrug my reply.

"As ready as I can be," I add and he nods as he pulls me to his side. We dodge a group of rowdy students loitering by the Arts block. We get to my car without incident then Mal stands guard as I unlock my door, shoving my bags over to the passenger seat floor space, and drop into my seat.

"You want a ride back?" I stick my head out my open door to offer as I start the engine, but Mal shakes his head as he gently pushes my door closed then slaps the roof of my car for me to get going. So I do, waving as I back out while Mal remains there until I drive around the corner, out of sight.

My steering feels off as I pull out onto the main road, but I don't think much of it until a few minutes later when I feel and hear a weird thumping coming from the car, so I pull over to the side of the road as soon as I safely can. I pause before getting out, taking in my surroundings uncertainly because where I've stopped is beside a large grassy ditch that borders a small bit of bushland, and this stretch of the main road is barely lit.

I shake off my reservations because, while it's creepy, this is a main road with near constant traffic so I should be fine. I step out and walk around the front of my car to the grassy side then to the back of my car where I see I've got a flat tyre. *Great.*

Good thing my dad taught me how to change tyres along with a few other things before I was allowed to drive alone at seventeen. I pop the trunk and start shifting the junk in there to get to the spare and then haul out its awkwardly heavy weight. I collect the jack and lug wrench also before kneeling down to set the jack up under the car, which is difficult to get right in the dark. I get back up to check if I have a torch in the back when an approaching car slows, switching lanes to park a few metres behind me. I shield my eyes from what feels like their high beams, as the driver gets out. I smile thankfully as they make their way over, obviously intending to help.

"Thanks for stopping, but I just need more light. If you could pull up closer that would really help a lot." I don't want to sound ungrateful, but I get nervous when I'm able to make out the male form approaching and would feel better if they didn't get too close considering where we are. Stupid maybe, because he could no doubt get it done faster than I can but his presence is making me anxious.

"Too bad I'm not here to help," he answers when he's closer. Chills slither down my back as I recognise the voice a second before his face clears the harsh light of his headlights. I take a step back away from him.

"Oh, God. No," I barely get the whisper out as my mind fails to decide how to get away from him fast enough before Snake rushes me and we go tumbling down the ditch—away from anything I could have used to protect myself and out of view of the road.

"I'm not, God. But I'll have you on your knees before me soon enough," Snake growls when our fall comes to a stop at the bottom with him on top, pinning me to the ground as I gasp to catch the breath that was knocked out of me.

I start to struggle and manage to dislodge him from his sitting position on my hips when I roll to the side. I immediately try to scramble away, but he grabs a handful of my hair and pulls back harshly until he manages to get a hold of my left arm, yanking it back so ferociously, I hear a horrible cracking sound and feel a searing pain in my shoulder as it dislocates. I scream out, before he forces my face into the muddy grass.

"I'm not playing this time, bitch. The more you fight, the worse it's going to be for you. I don't mind tearing you apart, so if you want to live, I suggest you stop," Snake snarls in my ear then flips me over onto my back before pinning me with his knees centred on my ribcage. He leans all his body weight into me as he secures my wrists in one hand then moves to undo my pants with his free hand.

If he thinks I'm going to make this easy for him, he has another thing coming.

I don't care what he does, I will not stop fighting.

I try to buck him off, and he leans back to slap me in the face so hard I see stars, but I buck again, and he loses his balance from putting so much force into the slap. I sit up and jump to my feet instantly, but Snake grabs my injured arm, jerking me back down. I land so hard I almost pass out from the pain that radiates up my arm when I land wrong on it, and I'm sure it's now broken too.

The pain makes me pause long enough for Snake to bounce to his feet. He begins kicking me, repeatedly, landing hard blows to my ribs and stomach with his boots as he shouts in frustration.

He stops and pushes me out of the foetal position I took and then leans down to rip the front of my shirt away, panting heavily in exertion and anger. The pain radiating all over my body is so excruciating, I have to fight to keep my eyes open and to stay conscious as Snake presses his body over mine to pin me.

He fumbles one handed with my zipper before shoving his hand beneath my underwear to roughly force a finger inside of me, groaning happily as I cry out in pain.

I try to kick and buck, but it fails to budge his hold on me this time. I'm gasping for breath. The threat of passing out is real as I try to force my brain to come up with something. Then, suddenly, his weight is thrown off me, and I scramble back with a whimper. I find Mal has Snake pinned to the ground with his forearm pressed against his throat while punching him in the face. Mal leaves Snake when he goes limp and approaches where I sit with my good arm wrapped around my legs, shivering in the cold grass, unable to move as my eyes flit between him and Snake's unmoving body.

"I've got you, baby girl," Mal murmurs, bending down to wrap me in his warm hoodie before lifting me effortlessly into his arms. He takes me up the steep grass to sit me in the backseat of his SUV. He calls triple zero to get an ambulance and the police on their way, continuously rubbing down my good shoulder the whole time to try to warm me.

But it's the shock and pain, not the cold that has me shivering.

I whimper and reach out to latch onto Malcolm's arm when he goes to walk away. I gasp because I've used both hands and the pain jolts me.

"I'm just going to make sure he can't get away before the police get here, Aela. I can't let him take off," Mal tries to reason with me, but I whimper again.

"Don't leave me," I plead and his eyes soften as he moves to cup my injured cheek.

"Here, hold this, and you'll be able to watch me the whole time." Mal passes me a large torch, and I keep the beam glued to his back as he returns to where Snake hasn't moved.

Mal lifts Snake's limp body over his shoulder fireman style and trudges back my way, seeming to take some pleasure in dumping Snake to the ground a couple feet in front of me before stepping over to block my sight of him.

"Arm or ribs?" Mal asks, gesturing to where I'm holding my injured arm to my chest and curled around it protectively.

"I think both," I say carefully, trying not to expand my lungs too much with my breathing so I don't make the pain in my left side worse.

"Anything else?" Mal asks. I notice he's flexing his hands, the knuckles of the right one are still dripping blood, and I ignore his question to nod to them.

"You're bleeding," I tell him then turn at the distraction of flashing lights to see an ambulance approaching.

"It's just a scratch," Mal assures me as the ambulance pulls up behind us, followed by a police car. The officers take Mal back towards their car to question him but stay within sight when I panic, and Mal demands to stay close. The paramedics split up so the guy is checking on Snake while the lady gently inspects my injuries as I list them to her.

Once the medic attending to Snake confirms he is just unconscious, he calls for an officer to come collect him before stepping over to help move me to the ambulance. I assure them I can walk. I call out for Mal as we get close, and he leaves the police instantly to be my side.

"I need you. Please," I whimper pathetically. I'm hanging on by a thread and having him there is the only thing keeping the blind panic at bay.

One of the officers tries to make him stay until the male medic yells commandingly over him, "For Christ's sake. Aela is in shock and needs to go to the hospital now, so how about you show some compassion and let her have the comfort of having her boyfriend close, since you will have to wait to get her statement at the hospital anyway."

I squeeze his hand in appreciation where it's gripped in my right hand as we continue shuffling to the back of the ambulance. He turns to wink good-naturedly at me.

"He's not my boyfriend, though," I clarify, and the medic chuckles as he carefully lifts me into his arms since I can't climb into the back.

"It gets the sympathy vote a little more, so don't tell anyone differently, and he'll have a better chance of being allowed to stick by your side," the medic murmurs quietly, lowering me to the stretcher.

He rifles through a bag on the shelf above me, producing a green inhaler I remember from when I broke my arm climbing in the backyard tree when I was twelve. The guy chuckles at my sigh of relief when I see it.

"I see you're familiar with these babies, so inhale it, and you'll feel better by the time I get you to the hospital," he jokes, handing it over when he finishes assembling it.

I manage a small smile of gratitude before I put it to my mouth, cover the diluter hole, and take as long of a draw as I can on the painkiller while Mal takes a side seat after the medic hops out.

"Our cars are going to be trashed left there. Sorry," I tell Mal with a wince once we're on our way. He shakes his head while focusing on his phone.

"It's all good. I've got a buddy collecting them who won't charge us for it and will even fix your slashed tyre," Mal replies and I smile.

"You're such a good friend. Thank you, Malcolm."

He shrugs before looking up at me with a teasing look. "That's what good boyfriend's do."

I giggle then frown as I continue inhaling on my tube.

"Slashed. He had it all planned. What an arse-muncher," I

complain and can hear the slur in my own voice this time. I don't care, thought. Mal chuckles as he puts his phone away to watch me.

"Feeling okay?" Mal sounds amused, and I nod with the tube still in my mouth because it's true. I feel light, airy, and carefree. The numbed pain is only in the far back of my mind now.

"These things are like magic wands. You want a suck on my wand and we can play wizards?" I ask as I offer him the green tube of goodness, but I'm not sure that's what I say when Malcolm doubles over in laughter. I ramble about Harry Potter being stoned though I can't keep track of my own words as my eyelids lower.

These things aren't meant to knock you out, but I fall asleep listening to Mal chuckle and chat to the medics before we even arrive at the hospital, which is only across the road from campus, for goodness sake.

Things are blurry after that as I fall in and out of consciousness. Until I wake up in a glaringly bright room bathed in daylight. In a hard, uncomfortable bed, wincing as I try to get comfortable while taking in what's clearly my small hospital room.

It's all generic white except for the three vases of flowers on the window sill and colourful form of Malcolm asleep hunched over in the chair beside me.

I have a drip in my right hand, a pink cast covering from my left knuckles to above my elbow that's propped in the air on a brace and it hurts my ribs if I take more than shallow breaths.

I turn back to look at Mal. I can't believe he stayed the whole night. I feel bad, not just for him but for his little girl who's probably missing him. I clear my throat to call to him, which kills my ribs, but the noise has him instantly jerking awake.

"Morning, baby girl. You feeling okay?" He asks, his voice

rough with sleep. I nod, though I feel like I've been hit by a truck.

"You didn't have to stay all night with me. What about your daughter?" I ask as he rubs his face in an attempt to wake up more.

"She's with my parents, and I didn't mind staying until you were okay with me leaving," Mal replies, getting up to stand beside my bed to take my hand, being careful of the drip as I tear up.

"I can't thank you enough for everything you did last night, Mal," I whisper. He smiles while offering me the opened water bottle from the table, which I gratefully take.

"You don't need to. You're like the little sister I never had, even though I've only known you a couple of years. I'm just glad I was there," Mal states. He then leans down to kiss my forehead.

I hear a throat clearing so I look to the door to see Alex giving Malcolm a hard stare as he straightens back up.

"Sorry to interrupt. Without actually being sorry," Alex strides in, placing a huge bouquet of white lilies and red roses beside me on my bed before leaning over to kiss where Mal just had, then finally looks at me and smiles.

"Hey, good looking," I sputter a laugh but stop with a wince when my ribs protest as I look at him doubtfully.

"You're crazy. Who do you think you're fooling. I'm pretty sure I look as bad as I feel, if not worse. What are you doing here? Not that I'm not grateful for the company and flowers," I ramble while Mal gathers his things and Alex commandeers his seat, dragging it closer to me.

"I'll leave you to it. Call if you need anything."

Mal taps my feet in farewell on his way out as I say goodbye and then turn to Alex expectantly.

"First, you will always be beautiful. Even with your primitive dried mud and grass hairstyle and beaten black and blue. Also, there's a group out there waiting to see you. We tried camping out in the lounge area overnight, but there's a bitchy nurse who hates me who made it clear we wouldn't see you until morning and threatened to get security, so we went home to sleep. I just now happened to get lucky and slip in before the nurse caught me. Admit it. You're happy to see me first."

I fight back the tears at his words and mentally curse myself to get a grip as I look away, touching the flowers to distract myself.

"They're beautiful. Thank you," I choke out, turning to see Alex shift in his seat looking awkward.

"Actually, they're from Dec. He asked me to pick them up and say they were from me. He couldn't... be here. He's really messed up over you," Alex murmurs. I huff sceptically as I push the flowers away, ignoring the pang of hurt in my chest. When Alex mentioned a group waiting to see me, I'd stupidly thought Declan was one of them. I have to focus on the ceiling to control the tears, taking a stuttering breath.

"I appreciate you coming, Alex, and I don't want to be rude. But I need to be alone right now," I tell him without being able to look his way.

Alex gets up, leaning over to press a kiss to my cheek as I bite my lip to fend off the tears welling in my eyes.

"He really does love you, Aela," Alex murmurs.

Alex then leaves just as the dam I fought to hold breaks and the tears spill. I curl into a foetal position in an attempt to control the pain of my ribs protesting at my sobbing and the searing pain in my chest.

"Cheeky devil that one. Mouse, how are you— Oh, sweetheart. Do you need more pain medication?" I hear my mother entering the room and attempt to hide my face, but she rushes around to envelop me in her typical perfume scent as she carefully rubs my back.

"Talk to me, sweetheart," Mum urges, smoothing back my hair like she always used to when I was sick or upset. The familiarity of it all works its magic, soothing me enough to allow me to be able to catch my breath after a while. I look up to meet her gaze, and she smiles, still continuing to pet me and her eyes turn knowing as they search mine.

"It's the guy, isn't it, the tattooist whose friends have camped out here?" she presumes, and I nod as Mum hands me a bunch of tissues.

"Tell me the story. I want to hear it all." She lowers the left railing on my bed and gets as comfortable as she can at my hip. I take a second to gather myself before telling her everything (excluding the sex) from the very beginning of my crush to now—about how talented Dec is with his other art forms but isn't confident enough in his ability to do something he really loves and stuck with tattooing because it pays enough.

I gush for over an hour while she attentively listens and mops up my tears. I even gingerly show her my tattoo, which she agrees is beautiful but is something we'll keep from Dad for as long as we can.

She smiles when I finally run out of energy and words, looking a little glassy-eyed as she leans over to kiss my forehead.

"Relax, sweetheart. I'll let the others come in before the nurse grumbles that visiting time is over. But never make me have to take a call like I did last night ever again, please. I think my age doubled in that first hour," Mum gently scolds, then smiles as she squeezes Dec's flowers into one of the vases that already contains a small bunch of roses.

Chapter 28

DECLAN

TWO BREAKS IN her left arm, a dislocated shoulder, fractured ribs, internal bleeding, and bruising as well as minor bumps, bruises, and scrapes. The words have been on loop in my head since Malcolm informed me of Aela's condition.

He also confirmed that he was the "boyfriend" the nurse referred to and that there is definitely nothing between them, but I still left the hospital when her family turned up looking just as devastated as I was.

I didn't deserve to be there.

I was the reason she was being admitted in the first place, and she probably wouldn't want to see me when she came out of surgery anyway.

So, I went home, where I quickly became sick of my own company, so I then went down to the bar where I drank my weight in scotch before stumbling back to crash on the couch in the shop. I woke up when Alex stopped by to try to talk me into going to the hospital. I gave him some money for flowers with strict instructions on what to get and say, and then stumbled back to my workspace instead of upstairs because I can't deal with the memories of her in my bed right now.

I slept until six and then rose to head back to the bar with plans to do it all over again, which was going well, until Alex finds me, taking the seat beside me silently. Judgingly.

"Don't. Just shut up and have a drink with me," I order without looking at him, waving to get the barmaid's attention.

"How about we go get some coffee in you, instead?" Alex suggests, and I shake my head as he tries to get me to stand with him.

"I've been drinking bourbon. It's not good to mix drinks, so sit your arse back down." I take another gulp.

"You want to do this here? Fine." Alex snatches my drink from in front of me. I turn to level a glare at him as he holds it out of reach.

"What the fuck? I'm not playing keep-away with you," I complain, but he continues stubbornly.

"Tell me why Aela, and I'll give it back," he demands, and I flinch at just her name.

"Why Aela what?" I ask and his eyes soften a little.

"You know what I'm asking. Why Aela?"

I pause then blow out a breath before gesturing to my glass. "I need a drink to answer that."

Alex pours half my drink into an empty glass then hands it to me. I gulp it down and slam the glass on the bar before facing him.

"She's like a silent siren. Your eyes would likely pass her without a thought in a crowded room if you didn't know her because she deliberately blends in. But close up, when you get her undivided attention, her beauty radiates and draws you in. You want to kiss the freckles on her nose, drown in her Caribbean sea-green eyes and devour her luscious lips. And then she smiles... Holy hell. You feel it every time like a physical caress. It grabs you by the balls and owns you. She's so goddamn sweet too, genuine, smart, and passionate, and to tie off the perfect little package, you realise she doesn't know any of this about herself. The little idiot thinks she is plain, boring and awkward when she's beyond beautiful both inside and out. And that's it, you're gone. She's a life changer, and you would do anything to be the person who shows her all of this about herself, every day for the rest of your lives," I go quiet and rub the ache in my chest that seems to be a permanent fixture these days.

Alex returns my glass so I slam the last of my drink down before continuing, "Then you lose her because your life is poison, and you're left just a big black hole of shit that you can't come back from," I finish and scrub my hands over my face.

"Right. It's time to get coffee in you. Then we can think up a game plan. I watched her fighting back the tears because you weren't there today. We have to sort this shit out so you can be together. I won't even give you crap for all that poetic bullshit you just spouted," Alex jokes, and I push him as I slide from my stool.

"It was the alcohol talking," I argue, and he chuckles.

"Sure bud."

***

The next afternoon, I'm nursing a killer hangover as I try to sort out all the paperwork at the counter since Kit is at the hospital again today, needlessly acting like my secret insider as she sends me stupid updates.

"The male nurse is flirting with her."

"Did you know our girl hates orange jelly? That's messed up."

"Mum is a total boss and the brother's hot if he could lose the stick up his arse..."

I rub my face then sip my coffee before stuffing the papers back where they go. I hold my head in my hands, propping my elbows on the counter in front of me.

The bell over the door rings as the glass slides open, and I don't even bother looking up.

"Sorry, we're closed. No one's in until five," I call out then drag my head up at the sound of heels determinedly tapping their approach on the tiled floor. I take in the form-fitting, beige pantsuit, the crisp white shirt, and pearls, and then my eyebrows shoot for my hairline in surprise when I see who it is.

"Uh… can I help you?" I move back when she shoves her bag onto the counter in front of me and silently searches my face for a long, awkward moment before she smiles.

"Declan, right? I'm Evelyn Montgomery, but I think you know that from the look on your face and because I recognise you from the hospital the night Aela was admitted, which is strange since she thinks you were never there."

She holds out a dainty, perfectly manicured hand so I reach out automatically and shake it until she pulls back to look around the room, walking over to the corner to inspect the metalwork there.

"You made this?" I struggle to find my voice, but she doesn't wait for my reply before continuing.

"My daughter's right, you're very talented. Can I see what else you've done apart from tattoos?" She lets herself through the little swinging door then heads down the hall, admiring the pieces on the walls. I jog to catch up as she starts upstairs like she knows where she's going.

Evelyn rifles through my sketch pads as she peruses the many metal pieces around my apartment before finally turning to me as I stand awkwardly in my own doorway (and make a mental note to get Kit a thank you gift for making me clean my apartment the other day.)

"You're probably wondering what I'm doing here, huh?" Evelyn asks, looking a little amused as she eyes me while holding a sketch of her daughter, naked in my bed. *Shit.*

"I've been bored since retiring early and have been looking

for a project that interests me. I have an offer for you. I want to help you set up your own gallery and have even found a few places available to look at already."

Evelyn holds her hand up with a cut off sound when I move to object.

"Before you say you can't afford it, let me tell you it will be a partnership with me. I have contacts from my time at the Arts Centre who have more money than they know what to do with. We could do this with very little risk of loss to anyone, let alone yourself."

She pauses to pull out a thick folder of papers she places on my coffee table.

"I'm sorry. I had planned to sit down and go through this with you, but I just heard Aela's being discharged, and I want to be there to take her home. So, read it over and call me if you have any questions. Unless you want to come see her?" Evelyn pauses to give me a hopeful look.

It kills something inside of me to shake my head negatively when my whole being is straining to say yes.

"I want to, Evelyn. But I can't right now. I'm waiting on some important calls. After everything I've put her through, I need to make sure Aela's safe," I reply. Then the woman walks my way with a small smile.

"You may not be what my husband wants for our girl's future, but I think you're a good man and are good for her. Aela has a new confidence that I think is thanks in part to you, and I know you care strongly for her because you both look like you're going through hell, and I'm not talking about her injuries. So know that you have me in your corner. Just don't keep Aela waiting too long because she already thinks you stopped caring from your no show. I think you two have found something people search their whole lives for, and it would be a shame if you didn't sort it out."

Evelyn leans in to kiss my right cheek while tapping my left, grinning as she pulls back, "Call me Evie from now on. Welcome to the family."

With that, she exits my apartment, leaving me standing there feeling bewildered. That woman is like a mini tornado—in ridiculously high heels.

"Declan, where you at, son?" I hear Buzz shouting downstairs, which breaks me from my daze. I jog down to meet him as he rounds the counter. "Who's the fancy pants chick?" Buzz points over his shoulder with his thumb to the door, and I give him a small smile as I run a hand through my hair, still trying to get my head straight.

"That was Evie, Aela's scary-as-hell mother," I inform him. Then Buzz walks back to try to get another peek at her before turning with his brows raised in disbelief.

"I must have missed something because she was sweet as sugar like her daughter when she passed me with a smile on my way in. She packing heat or something?"

I bark out a laugh, though the image of Evie armed with a gun is intimidating.

"No, she's got a take charge, no nonsense attitude. I barely got a word in the entire time she was here. Apparently, she wants to set me up with a gallery. Not just a showcase in one, but my very own place. That's crazy, right? And she wants me to get back together with Aela. Most parents would lose their minds and then ship their daughter off to a convent to get her away from me if we were ever introduced. Not that I ever was. But not Evie. She literally welcomed me to her family."

Buzz listens as I ramble, looking either surprised or impressed or maybe a little of both. I can't really tell.

I finally control my mouth and wait for him to comment for a long silent moment before he smiles, moving to slap me on the back.

"Son, that's great news. I'm happy for you. What's this about you and Aela, though. Since when did you split?" Buzz pulls back to place his hands on his hips as his brows lower over his eyes. "What did you do?" he demands.

I sigh before stepping back, which I try to cover with a back scratch because I know, once I tell him, he'll slap the back of my head. He is who I picked up the habit from, after all.

"I pushed her away in a failed attempt to protect her." Sure enough, I have to hold my hands out defensively in front of me when his arm swings out my way. "I still stand by it because up until this morning when you finally returned my calls, I didn't know if your guys were going to retaliate for the disrespect I showed at the headquarters. I've heard their gloating, remember? And I didn't want anything coming back on Aela," I add as Buzz shakes his head.

"You're an idiot. And don't think I won't get in that hit you dodged later when you least expect it," he warns with a glare. Then we're both distracted when Alex rushes through the door, panting.

He commandeers the remote to the television as he tries to catch his breath. "Fuck, I have got to quit smoking," Alex complains as he focuses on the control, completely missing my confused expression as I watch him.

"What the hell are you doing? I've been waiting for you to call for hours now," I exclaim as the television blares to life with music before he switches channels.

"That's why I ran here. It came on while I was waiting at the station, and I thought you would want to see." He points to a news update on the screen, so Buzz and I move to get a better view as the reporter begins to speak.

"It's been revealed the inmate killed while in custody was arrested only days ago for a long list of charges, including the stalking and assault of a university student on the Gold Coast. So far, the police have no suspects for the murder..." I stop listening as Snake's mug shot is displayed, turning to Buzz with my jaw clenched.

He feels my glare and turns to give me a shrug while shoving his hands in his pockets.

"We heard Joe ordered an apology present for you. You're welcome. And that's why I brought that." Buzz gestures to a case of Jack Daniel's sitting on the floor next to the counter. Alex slaps his back in appreciation as he makes his way to the box and opens it.

"Hell, yeah. Celebration time. I'll get us some coke and glasses." Alex exclaims, taking off down the hall.

"I wanted him for myself," I bite out. Buzz shrugs again unrepentantly.

"Let it go, son. He was going to be locked up where you wouldn't have gotten to him for years." Buzz dismisses me with a wave of his hand, ducking to lift the box onto the counter as Alex returns with three coke cans and glasses. Alex steps up to play bartender, so I drag a couple of stools over from a corner in the waiting area.

We settle in with our drinks, and as Alex pours the second round, Buzz gets his slap on the back of my head in and then nudges me with his shoulder, almost sending me off my stool.

"So how are you going to make it up to Aela?" he demands, ignoring my glare as I resituate myself in my seat and fight the urge to rub my skull.

"I don't think I can yet. I still have the original problem with Joe about the drugs to deal with. Unless he's decided I've had enough trouble and will drop it?" I ask half hoping, which has Buzz shaking his head.

"No. But I could take this place off your hands so you can take the pretty lady up on the gallery offer," Buzz suggests with a side glance my way.

I stare at him as Alex asks what he's talking about.

"I did tell you I was looking at getting another spot. If I had known at the time that you were ready to realise your full potential as an artist, I would have made you an offer on this place sooner," Buzz adds. He takes a mouthful of his drink as Alex looks between the two of us expectantly.

"Just think about it. I reckon it's the answer we've been looking for, and then you'd have no reason to delay your grovelling at Aela's feet," Buzz continues with a smirk before Alex injects himself between us, leaning over the counter so his head blocks my view of Buzz with a questioning look on his face.

"You see me, right? I am actually here, so you must hear me, too. Now back up a little and explain all this crazy talk. Selling the shop? What the hell?"

I sigh and push his ugly mug back because it's too close for my liking and catch him up on what's happening before turning back to Buzz as I think out loud.

"I'll have to think it over and speak to my crew first. Plus look at the pile of paperwork Evie left me. Then we'd have to find a place if I agree and sort everything out, which will take a while. And you won't be getting Kit. I'll take her with me. She can't stand all that shit any more than I can, anyway. Then there are my personal clients. The one's I've started on I will take with me. I won't leave them in a lurch and you know I hate not finishing something I start."

Buzz holds his hand up to silence my rambling.

"All the details can be hammered out as we go. Why don't you grab this paperwork and we'll go over it. Then, if it's all legit and as good as it sounds, we'll get the ball rolling?" he suggests.

I nod then finish my drink before going to retrieve the thick folder. It makes a dull thud sound when I drop it onto the counter in between us all. Alex raises his brows as Buzz opens it with his reading glasses perched on the end of his nose.

I'm grateful he's willing to do this because my pounding headache has doubled its enthusiasm by the third page of business jargon, but Buzz seems to understand it.

I back off to cradle my topped up drink and watch curiously as Alex texts away on his phone with a happy grin.

"Who're you messaging?"

Alex's head shoots up with a guilty look before he steps back like I'm going to grab his phone, which makes me want to do it out of curiosity.

"No one. I was playing Angry Birds since I'm no help with any of that shit." He waves his hand to the paperwork then shoves his phone into his pocket as it vibrates with another incoming text.

I raise my brows at him but turn around when the front door slides open.

"You arseholes are having a party without me? What are we drinking to? Have you two been named King and Mayor of Douche Ville?" Kit asks. She strides into the room then slaps the back of my head with a glare before rounding the counter and shoving Alex out of the way to put her bag in the storage space she uses.

"What have I done?" Alex complains with his arms out as she turns her glare on him.

"You exist. That's enough," Kit bites out then turns to lean over the counter to kiss Buzz on the cheek with a small smile. "Hey, Pops," she greets him happily, and he murmurs his reply distractedly as Alex gives me a confused look.

"Is this the day of the month you hate all men or what, dragon lady, because that was harsh even for you," he asks Kit who growls as she turns to slap his chest.

"You're a damn pig. And you. I've dealt with tons of stupid skanks showing up here trying to see you after you've ditched them, throwing hissy fits when I deny them access. I've always assured myself you were a good guy. You just needed the right girl. But after seeing Aela delay leaving the hospital in misguided hope that you would drop by, which she held until the very end where she had to face reality and forcibly hold her shoulders back and head high, I've given up on you along with her. You're worse than Alex, Declan. I hope your balls shrivel up and fall off, the next time you get laid, and I'm not skank intercepting anymore," Kit lashes out. I sit speechlessly as she tears up before spinning around and storming off down the hall. The slamming of the backroom door echoes in the resounding silence. *Fuck.*

My stomach drops as I hope what she said isn't true, but I know Kit wouldn't have said it if it weren't.

"This looks like a sweet deal to me. Sign up and get the ball rolling while I go calm the girl down. Don't let her words get to you too much. If Aela is your one, it's never too late." Buzz pats me on the back as he slides the file back to me before heading down the hall after Kit. Alex offers me a pen from Kit's collection beside the Mac in silent encouragement when I look up to him feeling lost.

If I am too late, then all this is for nothing. Whatever expression I give him has Alex giving me a small smile.

"You remember all that poetic shit you spouted when I asked you why Aela?" he asks quietly and I nod before he continues.

"I already knew what she meant to you. I asked to remind you of what you were fighting for. It's time for the next round, man," he pushes and the moment feels weighted as I take the pen, holding it over one of the tagged boxes to sign while I nervously play with Evie's business card with my free hand.

I close my eyes as I take a deep breath then force it out in a huff as I do the only thing I can.

Chapter 29

AELA

I SPENT TWO days doing nothing but resting in the hospital. Yet all I want to do when I get home is curl up in bed and sleep.

Mum and Kara brought me home and tried to stay to hover over me, but I sent Mum home and Kara to work after assurances that I was fine.

I'm not fine, though.

The two weeks before Snake's attack, I had kept myself busy, and a small part of me believed Declan would come back, so I didn't hurt so much.

Now, I'm stuck with nothing to distract me from the knowledge that he's let me go, which he made clear by not bothering to visit me in the hospital when even Alex stopped by a couple times. From the moment I woke up after the surgery to fix my arm, all I wanted was to see his face. Every minute that passed I waited expectantly, hopefully, but he never came. That stubborn hope held out until we reached the car park when I had to face the reality that he wasn't coming, and I have to let him go.

Of course, I decided to make a martyr of myself instead, when I spied one of his shirts over the back of my desk chair. I changed into it, breathing in his scent that's soaked into the soft cotton as I gingerly pulled it over my head, being careful of my ribs.

I decided I would allow myself this day to be heartbroken while surrounded in his comforting scent that I need so much right now. But come tomorrow, I will get up and immerse myself in studying for my exams and any classwork I may have missed, even though the doctor excused me from school until my ribs healed more. But if I complied, it would cut out some of my exams, and I'm not having that.

So for today, I take a couple of prescribed painkillers and cry myself to sleep as I envision having Dec wrapped around me to put me to sleep and not just the shirt he left behind.

Just like he left me.

***

I get away with hiding out in my room for nearly three days before Kara busts in, determined, shoving all the books surrounding me on my bed to the floor before she levelled me with a look.

"Up and shower. We're going out, and I will not hear excuses why you can't. I'm driving, and you're going to let your hair down and remember how to have some fun if it kills us," Kara demands as I remove my reading glasses to look at her incredulously.

"You're kidding. My arm is practically swallowed in a cast, I have fractured ribs and rainbow bruises, and you think it's a good idea to go out?"

Kara moves to carefully but forcefully to get me up from the bed. "When I'm done, no one will be able to see the bruises in the darkness of a club, and it's not a dance club, so stop giving me that look. I'm not a total idiot." She rolls her eyes at me before heading into my closet as I stand there in disbelief.

"Do you need help to wash your hair or whatever since you can't get your cast wet?" She pops her head out to ask, and I shake my head indignantly at the thought. I'll find a way to manage without needing her in the shower with me like an invalid.

"Then snap to it, bitch."

She moves back out of sight, and I grumble a string of curses as I march into my bathroom. It's a struggle, but I manage to wash with one hand then blow dry and brush my hair before heading back out to my room where Kara is contemplating two outfits laid out on my bed.

"Do you feel like jeans or a dress?" she asks, hearing my approach. and I huff as I begin to struggle into my underwear.

"If I really had a choice, it would be leggings."

Kara shakes her head dismissively at my choice, before lifting up my long, black maxi dress with a black elastic belt and a detailed silver clip at the front, shoving it towards me.

"You should be both comfy and gorgeous in this," she announces, and I give a harsh laugh as I snatch it from her hands.

"You're mental. Nothing will make this gorgeous." I hold up my permanently bent arm, encased in the bright pink cast.

"I think it's cute, but I hear you. Luckily, there are these amazing things called jackets," Kara says sarcastically, holding up my tiny black cardigan.

I grudgingly accept it. She leaves me to awkwardly dress myself. I groan at the glittery black heels she left out for me to wear but slide them on anyway before making my way to her room where she's sitting at her vanity, applying her makeup.

"Just so you know, if I fall and break something else tonight, don't be surprised when you wake up to me shaving off your hair," I warn. Her eyes meet mine in the mirror, and she moves her eyeliner pencil away to smile at me.

"But you look gorgeous, and I will be glued to your side to catch you if you stumble so you and my hair will be safe," Kara promises, not the least bit concerned.

I cross my arms over my chest to make sure I get the seriousness of the situation across before continuing.

"I hope so for your sake because I'm talking eyebrow removal and all. I may even shave your upper lip so you grow a lady 'stache," I add. She laughs, clearly not feeling the gravity of my forewarning.

"I got it, babe. Now take a seat so I can work my magic." Kara hops out of her seat and pats it for me to sit.

I sigh then give in. Following her orders to close and open my eyes and lips on her demand while she expertly smears, pats, brushes, and coats my face with piles of makeup until she's happy.

"Done. Check it out, hot stuff," Kara says with enthusiasm so I turn in my seat to face the mirror though I don't really care what I look like after looking like a shadow monster the past few days. My skin is back to being one colour apart from the bronzer over my cheekbones, and she's given me a glittery, smoky eye with light pink lips. I smile at her through the mirror since she's waiting expectantly.

"You're a genius," I state as she begins gathering my hair into a deliberately messy braid that she tosses over my shoulder and moves off to change into a pair of grey skinny jeans, a slinky black top, and stilettos with a chrome heel.

"All right, let's go." Kara gestures out the door as she grabs her purse.

***

"Seriously?" I stop walking in protest because Kara has led me to the stairs at the entrance of Ruby's.

"What? It's ladies night, so we get free entry and cheap drinks." She pauses with one heel on the second step, "Don't tell me you have a problem with seeing strippers. They don't have anything you don't see every day," she argues as she takes another step and I huff.

"Why here. You know Alex works here, right?" I ask, and she shrugs as she takes another couple of steps.

"Yeah, he may have set us up for free drinks and VIP treatment. Free drinks are hard to turn down on a student's budget. Now, come on. There's a drink being poured with my name on it." Kara steps back down to take my hand, leading me up the stairs.

"Good evening, ladies." The burly bouncers in matching black suits, greet us in sync with a smile, their hands held out for our I.D. Kara smiles brilliantly as they look us over admiringly, barely looking at our cards before handing them back and wishing us a good night.

"Don't work too hard, boys." She winks flirtatiously as I start through the door. I have to reach back to drag her in as the younger one steps towards her with a grin.

"Glued to my side, remember?" I remind Kara grumpily.

She pats my hand with a barely apologetic look, before turning to give her name to the reception lady, who gives us wristbands and is super polite, but I barely look at her.

I'm too busy glaring at Kara before she drags me through another set of glass doors into the dimly lit club. The main floor is decorated luxuriously in red and black velvet, leather and glass, with the bar and stage bathed in blue lighting. Kara heads straight to the bar that's currently empty, leaning over it with a playful grin to where I spot a bartender with a familiar head of dark hair crouched down with his back to us restocking the fridge.

"What does a girl have to do to get an Orgasm and Screaming Sex with a bartender around here?" Kara calls out, making me look at her in surprise. Alex turns around with his signature grin, shutting the fridge to stand and lean our way when he sees it's us.

"You can get both at once from me anytime, babe. All you gotta do is ask." Alex winks as Kara snickers. Then he moves over to take a few bottles from the mirrored shelves behind him and two shakers.

"You two are a sight for sore eyes tonight. Looking lovely, ladies," he continues. He expertly pours the bottles simultaneously without needing to look as he smiles at us.

"You know, something about being behind this bar makes you seem totally fuckable," Kara replies with a grin.

I start to feel awkward like a third wheel, as they eye each other teasingly.

"You want to see if it's the same in the backroom?" Alex gestures with a tilt of his head to a dark door at the end of the bar as he juggles the shakers. Kara bites her lip thoughtfully before grinning as Alex pours our drinks.

"Nope. You may have better luck after I've had a few of these, though." She winks and they both chuckle quietly.

I take a sip of the creamy drink placed before me, and after an extremely lengthy pause, their sexual stare down finally breaks as Alex wipes down the counter with a smirk.

"What was with the drink order?" I ask Kara quietly. She grins playfully at me.

"It's a new rule for ladies night, courtesy of Alex, actually. To make it more interesting, all drinks have to be sexually named," Kara explains and Alex bows.

"Happy to have changed your life in such a profound way," he jokes, then moves down the bar as a couple waves him down. "You're in the reserved section, stage side," Alex calls over his shoulder.

I turn to Kara curiously before she gestures for me to follow her. I admire the water feature wall at the back of the unoccupied stage and the pretty chandeliers until I hear Kit calling out over the music.

I look to see her waving from a leather chair in a little wrought-iron fenced-off seating area that we're headed to. The bouncer standing in front of it unlatches the rope barring the entrance. I'm immediately assaulted by hugs, squeals and a cloud of mixed perfumes from two of our friends from high school, who we haven't seen in a while due to conflicting schedules— Jen who is studying to be a nurse, and Charli who just returned from a round the world trip. They're identical twins with long, sandy blonde hair, brown eyes and are always perfectly put together.

After their exuberant greeting, I quickly step over to nab the seat against the railing beside Kit where my back is to the bar. As the other three slide into the long bench seat on the wall. I can barely make out what the girls are talking about over the music, so I sip my drink and take in the room as it slowly fills up.

"How are you doing, babe?" Kit asks in my ear, and I turn with a smile.

"I'm getting there. How long has this thing been planned?" I ask, noticing the reserved sign hanging on the little railing.

"Kara invited me this morning." She admits with a grin. I nod, glaring at Kara for rushing me, but she's too busy talking to notice.

At nine, the DJ mans the sound system I can just see on the level above us and starts the show, introducing the dancers for each set. Kit and I become entranced, watching the performers. Cheering for the experts on the pole and sniggering quietly about the not so great—like the one who literally walked back and forth—looking dazed as she took her ensemble off and gyrated a little.

I watch in amazement as a crazy talented dancer does some serious tricks at the very top of the two-storey pole before coming back down in a rush that makes me gasp in horror, but she quickly halts her descent to lower her feet gracefully to the floor. I'm so caught up I fail to notice the feel of someone standing behind me until there's a brush of air against my ear while I clap.

"My thoughts exactly, trouble. You're breathtaking as always." I pause at the voice I've missed so much but refuse to acknowledge him, forcing myself to keep my gaze locked on the stage.

"Care for a free lap dance?" he murmurs in my other ear after a moment, and I feel him playing with my braid. I tug away from him to place my glass on the small table while attempting to ignore his presence, feeling the girls watching me one by one.

"Come on, sugar. I'll make it worth your while in the private room," Dec continues in a teasing tone.

My control fails when I feel his fingertips run lightly down the nape of my neck. I turn to find him leaning against the railing. Dec's changed so much in such a short time that I have to work to control my shock so he only sees annoyance. He's lost a bit of weight, grown a bit of scruff along his jaw that gives him a ruggedly sexy edge, and I can't tell if it's just the lighting in here, but his eyes seem dimmer than usual too. I stop my perusal to level him with a glare.

"I don't want anything from you, but for you to leave me alone. You haven't had a problem doing it these last few weeks, so you can just continue, thanks," I snap, turning to rise from my seat and leave our area as Kara yells for me to wait.

I weave my way through the crowd, feeling Dec right behind me, but ignore him, sliding into a tight spot at the bar where I lift my cast to rest on top of it.

Alex acknowledges me with a look as he finishes an order and then leans my way expectantly.

"Something strong and hard," I call out and see he's about to make a smart remark but changes his mind and turns to the bottles.

"Should you be drinking with your pain meds?" Declan yells in my ear, and I shove him away with my plastered arm.

He doesn't take the hint and makes his own space beside me with an adamant look. I roll my eyes before taking the drink Alex offers me.

"Yeah, well, there are some pains medication can't help with that I'm hoping the alcohol will." I see him wince before I move to return to the girls, but he takes hold of my good arm.

"Aela, we need to talk. Please, come with me," he urges and again, I shake him off, trying to mask my emotions as I face him.

"No. We needed to talk. But you pushed me away and shut me out. So no, I'm not going to stop and hear what you have to say in a damn strip club," I argue then turn away just as a guy approaches from behind me with a concerned frown Declan's way.

He's cute. Tall and tanned, brown hair and eyes, and well-dressed. I'm not interested, but I smile politely as our eyes meet while I step to pass him.

"Is he bothering you?" Before I can say a word, Declan is in his face intimidatingly, muscles bunched and ready for a fight.

"Do not speak to her. You want some arse, go pay for a dance," Dec orders but the other guy doesn't step down. Instead, he leans into Declan, but thankfully, before it can get out of control, two bouncers appear and separate them. Declan moves to grab me, but I pull out of reach in refusal.

"Go away, Dec," I demand. Ignoring what feels like every cell in my body screaming to be with him, I turn away.

Declan keeps his distance the rest of the night but is never far away as the girls get rowdy and mess around on the amateur pole near the toilets. Kara drops by the momentarily quiet bar to have a chat with Alex that's filled with heated glances and flirty touches, which gives me hope for them, but it doesn't take her long to notice my weariness and leave him to call it a night.

I stew in a mix of emotions in silence on the ride home until Kara mutes the stereo with a quick glance my way.

"Let it out," she urges knowingly, looking back to the road.

I remain silent for a moment before it bubbles up and explodes out of me in one loud, ugly rush.

"How dare he? Weeks of nothing, then Declan just shows up wanting to talk at a strip joint, looking all deliciously rugged and handsome and smelling lick-able, teasing me like he didn't tear my heart out and dismiss me when things got too hard for the poor baby to take. Then he starts a fight with a guy who was just making sure I wasn't being harassed by a creep. Who does that? And he doesn't get the right to look hurt and make me feel bad when I turn him down. Stupid jerk-face," I run out of steam and lean my head against my window.

Kara takes a minute before looking at me again.

"I'm going to say something, and you're not allowed to get angry because you know I'm always on your side." She pauses to peek at me again so I nod. "I know you're hurting, babe, but do you really want to stubbornly push him away when he finally shows up? Yes, he's really late and should have started with some major sucking up, but he's a guy, and we all know guys are stupid. What's important is he showed up and wants to fix his mistakes," Kara tries to reason as we pull into her parking space. I automatically check around us before getting out, which she catches, giving me a sympathetic smile.

I head straight to my room once we're inside, slip out of my clothes and into a singlet on my way to wash my face. I retrieve my phone from my clutch to check my alarm isn't set since tomorrow is Sunday and find I have a text from Declan from two hours ago.

"Sorry I'm such a screw-up, but I am not giving up on us. Xx"

***

The week of exams is an exhausting blur of studying and tests, and I have never been so happy to reach a Friday afternoon in my entire life as I step out of my last exam for the semester.

The girls from my study group, Mia and Jules, who are also in my class, talk me into going for a celebratory drink at the tavern across the road where many students and even some teachers are heading to unwind. I send Kara a text as we walk over to tell her to stop by if she wants.

It's only three in the afternoon, and the place is already packed with others celebrating the end of exams. Jules instantly disappears in the crowd due to her tiny frame she blames on her Filipino descent to head to the bar, so Mia and I snag us a table in front of the open bay windows so we can enjoy the fresh air.

Jules finds us five minutes later with three Corona's with lime, and Mia wrinkles her nose at hers before gulping it down. She then ties her long red locks into a messy bun because the air-con and slight breeze coming through can't compete with all the radiating body heat packed in here.

I sip my beer since I plan to drive home later, which is difficult enough with my cast, and I'm still taking my prescription when needed.

We share a few laughs, and the girls have a couple rounds before Mia drags me up to dance with her while Jules clings to the table, adamantly refusing. The space everyone is dancing in is full of writhing bodies, and Mia squeezes us through until she is happy with a spot. She turns to face me, swinging her hips with her hands in the air along with everyone else.

We start busting out horrible dance moves for a laugh and have a great time as the songs change until a pair of strong hands grip my hips and someone presses against my back. I look over my shoulder to see an unfamiliar guy grinning back at me while thrusting his groin into my arse. I smile politely before trying to extract myself from his grip, but he follows me, sliding his hands around to rest on my stomach. I look to Mia for help, but she's laughing, finding the situation comical. So I make myself relax and plan to give him this song before I put an end to it. It's just a dance, after all, even if I can feel his junk grinding into me.

I put my good hand over his to keep them from wandering and bop along to Jimmy Eat Worlds' *In the Middle*, one of my favourite songs. I'm yanked back suddenly before his arms disappear from around me so I turn curiously, stopping when I see Declan gesturing for the guy to take a hike. Declan turns my way with a sheepish grin as he steps up to wrap his arms around me.

I hold my hands up to stop him with a glare.

"What are you doing here?" I yell to be heard over the music as Dec swings his arm around my back, bringing me against him despite my refusal.

He leans down to my ear, "A feisty little birdy told me you were here, so I came with Kara and Alex because I'm tired of you ignoring my texts. I've resorted to stalking you again," he replies. The rumble of his voice sends a delightful shiver down my spine I try to ignore.

"I didn't reply to them because that was a chicken shit move. You can't just send a daily apology text and expect it to be enough," I argue. He nods in agreement as his other arm snakes around me before I push him back, using my cast to get some leverage.

"No, Declan. You can't just show up and scare off someone I'm dancing with to take their place. I—" He kills my argument by suddenly yanking me against him and dropping his head to cover my mouth with his.

My body melts instantly into the warmth of him as he

invades my senses. My hands latch onto his navy shirt with a mind of their own as he takes my mouth, his tongue sliding out to glide over my bottom lip before he tilts his head for better access. His left hand moves up to the back of my head to keep me from retreating. Not that I could if I wanted to—which I don't anymore.

His tongue forces its way slickly into my mouth to caress mine. He tastes slightly minty like he'd prepared for this, which annoys a small part of the back of my mind, but it isn't enough to make me want to stop.

He smells, feels, and tastes too good after being deprived of him for so long.

My tongue automatically tangles with his as his hands move to cup my face, and he deepens the kiss. I'm pretty sure if he released me right now, I'd be a puddle on the floor. I feel like I've been turned to mush, and my legs will no longer hold me.

This kiss is everything—apologetic, needy, dominating and Declan staking his claim on me for all to see.

I hear catcalls and cheers of encouragement, but they sound far away. I can't be certain they're even for us, not that I care.

Eventually, Dec slows down and pulls back to nip and lick at my kiss-swollen lips. I open my eyes just in time to see him release a giant sigh then open his eyes that instantly meet my gaze as he leans his forehead against mine.

"Why do I always lose myself in you? I came here intending to talk and grovel, but then you're yelling at me, and all I could think of was kissing you until I couldn't take it anymore. And holy hell, that kiss. Nothing can make me give up on us. You've pulled apart the guy I used to be like a puzzle then put me back together in a new way that revealed there was an empty space that only you can fill. I won't be without you, Aela. I can't. I'm so sorry for pushing you away—even if my intentions were good. I'll do anything to make it up to you, baby. I love you."

Declan's eyes are glued to mine during his declaration, revealing the sincerity of his words in his stormy gaze.

It's all too much—the kiss, his declaration of love, and how much I need him. It's overwhelming and scares the hell out of me.

I pull away as my eyes well up, and my hands feel cold and clammy as they shake.

"I won't let you hurt me again, Declan. I can't."

I turn and rush out of the bar without a word or glance at any of my friends. I barely register my run across campus until I'm in my car, tears falling as I start the ignition. I wait until I'm back in control and then head home, ignoring my phone blasting from my bag.

My mind is in such a whirl once I get home, I can't even recall if I locked my car or the trip up to the apartment when I crawl into my bed, but I couldn't care less as I turn the radio on to drown out the noise my phone is making as it continues to go off where I left it in my bag beside the front door.

I'm exhausted and refuse to cry anymore over this but feel lost about what to do with myself. I have no studying to do now we're on holiday, and I'm not scheduled back at work for another week.

So I just lay there, staring out my window at the view of the Broadwater as the sunset colours the sky in shades of pink, purple, and orange.

I obviously fall asleep because I suddenly wake to a quiet knocking on my door and my view is now dark, lit only by streetlights and the surrounding buildings.

I hear Kara whispering before my door creaks open, and she softly calls my name, but I remain still, imitating sleep before the door clicks shut. I think I hear Alex murmuring as they head back down the hall before another door closes.

I bury deeper into my blankets, curling around my casted

arm, and try to ignore Declan's faint but still present scent on my shirt as I wait to fall back to sleep.

***

I drag myself out of bed in the morning, feeling hung-over after a disturbed night's sleep and stumble into the kitchen to get the Nespresso brewing before using the main bathroom to relieve myself.

I head back to retrieve my coffee and come to a standstill when I find Alex sipping it as he leans against the bench in nothing but a pair of black boxer briefs with a satisfied smile and his hair mussed up more than usual.

"Good morning. Sorry, I claimed the first cup and put another on for you. I couldn't wait."

The machine stops its whirring and Alex cheerfully hands over the fresh cup as I frown at him.

"You two interrupt my sleep with your wall pounding and porn noises, and then you steal my coffee and assault my eyes with too much skin first thing in the morning? Not cool, Alex," I grumble. He chuckles, which has me glaring over my coffee at him. "Tone down the watts of that smile. It's too bright, too early," I add, then head to the couch to curl up with my cup.

"No wonder Dec can't get enough. You're even adorable first thing in the morning," Alex muses as he gets comfy on the opposite side of me. I send him a silent glare because I know I look like hell. I haven't bothered to brush my hair, have my glaringly pink cast, and I'm still in my oversized white tee that reaches mid-thigh, thankfully covering my 'bite me' boy shorts.

I try to focus on the news program, but my eyes wander against their will because he's sitting in my peripheral vision with so much tattooed skin on display.

"Seriously. Cover up or get out," I demand exasperatedly.

Alex laughs out loud before reaching for his shirt that was handily discarded over my bag on the other couch. He lifts up off his seat as he struggles to reach it, so I catch a glimpse of his Adonis arse framed in his underwear before he sits back and pulls his shirt on over his head.

"Better?" he asks with amusement. I nod which has him chuckling again. "You know, I've never had a chick complain about my lack of clothing until I met you and Kara."

I shrug while flipping channels. "Maybe we're just not that into you," I offer, and he shoves my leg playfully with a chuckle.

"Oh, Kara's into me. She called me God repeatedly last night and praised my trouser snake," Alex argues smugly, and I shake my head.

"You are too much sometimes, you know that? I don't know how you don't get your arse kicked by the women you molest," I complain half-heartedly as he grins.

"I know you love me, really," Alex insists with a poke to my cheek. I shake my head but can't hide my grin.

"You two are loud arseholes," Kara complains as she stumbles out from the hallway to the kitchen, looking a little worse for wear in a black silk slip.

I grin at her state as I call out, "Funny. That's what I thought about you two all night."

At the same time, Alex says, "No, but I'd like to get up in yours." I smack his arm with my cast-free hand in disgust as Kara snorts derisively.

"What are you even doing here? I thought your motto was to have fun with the clit, then time to split?" Kara complains. It's only because I'm looking at Alex that I see his smile dim as he steels himself, guarding his emotions before he shrugs nonchalantly sipping his coffee.

"You wore me out, sunshine. I couldn't leave if I wanted to," he explains.

I feel like an awkward third wheel. I gulp the rest of my coffee then get up to rinse my cup, finding Kara in the kitchen, biting her thumbnail as she waits for her mug to fill. It's a nervous habit of hers since we were little.

"I'm going for a shower," I needlessly inform them as I go to my room to give them some space to sort out their own problems.

An hour later, I'm freshly showered and dressed with my hair done and have avoided them as long as I can. I hesitantly walk back out to get some food, and all is quiet. I exit the hallway to find Alex in the same spot, but Kara's now cuddled up to his side as they watch her favourite zombie show that I can't watch because anything with zombies gives me nightmares. Sad but true.

I try to not disturb them as I head to the kitchen and make some toast, but Kara must hear the fridge open because she calls out, "There was a delivery."

I look over and see her hand up as she points towards the corner of the kitchen bench against the wall where I notice our vase is filled with a rainbow of roses.

I lean over the bench to grin at Alex. "Where did you pull them from?" He shakes his head in reply as Kara sits up to face me.

"They're not from him. Read the card," she demands and then resumes snuggling while Alex plays with her hair. I look again and recognise the scrawl on the little white card propped above the flowers on a plastic stand.

I sigh heavily as I pull it off to read:

Aela,

Sorry for freaking you out. I'm going to be really busy for a bit so I'll give you some space, but I will see you soon and continue our talk because I'm not finished. I. Love. You.

Yeah, you have to get used to that because I plan on telling you it every day for the rest of my life. Love, Dec.

I groan and then walk over to grab my phone out of my bag and see I have fifteen missed calls from the girls and Declan, along with a handful of texts.

I reply to Jules and Mia to apologise and let them know I'm okay before going to Declan's. I ignore the apologies but curiously click on the YouTube link and watch as it starts loading *Never Gonna Give You Up,* by Rick Astley. I burst out laughing as the old pop song starts playing before I shut it off and send him a simple 'thank you.'

Alex and Kara are watching me curiously when I look up then remember the toast I came out for and rush back to reheat it, unable to contain the stupid grin on my face even though I know it isn't smart to fall for Dec's charms again.

I decide to spend the day relaxing in the sun and ask the lovebirds if they want to come to The Spit.

"I get to have you two beauties in bikinis all to myself? I'd be certifiable to refuse," Alex jokes then we get ready to go, stopping to get supplies to fill the esky with drinks and food and for Alex to get swim shorts because we refuse to let him skinny dip.

I enjoy my first peaceful day in what seems like forever. Soaking up the sun and sea air with a good trashy romance novel and watching in amusement as the other two frolic in the water. It's exactly what I need to recharge and feel more like myself.

***

I've enjoyed my time off with Kara keeping me busy shopping, going to the theme parks, catching movies and being pampered at a salon and a day spa.

However, a week of only getting a daily short, sweet text with a link on the end to one super cheesy love song after another from Declan, leaves me confused and edgy. Seriously, I spent two nights cleaning the apartment from top to bottom until it was spotless, not caring that my cast slowed me down. I even bleached all three bathrooms.

Kara becomes concerned enough to invite me to a gallery opening just to get me out of the house, despite knowing I've spent years avoiding these things after being dragged to way too many by my mother. I gratefully accept this time, though, for the distraction and something to do.

It's in the evening, so Kara decides we should go shopping for something to wear, and we hit another shopping centre. I keep checking my phone, waiting for my text for today. I even breakdown after lunch and try to call him before I can talk myself out of it while Kara's in the toilets, but it rings out before going to voicemail.

Kara leads me into a more formal boutique than we normally shop at, and I decide to humour her as we admire the racks of expensive cocktail dresses and gowns.

"Whoa. Aela, I've found your dress, babe." I turn from the pretty black silk I'm holding to see Kara on the opposite side of the room so I head over to see what she's got.

Kara looks excited as she holds up a beautiful chiffon and satin, knee-length dress in swirling shades of green and blue with a strapless, sweetheart neckline and crystal detailing under the bust.

"Trust me, this is it. Don't even waste time trying it on, just get it," Kara urges as I take it from her then spy the price tag and balk.

"I am not paying that much for a dress. Shoes maybe but never a dress," I argue, but Kara holds the dress against my front, picturing me in it before the mirror. She shakes her head adamantly.

"You can wear this dress for anything, and it suits you perfectly. Honestly, it even matches your eyes. If you don't, I'll send your mum a photo, and I bet she will transfer money to my account and demand I get it for you," Kara orders.

It is a pretty dress. And the satin is so soft.

I swish the dress in front of me longingly.

I end up caving far too easily but put up a fight when Kara suggests new shoes because I have a pair of nude pumps that will work just fine.

Kara seems more excited than normal for one of these things. When I ask about it, she explains a few of her friends have some pieces being displayed. I let it go but not without noticing how vague her reply was.

I keep my makeup light but decide to put a little extra effort into my hair to do the dress justice. I struggle to work around my cast to put two small braids on each side then pin it up in a loose looking pile of curls, securing it with a ton of hairspray.

My hair doesn't usually comply with my effort and look good unless I'm messing with it when I'm bored. So I'm happy it actually turns out great. I slip into the dress and heels then check the finished result in the floor length mirror, wincing at my bright pink graffitied cast that stands out like an eyesore against my dress. But apart from that, I look nice. Of course, the first thing I think of is I wish I were seeing Declan like this.

"You need any help— Oh, wow. Don't move," Kara exclaims as she enters my room then holds her phone up to take photos of me with the view out my window for a bright backdrop.

"Selfie time. Then we'll be on our way, babe,"

Kara excitedly makes her way to me with a spring in her step, her blush coloured chiffon dress floating around her legs fluidly.

We take a few more pictures together until she's happy, then we make our way down to the garage.

Kara drives her car, babbling excitedly while multitasking,

uploading pics to Facebook from her phone which has me nervously clinging to my armrest, cringing at how many close calls we have with other cars as we make our way towards the Sundale Bridge.

"Give me the damn phone, and I'll do it for you before you drive us into the water," I snap anxiously.

Kara rolls her eyes like I'm being dramatic but hands her phone over without comment, nonetheless.

We safely make it to the parking lot of the busy wharf on Seaworld Drive where all the popular boat tours and luxury yachts are docked. Then I follow Kara over to the cute double-storey, white wood slatted boutiques that have a seaside feel.

We pass a fancy looking salon and a beach cruiser store, our heels sounding loud against the wooden walkway as I admire our surroundings.

My eyes land on a swinging wood and brass sign up ahead that's made to look old and rustic which reads 'Missing Pieces Gallery.' I peek through the window at the packed front rooms and smile as Kara gives an excited squeal.

We step up into the entrance of the gallery, and I admire the polished, dark-stained wooden flooring and glossy white walls. We follow the flow of the crowd to the left room, and I take in the wide collection of varying pieces on display from sculptures of metal and clay to beach photography, landscape paintings, portrait sketches and more. The metalwork reminds me of Declan, of course, because there's always something around to bring him back to the forefront of my mind.

I turn my head to get Kara's impression, but she's no longer beside me. I can't even see her in the crowd. I move more into the room to peruse the art, starting with the impressive sketch of a naked woman grinning over her shoulder. The only colour in the piece is the red of her lips, the brilliant green of her eyes, orange flames of her hair and a beautiful burst of colourful flowers trailing down her back. There are three others similarly done in a collection by the artist on the small side wall. I make a mental note to come back to these because I'd love one for my room or maybe a present to put away for Kara.

I move along to the beach photography, then to a sheet of metal that has been used as a canvas that's been heated, bent and painted to present a three-dimensional piece of lovers entwined in shadows.

I can't take my eyes off it. My hand twitches with the urge to reach up and follow the curves that make up the bodies. It's beautiful and captivating. I look to find the artist's name, gasping when I find the familiar mark of Declan's signature burnt into the corner.

I look around for more pieces from him I might recognise, but my eyes land on something even better that's leaning against the doorframe at the other end of the room, which has me making my way over before I consciously decide to take a step.

"Hey, beautiful," he murmurs with a soft smile once I'm close enough to hear, and the part of my brain that controls my voice seems to short circuit as I take him in.

I've seen Declan dressed up before. Even wearing the same suit and shiny shoes he's in now, but there's something different. Something more about him.

There's a light of contentment in his eyes and strength in his stance. As though a weight has been lifted off his shoulders that I hadn't realised was there until now seems to be gone. It makes my heart feel light, like it could fly out of my chest. It also makes him even more ridiculously attractive.

As if he needed it.

Dec's rocking that suit and new aura, and if it wasn't for the crowd of people shuffling around us, I would be all over him in under a second.

Okay, Aela. Get it together and find your words. I have to

force myself to concentrate to reboot my brain. I look back to his artwork across the room before turning back to him.

"Declan, wow. This is amazing, you and your work. You have something in a gallery. That's huge. Congratulations!" I stutter out then lean in fast to give him an excited hug that has him chuckling.

"Thank you, but I have slightly more than that. I'm a part owner of this place." I lean back to look at him with surprise and he takes my good hand in his.

"Come with me and I'll explain," Dec leads me to the gleaming wooden staircase in the centre of the floor space beside the counter, and then we weave our way through the staircase traffic.

At the top, there's another open showroom to the right and two rooms to the left that have wooden-framed glass doors. They're lit up so I can see one is an office while the other has a large workbench inside.

"There you two are. Aela, you look lovely."

I turn in surprise at my mother's voice to find her stepping through the crowd before she envelopes both Declan and me in a hug.

"Give us a minute, Evie. I haven't talked to her yet," Dec excuses us, and the shocks just keep coming as Mum steps back, releasing us with a dismissal wave.

"I'll go back to Nicola and the others. Don't you keep him long. The man's got to mingle and make us some money," Mum points playfully at me as she says this, then turns to go through the crowd.

I spot our friends and family ahead of her, mingling in the corner near a bar setup where Kara waves at me mischievously.

Dec tugs on my hand still clasped in his then continues to the office, gesturing for me to sit on the small leather loveseat as he shuts the door, cutting out the noise of the other room and then leans against it.

"Sorry about all this. I didn't intend to leave you out of the loop, but we've been insanely busy setting everything up. I wanted to tell you so you would know I'm serious that I don't intend to ever let you go. Ever. But you never gave me the chance to tell you, and it's too much to explain in a text. Then I got out voted because Kara thought it would be better to surprise you with it, and they all decided it was romantic. I don't know about that, but I do know I've missed you so damn much."

Dec pushes away from the door to take a seat beside me, his knee touching mine as he takes my hand.

"Your mum is brilliant, by the way. This is all her idea.

Evie came into the shop a few weeks ago like a mini tornado and literally blew me away with an offer to be her partner in this with a folder full of places to look at and the paperwork ready to go. Then Buzz ordered me to let him buy me out of Ink Fix. They are lifesavers because I needed to get you back but didn't want anything else to happen to you because of me. I couldn't see a way out of the mess with Joe until they threw me this life raft."

He looks away for a breath.

"I'm sorry for pushing you away. I panicked because that night with Joe, I finally admitted to myself how much you meant to me. I was scared of what they would do to you because I declared it in the heat of the moment. I can't lose you, Aela. I feel like I've been living on autopilot since Grace died. I lost the other half of me when I lost my twin, and then my family fell apart and everything I knew, all that was certain and safe, was gone. I eventually got good at faking to be okay. I even fooled myself into believing it for a few years but really, everything felt like a burden. I couldn't appreciate anything or anyone and stayed away from women I thought I could care for because I already loved too many people who it would kill me to lose. Then you come into my life and literally knock me on my arse."

316

He pauses to smirk at me in reminiscence and I smile sheepishly.

"You changed everything. Like a burst of colour that couldn't be ignored, so bright that the dark faded, and I was able to appreciate what I had. When I forced you away, I thought I could learn to be okay as long as you were alive and could be happy, but I couldn't do it. It was like losing a limb I could feel but not see, all over again. I'm not trying to make an excuse for my actions. I just want to try to explain if you even understand what I'm trying to say because I have rambled on a lot. So I'm going to shut up now and you can yell at me, tell me to go to hell, or whatever you want, and that's okay because I was a dickwad and deserve it, but I still won't give up on us."

Dec nervously fidgets, pulling away to lean forward, his elbows on his knees like he's bracing himself, looking down at his clasped hands, entwining his fingers.

I watch through watery eyes for a moment as he prepares for the worst and then I smile because he looks so boyish. I reach out to take his face in my good hand and turn him gently to face me until his stormy-blue eyes meet mine.

"I love you too, Dec. But if you ever try to push me away again, I'll kick you in the balls and then ignore it," I warn playfully then lean in to kiss him but he pulls back.

"I won't. But can I just ask, what is with you women and balls? Kit threatened to pierce them, Kara said she'll burn them off with my blowtorch, and now you're going to kick them. You women are brutal—"

I shut Declan up by launching myself at him, covering his lips with mine as I wrap my arms around his shoulders, careful not to knock him out with my cast. Dec slides his arm out from between us so he can hold me to him tightly while shifting his right leg up to hook around and between mine from behind as he falls back into the couch.

I ignore the protesting of my injured ribs as his tongue slides out to meet mine, because I'll be damned before I break this kiss. I grip the back of his hair while tilting my head to get a better angle, and Dec groans when I tug on it, eliciting a shiver from me and a tingling in my core.

I hear a loud commotion seconds before he pulls away, chuckling when he looks up at the door.

I follow his look in a bit of a daze to see Kara, Kit, and Alex, gawking through the window as they holler, whistle and clap. I flush as I giggle then give them a finger wave before Dec looks back to me with a grin. I dip my head to give his lips a final peck before pulling up off him.

"We'll continue this later, trouble. I have a few things here in need of breaking in if you're up for it," Dec promises thickly, adjusting his erection in his pants, and I grin as I straighten my dress.

"Looking forward to it. I'll even give those bullied, blue balls of yours some loving. Now, let's go schmooze people into buying you bare." I wink then walk out the door with an extra sway of my hips for his viewing pleasure, hearing him mutter a curse.

***

Dec locks the door behind the last people to leave—which so happens to be our mothers—then sweeps me up into his arms to carry me up to the office, and we pick up exactly where we left off hours before.

I'm impatient after being without him for so long. I just want to tear off the clothes in our way and get to it, but Dec has other ideas. He unzips my dress then slowly drags it down my body, kissing every inch of skin revealed as he goes, as though greeting every inch of my body like a loved one he hasn't seen in so long.

It has me feeling cherished, and my heart melts, so I allow him to continue without protest.

"Are you sure you're up for more than this. I don't want to hurt your ribs or your arm?" he asks huskily against my stomach. I shudder as I run my good hand through his hair.

"I need this, Declan. I'll tell you if it hurts," I promise then feel him shudder as he releases a breath.

"Thank God. I will stop if you need me to, but I think it may kill me right now to do so. I need you so much, maybe more than air right now," he swears, making me giggle.

Dec dips to lick the skin beneath my navel, causing me to squirm with a gasp.

We both hold to our promises and don't leave the gallery until the early hours of the morning. We're exhausted and sore after christening every available surface in the place, paying special attention to his workbench and desk so Declan has plenty of inspiration—which he will need since he sold out of his pieces on display.

We head back to my apartment, neither of us able to wipe the content smiles from our faces or not be joined in some way, as Dec continues to be careful of my ribs despite me telling him I'm fine.

"I love you, trouble. Always," Dec murmurs in my ear after we settle into spooning positions in my bed.

I smile as I wriggle to get as close to him as possible until his hand at my hip tightens, and he makes a pleading whine in the back of his throat that has me giggling.

"I Love you too," I reply as I snuggle in and close my eyes at the feel of his lips pressing against my shoulder.

Always. I can live with that.

Chapter 30

EPILOGUE

"OH, GOD. HELL, I'm dying. Stop. I have to stop," I gasp, trying to catch my breath while Dec laughs and I shoot him a glare.

"I told you not to push it," he points out as he runs backwards on the treadmill beside me, barely even breaking a sweat though his machine is set higher than mine. He's just messing around to entertain himself. *Show off.*

"You can shove your 'told you so' where the sun doesn't shine, and I hope you trip and break something. It's been over two months. I need the workout," I complain, folded over with my feet braced on either side of my machine and my arms –that are now finally both unhindered by plaster- awkwardly wrapped around my ribs.

"We can go back to our room, and I'll give you a proper workout." Dec grins down at me suggestively before spinning to face the right way, and I shake my head in a negative as I force myself to stand straight.

"Kara's home and you know Alex will be around just like every other day of the last two weeks since you moved in, using visiting you as his excuse regardless if you're there or not so he can bug Kara until she kicks him out. It's hard to be in the mood with that going on," I argue while Dec stops his machine when he sees I've given up. He steps over to join me on mine with a grin.

"We could sneak into the showers here or go up to the pool area and scope that out," he suggests, and I flick him with my towel.

"What kind of girl do you think I am?" I object, fighting a smirk when he loses his grin before taking me in his arms and pressing kisses to my sweaty face. Completely ignoring my protests.

"The best kind. Mine," Declan murmurs in my ear. I let the smirk slip free as I stretch up to press a quick kiss to his lips.

"Ooh... twenty points for charm," I tell him and then push him away to leave.

"So, yes to checking out the pool?" Dec insists when he catches up with me. I laugh as I continue down the steps with a shake of my head.

"What's going on with our best friends anyway?" Dec grumbles while we wait for the elevator. I shrug before I finish sipping from my water bottle.

"I don't think even they know. But it's fun to watch," I reply as the bell sounds and the doors to the lift open.

"I bet you Alex will wear her down again, and she'll give in." Dec grins as I press the button for our floor, and I smirk, knowing how Kara is with guys.

"Twenty bucks says she'll own him first," I wager and Dec chuckles as he nods.

"I'll see your twenty and raise you a sexual fantasy of the winner's choice that the loser has to comply with," Dec offers, holding his hand out for me to shake as I laugh.

"This is about pool sex again, isn't it?" I assume, and he uses his offered hand to reach out and pull me against him.

"I have the mental image of you riding me in a dimly lit corner of the pool, wet hair trailing through the water with nothing covering you but that tiny black bikini top of yours, bare skin glistening as you throw your head back and come around me. I will do anything to see it become a reality,"

The guy has a way with words.

I can practically feel the moment he describes, the water lapping around us while being wrapped around his strong, warm body.

I suddenly can't think of anything I want more.

"You're on. But I can't deny you something you want that badly, and I could do with a cooling off. So… race you to the top floor?" I bite my lip in anticipation as I watch Dec's eyes darken with arousal.

Well, this just became even more entertaining.

I can't wait to see who comes out on top. In our bet, of course. I'm sure we'll tie in the pool.

Coming Soon

Kara and Alex's story,
Drive Me Crazy

Acknowledgments

First and foremost, I have to thank my husband, who patiently put up with many hours of being ignored as I immersed myself in the lives of these characters. Who talked me out of my funks, encouraged me when I was ready to give up, and in general, puts up with my craziness with little complaint. I love you most and always, Michael, and am thankful every day to have you in my life.

Thank you to Chritty, who put up with my three a.m. plot texts, couldn't get enough sneak peeks, loved my characters before I could even get them written down and cracked the proverbial whip when I procrastinated. You are the best sister ever. I love you to bits, and I'm sorry for convincing you to eat a raw chili when you were five, but it's really time to let it go! Haha.

A HUGE thank you to Rogena, of RMJ Manuscript Service. Editor extraordinaire with the patience of a saint and the ability to produce diamonds out of coal! Honestly, there's not a single page in this book that didn't benefit from your magic and I can't thank you enough for all your work. Anyone looking for an editor or formatter, I can't recommend Rogena enough!

Thank you to the rest of my family, both by blood and marriage. Words can't describe how much you all mean to me. Thank you for your unwavering love and support despite my sometimes lacking and awkward social skills. I'm sorry you're all stuck with me!

Thank you to the few friends I chose to share my journey with, who repeatedly urged me to realise my dreams of becoming an author, your encouragement was invaluable. A special shout out to Jenny Hitler! Aka Jaime, for the late night company after work.

Thank you to Frina Art from selfpubbookcovers.com for the beautiful cover.

And many, many thanks to YOU for choosing this book and taking the time to read it. I hope Aela and Declan were able to burrow themselves into your heart like they did mine, and whether you loved or hated their story, I would appreciate your feedback. Leave a review on the site you purchased it from and/or contact me. I'd love to hear from you!

Strive for your dreams and never let anyone, including yourself, tell you that you can't do it. You really can achieve anything if you're willing to work for it. Never give up!

About the Author

ASH HOSKING is an admitted daydreamer and hopeless romantic with a dirty mind from the Gold Coast, Australia. She lives with her sweet husband and adorable furbaby, Prim, who loves to snuggle on Ash's lap to keep her from getting anything done. When not at her day job in catering, she can usually be found either working on her next book or reading, including on her lunch breaks. She enjoys warm days at the beach, is addicted to Zarraffa's mocha fusions and can never say no to a Tim Tam. Contact or follow Ash at:

Facebook: Ash Hosking
@ashhoskingbooks

Instagram: ash.hosking

Email: ash.hosking@gmail.com

www.ingramcontent.com/pod-product-compliance
Lightning Source LLC
Chambersburg PA
CBHW060511180626
46817CB00002B/344